W9-ANG-136

ALSO BY STEPHEN DOBYNS

NOVELS
Saratoga Strongbox (1998)
The Church of Dead Girls (1997)
Saratoga Fleshpot (1995)
Saratoga Backtalk (1994)
The Wrestler's Cruel Study (1993)
Saratoga Haunting (1993)
After Shocks/Near Escapes (1991)
Saratoga Hexameter (1990)
The House on Alexandrine (1990)
Saratoga Bestiary (1988)
The Two Deaths of Señora Puccini (1988)
A Boat off the Coast (1987)
Saratoga Snapper (1986)
Cold Dog Soup (1985)
Saratoga Headhunter (1985)
Dancer with One Leg (1983)
Saratoga Swimmer (1981)
Saratoga Longshot (1976)
A Man of Little Evils (1973)

NONFICTION
Best Words, Best Order (1996)

POETRY
Common Carnage (1996)
Velocities: New and Selected Poems, 1966–92 (1994)
Body Traffic (1990)
Cemetery Nights (1987)
Black Dog, Red Dog (1984)
The Balthus Poems (1982)
Heat Death (1980)
Griffon (1976)
Concurring Beasts (1972)

Boy

in the

Water

Boy
in the
Water

A Novel

STEPHEN DOBYNS

METROPOLITAN BOOKS

Henry Holt and Company   New York

Metropolitan Books
Henry Holt and Company, Inc.
Publishers since 1866
115 West 18th Street
New York, New York 10011

Metropolitan Books is a registered trademark of
Henry Holt and Company, Inc.

Copyright © 1999 by Stephen Dobyns
All rights reserved.
Published in Canada by Fitzhenry & Whiteside Ltd.
195 Allstate Parkway, Markham, Ontario L3R 4T8

Library of Congress Cataloging-in-Publication Data
Dobyns, Stephen. 1941–
Boy in the water : a novel / Stephen Dobyns. — 1st ed.
p.   cm.
ISBN 0-8050-6020-0 (alk. paper)
I. Title.
PS3554.02B69   1999   98-56106
813'.54—dc21   CIP

Henry Holt books are available for special promotions and
premiums. For details contact: Director, Special Markets.

First Edition 1999

Designed by Paula Russell Szafranski

Printed in the United States of America
All first editions are printed on acid-free paper. ∞

10 9 8 7 6 5 4 3

For Michael Fischer and Suellen Mayfield

Everything that happens is as normal and expected as the spring rose or summer fruit; this is true of sickness, death, slander, intrigue, and all the other things that entertain or trouble imprudent men.

—Marcus Aurelius, *Meditations*

Boy
in the
Water

PROLOGUE

Like a black island on a turquoise sea, the dark shape floated on the surface of the water, lit from beneath by a string of underwater spotlights evenly spaced along the twenty-five yards of the swimming pool. They gave off the only light apart from the glow of a red exit sign above the door. The shape at first looked like a barrel or log. It took a moment to realize that it was a body: a boy, naked except for a pair of white Jockey shorts. He was small for his age and quite slender. Perhaps he was thirteen—an eighth grader. Only the boy's torso and the back of his head rose above the surface; his arms and legs hung down toward the black lines that ran the length of the pool's bottom. His elbows were bent and his fingers were curved and relaxed, as if he had been holding something but had just let it go. The underwater lights made the air shimmer above the water and formed rippling shadows on the green cinder-block walls and tile ceiling.

Something small with pointed ears and a bedraggled tail stepped gingerly across the boy's back, tentatively lifting and shaking one paw after another as it moved along the boy's shoulder blades. It mewed and the sound echoed throughout the pool area. When the creature turned and its full silhouette became visible against the turquoise, one could see it was a kitten stranded on this dark island, stepping lightly from one part of the boy's back to another, seeking the highest spot, while its movement caused the body to bob and turn very slightly. As a trickle of water ran across the boy's skin, the kitten reared up like a miniature horse to keep its paws from getting wet.

One side of the boy's body was white as parchment, lit up by the row of underwater lights. The other side was dark. His long red hair floated on the water in a ragged fringe. The kitten continued to mew and pace across the body as the turquoise light flickered and the boy's shadow drifted like a dark swimmer across the left-hand wall. The kitten's fur was orange-colored, and the orange of its fur and the red of the boy's hair seemed significant, as if there were a family connection. It was warm and humid in the large room and the air smelled of chlorine and mold.

Two men stood at the shallow end, watching. Their backs were to the door and together they formed two black silhouettes.

"When did you find him?" asked the one in an Irish fisherman's hat.

"Half an hour ago."

"And we're the only ones who know?"

"Except for whoever put him there."

The kitten paused and arched its back, and its damp fur bristled. Then it began to mew frantically.

"Do we call the police?" asked the bareheaded one.

"Let someone else do it."

"You're taking a chance."

"I see no reason to think so."

Both men wore heavy overcoats, giving off an odor of damp wool.

"And is this what you were expecting?"

"No, but it will do."

Outside it was snowing, as it had been for the past ten hours. More than a foot had fallen and the snow spread its white, uninterrupted surface across the lawns and playing fields to the edge of the forest. A half-moon glowed dully behind the clouds so one could make out the school's buildings: five two- and three-story structures built in the nineteenth century and laid out in the shape of the letter *H*. The bridge of the *H* was Emerson Hall, the administration and main classroom building, with its illuminated bell tower. Lights were spaced along the driveways and sidewalks, creating brilliant circles of white. Beyond the school buildings on a curving driveway stood a row of six dormitory cottages for students, and further along the driveway and scattered among the trees were five small houses where faculty lived. Lights burned in the windows of two of the cottages: Shepherd, where a dozen students and two teachers were eating popcorn and watching *Die Hard 3,* and Pierce. Here, in the faculty apartment on the top floor, a tall, thin man was hurriedly taking clothes from the bureau and closet and dumping them into the two suitcases that lay open on the bed. It was the Friday night after Thanksgiving and most of the students were gone.

Lights also burned in four of the five faculty houses. In one a woman was mending a tear in a blue denim skirt. Beside her was a bowl of red-and-white peppermints and every so often she would stop her sewing, unwrap the cellophane from a candy, and almost tenderly put it in her mouth. In another house, a boy and his mother were watching the last minutes of a college basketball game. In a third, a man and woman were making love on a blanket before the fireplace, in which three logs were burning. Their damp skin flickered orange in the firelight. In the fourth house, a bearded man was cleaning a double-barreled shotgun in the basement, gently pushing an oiled cotton swab down the length of one of the barrels. Upstairs, his wife watched television.

Over at the school garage, in his overheated office, the night watchman was sleeping with his head on the desk, his arms hanging down so his knuckles brushed the floor. He snorted as he breathed and a trickle of saliva had made a kidney-shaped stain on the green blotter beneath his mouth. Upstairs in a small studio apartment, the assistant cook lay on his single bed, studying the cracks in the ceiling. He was smoking a cigarette and the smoke spiraled upward, forming a nimbus around the bare bulb that hung from a black wire. Next to him on a small bedside table was a half-empty bottle of Budweiser and a saucer overflowing with cigarette butts. In the apartment behind Stark Chapel, the chaplain, a woman, was lying in bed reading an Ellery Queen mystery. Across from the chapel in the library, an overweight, balding man was sitting at a desk leafing through the week's magazines, licking the index finger of his right hand as he turned the pages. The half dozen other faculty and staff who lived on the grounds were away for the holidays.

The snow swirled around the security lights along the sidewalks and driveways. It seemed to plunge through a hole in the sky above the floodlit bell tower. It accumulated on the scaffolding where workmen had been repairing the roof of Emerson Hall. It dusted the heads of the alligatorlike gargoyles protruding from the cornices of the buildings. It collected on the vines of dried ivy clinging to the brick walls. It drifted through the broken windows of an unused dormitory and mixed with the dust on the floor. It formed delicate caps on the gilded tips of the iron fence posts lining the driveway. It gathered on the soccer goals and bleachers in the playing fields. It gave white cloaks to the pines. It seemed to bring the trees closer—the White Mountain National Forest that surrounded the school on three sides, three-quarters of a million acres stretching across north-central New Hampshire, a vast expanse of wintry dark, spotted with ice-covered lakes. The silence was so profound that a person standing motionless in the middle of the playing fields might have supposed that he had been struck deaf. Then a dog barked out in the woods, or perhaps it was the high yelp of a coyote.

South of the school, a quarter mile beyond its front gate, ran the Baker River. Then Antelope Road, extending through the woods between the tiny villages of Brewster Center and West Brewster, where a few of the faculty lived. Beyond Brewster Center lay the road to the city of Plymouth, twenty miles away. Not much was moving except snowplows at this time of night—sometimes a tractor-trailer out on the interstate, heading up to St. Johnsbury or down to Boston, leaving a cloud of snow in its wake.

The two men made their way out of the gymnasium, the one in the hat tugging at the door with his gloved hand to make sure it was locked. They turned up their collars and the bareheaded man put on a blue ski cap. They buried their hands in their pockets and seemed to pull their necks down into their collars.

"Where's Hawthorne?" asked the man in the ski cap.

"He went down to Concord to visit his friend Krueger."

"What a shame he was gone just when something like this

happened—a boy dead in the pool. What kind of headmaster is he, anyway?"

The other man laughed and began to move away from the building out into the snow. "One whose tenure at Bishop's Hill will be blessedly brief."

The men chuckled together as they made their way along the path, lifting their boots above the surface of the snow, like shore birds walking through water. The wind was beginning to pick up, blowing the snow in gusts across the playing fields, creating white billows that swirled and rose, as if the snow had a sort of life, enwrapping the men as they walked and smoothing out their footprints until, as the night progressed, there was no evidence that the two men had ever passed that way at all.

Part One

1

Burnt flesh newly whole, pink skin puckered on the back of the hand, a moonscape of scar tissue extending from the sleeve of a gray sport coat. In the correctness of dress, only the scars were out of place. As he reached out to shake the hand, Kevin Krueger tried not to hesitate. This was his friend, Jim Hawthorne, his former teacher, a man he loved, a man to whom he owed his career.

"Been a long time," said Krueger, squeezing the hand. "It's great to see you."

Bright morning light cut a yellow wedge across the office floor, the northern light of a fall day under a blue New Hampshire sky. The gold dome of the state capitol seemed to blaze under its regard.

His visitor noticed Krueger glancing at the scars. He gripped Krueger's hand firmly, as if to show he had entirely healed. "We talked on the phone."

"But I haven't seen you for nearly a year."

"Since before the fire." Hawthorne let go of Krueger's hand and stepped back. He was tanned and muscular, as if he spent part of every day at the health club, which was probably true. After all, he had been recuperating. Or perhaps it was that California glow. His hair was lighter than Krueger remembered, nearly blond and finely textured. Then, with shock, Krueger realized that Hawthorne's hair must have been burned off.

"You look well," said Krueger, hesitating whether to remain standing or sit down.

Hawthorne considered this estimate with amusement. "My doctor says I've been putting myself back together, but it feels like loafing. Now I want to return to work."

Renovation was going on in one of the state offices down the hall and the sound of an electric saw shrilled through the air. The work had begun on September 2 and after nearly three weeks Krueger still hadn't gotten used to the noise. He noticed Hawthorne's jaw tense, then relax.

"But not in your field?" said Krueger, turning to shut the window behind him.

"It's still school administration."

"Another sort of school . . ." Krueger let the remark hang. He didn't wish to bring up the fire, but that meant their talk stayed on a level of superficiality that he had never experienced with his friend. Was he afraid Hawthorne might cry? Or he himself would? After all, he had baby-sat for Lily at least half a dozen times in Boston. In his mind's eye, he could see her sparkling blond curls.

Krueger had met Hawthorne seven years earlier at Boston University, when he had begun graduate study in clinical psychology. Jim Hawthorne had been his adviser as well as teacher. Hawthorne was now thirty-seven. His birthday was in February, the same month as the fire. Only six years separated them and the two men had made many trips to various agencies and residential treatment programs throughout the state, especially to Ingram House in the Berkshires, where Krueger had done the work that resulted in his thesis. And when Krueger had said he was interested in a job with the New Hampshire Department of Education, Hawthorne hadn't protested but had made the necessary calls from San Diego, even though he would rather have seen Krueger working in mental health. Yet if Krueger had taken a position someplace else, Hawthorne wouldn't have been here this morning and Krueger wouldn't have had the opportunity now to assist him.

"I've been on the phone with members of the board," said

Hawthorne, "and they've sent me cartons of papers. Without actually visiting the place I don't see how I could be any more prepared."

"All this in six weeks?"

"They want someone in residence before the semester is much advanced. Classes began two weeks ago. And I was ready to make the change." He looked uncertain for a moment. "You know, it's time to make a fresh beginning."

Krueger wondered what Hawthorne meant by being "ready." His dark gray jacket, blue slacks, white shirt, even his tie looked new. But of course his other clothes had been destroyed. In fact, in terms of property, he'd probably lost everything. But what had he lost of the rest—of his essential self, what people outside their profession might call the soul?

"There's no real town nearby, at least for twenty miles," said Krueger.

"I like the country. Perhaps I'll learn to ski."

"You could get stuck after the snow begins. The roads can completely shut down."

"You're not very optimistic."

"These places, they develop their own ways of doing things. They get terribly ingrown: cousins and high school chums working together for years . . ."

"That's probably why the board insisted on an outside hiring."

"Of course, of course." Glancing at Hawthorne's hand, Krueger saw how the scar tissue extended up the backs of his fingers, how the little finger had no nail but ended in a sort of pink fragility.

Hawthorne was thin and handsome and somewhat gaunt, with dark indentations beneath his cheekbones. He wore glasses with pewter frames that kept sliding down his nose which he pushed back up with his thumb. Krueger was a few inches shorter and stocky, with a receding hairline, bushy eyebrows and a thick mustache, as if these bristling growths were soft bumpers between him and the world. These were men of similar backgrounds who had gone to similar New England schools and universities. They read the same magazines and newspapers, the same books. They felt at home in the same fashionable sections of Boston or San Diego, New York or San Francisco. But one had suffered great tragedy and the other kept trying to imagine it.

Krueger had felt inadequate to the task of helping his friend. He had written. They talked on the phone. Hawthorne's life had taken a turn impossible to anticipate and Krueger had been struck with wonder and compassion.

"It's hardly your sort of school," he said.

Hawthorne suddenly grinned. "On the cutting edge of failure, much like myself."

"You're a clinical psychologist with a tremendous reputation."

"The school claims to specialize in youngsters with special needs."

"You know what that means. Highly structured environment, empathy development, special needs—it's code. The school's just a dumping ground."

"It's been around a long time."

"In name only. Even ten years ago it was different. They started that business about special needs when enrollment began to fall. Their accreditation hangs by a thread."

"You think I can't save it?" There was a hint of something in Hawthorne's voice. Not anger or bravado. Perhaps it was no more than a touch of metal.

"I think it's an impossible task. Bishop's Hill needs an endowment, a new student body, a new faculty, and a new physical plant. They'd do better to tear the place down and start over."

"The board's given me complete control."

"But what about the staff? Do they know you're coming?"

"They were notified on Thursday."

Krueger almost smiled. "They must be jumping. And why did you decide against a residential treatment center?"

"Maybe I need a break." Hawthorne sat down at last, perching on the edge of the chair. Glancing around the office, his eyes settled on the photograph of Krueger's wife, Deborah, and their son and daughter. He looked away. "Maybe I just don't want that work anymore."

Krueger began to speak quickly. "I've been hearing about Bishop's Hill ever since I came here. The faculty keeps leaving, many are barely qualified. Parents complain. The health department came within an inch of closing down their kitchen. And there were other stories, allegations even."

"That's why they were eager to have me."

"What happened to the previous headmaster?"

"He's been gone several years. They had a sort of halfhearted search but it was only this summer that they decided to make a new commitment."

"It was either that or sell out to the Seventh-Day Adventists." Krueger rubbed the back of his neck. He hoped he wasn't getting another of his headaches. Hawthorne had been one of the preeminent administrators at one of the preeminent treatment centers in the country. He could probably go anywhere. Instead, he was choosing a fifth-rate institution on the verge of closing. "You'll be buried there," added Krueger.

Hawthorne seemed not to have heard. "What sort of person is the acting head?"

"Fritz Skander? He's the bursar. I've talked to him on the phone. Well-spoken, kind of upbeat and ironic at the same time. He was hired to teach math, then worked his way into the management end of things. He's been acting head for two or three years. Personally, I thought he'd be the one to get the job."

"He has no background in psychology or administration. He has the ability, but I have the résumé."

"You have tremendous ability. What about your research, your writing?"

Hawthorne began to speak, then turned away. A bony, angular face with a jutting chin—the morning light emphasized every wrinkle that had appeared since Krueger had seen him last, and again he recalled Lily's glorious curls. The mother, too, had been blond.

"Skander will be associate headmaster and continue as bursar, as well as teaching a section of geometry. The board chairman kept saying how everyone would have to bite the bullet. Otherwise, there's a psychologist at the school, a couple of mental health counselors. I've looked over the records of about half the students. I'd like to hire another psychologist as soon as possible."

"And the physical plant?"

"Serviceable but failing. There's a fund drive to replace the roof of the main building, Emerson Hall. Several of the dormitory cottages need substantial work."

Hawthorne ticked off various problems on his fingertips: a crack in a boiler, the need to replace a stove in the kitchen, faulty wiring in one of the dorms, cracking plaster. Krueger asked questions and his friend responded. Despite the difficulties, Hawthorne was eager to face the challenge. It was a new undertaking to fill his mind. As he said, a new beginning.

Krueger had heard from Hawthorne two days earlier after a silence of six weeks. He was leaving San Diego and would fly into Logan Sunday evening, then stay at a hotel and drive up to Concord on Monday. In his initial surprise, the only detail Krueger found odd was that Hawthorne would stay in a hotel. He probably had dozens of friends in the Boston area. It was only after Krueger hung up that he began to wonder about Hawthorne's whole enterprise.

"Why's Jim coming to New Hampshire?" Deborah had asked.

"He's taking a job at Bishop's Hill. Headmaster." Saying those words, Krueger had thought they sounded crazy, as if his friend had taken a job flipping burgers. Even though it was the weekend, Krueger made some calls. Maybe something had changed at Bishop's Hill in the past few months. But nothing Krueger heard had encouraged him and what had started out sounding insane only appeared more so. Perhaps, he thought, Hawthorne was planning a book and the school was connected with some new area of research.

Now, talking to Hawthorne, Krueger felt in no way persuaded, especially since the research and writing appeared to be a dead issue. But even if Hawthorne's only intention was to keep the school afloat and even if the board had committed itself to a new financial effort, it seemed too little too late. Krueger rubbed the back of his neck and wondered where he had put his aspirin.

"Maybe you can do it," said Krueger, trying to be optimistic. "It's astonishing that the place is still open. And of course it's expensive. Dumping grounds usually are."

Hawthorne rose from his chair and walked to the window. Sunlight illuminated the white bark of the birches on the far side of the parking lot. Hawthorne looked both ready and stoical, like a man about to lift something heavy. But mixed with his stoicism was sorrow. Not that his brow was creased or his shoulders were bent; he seemed perfectly calm. Indeed, in the strong chin, Krueger believed that others would see determination. But Krueger couldn't help but imagine the awfulness of Hawthorne's memories. If it had been his own wife and child, he didn't see how he could live.

Hawthorne walked over and squeezed Krueger's shoulder. "Jesus, it's great to see you. You remember those basketball games we used to have? Maybe we can do that again."

The warmth of his smile was a great reassurance. Krueger tried to speak but could only nod a little foolishly.

"I wanted to come out to California in February."

"I couldn't have seen anyone. I was dead. Dead inside at least."

"Even so . . ." Krueger tugged at his mustache.

Hawthorne turned again to the window. "What other problems do you think I'll have at Bishop's Hill?"

With relief Krueger returned to the subject that, though bleak, was at least precise. "Your presence should do wonders for morale. I'll bet even the non–psychology types have been reading your articles. You'll have to be firm, of course. I'm sure they've been worried by how things have drifted along. The main thing is the children—teenagers really. They're the ones who've suffered."

"Anything more than educational neglect?"

"A tenth grader was arrested for shoplifting in Plymouth in May. Some drunk driving. Marijuana. The school uses a totally antiquated merit system with so many checks resulting in punishment. On the other hand, a new teacher joined the staff in January. I don't think it's an us-against-them scenario. There's even a new cook."

"Then what's the problem?"

"I'd like you closer to Concord, where I can see you." Krueger gave a laugh, but it sounded false to his ears. "And it's not your area of expertise."

"You think I won't be able to do it?"

"You're a tremendous administrator."

"That was before."

Krueger turned in his chair. "I'll be frank with you. I don't understand why you want Bishop's Hill. It's a pseudo–prep school for kids who have managed to stay out of agencies or institutions only because their parents have money. It's a sinking ship. I don't know if anybody could fix it and I don't know why you want to."

"I told you, I want to do something different."

"And that's sufficient reason to go to Bishop's Hill? You could go to one of the best places in the country and you're choosing one of the worst. The money must be terrible." Krueger tried to make it a joke, but it didn't sound like a joke.

"I'm not doing it for the money."

"So what *are* you doing it for?"

"Simple professionalism."

"It'll be like trying to empty Lake Winnipesaukee with a pail."

"Maybe that's what I'm good for right now. Listen, I have to start completely over. Can't you see that the fire was my fault? When this position opened up at Bishop's Hill, I jumped at it."

"You know as well as I do who caused the fire."

Hawthorne ignored him. "If Bishop's Hill doesn't work out, then I'm finished. I don't mean I couldn't get other jobs. Just that this is the last chance I'm giving myself."

The silence that followed was filled with the whine of the saw. Krueger heard his secretary laugh and a door slam. He thought of how far Hawthorne had traveled from Krueger's own life. "You'll spend the night? Deborah'd love to see you. And your namesake, he's already four."

"I'd like to get up there as soon as possible. About how far is it?"

"Two and a half hours door-to-door. The color should be just getting started."

"I had some stuff shipped from San Diego. It'll arrive next week."

"But you'll stay for dinner?"

"Thanks, but I still get tired pretty easily."

Krueger stood up. His chair spun back and hit the wall with a thud. "We need to talk more. Stay for lunch. If I were the one going up there, I think I'd move into it gently."

"You think I'll fuck up, don't you?"

"Of course not, but they've had lots of time to get fixed in their ways." Krueger was aware of not answering the question. What did he know of his friend's mental state? Only that Hawthorne had chosen to bury himself in a backwater, which was itself evidence of eccentricity. Perhaps something worse than eccentricity.

Hawthorne had paused at the door. "As you say, the children come first." It seemed only politeness that was holding him back.

Krueger gave up. The conversation had exhausted him. "Give me a call once you get there. Or I'll call you. You know that my office is at your disposal."

Hawthorne grinned. "It's been a while since I've gone to school."

They shook hands again. This time Krueger kept his eyes away from the scars. He wondered how much was hidden by Hawthorne's clothes, whether his entire body had the shiny delicacy of the wrist. Although Krueger felt guilty, he was comforted by Hawthorne's grip. It seemed evidence of something positive. I'm grasping at straws, he thought.

After he had shut the door, Krueger was struck by something Hawthorne had said. What had he meant by saying the fire was his fault? That kid Carpasso had set the fire. Everyone knew that.

The girl sat on the edge of the stage with a cigarette hanging from her lips and stared at her toes in their small, golden thongs. The toenails had just been painted a shade of red called "Passion Juice" and were not entirely dry. They sparkled in the intensity of the spotlights. The girl's back was bent and a strand of peroxided hair fell forward, concealing one side of her face. She picked at a dab of red on her toe and blew smoke from the corner of her mouth. Around her left ankle was a gold chain with a heart, a gift from her father six years earlier.

She seemed alone in the room despite the two dozen men and the waitresses in their skimpy dresses weaving between the tables. A few men clapped as Gypsy, naked and businesslike, walked briskly from the stage to the dressing room, carrying a little blue dress in one hand and a pair of black high heels in the other. She had just finished her number, and briefly there was a kind of silence. Someone whistled shrilly; a chair scraped; the neck of a beer bottle clinked against the rim of a glass.

The music began again. The girl dropped her cigarette and ground it into the tile. By the time she was on her feet she was already into her dance, sashaying up the remaining two steps and across the stage, her eyes focused on the spotlights so everything would be a blur when she looked away. The music was the long disco version of the Stones' "Miss You," and she matched her steps to the staccato precision of the drums and bass, snapping her fingers and lifting her knees so they flashed in the lights. She thought of the music as antique—the song was twenty years old—and she imagined that her parents had once danced to it, her father taking Dolly's hand, then spinning her away.

The girl kept her head raised as she moved to the chrome pole in the middle of the stage. She was the cool one who never let her eyes drift below an imaginary line, as if beneath that line were only fog, like early-morning fog at Rye Beach. When she table-danced, men would often say, "Why don't you look at me?" And sometimes they whined and sometimes they called her "Bitch." She wanted to say, "Fuck you," but she'd just smile as if her thoughts were in exotic places, Zanzibar or Rio de Janeiro. And when the men tucked ten- or twenty-dollar bills under the thin gold chain around her waist, she would stroke their cheeks just once and draw her nails lightly down the stubble on their faces, but she still wouldn't look at them.

Gripping the pole with her right hand, the girl swirled around it with her head back and her nearly white hair streaming behind her. She had pinned it up but, as she spun, her hair came free and she could feel how the men grew attentive, as if her hair's very loosening were a sign of her wildness. The girl focused on the mirrors on the ceiling above the stage, watching the pretty, heavily made-up face of her reflection stare back at her. At one moment she was amazed by her beauty and at the next by what she saw as her ugliness: her lips not enough of this, her nose not enough of that, and the blue of her eyes insufficiently dazzling. She wore a mixture of pastel-colored veils that fluttered in the breeze from a fan at the edge of the stage: a two-piece costume made by an ex-dancer who had gotten fat and now designed costumes for other girls, polyester delicacies whose only function was to be ripped away in a fantasy of sexual abandon. The veils whirled and eddied around her in varying shades of blue, green, and red—pulsings that let the girl imagine herself a multicolored bird of Eastern mythology, beautiful but deadly. The stage was eight feet wide and formed a runway between the tables where the men sat. The dancers called it the meat rack. As the girl spun round the pole, the veils separated and came together, giving glimpses of her tanned body and revealing her small breasts—too small to the girl's mind, small and undeveloped, almost boyish. They embarrassed her, but after all, she was only fifteen.

As she spun, she kicked off one slipper, then the other. Her movements were a mixture of sensual languor and military precision as she keyed them to the rhythm of the song: "I been sleeping all alone; Lord, I miss you . . ." She had begun work that day at one and now it was rush hour on a Monday afternoon, September 21—men leaving work in Boston and heading to suburbs along the North Shore. A few would stop for a beer and to watch a pretty girl show her naked body.

Some would pay to have the girl dance for them alone—one man at a table with a beer and a shot and the girl weaving back and forth with her pubic hair trimmed into a heart shape or diamond shape, whatever had become the newest fashion among the girls, the same way they would get boob jobs or even lip jobs and rush to one surgeon after another. And this girl, too, though she needed every penny she earned, had gone to get implants—it only made sense, she told herself, because her breasts were so small. The doctor had refused, saying she was still growing, but he didn't say anything else; that is, he didn't report her, though he could tell she wasn't eighteen.

The club had no windows, so it could be any time of the day or night. Mostly it seemed like one unchanging minute. One dancer replaced another, one song replaced the next, and even the men looked the same in their longing and feigned boredom—small but endless variations of the same sixty seconds till the club closed at one in the morning and the girls went off to whatever domestic deficiency they called home. By then the girl would have danced on stage a dozen times and, if she was lucky and the club was busy, she would have danced at a dozen tables. She would have washed a dozen times and changed her makeup a dozen times and still she'd feel the places where men had touched her ass or tried to rub against her breasts and tell her what a fox she was or what a bitch and how they wanted to push her down on the floor and do things to her. One fat man had come back night after night to say how he wanted to piss in her mouth, until she had complained and Bob had told the man not to come back, because he wasn't spending any money. But if the man had been buying drinks, then Bob would have told her to get used to it and what the hell did she expect. She would have accepted it because Bob knew that her ID was phony, but he wouldn't let her go unless there was a problem, because he got his percentage and many of the men liked babies, liked little girls, even if their tits were small and they looked like boys from the back, the cheeks of their buttocks tight and shiny.

The girl's sweaty fingers squeaked on the pole. She drifted to a stop, putting her hands down low on the cold metal, then kicking her feet so they rose up and curled around the pole until she was upside down with the veils swirling over her head and the sequined V of her bikini bottom catching the light. She imagined the sequins sparkling, the men slowing their drinking to watch, the stupid pigs, the hairy scum.

One man whistled, and one of her regulars yelled her name: "Misty!" She was Misty. She slid down onto her shoulders and did a backward roll and when she stood up the top part of her costume fell away into her hand. Tensing, she waited for the jokes about her flat chest, the jeering that sometimes came—not all the time, but enough to grind her guts. But this time no one shouted about tiny tits or banana body and Misty let the veils drop at the side of the stage, then did a slow cartwheel back to the pole as Mick Jagger sang about "some Puerto Rican girls who're dying to meet you." It amused her that the thousands of dollars Dolly had spent on gymnastics classes now let her be such a hotshot, as Bob called her, doing tricks that none of the other girls could match.

A handstand let Misty slide her feet up the pole again, gripping it with her thighs. As she turned, she extended her tongue, flicking it against the shiny metal, which tasted of salt from the other girls' sweaty hands. A man pounded his fist on a table so that a bottle overturned, and he or someone else whistled. But she had detached her mind from where she was and thought how good it would be to get back to the apartment she shared with two of the other dancers, how she would take a long bath and listen to her Walkman in the tub—Charlie Haden and Pat Metheny on the CD *Beyond the Missouri Sky*, because away from the club she hated to listen to any music she could dance to. And she thought how she wouldn't be working tomorrow and she would take the T to Revere Beach, then to a movie or the Cambridgeside mall, where she could walk and walk and look in the shops, but she wouldn't buy anything—she was saving her money. She'd spend the whole day by herself and if anyone spoke to her she would tell him to fuck off, fuck off, because she'd been dancing too much, getting her ears too full of those people's cheap noise. Isolation was what she wanted, because in two months at the club she had seen girls burn out on stage—dancer meltdown. It scared her because it seemed so easy and she thought, I could do that. I've got to be careful.

Misty arched back in a slow flip, then she spun away from the pole and sent her hands into a splayed-fingered ballet around the gold clasp that held the bottom part of her costume in place, inserting her thumbs under the elastic and pulling the waist band from her waist, letting it snap back, then pulling it again and holding it with her elbows out to the side, striding to the music along the perimeter of the meat rack. But because she'd been staring at the lights, she could see little except thick masculine shapes and the lights of the video games and three pinball machines along the back wall, and she realized that was a mistake because she wanted to find out if the man was here, the one with a sport coat and tie who had been coming for the past several days and drank only Coke and watched only her. He didn't seem hungry or excited, though; it was as if he were seeing not a naked young girl but a piece of furniture, something not special or collectible, only part of his job. That had worried Misty and she thought he might be a cop, but Bob swore he knew all the cops and he'd never seen this guy before. Even so, Misty hoped she wouldn't see him again, because if he wasn't a cop or a nutcase, then he could be a PI. It was Gypsy who said he might be a PI, and Misty had to ask what that meant. "Private detective, dummy," Gypsy told her, not mean but sarcastic, as was her way.

If the man was a detective, then Misty knew what would be coming next. Partly that frightened her and partly she felt relieved, because she already had four thousand dollars put aside, and though she meant to save more and have ten grand by Thanksgiving, she was worried she might blow it on something else or melt down or buy drugs and forget about her plan—about the only thing that mattered in her life, the reason she had been shaking her butt in men's faces since the July 4 weekend, when she had started work, getting her ears full of the noise, the men's talk, words that were meant to be sweet or sexy or macho but that made her hate them, made her want to reach into the men's pants and rip away their pricks like yanking weeds out of the ground.

Misty went into a forward roll as Mick sang, "I guess I'm lying to myself because it's you and no one else," and when she came onto her feet she was holding the bottom part of her costume in her left hand and keeping the splayed fingers of her right mockingly across her pubic hair as men shouted. She turned her eyes away from the lights now because she wanted to see who was there, wanted to drag her eyes across each male face. She was naked except for the chain around her waist and the chain around her ankle. Her skin was a light bronze from the three times a week she went to the tanning parlor. No strap marks or bikini lines: she never showed her skin on the beach. Just above her buttocks and around her coccyx was her one extravagance, a tattoo of the biological symbol for woman in bright blue and red and the size of a closed fist so the scumbags would know they weren't looking at a boy when they stared at her ass, the tight, muscular buttocks each forming half a golden peach. She bent forward and ran her spread fingers down her thighs to her ankles, gripping them as she turned a slow 360 degrees, showing her tattoo to the entire room.

Then, at the end of the bar, she spotted him in his tie and sport coat and this time he wasn't alone. Misty recognized the other man even before she saw his mustache, knew him just by the curve of his shoulders, the thick graying hair he was so vain about. She believed she could have spotted him if the room had been pitch dark. Even at this distance she felt she could see the black hairs on the backs of his hands and the yellow flecks in his brown eyes, turd-brown eyes, she called them.

Misty began spinning around the perimeter of the stage with her arms outstretched. Several of her regulars called to her but she ignored them. On the far side from the two men, she fell to her stomach, then she wriggled snakelike across the tiles with her tongue darting and her fingertips fluttering against the cheeks of her ass. Reaching the edge, she pushed herself up into a handstand and came down with her back to the men, bending over with her legs wide apart, down, down until her hands rested on the floor and her peroxided hair dragged on the tiles as she looked back between her legs at the two men at the end of the bar, the one she didn't know and the one she hated, pursing her lips and kissing the air, before gripping her ankles and dragging her red nails up the backs of her legs, leaving parallel scratches on the backs of her thighs till the heels of her hands touched her buttocks. She let her fingertips play against the black diamond shape of her pubic hair, let her fingertips caress the creases of her vulva, and all to the same precise beat of the song, "Miss You," which was now coming to an end. Then she dug two fingertips of each hand into the bristly pubic hair and began to draw the flesh apart, holding her vagina open with two fingers of one hand as she inserted the index finger of the other, listening to men shout and hearing Bob's angry voice because she had broken the club's primary rule, the rule that stood at the head of a hundred other stupid rules and that would cost her the job, but what did it matter? This was her last night, she was already out of here.

The music stopped, not because the song had ended but because Lucy at the bar had flicked the switch. Misty stood up and walked to where she had left her costume and cigarettes, striding as purposefully as a soldier, with her chin raised. Men were shouting and whistling. She shook a cigarette out of the pack, stuck it in her mouth, and lit it, clicking the Zippo shut as she blew a mouthful of smoke at the ceiling. Then she walked quickly to the dressing room. She heard someone calling to her, "Jessica, Jessica!" But that wasn't her name. Her name was Misty.

She went through a door that swung shut behind her and tossed her costume onto the table. Out there she had felt mean and proud of herself, but all of a sudden she could feel herself choking up as tears filled her eyes.

"What in the fuck's wrong with you?" said Gypsy angrily. She stood in front of Misty, six inches taller in high heels and a mountain of red hair, with her artificial breasts shoved between the two of them like small haystacks scantily contained by pink polyester. "You've just thrown away your job—an easy grand a week into the trash. You know that Bob won't take that shit."

"I'm quitting anyway," said Misty, wiping her hand across her eyes and going to her locker. She worked the numbers of the combination. "You can have my costumes if you want them."

"Who's the guy you were showing your pussy to? I hope he's paying you big money."

Misty pulled on her blue jeans. "My old man," she said. She didn't look at Gypsy.

"You were sticking your fingers up yourself for your father?" Gypsy had lowered her voice. There was still shouting out in the club.

Misty drew a blue University of New Hampshire sweatshirt over her head. It hung halfway down her thighs. "Not my father, my stepfather. My father's dead." Her voice was neutral—the practiced tone she thought she had perfected. She tied her money belt around her waist and shoved it under her jeans. Then she stuck her feet into her Tevas and adjusted the Velcro. She grabbed her green backpack off the hook and collected a couple of loose dance tapes from the shelf along with a squirrel-sized brown teddy bear that was missing an eye. The bear's name was Harold; she couldn't remember a time when she didn't have him.

Misty wished she could wash the makeup off her face and body but she didn't have the time. Maybe later, depending where Tremblay took her. She hoped the detective would stay with them. She was afraid of being alone with Tremblay. Misty dug a blue Red Sox cap out of her bag, then twisted up her hair and pulled the cap over it, turning the cap around so the bill pointed down her back. Taking a towel from a hook, she rubbed it across her mouth and face, trying to remove her lip gloss. The towel smelled of sweat and cheap perfume.

There was a hammering on the door and Bob entered without waiting for a response. He was tall and he shaved his head to look mean. "You're done. You're outta here!" He stood holding the door open. Misty could see her stepfather standing just beyond him. Tremblay was brushing his thumb against his gray mustache, and he wore a little smile to indicate he wasn't surprised. He was never surprised.

"Where're you going to go?" asked Gypsy, already taking the costumes from the other girl's locker and putting them in her own.

"School," said Misty. "I'm going to school. I'm going to start tenth grade." She tossed the dirty towel at Bob, then walked past him without saying a word.

The bigger of the two men walking along the edge of the surf was laughing and scuffing his heels in the sand. It was a cool night on the first day of fall and the men wore dark jackets. The moon to the east was a little past full and seemed to lay a silver finger on the water off Revere Beach as the surf advanced and retreated with hisses and melancholy sighs. There was no wind.

"If you could of seen him, Sally," he was saying, "I almost pissed myself. That would have made both of us. He was wearing these light pants and suddenly I seen this big wet spot. I couldn't help it, I snorted right through my mask."

The smaller man chuckled appreciatively, but all he wanted was to go home. It was past two-thirty and he had an appointment at eight the next morning to look at a greyhound puppy, "a guaranteed champion," he'd been told.

"He didn't even notice what he'd done. 'Jesus, you piece of shit,' I told him, 'look what you done to yourself. Didn't you have a mommy?'"

The smaller man chuckled again. His name was Sal Procopio and he was twenty-six. The guy with him, Frank, was a little older. Sal didn't know Frank's last name, or rather, he'd heard Frank give several—all of them French, so maybe he was a Canuck. For that matter, Sal didn't even know if the guy's first name was really Frank, so maybe that was phony as well. In fact, the longer he knew Frank, the less he knew him, as if each new fact took away a piece of knowledge instead of adding to the small amount already accumulated. Sal wasn't sure how he felt about this.

Frank laid an arm across Sal's shoulder, squeezing the muscle. With his other hand, he accompanied his story, spreading his fingers or closing them into a fist. "But, hey, I didn't have a lot of time. The longer you're inside, the bigger chance you take. You hear what I'm saying? What if a cop had wandered in? It could be anybody, some alkie wanting another drink. The chickenshits are worse than the tough guys. They don't fuckin' move! This guy just stood there and pissed himself. 'What's wrong,' I tell him, 'ain't you seen a gun before?' Asshole in a liquor store. You'd think he was a virgin. These guys get stuck up all the time."

Sal tried to keep his feet out of the water but Frank kept bumping him. Although the tide was going out, every so often a large wave sent the foam right up to his basketball shoes. The two men were walking south. Few people were visible: some couples making out but no one nearby. Sal had brought girls to Revere a few times when he was a kid but he didn't like getting sand in his Jockey shorts and he didn't like being seen. People knew what you were doing. Even under a blanket, they could tell what was going on. If you couldn't afford a motel, then you had no business with a girl in the first place, that was how he saw it.

Frank gave his shoulder another squeeze. "So I tell him to get a move on. I should never of been friendly in the first place. 'We're closing in ten minutes,' he says. His back was to me and he hadn't seen the mask. So I put the barrel against his ear, smacking him a little so I could hear the clunk against his skull and I asked him as sweet as I could, 'You ever seen one of these?' He cut his eyes toward it and I cocked it. That little double click—it's almost like music. That's when he pissed himself. Jesus, I laughed."

Sal tried to laugh as well, but it ended up more like a grunt. He'd been out in the car ready to take off at the first sign of trouble, even

27

though he'd sworn to wait. This was their fourth job together and Sal wanted out. In the morning, he'd get this greyhound pup, train him, and make a bundle. It was honest work, pretty much. His only worry was that Frank would get mad when he said he didn't want to drive anymore. He'd seen Frank's temper in a bar about two weeks earlier. Frank hadn't been drinking but that only made it scarier, that he'd try to beat a guy to death cold sober. If he hadn't been pulled off, Frank would have killed the guy, just beaten his head in with the pool cue. And what had the guy done, for Pete's sake? Called him a loony when Frank got mad and threw down his cue. Five bucks on the game, and Frank was ready for the slammer. Shit, Sal had been called worse than that, a whole lot worse.

Frank stepped away as another wave came up the beach. The foam glittered and slid toward them. "But the kid wouldn't do shit. He wouldn't get the money and wouldn't budge. A red light on the video camera kept blinking. So I grabbed his hair and shoved the pistol right into his mouth so it jams against his tonsils. 'You got two seconds,' I told him. No way was he going to fuck with me, piss or no piss. He straightened up, though he was bawling. Nodding and gagging all at once. At least he emptied the cash register."

"How much?"

"A couple of grand or more. We'll count it out."

The two men had met at a bar across from Wonderland in May. Frank was from New Hampshire, at least that's what Sal thought. He was about five ten, with a narrow face and thick dark hair that he slicked back with gel. Frank wouldn't say much about himself. Sometimes he talked about cooking, so maybe he'd been a cook. He told a lot of jokes and had no trouble talking to women. He was always upbeat, or pretty much. He didn't seem to have a job and Sal figured he made his money at the track, until Frank asked him to drive for him. Before that Sal had already told him about his troubles with the law. Frank had been sympathetic, like he'd had cop problems of his own. And Frank didn't drink much or do drugs. He seemed like a guy who was always in charge so Sal figured he could do the driving. After all, he'd be sitting in the car; if anything bad happened, he could drive away. That was in June. Now Sal didn't trust Frank anymore. He'd seen him in fights, he'd listened to stories that he'd thought were total bullshit, then he got to be unsure. Frank didn't have a lid, was how Sal put it to himself. If he thought of doing a thing, he'd do it. He was like a drunk but he never got drunk and Sal almost laughed at that, though he didn't feel like laughing and only wanted to get his cut and go home, have a glass of milk, eat a couple of Devil Dogs, and hit the sack.

Frank carried a small backpack. His Chevy pickup was parked in the lot. Sal's was farther up along the curb. They always met at Revere Beach. Frank had talked about being followed and being careful, and at first Sal had thought that sounded smart. But now he thought, who the fuck was going to follow them? Earlier Sal had meant to tell Frank that tonight was his last job, but he didn't know how to bring it up without sounding chickenshit. Then he thought, why say anything? The next time Frank called, Sal would say he couldn't do it, that he'd had enough. Then he thought of moving, getting a whole new place, so he wouldn't have to see Frank again. The more he thought that, the more he liked it. He liked the idea of Frank calling and there being nobody home.

"Did I tell you the one about the two cannibals who cook themselves a clown?"

"Yeah, you did," said Sal. " 'This taste funny to you?' I liked it." He tried laughing again but his throat hurt. The sand curving ahead of them was divided into two shades of darkness, showing how far the tide had climbed the beach.

Frank was laughing. He put his arm across Sal's shoulder again, hugging him to him. "You know, I did a guy the other night."

" 'Did a guy'?" Sal felt Frank's fingers gripping his shoulder.

"Yeah, I fixed him."

"You shot him?"

"Doesn't matter how I did it. It got done, that's all." Frank kicked up a spray of sand. "What's more it felt good. Felt like I was creaming my jeans. He was a guy I'd known a long time. I hadn't seen him for a while, but he'd been in my head. He was from Manchester, like me. Buddy Roussel—shit, I'd known him way back in school. Ran into him in a club."

"What'd he do?" Sal tried to step away and got his feet wet.

"Jesus, what didn't he do? He got me in trouble in school when some equipment was stolen, a bunch of bats mostly, a couple of old gloves. Then he told this girl some stuff about me, that I'd slapped another girl, which was a lie. She'd tried to hit me and I'd put up my hand, that's all there was to it. I couldn't even get work because of him. There was a kitchen job I applied for and Buddy said something to the owner. I couldn't find out what he'd said, but it was total bull-shit. I'd done lots of cooking. I was good at it. But it didn't make any difference. Buddy'd already been at the guy. A fast-food joint, what do they cook anyway? Burgers and ice cream—that's not food, not real food anyway."

"Sounds like a long time ago." Sal's stomach felt like it got when he was outside in the car and Frank was in the liquor store with his gun—partly it was cold, partly it was fluttery.

"Yeah, what goes around comes around. Course I was willing to let bygones be bygones, but he had to shoot off his mouth. He said he figured I was locked up somewheres. What'd he have to say that for? He had a girl with him, like he was saying it just for her. So I made like I was leaving and waited outside. I got him when he came out. Just like the end of a movie. Boom—*The End of Buddy Roussel,* starring Francis LeBrun. He was still with the girl, but she didn't see my face. Shit, she was too busy screaming at Buddy to get the fuck up off the sidewalk, like she didn't even know he was dead yet, the stupid cow. But I don't know what Buddy might have told her. Like my name or where he knew me from. Anyway, now I got to change my game plan sooner than I meant to. I got a cousin north of Plymouth and I'd already been talking to him about a job, something legitimate. The trouble is, it means the end of our party. No more liquor stores for a while. I hate to disappoint you."

A young couple were wrapped up in a blanket with only their toes showing. The men didn't speak as they walked past. Frank was still scuffing his heels as if he enjoyed making cuts in the sand that the tide would erase. No more liquor stores, thought Sal. He wondered why Frank was telling him this stuff. Again he thought how he wanted to get his share of the money and go home. Tomorrow he'd start looking for a new place. Even Providence wouldn't be too far away. It didn't matter that Frank was leaving. He could always come back.

"This cousin of mine, Larry, he's never been in trouble. He's a real good cook and even took some classes up in Vermont, at least for a while, but it was too chichi, you hear what I'm saying? Fuckin' sauces up the wazoo. Now he's cooking at a school. He said he'd give me a job any time I wanted, full time, part time, it didn't matter. Larry's dad was the brother of my old man, the cocksucker. Both dead now, but he was okay. Worked in a hardware store. He gave me my first hammer when I was six or seven. Means a lot, your first hammer." Frank paused to light a cigarette.

Sal saw Frank's face flare in the light of the Bic: dark eyes squeezed half shut against the smoke, dark hair combed back from his forehead. Why's he telling me this? Sal asked himself. He glanced back at the couple on the blanket about fifty feet away.

"That's too bad about you going away," said Sal. "We were doing all right."

"Yeah," said Frank philosophically. "Everything gets fucked sooner or later."

"You really killed this guy?"

"Deader'n a doornail."

"Didn't it bother you?" Sal tried to keep the surprise out of his voice.

"Sometimes there's a fuss, and I hate fuss. This time there was no fuss. First he was there, then he wasn't."

Sal wanted the night to be over. He wanted to be someplace with other people and lots of activity. "It's about time to split up the money, wouldn't you say?" They were again walking side by side on the packed sand. Frank's cigarette made a red streak as he moved it to his mouth. Sal could feel his wet socks bunch between his toes.

"I got bad news about that," said Frank, sounding apologetic.

"You mean about the money?"

"Yeah, the money."

"You mean you didn't get as much as you thought?"

"No, I got it all right. He had a whole bunch of fifties."

"Then what's the problem?"

"I just don't want to give you any."

Sal didn't think he'd heard right. "Say again?"

"This going-away business, I don't know how much I'll need. So, you know, I'm going to keep your share."

"I thought you'd be getting a job." Sal forgot that his feet were wet, hardly heard the splash of his footsteps.

"Actually, I got two jobs. I met a guy who offered me a sweet deal at this place. He looked me up a couple of weeks ago. Wants me to do a number. I didn't have to go find him or anything. He'd heard of me in Portsmouth. Where I was before here. Did I tell you what they call a female clone?"

"Yeah, a clunt. I thought you were going up to this school to cook."

"Jesus Christ, can't you keep anything straight? Why the fuck would I stick myself up there in the boondocks unless I had a good reason? The number came first, the cooking came second, Buddy Roussel came third. The school's going bust; they're dying for students. They'll take anybody day or night. It made the whole business a piece of cake."

"I still don't see why you can't give me the money. I want to buy a dog, a greyhound." His stomach was hurting again

"Jesus, you'd be better throwing the money into the street. I'm doing you a favor."

"By not giving me the money?" Sal stopping walking. They were both in the water.

Frank flicked his cigarette through the air. It made a red arc into the surf. "I fuckin' told you. You fuckin' stupid? I'm in a jam and got to move fast. And this other job, the big one, after I take care of it, then I'll have to disappear. Get up to Quebec or someplace and live fat."

"I could lend it to you."

"You're not going to be lending it to me, asshole, I'm going to be taking it."

"What about me?" Sal thought about what Frank had told him about killing that guy Buddy something.

"You, nothing," said Frank. "You don't even exist. Jesus Christ, you're dumb. Did I ever tell you how you brainwash an Italian?"

"Then keep the money." Sal took a step deeper into the water. "I'm glad to do you the favor. We're buddies, right? Keep the whole thing."

"You didn't say if I'd told you the joke."

"An enema, goddamnit. That's how you brainwash an Italian. You give him an enema!"

"Don't talk to me like that, Sally. I always been polite to you."

Sal stood up to his ankles in the water. His head felt full of yelling, and in the midst of the clamor he realized he was going to piss himself just like the kid in the liquor store.

"Bishop's Hill," said Frank. "Bishop's Hill Academy. I love names like that. You can almost smell the money. Me, I never got past tenth grade. Thought of taking the G.E.D. at one point, but why bother? I don't need a fuckin' piece of paper saying I can count. But this cooking job at Bishop's Hill, it'll be like being in school again, except nobody's going to be shouting at me or pushing me around or making fun of me. Shit, I'll even get paid. Can you beat that?"

"Let me go, Frank."

"No can do."

"I'm a friend, right. I won't say anything. You can even have my car. Let me go."

"I already got a car."

"I got the money from the other jobs at my place. I'll give it to you. Just follow me back."

Frank zipped up his backpack, then swung it onto his left shoulder. "I'm not dumb, Sally. Stupidity's not my problem. It's like an insult to think I'm dumb."

Sal stepped deeper into the water. There was something in Frank's hand but it wasn't a gun. It was something small.

"You do a little business for a while," said Frank, "then it comes to an end. It's fall and I got to go to school. Did I tell you that joke about what elephants use for tampons?"

The ice pick in his hand was tilted so it wouldn't catch the moonlight. Frank grinned and rested his arm on Sal's shoulders, a friendly gesture. Sal tried to step away, but it was too late. Perhaps he felt the prick of the needle point at the base of his skull but most likely it happened too fast to feel even that. Frank shoved the ice pick upward into the softness, then gave it a little swirl, cutting a cone shape into "the gray stuff," as he called it. Then he slipped it out. Sal's whole body was twitching and jittering. He grabbed Sal's shoulder with one hand and the seat of his pants with the other. He walked him deeper into the water. Sal himself wasn't walking; he was dead weight.

"Sheep, asshole, that's what elephants use for tampons." He lowered Sal into the water so he wouldn't splash. It was like those baptisms he'd seen on TV. He liked the idea of making Sal clean again.

Frank pressed his foot down on Sal's back to force the air out of his lungs—the bubbles burst around him like farts, like farting in the bathtub, and that made Frank chuckle.

"Think of it this way," he told Sal, "I'm saving you from ever being sent to jail."

Frank turned and walked back to shore with the water running off his clothes. He was going to school. He was almost excited.

2

Because she was interested but still expected to be bored, the woman sat in the back row over by the window so if she wished she could turn her attention to the late-afternoon sun laying its orange light across the playing fields, where some half-dozen young men were kicking a soccer ball as if it represented the very acme of earthly endeavor. Her name was Kate Sandler and she had been teaching Italian and Spanish at Bishop's Hill since January, when her predecessor, Mr. Mead, had given the school two days' notice before relocating to the west coast of Mexico, "for his health," he had said, "both mental and physical." As a divorced mother with a seven-year-old son, Kate had felt lucky to get the job. Now, three weeks into the fall semester, her sympathies lay with the absent Mr. Mead. Kate was trim, athletic, and thirty-four with shoulder-length black hair that she wore in a ponytail at school. Reaching back from her left temple was a white streak about an inch wide that had made its appearance while she was still in college. At the time she had been sorry to turn prematurely gray but the white streak had been the extent of the change and now she valued it as something that made her memorable to clerks and garage mechanics.

Eighteen of Kate's colleagues sat in front and to her left; the remaining three or four probably wouldn't appear. Kate thought of them all as survivors—some she liked, some she didn't, others she hardly knew. Now she felt herself to be a part of them. She, too, was a survivor. In the spring semester, she had been invited to several dinners, she had gone on one rather dreary date, and once, when her daffodils were in bloom and she was feeling optimistic, she had invited an older couple over to her small house for lasagna. Still, there was no one to whom she felt particularly close.

The meeting was scheduled for five and it was nearly that now. Her colleagues were beginning to look attentive, turning from their slouched positions and perfunctory conversations. Green shades were drawn down over the top half of the high windows, giving an aquatic tint to the ceiling. The dark oak woodwork had been recently polished and the air retained the faint aroma of Murphy's Soap. Next to Kate, Chip Campbell, the history teacher and swimming coach, patted her knee and said, "Let's *vamos,* buster!" But whether he meant that they should leave immediately or that he wanted the meeting to begin, Kate couldn't decide. Chip had a round red face and the look of a former athlete who has gone to seed. His short sandy hair was brushed back in a ragged flattop. He had taught at Bishop's Hill for twelve years. Before that he had taught in public schools in Connecticut until, as he said, he couldn't stand the bullshit anymore.

Directly in front of Kate sat Alice Beech, the school nurse, in her white uniform. She glanced over her shoulder at Chip, then smiled at Kate before turning away. Chip directed a mocking smile at her back. He and a few others claimed that Alice was a lesbian, but Kate had no proof one way or the other. Nor did she care. Alice was an unattached single woman in her midthirties. Her short dark hair was perfectly straight and clung to her skull like a cap. The nurse had always been pleasant to Kate, and sometimes they sat together at lunch.

People grumbled about attending a meeting so late in the day but their annoyance was offset by curiosity about the new headmaster, Dr. Hawthorne, who'd been observed since his arrival three days earlier but not officially met. A number of faculty had asked Fritz Skander what they were in for. Skander only smiled and said, "I guess we'll find out." But Hawthorne had made his presence felt right from the start when he indicated that he wanted faculty cars parked in the lot behind Douglas Hall, not in the circle in front of Emerson. And there were other indications: the grounds crew had grown more active and a number of litter baskets had suddenly appeared. And Kate had seen him at lunch talking to students—a tall man in his thirties with a thin, angular face and light brown hair.

The heavy door at the front of the room opened and Fritz Skander entered, followed by Hawthorne, Mrs. Hayes—the school secretary— and a third man whom Kate recognized as one of the trustees, Hamilton Burke, a lawyer from Laconia. Burke was about fifty and portly in a three-piece blue suit. He looked as serious as if he were standing before the Supreme Court.

Skander seemed especially genial and winked at several of the faculty who caught his eye. He was perhaps forty-five, rectangular without being heavy, and with a full head of thick gray hair that crossed his brow in a straight line. He was a man with a lot of charm and fond of wearing humorous neckties. When Kate had met him in January she had thought they would become friends but she hadn't learned much more about him than she did at that first meeting; and while Skander was affable, even effusive at times, Kate came to realize that was just his manner and didn't necessarily reflect his interior self. Skander was several inches shorter than Hawthorne, who was also smiling, although his eyes were alert. Kate couldn't blame him for being tense, if that was what it was.

Mrs. Hayes looked motherly and somewhat anxious—a stout woman in her early sixties in a flowered dress who was reputed to have a temper. Now she appeared particularly eager to help and, indeed, that was often the case. But her evident strain made Kate conscious of how she herself was looking at her new boss, and she realized she too had some skepticism, even suspicion, having to do with her sense of Bishop's Hill as it had developed over the past eight months. Not that she could entirely fault the school. After all, there was so little money.

Fritz Skander went to the podium, joined his hands together palm to palm, and pressed them to his lips for silence, though by that time the room was mostly quiet.

"I know it's frustrating to have to meet so late in the afternoon. You all have terribly busy schedules with far too many demands on your time." Skander spoke in a sort of stage whisper that suggested intimacy, and Kate had to lean forward to hear. "We wanted to take this opportunity," he continued, "to let you get just a little acquainted with Jim Hawthorne, our new headmaster. I think you'll realize, as I have done, how lucky we are at Bishop's Hill to have someone of his reputation and experience ready to take the helm."

Mrs. Hayes had sat down to the left of the podium, next to Hamilton Burke. Hawthorne stood next to Skander with his hands behind his back. He looked cordial but serious and Kate thought his face reflected a sobriety that he brought with him, not a temporary nervousness or tension but a gravity in his nature, as if he wasn't a man who laughed much. Behind them on the high wall were six marble panels with the names of young men from Bishop's Hill who had fought in six wars from the Civil War to Vietnam. Small black crosses indicated the boys who had died, and whenever Kate was in this room, known as Memorial Hall, she wondered about them and what their hopes had been. The panels gave an indication of the school's long history, all the more affecting, Kate thought, considering how close Bishop's Hill had come in the past year to shutting its doors.

Skander's voice remained at the level of a soothing purr as he spoke of Dr. Hawthorne's years as director of a school in San Diego, his time at Ingram House in the Berkshires, his many articles, and his professorship in the Department of Psychology at Boston University. Hawthorne's experience was in clinical psychology working with high-risk adolescents and Kate realized that his appointment signified a shift in the ambitions of the board of trustees. For although Bishop's Hill promoted itself as catering to young men and women with special needs, that had, in the past, seemed more advertisement than actuality.

"I'm sure I'm not the only one," said Skander a little louder, "who wishes that our relationship with Jim Hawthorne will last many years. Obviously in these three days I can't say that I have gotten to know him. But already my wife and I see him as a friend as well as a colleague, and I look forward to that friendship deepening and becoming a sustaining timber not only of my professional life but of my private life too. Won't you help me welcome him." Skander stepped back, beaming and clapping his hands. His head was tilted to one side and his dark eyes crinkled at the edges, which gave a touch of whimsy to his enthusiasm. It made him seem inoffensive and endearing. As he clapped, his jacket opened and Kate saw a red necktie patterned with the white silhouettes of dogs.

The faculty and staff began applauding as well; two teachers, then two more stood up. Roger Bennett, the math teacher, whistled with an ironic cheer. His wife, the school chaplain, was absent from the meeting. Bennett was a tidy, small-boned man, and beneath his heather-green tweed jacket, he wore a bright red crewneck sweater. He glanced around at his colleagues, grinning and making quick lifting motions with his open hands, urging them to get to their feet.

It seemed to Kate that the sudden release of energy merely masked the staff's anxiety. Hadn't she heard them wondering what changes lay ahead? More than half taught at Bishop's Hill because they couldn't go elsewhere. They lacked the credentials to teach in public schools, and any private school, unless desperate, would examine them with care. Just the fact they taught at Bishop's Hill was suspect. In some cases there were other shadows on their records—an affair with a student years before, possibly the striking of a student, perhaps a breakdown or time spent in a rehab center. Some were just too old. So if their positions were in jeopardy, for many it meant the end of the line as far as teaching was concerned. And still they clapped—thankfully and heartily—even though most would have preferred Skander as headmaster. Whatever his shortcomings, at least he was a known commodity.

On the playing fields, a wrestling match had developed among four of the soccer players. From this distance Kate couldn't tell how serious it was. Hurrying toward the group rolling on the ground was a man in jeans and a white jacket. It looked like Larry Gaudette, the red-haired cook, who had come to Kate's small house the previous spring to help her shovel snow off the roof. Gaudette dragged two boys away by their ankles. What at one moment had been a picture-perfect scene of boys kicking a ball across the playing fields had turned into something ugly. It reinforced Kate's idea of Bishop's Hill as a place where things went wrong. A number of the faculty and staff applauding Jim Hawthorne had assignments in the dormitory cottages and Kate wondered who was left to monitor the students, one hundred and twenty boarders ranging from the gloomy to the criminal. Then Kate stopped herself. She certainly had students who were intelligent, even students she thought of with great affection, but in every instance there was a reason why the student was at Bishop's Hill and not someplace else. And none of those reasons pointed to a quality to be found here and not elsewhere. Indeed, many were at Bishop's Hill simply because no place else would take them.

Jim Hawthorne stood at the podium with his hands holding the edges as he waited for the clapping to subside. He adjusted his glasses and brushed back a lock of hair that had fallen across his forehead, a gesture that made him seem suddenly younger. Chip Campbell leaned over to Kate. "There's a handsome guy for you."

Without doubt Hawthorne was in good physical shape—he was even tan—but was he handsome? Perhaps more distinctive than handsome, thought Kate; there was something too serious to be considered in the category of conventional good looks. Kate saw that Alice Beech had turned and was looking at Chip. Since she was directly in front, Kate couldn't see the nurse's expression but she guessed it was disapproving. She was glad she had kept her mouth shut. She could have easily said something stupid just to be sociable. Alice turned back and her starched white uniform rustled. Chip raised his eyebrows at Kate and winked.

The teachers who had been standing took their seats. Out on the field, Kate saw Gaudette talking to one of the soccer players while the others trotted back to the gym.

"I want to tell you," said Hawthorne, "how glad I am to be here and how glad I am that we'll be working with one another. However, I don't want there to be any doubt about the enormity of our task." He paused and looked out at his audience. Kate felt his eyes move across her. There was a slight burr in his voice that Kate found attractive and a slight accent that she associated with Boston: the broad *a* and a mild reluctance to confront the letter *r*.

"The school's increasing debt, the low salaries of everyone who works here, problems with the physical plant, decreasing enrollment— at the moment the only circumstance in our favor is your own willingness and the board's decision to give the school one more chance, a chance that I'm afraid will be our last."

Hawthorne went on to cite further problems—lack of money, vacancies among faculty and staff, electrical and heating problems, broken equipment, low test scores of students. Kate already knew much of this but together it formed a depressing catalog. Hawthorne, while not exaggerating, was making certain that nobody held out any false hopes. The list was being made dire because dire solutions would be called for.

"If the school doesn't begin to turn around this semester,"

Hawthorne continued, "we will lose our accreditation before the end of the year. If that happens, then we won't open next fall. That's one possible calamity among many."

Kate glanced at her colleagues. A few looked as if they were being scolded. Chip was digging at his thumbnail with a toothpick. Did any look hopeful? Kate thought not. Most were keeping their faces purposefully blank. Some students ran down the hallway outside and Chip heaved himself to his feet and walked to the door, where he looked out threateningly, ready to catch someone doing what he shouldn't.

If it hadn't been for her ex-husband in Plymouth and the terms of her divorce, Kate would have returned to Durham to finish her Ph.D. in Romance languages. Her choices were teaching at Bishop's Hill or finding a job in an office. Even if she had wanted to teach at Plymouth State, there were no jobs available except for tutoring. And Plymouth was a thirty-minute drive, while Bishop's Hill was less than ten. Most days she could be home when Todd got back from second grade. Even today she had been home to fix him a snack. Then Shirley Hodges up the road had agreed to watch him until Kate returned around six-thirty or seven.

"Despite our history at Bishop's Hill," Hawthorne was saying, "we cannot pretend to be a traditional prep school. Over the past ten years our attention has been increasingly focused on what was once called 'the problem child,' and if Bishop's Hill is going to continue, then it will have to be in the area of helping such children. But instead of using the phrase *problem child*, I'd rather talk about children at risk. Reading their files, I've been dismayed by the psychological and physical handicaps, the divorces, delinquency, academic failures, sexual and substance abuse—I'm convinced the only way to help them academically is to help the whole child. And because one of our first obligations is to strengthen deficient ego functions, we need to think of our work as a twenty-four-hour activity. The entire day at Bishop's Hill is our milieu and this milieu is our primary teaching tool. Along with educating our youngsters, we are trying to teach them age-appropriate behavior, to offer a counterdelusional design to break down their defenses and enable them to become productive members of society."

With surprise Kate realized that Hawthorne was sincere, and she saw that she had expected something specious about Bishop's Hill's new headmaster. She had thought he would be like the others, someone who couldn't get a job elsewhere and for whom Bishop's Hill was the last stop. At best, she'd seen his hiring as a cosmetic change: a good-looking professional man to handle the fund-raising. This insight made her more attentive, and her colleagues, she noticed, were more attentive as well, sitting straighter, and two or three of them were even taking notes, although their faces, if possible, were stonier.

Hawthorne spoke about theories of alternative behavior, how that didn't mean enforcing rules that led to punishment but called for the substitution of other responses that in turn meant increased interaction with every child. He wanted to dismantle the school's system of merits and demerits. "We can't punish behavior unless we're willing to teach the child alternatives that he or she can substitute. A merit/demerit system is how you create a prison. We must be careful to be neither baby-sitters nor prison guards curbing our students' actions till their sentences are up."

It occurred to Kate to wonder why Hawthorne was there. Not why he had been hired but why he had decided to come to Bishop's Hill. Unlike Fritz Skander, he had nothing casual about him, no trace of the easygoing administrator. He appeared thoroughly professional. Why should Hawthorne want to settle in rural New Hampshire, where people's main links to the outside world were the satellite dishes attached to the sides of their dilapidated barns? And with that question Kate felt a rush of fear she couldn't understand. After all, she held her job lightly no matter how much she cared for her students. Were she fired, she would find another. Even though she had no wish to work in an office or a store, such a situation would hardly be permanent. Then it seemed to her that fear was what she saw on the faces of her colleagues. Whatever the past had been, the future would be different and the angular man at the podium represented the moment of change. Even his angularity made Kate uncomfortable. It made her think of sticks shoved in a bag, chafing and poking at the insides.

"We're here to help these children in their transition to the adult world," Hawthorne was saying. "They have been injured and their sense of cause and effect is based on a distorted sense of survival. Even those of you who have been victims of their anger must realize that it is characteristic of damaged children to display anger when it would be more appropriate for them to be sad."

The reference to anger made Kate think of her ex-husband, whom she hadn't seen since July, when the divorce was finalized. She supposed even George's anger existed because he lacked the courage to show his sadness, but after a point Kate no longer cared, especially when he had drunkenly tried to knock her down. Every Saturday morning Kate drove Todd in to the YMCA in Plymouth for his swimming lesson. George would pick him up. Then on Sunday evening he would drop Todd off at the library for Kate to pick up. She wouldn't ask Todd about his time with his father. She knew that George would again have told Todd what a terrible mother she was and would have grilled him as to whether she had a boyfriend or whether any man had been sleeping at the house. He had even made Todd reveal her uninspiring date with Chip Campbell the previous spring, a dull dinner followed by a bad movie to which Chip brought a thermos of martinis. And at least once George had yelled at Todd and called him a liar. She had tried to ask Todd if there had been other kinds of abuse, but Todd was oddly protective of his father, as if George were a younger sibling who was especially clumsy or weak.

Kate shifted her legs and the afternoon light reflected on the gold ankle chain with the letter *K* around her left ankle. She had bought it the day her divorce had been finalized. At first she had intended to get a golden heart but that seemed sentimental. Even with a *K*, though, the chain represented her future, a new future. She had also wanted it to mean hope, but as her life continued without dramatic change, the chain came to mean no more than "on-goingness." And what changes did she still hope for? If not romance, at least some form of male companionship. The very fact that George was jealous made her wish for something just so it wouldn't seem that she was agreeing to his terms. And he wasn't really jealous. He had for her neither love nor liking; rather, he hated the idea of another man's fingerprints on what he still saw as his property: his hunting rifles, his Dodge four-by-four, his ex-wife. What appeared to be jealousy was the result of frustrated ownership, not affection. Surely that was why he was so insistent that Kate stay in the area and not because of Todd, whom he never called except to question him about his mother's behavior and whose visits with his father were mostly spent in front of the television.

Kate smoothed her green cardigan down over her breasts. She found herself trying to determine the last time she had been held. Two summers ago she had taken a seminar for secondary school teachers in

Romance languages at UNH and had gone out half a dozen times with a Spanish teacher from Portsmouth. Todd had been staying with her parents in Concord. Was that the last time she had been embraced—fourteen months ago? She had had no strong feelings for the man, whose last name she couldn't recall, but now he stood as a high point in her romantic life. How pathetic, Kate thought. Here she was, still young, reasonably attractive, and in good physical condition and she could almost feel the skin decaying on her bones. Her sense of waste heightened the anger she felt toward her ex-husband. There were plenty of places where she could take courses next summer. Even California wouldn't be too far. She would apply and take Todd with her. To hell with George. But the summer was nine months away. It was only September and she still had the winter to get through.

"If we see teaching as a twenty-four-hour activity," Hawthorne was saying, "it will require a great deal of communication not simply among the faculty but among everyone at Bishop's Hill. Our job is behavior management and behavior change—education is part of that but our primary instrument of change is Bishop's Hill itself. We'll need to have regular staff meetings, which won't just be the usual, depressing rehashes of inappropriate behavior and who did what to whom. The point won't be to discuss what's been done but what might be done. And we'll all need to pool staff resources to think up alternatives that might be of assistance."

Kate perceived that whatever changes were initiated by the new headmaster she herself would be asked to give up more time. This thought was followed by resentment. She saw herself as a responsible teacher whose homeroom duties, six sections of languages, field hockey chores, and occasional mail room and dining hall duties kept her fully occupied. What right had Jim Hawthorne to demand more of her? By redefining their endeavor and calling it a milieu—Kate automatically suspected other people's jargon—he was making her job something else. But along with irritation she felt sympathy for Hawthorne, who surely was arousing the resentment of her colleagues. They were used to their routines. It wasn't necessarily that Hawthorne was asking them to do more work—he was meddling with their complacency.

Yet Hawthorne was right about the students. Many were disturbed and troublesome. They acted out and lost their tempers. They were unhappy and felt unloved by their families. Even the best seemed to be trying to accommodate themselves to what Kate thought of as a reform school mentality—following orders out of fear of punishment rather than to be successful. And she was reminded of the new girl who had appeared in Spanish I on Tuesday—Jessica, her name was. She had an ankle bracelet like Kate's, though thicker and shinier. Her room-mate, Helen Selkirk, also took Spanish. Helen had talked to Kate about the girl after class, saying that Jessica had made Helen switch to the top bunk, threatening to wet her bed if Helen didn't move. But that hadn't been the most disturbing thing. What had Jessica said? "Who do I have to fuck to get along here?" In class the next day—pretty and blond and fifteen—Jessica had seemed to exude the ani-mated naiveté that passed for innocence among adolescent girls. Yet what was her history and what dreadfulness in her past had led to her question? And when Helen told Jessica that she didn't have to fuck anyone, she hadn't believed her. "Sooner or later you got to do it," Jessica had told her, "that's just how things are."

Kate studied Hawthorne standing behind the podium—his dark gray jacket, his white shirt and tie. She saw he wore a wedding ring, though she'd heard nothing about a wife. She wondered how she felt about that and detected a trace of disappointment. It made her scold herself again. Perhaps Hawthorne's wife was someone with whom she could be friends. God knows, she'd be glad to find someone to talk to. As Kate listened, she felt that Hawthorne knew what he was saying was unpopular and that he didn't care. No, that wasn't right. He cared but it wouldn't make him change his approach. He meant to take Bishop's Hill forward and those who didn't follow would be cut loose.

Kate glanced out the window—the shadows were lengthening across the playing fields and the light was increasingly golden. A red-haired boy in a red sweater was walking toward the trees, presumably to have an illegal cigarette. She recognized him as an eighth grader, although she couldn't think of his name. He kicked a stone and it glit-tered in the light as it flew through the air.

Sitting on the grass near the back of Adams Hall, Kate saw, was the girl she had been thinking about—Jessica. She wore jeans and a blue sweatshirt and she sat with her knees drawn up as she watched some-thing hidden by the edge of the window. Kate pushed back her chair. A man was splitting wood. He had his shirt off although it wasn't warm.

He would position a log on the chopping block, then stand back and swing the ax lightly over his shoulder, letting it gather momentum as it plummeted downward. A second after the log split in half, Kate heard the noise, a faraway thud. At first she couldn't identify the man—dark-haired and muscular with a narrow face—then she realized she had seen him before. He, too, had just come to Bishop's Hill. He was Larry Gaudette's cousin and he worked in the kitchen. Indeed, the previous day he had made bread and the wonderful smells coming from the oven had cheered everyone. Kate had noticed him in the dining room yesterday afternoon, but then he had his shirt on and was wearing a Red Sox cap.

Jessica sat about fifteen feet away from him. Kate didn't know how long the girl had been there but she felt that the wood splitting had been continuing for a while, at least she'd been aware of the sound of the ax at some low level of consciousness. The man swung the ax, kicked the pieces aside, then positioned a new log and brought the ax up with one hand, gripping the handle with the other when the ax reached the top of its arc. The movement had an easy grace. Kate wondered if the two had spoken or if the man knew that Jessica was watching, though she suspected he knew even if no words had been exchanged. In her baggy jeans and sweatshirt, the girl looked sexless, but her roommate had told Kate how Jessica had a garish tattoo on her bottom. "One of those woman symbol things," Helen had said.

The beginning of applause brought Kate back to the room. Hawthorne had come to the end of his talk. She turned forward and began to clap, thinking as she did that the applause lacked the enthusiasm of the applause fifteen minutes earlier. Nobody stood.

Hawthorne held up a hand for silence. His slight smile suggested to Kate that he wasn't sure what to do with his face. It occurred to her that he wasn't as confident and inflexible as he at first seemed.

"I expect some of you have questions," he said.

Chip Campbell got to his feet and raised his hand. "I'd like to hear more about these regular meetings." He glanced around him with a certain severity. "I'm sure we all would."

"We have about 120 boarders and a dozen or so day students divided between the upper and lower schools. The faculty of each school would meet weekly to discuss what they see as problems and difficulties among the students, as well as what we can do to help."

"Some of us teach in both schools," said Chip. Dressed in khakis and a brown tweed jacket over a Bishop's Hill sweatshirt, Chip stood with his hands on his hips. He had a thick red neck and oversized red ears that his short hair made seem larger.

"I'm aware of that," said Hawthorne. He spoke patiently but coolly, as if he were discussing numbers or automotive mechanics rather than people. "Those faculty would need to attend both meetings. And I'll be attending both meetings myself, as well as the meetings of the nonacademic staff."

"That's a lot of time," said Campbell.

"Yes." Hawthorne seemed about to say more, then didn't.

Chip glanced around at his colleagues, obviously hoping that one or more would continue this line of inquiry, then he sat down. When Kate had gone out with him that spring, Chip had barely been able to drive by the end of the evening. On the other hand, she was impressed that he had taken a thermos of martinis to a movie. And she even slightly blamed herself for his condition. After she turned down his offers of a martini, he had drunk the whole thermos himself, as if the contents would spoil if he didn't act quickly. Chip had asked her out two other times, but each time she'd been busy, or said she was. Kate had already spent a quarter of her life with one alcoholic and she worried about her brief attraction to Chip, as if it suggested too much about her failings.

Mrs. Sherman, the art teacher, had her hand up. She was a rather flamboyant woman in her midfifties who wore a beret. "I'm worried about what you say about the demerit system. I often feel almost incapable of controlling some of my students and without the demerit system I think I'd be completely at sea. Isn't there a danger of too much permissiveness?"

"I don't believe it's a matter of permissiveness," said Hawthorne, "but of giving the students increased responsibility and trying to remove a them-against-us type of thinking. Our kindness to them must be separated from any notion as to whether they deserve it. The student who acts out and the student who never opens his mouth may be equally in need of help, and those are issues best addressed by the weekly meetings as well as other methods." He went on to discuss the role of the two counselors now at the school and how each would be responsible for half the students and would work with him and the school psychologist. Sometime during the year Hawthorne hoped to hire a second psychologist. And he spoke of increasing the students' sense of connection to the school by instituting a buddy system between upper and lower classmen, starting discussion groups within each grade, and assigning students to the grounds crew, the kitchen, or the library to help with certain tasks.

Further questions were asked, ranging from the smallest of issues—a broken desk in a classroom—to the philosophical—hadn't Freud been generally discredited? But behind them all lay the concerns about time and how the students could be controlled. Ted Wrigley, the other language teacher, was worried about what he called the ethical dimension of increased student surveillance. Wasn't it a form of spying?

"Our job," said Hawthorne, "is to help prepare these youngsters for the adult world, to educate them in a variety of areas all the way from mathematics to how to interact with one another. Let's say a girl comes to class with cuts on her arm or stops eating or refuses to brush her teeth. Surely you wouldn't ignore symptoms like that. If we pay more attention to students' behavior, we can do much to prevent these kinds of problems from developing, or at least keep them to a minimum."

"Will these be one-hour meetings?" asked Roger Bennett, getting to his feet and smoothing back his blond hair. The fact that his wife was chaplain gave him a degree of unspoken authority, as if he were dean or associate headmaster. "Many of us have already committed our afternoons. What will be gained by making our busy schedules even busier?"

Kate again turned her attention to the playing fields. The shadows were longer; the girl was gone. But the man was still splitting wood—setting a log on the chopping block, then stepping back with his ax. His movements had a machinelike refinement, as if he could easily split logs all day. Kate wondered if he, too, would be included in these meetings, if he would be called upon to say how a girl had watched him splitting wood and what this might signify. Kate almost smiled. Couldn't one say that everything had bearing on something? Really, it was impossible to provide for every contingency. If kids wanted to get in trouble, it would be hard to stop them. But wasn't that the very attitude Hawthorne was arguing against?

The questions continued. Could students still be sent to the head-master's office if they acted up? Could bad behavior be punished with failing grades? The questions were as much about allaying the anxieties of the faculty as about looking for specific direction. "But it sounds like a treatment center, doesn't it?" asked Herb Frankfurter, one of the two science teachers. The librarian, Bill Dolittle, seemed to agree. "Do you really think this will make them better?"

"You're right," said Hawthorne, "we don't want to run a treatment center. The students haven't been sent here by psychologists, nor have they been mandated here by the court. Their parents pay a lot of money for the privilege of enrolling them at Bishop's Hill. But some of their conditions are similar, though perhaps not as severe. I don't expect we can solve any huge problems, but, yes, I feel the students can be helped."

"Without a demerit system," said Tom Hastings, "I'll become an even greater victim of their verbal abuse. You wouldn't believe some of the stuff I get called." Hastings, the other science teacher, was about Kate's age. Whenever he got nervous, he stuttered, and the students teased him.

"I bet I've been called the same," said Hawthorne. "However, they can't abuse you."

"Isn't being called m-m-motherfucker a form of abuse?"

"As long as you can walk away, you can't be abused. They're stuck here, you're not. And don't get caught up in the meaning of the words. These are damaged kids. If you were a doctor and a kid came in with a broken arm, you wouldn't take offense. For a boy to call you motherfucker is like a broken arm. And if a boy or girl is disturbing the class, you can make them take a time out or send them to my office. You can do all sorts of things, but to punish them is to avoid the prob-lem. Basically, it's a form of irresponsibility. And, let me tell you, it doesn't do any good."

There was a note of impatience in Hawthorne's voice. Kate's col-leagues glanced at one another. The new headmaster's tone had unset-tled them.

Hamilton Burke got to his feet and put a hand on Hawthorne's shoulder. "These issues will be worked out over the next weeks and I'm sure nobody will have anything of which to complain. In the meantime, it's getting late. The board of trustees is hosting a little reception across the hall in the Peabody Room so we can continue our chat more informally. I hope you'll all join us for a drink and a snack."

Skander began applauding again to signify that the meeting was over. This time the applause was very brief. Chairs were pushed back.

"Welcome to Hawthorne's gulag," said Chip. "I'm sure not going to let any student of mine call me a motherfucker, no matter what this guy says or where he comes from."

Alice Beech turned abruptly toward Chip and her white uniform seemed to hiss. "Then it's clear you heard very little of what he had to say."

Bill Dolittle joined them. Besides being librarian, he taught two sections of English. He was portly, balding, and reminded Kate of a friar—a rather sexless middle-aged man who liked his wine and comforts. "I'm impressed by his seriousness. It's certainly a new idea to try to actually help out students."

"Sounds like Do . . . little likes the new headmaster," said Chip, mockingly. "Is that right, Do . . . little? Have you found yourself a friend?"

"I wish you'd stop that joke," said Dolittle, pursing his lips. "I work as hard as anyone else around here and much harder than some."

Roger Bennett came up behind Chip. "So what do you think?" Bennett raised his eyebrows ironically, as if answering his own question.

"All I know," said Kate, "is that I'd like a glass of wine."

Jessica Weaver sat in her bunk, writing a letter. It was the lower bunk she had chased her roommate out of, the jerk. If possible, she would have chased her from the room altogether, but she didn't want to call too much attention to herself. It would be dumb to wreck her plans by being foolish. After all, that's what had happened last time and that's why she was at Bishop's Hill.

Jessica had tucked two blankets under the mattress of the top bunk, letting them hang down and enclose the lower bunk so she felt like an Arab in a tent. Two of her biggest schoolbooks were piled to make a small table and on them burned a red candle in a saucer she had swiped from the dining hall. The candle gave enough light to see by and even warmed the small space, making it cozy. Leaning against the books was her stuffed bear, Harold, whose one eye was focused fondly upon her. Jessica was listening to her Walkman—*Beyond the Missouri Sky* again, programmed to play the last song, "Spiritual," over and over. So arranged, Jessica could imagine she was almost anyplace and not at Bishop's Hill in the few minutes dividing Friday night from Saturday morning. She wore blue flannel pajamas and sometimes she paused in her writing and chewed the black plastic tip of her pen.

She was writing to her ten-year-old brother, Jason, but she wasn't going to mail the letter to their home for fear that Tremblay would intercept it. That would be a disaster. No, she would send it to Jason in care of a friend of his in school as she had done before. She tried to write three times a week, telling Jason the news and how their plans were progressing. She described how the headmaster had spoken to the students that morning, saying all the stuff he would do for them. Jessica hadn't believed it but at least Hawthorne hadn't talked down to them. And when some of the students acted silly, Hawthorne hadn't gotten mad but just waited for them to finish.

And now she was telling Jason about her intentions. "There's a man here who I think will help us. I've only talked to him a little but I've been watching him. He works in the kitchen but he's not like that. Not like a kitchen person, if you know what I mean. I like him. After all, I'll be paying him $2,000 and he doesn't have to do much. Just get you out of the house and I'll do the rest."

She considered what "the rest" might be. Her father's younger half brother, Matthew, lived in Washington and worked for the government, something in the Department of Labor, although she didn't know what. He wasn't in charge, she knew that much. She hadn't seen Matthew since her father's funeral, but she'd talked to him on the phone and had written to him. Now, however, she meant to appear on his doorstep with Jason. Surely if Matthew knew what Tremblay had done, he would protect them. He'd probably kill Tremblay, smash him with an ax, so she knew that she shouldn't tell Matthew just yet. He certainly knew that her mother wasn't good for much. Even if Dolly was sober and not taking pills, she was still frightened. A sodden chipmunk, that's what she was. She wouldn't stop Tremblay. She didn't care what he had done. And though that wasn't completely true, it was at least true that Dolly was too scared to protect them.

Again Jessica thought of how Tremblay would come to her room at night. She didn't mean to think of it but the pictures seemed trapped in her head. Now he said he'd do the same to Jason unless she stayed at Bishop's Hill and kept quiet. And she knew he would; he wasn't scared. Jessica thought of how she used to hear him getting up to go to the bathroom, how she would count his steps—one, two, three—it was twelve steps from his bedroom to the bathroom, and if there was a thirteenth step, then her whole stomach felt nauseous because it meant he was coming to her room. Four, five, six—she could tell by his steps how much he'd been drinking and sometimes she knew there would be a thirteenth step even before she heard it.

She'd kill him if she could, and if he touched Jason, she would kill him for sure. When Jessica was smaller, she would think of spraying bug spray in Tremblay's mouth when he was passed out. Now she would use a knife from the kitchen, one of those expensive butcher knives he liked to brag about. He'd promised he wouldn't touch Jason as long as she stayed at Bishop's Hill, but he had always promised her things and then come to her room anyway. Seven, eight, nine—hearing him stumble into the wall, sometimes knocking down a picture. Then Tremblay would pause and Jessica would listen to him breathe heavily, already knowing what he wanted, that he wouldn't stop at the bathroom but would continue down the hall. Ten, eleven, twelve. And she would look at the light under her door and wait to see his shadow fall across it.

"Just make sure you don't make Tremblay suspicious," she wrote. "It would be best to do it when he is away on a business trip, so you need to find out about his schedule. Don't ask him about it. Maybe Dolly knows."

Jessica had stopped referring to her as "mother" when she married Tremblay. She'd become Dolly—a stupid big sister with whom Jessica was obliged to live. The candle flickered and she stared at the page. LeBrun could fuck her if that's what he wanted; she'd do anything to get him to help. But the thought of sex was awful to her. Men's moist, fat hands, their awful knees; their underwear that smelled of pee. At the club men would wiggle their tongues at her to show how much they wanted her, as if that would make her excited and dance even wilder rather than make her sick and want to puke on them. With LeBrun, she hoped the money would be enough—four thousand saved from table dancing, from pushing her small breasts into the faces of drunken men. Two thousand for LeBrun and two thousand for her and Jason to get to Washington and maybe beyond.

She hadn't asked LeBrun yet. She had to be sure. Yet the more she waited, the more dangerous it was for her brother. Even if Matthew wouldn't hide them, she could still go back to the titty bars. She had her fake ID. They would go to the West Coast, someplace warm. In December she'd be sixteen. Then she'd have five years until she came into her trust fund. She and Jason each had one and they had to be twenty-one before they got the money. And then Tremblay would have nothing because Dolly would no longer get an allowance or be paid child support. Jessica hoped Tremblay would be dead by that time. How brilliant if she could get LeBrun to kill him. But she was letting her fantasies get in the way. It would be hard enough to get him to rescue Jason, much less kill someone.

"Unless he's going on a business trip, the best time to get you out of the house is between Thanksgiving and Christmas," wrote Jessica. "Both Tremblay and Dolly drink more then. A few days before, you need to put a bag with some of your stuff over at Chuckie's. You can't take too much. No trucks or stuffed animals."

What she liked about her Uncle Matthew was that he looked like her father, even though he was only a half brother. There was another half brother, Eddie, in Tucson, but he never wrote or showed any interest. Even here at Bishop's Hill, Jessica had already gotten a letter from Matthew, a note really, saying he was glad she was safe and he hoped to see her sometime during the year but he was very busy right at the time.

"A few people here aren't bad. I like my Spanish teacher but my English teacher is a dope. He's also the librarian and he reads us dumb books. The kids are absolute nothings. My roommate cuts her arm with a razor blade. I don't know if she thinks it's cool or what. Some kids try to talk to me but I ignore them. They're all babies. But the woods are pretty and the trees right now are really beautiful. A couple of times I've gone for long walks by myself. People say there are moose and black bears, I haven't seen any, but LeBrun said they can't leave the garbage cans outside because the bears will get them and make a mess—"

The blanket curtain was suddenly pulled aside. Jessica looked up and saw the upside-down head of her roommate, her brown hair hanging down. She almost yelled she was so startled. Helen was talking but Jessica couldn't hear over the Walkman. She took off her earphones.

". . . completely crazy," Helen was saying. "You could start a fire with that candle. We could burn up. I knew I smelled something. If you don't put it out immediately, I'll tell Miss Standish. I'll go down there right now. What's wrong with you?"

Jessica leaned forward and blew out the candle, leaving Helen in the dark. Then she put on the earphones again so the bass repetitions of the song filled her ears. "Bitch," she said, but even she couldn't hear the word, it was so soft with her earphones on, almost a kiss. The song "Spiritual" had again reached the part that she liked—Dut-dut-dut-dut . . .

The French windows of the headmaster's apartment opened onto a terrace that looked out across the school's playing fields. The apartment was in Adams Hall, where classes were held, but it seemed homelike and included enough bedrooms for a big family—a feature that Hawthorne, now that he was single again, couldn't consider without bitter irony. At the moment he was leaning against the balustrade that divided the terrace from the lawn some half-dozen feet below. The night was cloudy and windless. In the distance he could hear coyotes yapping.

Hawthorne wished he could pray, but the sky looked especially empty, a black chasm disappearing above him. Lights burned in the windows of several buildings although it was past midnight. More lights lined the walkways. At the corner of the playing fields a security light cast a yellow tint across home plate. But between those lights and whatever existed overhead, Hawthorne sensed only emptiness. He zipped up his jacket and buried his hands in the side pockets.

If he could pray, what would he ask for? To see his wife and daughter once more? To gaze on their living faces? But if he believed in prayer, then wouldn't he believe that he would see them again? And there unfolded in his mind all the possibilities of an afterlife, as if he were pushing through one after another, expecting their faces to emerge from the confusion. If only he could see Meg and Lily one more time, he would surrender himself to any belief, do anything to breach the dark wall that kept them from him. Hawthorne felt a constriction in his chest; his heaven was empty and he was sure that when he died his own particular light would simply blink out. Meg and Lily were dead. He had brought their ashes back to New England to bury in Ingram in western Massachusetts, where they had lived before moving to San Diego. He had thought of driving out to Ingram before coming to Bishop's Hill to see if their stones were in place and how the cemetery looked at the beginning of fall. But he hadn't gone. Perhaps he would go later; he lacked the courage now.

Hawthorne hoisted himself up on the balustrade, kicking his heels against the small columns supporting the railing. Before him rose three stories of Adams Hall with its ivy and crumbling brick. At the corners of the roof were dragonlike gargoyles, looking foolish by day but in the moonlight full of menace. His apartment—or "quarters," in the idiom of the school—took up a sizable portion of the first floor and showed signs of having been lately vacated by Fritz Skander. Hawthorne had been willing to let him stay, but he understood the symbolism of the move: there was no way Skander could live in the headmaster's quarters. Anyway, there was a house for him on the grounds. It amused Hawthorne. Here he wanted to make a clean break and give himself over to a labor that would completely fill his mind, but already he was restricted by the customs of the new place. Maybe he would have done better digging ditches or dedicating himself to the improvement of an Indian tribe deep in the Amazon jungle—but such a tribe would also have its rituals, no better or worse than those at Bishop's Hill.

And Hawthorne was digging a ditch; or rather, bringing Bishop's Hill back from the near dead was equally labor-intensive. Unhappily, it wasn't intensive enough. It didn't block his other thoughts, because here he sat recalling all those aspects of his wife and daughter that formed the major continent within his skull, until he wanted to hammer his head with his fists and shout, Stop! Was this why people went crazy, to keep something out of their brains? All his training as a psychologist denied such old-fashioned ideas. He was overcome with hatred for the language of his trade, its clumsy diagnoses and efforts to describe the human condition, because here he was and his sky was still empty. But how else could he shut down his thoughts if not by ferocious work? Even his own death he had rejected—not for moral reasons but for a logic that, Hawthorne felt, approached the absurd. Meg and Lily now existed only in his seemingly limitless memory—again and again they moved across the stage of his thoughts. Meg might be doing no more than arranging flowers in a vase or Lily might be putting a pair of tiny shoes on the feet of a Barbie doll. Were Hawthorne to die, wouldn't it kill them once again since their only remaining life was in his head? Once he was gone, they would be nowhere.

As for the other distractions, the more common forms of self-medication—alcohol, drugs, women—he felt he knew too much to give them credence. Even if his heaven was empty, it held more than the illusion extended by alcohol, and this paradox almost made him smile—Hawthorne, a man to whom smiles no longer came easily. No, he had chosen himself a ditch to dig, though in the past week he'd found himself thinking more of Sisyphus shoving his boulder up the hill. Hawthorne wondered how long it had taken Sisyphus to realize he wouldn't succeed, that it wasn't a matter of working harder or of there being a right way or a wrong way. The boulder would never perch motionless on top of the mountain and allow Sisyphus to say, "I did it."

Was Bishop's Hill like that? Hawthorne couldn't let himself think in such terms. He had chosen to come to a place where he wasn't known, where the details about what had happened in San Diego remained vague. He wouldn't have to talk about it and deal with people's curiosity, whether kindly meant or not. He was well aware that taking the job at Bishop's Hill after having been at Wyndham was like a colonel, even a general, voluntarily returning to the ranks, becoming at best a sort of staff sergeant. Krueger had asked him if he meant to write a book but Hawthorne had none of that left inside him. After all, his being an innovator in his field had been one of the causes of the fire. Better to be a sergeant and concern himself with daily chores, better to dig a ditch. He would fully give himself to Bishop's Hill, and if that wasn't enough, the trustees would close the school and that would be that. Whether he succeeded or failed was beyond his concern. Like Sisyphus, he thought, pushing for the sake of pushing, the very Zen of pushing, and again he almost smiled.

Yesterday he had talked to the faculty, this morning he had addressed the students. After lunch he had talked to the staff—secretaries, grounds crew, housekeepers, the people who worked in the kitchen. The faculty had looked at him with fear, the students with suspicion, and the staff with disbelief. But no, that wasn't true, there were some who seemed to listen with open minds. And others might be convinced, although slowly.

That afternoon he had talked to the school secretary, Mrs. Hayes, about her computer skills. She had come into his office and refused to sit down, saying that she preferred to stand. In her self-presentation, not a single hair was out of place. Her old-fashioned dress, cameo brooch, string of artificial pearls, practical shoes—her display was seamless. It turned out she had no computer skills. The board had offered to buy her a computer but she had refused. Her old Underwood was good enough for her. Hawthorne told her that he had ordered several computers, a printer, and a scanner and would show her how they worked. In no time, Mrs. Hayes unraveled. One tear slid down her cheek, then another. She told Hawthorne that she knew he intended to let her go.

"I have no intention of firing you," he had said.

"That's what you say now, but I know differently."

"Please believe me. I need you here."

But she didn't believe him. She had worked at Bishop's Hill for more than thirty years but she understood that changes were necessary.

"I'm only asking you to familiarize yourself with a perfectly simple machine. It will make your job and mine far easier." He hadn't had the courage to mention the Internet and e-mail, all the things that could be done online.

In the end, Hawthorne spent his time reassuring her that her position was safe. "Has anyone told you that I mean to fire you?"

"People talk." Mrs. Hayes had patted her nose with a handkerchief. "And I know I'm not young anymore. I'm a slow learner."

Hawthorne wondered what would happen if Mrs. Hayes refused to use a computer. Well, then, she would stay on till her retirement; she provided valuable continuity. But what bothered him was that she didn't believe him. No matter what he said, she remained convinced that he would force her out of Bishop's Hill. And he again thought of the faculty members the previous afternoon, how they tried to conceal their doubts and fears—what would he have to do before they realized he was trying to save their jobs and not preparing to fire them?

At least Fritz Skander understood the difficulty.

"They need to trust you," Skander had said in his soft voice. "I can help you with that. I know them. It won't take long. They're basically good people."

Hawthorne had felt so grateful that he had shaken Skander's hand. In response, Skander had given him a smile of such warmth and willingness that Hawthorne's doubts receded.

"It'll be hard for a while," said Skander, "but they'll come around."

"I'm depending on you," Hawthorne had told him.

Skander patted Hawthorne's arm. "That's what I'm here for."

Hawthorne's meeting with the students had been less daunting even though they were less welcoming. But they were adolescents and Hawthorne felt he knew the breed. Their suspicion, indifference, and cynicism lacked the inflexibility that age gave a person. Although they were wary, it would be easier to win them to his side. They were quieter than kids in a treatment center, better able to keep themselves under control. And they were more sophisticated, more capable of channeling their energies in a single direction, even more analytical. So they had watched him.

He would always be available to them, he'd explained; if they had complaints they felt were being ignored, they could come to him at any time.

"What about the food?" one boy asked. "It sucks."

"We've hired a new assistant cook and yesterday he made fresh bread for lunch. Personally, I thought it was wonderful. The problem at the moment is the kitchen's budget but I'm sure it can be increased a little. The new cook has placed a suggestion box outside the kitchen. If there's a kind of food or particular dishes that you want made, just leave a note and maybe he can do it. I know he'd like to."

"Can we get wine with meals?" asked a boy.

"Or beer?"

There had been more joking suggestions. Hawthorne had waited for them to quiet down. But he liked their energy. Some seemed sullen or hostile but most were good-humored. He spoke about the difficulties the school was experiencing but also how the board was committed to making the school better. Money was being raised but they had to be patient.

Meeting with the staff, he had again spoken about the idea of a milieu and the need to prepare students for the adult world, not just by teaching the three Rs but by teaching them age-appropriate behavior and raising their sense of self-esteem. He knew the staff often had contact with students and he was sure they could make helpful suggestions. He would begin meeting with them weekly to discuss the school and the work it was doing. There would be refreshments; the atmosphere would be relaxed.

The fifteen or so men and women were skeptical but polite. Since most were hourly employees, they didn't share the faculty's complaints about spending extra time on campus.

Afterward at a reception, Hawthorne was introduced to each of the staff, including the new cook. The man told him a joke. What had it been? "Did you hear the story about two cannibals eating a clown? One says to the other, 'This taste funny to you?'"

Hawthorne had been surprised but he had laughed and chatted with the cook, whose name was Frank, a man about thirty with a narrow face and his dark hair slicked back with gel. Frank had seemed especially energetic and Hawthorne heard him telling jokes to others as well. Hawthorne was glad of his vitality. He seemed the only one not made nervous by the new headmaster and he looked at the scar on Hawthorne's wrist without embarrassment. Still, Hawthorne had found himself trying to draw a line between upbeat and hyper. But he also liked the man's cousin, Larry Gaudette, the head cook, who seemed serious, responsible, and even slightly critical of his cousin's joke telling.

Sliding off the railing, Hawthorne stood and stretched. It was nearly one in the morning and he had a few files left to read. He would spend the weekend going over student files, then start scanning them onto floppy disks. And he wanted to read the files of students who had transferred or dropped out. Some he would telephone. Even if he only got an earful of complaint, it might be useful to hear why they had left. If he worked all weekend, maybe he could keep his mind fully occupied. Skander had invited him to dinner on Saturday night and he looked forward to that. Hawthorne glanced up at the dark windows of Adams Hall. A sudden breeze sent the dried leaves of the ivy rattling and whispering. Strangely, he had a sense of being watched. He looked more closely at the windows.

Suddenly, Hawthorne had a shock. Somebody was standing at a third-floor window looking down at him. It was a man. There was something very odd about his clothes. With a feeling approaching horror, Hawthorne realized the man was dressed in a fashion that had gone out of style a hundred years earlier. The stern white face and thin beard, the somber clothing—the man stared down at Hawthorne with such anger that it was all Hawthorne could do not to turn away or cover his eyes. The figure was standing about a foot back from the glass, dimly illuminated by the security lights along the walkway. Hawthorne waited for him to make some sign but he stood at the window, forbidding and lifeless.

Forcing himself into action, Hawthorne ran across the terrace toward the French windows. Once inside he paused long enough to grab a flashlight from the hall table, then he hurried through the door separating his quarters from the rest of the building. He stopped to listen. The only noise was the wind moaning through a crack. Hawthorne ran for the stairs, taking them two at a time as he dashed toward the third floor. His shoes had rubber soles and made hardly any noise. He kept the flashlight off; there was enough light in the stairwell from the windows. When he reached the third-floor landing, he opened the fire door and listened again.

From farther up the hallway, he heard laughter, manic and inhuman. Hawthorne moved quietly through the door and down the hall. The laughter grew louder with breathless hysteria. Here the only light came dimly from the open doors of the classrooms. Touching the wall with one hand, Hawthorne moved forward, gripping the flashlight but not turning it on. The laughter seemed to be coming from a classroom halfway down the hall, which looked out over the playing fields. Hawthorne calculated that it was in this same area that the man had been standing. He paused at the doorway. His hands were sweating and he wiped them on his pants. The high tenor of the laughter, its tenacity without pause for breath, its noisy echo in the empty classroom—Hawthorne imagined it spewing forth from the dead mouth he had seen.

He flicked on the flashlight and stepped into the classroom, sweeping the beam across the desks and blackboard. There was no sign of the man he had seen at the window. Then, on the teacher's bare desk at the front of the room, he saw a set of jittering white teeth jumping and turning in the circle of the flashlight's beam. The awful laughter was coming from the teeth. Hawthorne gripped the doorjamb and watched the teeth hop about on the desk, approach the edge, then scuttle back to the center. He felt for the light switch and turned on the overhead fluorescent light. The white teeth and bright pink gums were a toy, a plastic toy. Laughing and twitching, they again skittered to the side of the desk, balanced briefly on the edge, then fell to the floor with a crash and were silent. Hawthorne kept by the door. It was the scientist in him, the clinical psychologist, who stared at his two hands and watched them shake, as if he had the D.T.'s or the palsy of the very old. The very peculiarity of it helped to calm him. In the silence there was only the hum of the fluorescent lights and the occasional low moan of the wind.

After making sure there was no one hiding in any of the rooms, Hawthorne hurried back down the stairs. At the bottom he paused, but there was no sound. He hurried through his quarters, out to the terrace, and down to the lawn, hoping to see someone running away, but there was nothing. He walked quickly across the grass. He had turned off the light but still held it in his hand. His heart was beating rapidly and he felt that if he relaxed even a little his panic would overwhelm him. About a hundred yards from Adams Hall he entered a grove of trees and stopped. He became aware of a peculiar but somewhat familiar odor. Almost without knowing it, he found himself thinking of France, where he had gone with his wife shortly after their marriage.

Hawthorne squinted. Seated under a tree and faintly illuminated by a light at the corner of Adams Hall was a boy in a sweater smoking a cigarette. The boy held it very precisely between his thumb and index finger, inserted it slowly into his pursed lips, and inhaled deeply. Then he slowly exhaled one, two, three smoke rings.

"Is that a Gauloise?" Hawthorne called out.

The boy leapt to his feet, sprinted away several yards, and then stopped. "Yes, it is," he said.

"I thought I recognized the smell. I used to smoke them in Paris, even though the first several made me dizzy."

"Would you like one?" asked the boy, turning. He appeared about thirteen, slight and with long red hair. He was trying to keep his voice calm but it squeaked nonetheless.

"No, thanks. I quit when my daughter was born." Hawthorne's voice faltered.

"You going to report me?"

"Not tonight. It's too late for reporting. Have you seen anyone else out here?"

The boy leaned against a tree and smoked his cigarette. "No, nobody. Why?"

"I thought I saw someone leaving Adams Hall. You're positive?"

"Absolutely . . ." The boy paused. "You're the new boss."

"Headmaster, yes."

"I heard you speak this morning."

"Oh? How did I seem?"

"Okay, I guess. I wasn't sure if you were serious. You know how it is—you hear a guy's scam, then you just wait and see. You going to let students smoke?"

"That's not in my hands. There are laws against it, insurance regulations."

"So I'm going to keep getting caught."

"I expect so. Do you really need to smoke?"

"I'm an addict," said the boy with some pride. He stood with his hands on his hips and the cigarette stuck in the corner of his mouth. His hair fell across his forehead in a wave.

"If you get desperate for a cigarette and you can't have one without getting caught, then come to me. We'll go for a drive and you can smoke. I like the smell of Gauloises."

"I don't always smoke Gauloises. I just got lucky."

"Well, whatever you're smoking. If I'm not too busy, we'll go for a spin."

"I bet you won't."

"Try me," said Hawthorne. "How come you're out so late?"

"I don't sleep much and I like to see what's going on. I don't mean I'm a Peeping Tom but I hate just lying there staring at the ceiling."

"What about the night watchman?"

"He's usually drunk and asleep. You'd have to step on him to get him up."

"What's your name?"

The boy hesitated, then said, "Scott."

"I'm Jim Hawthorne."

"I figured that."

"What do you see when you wander around?"

"All kinds of stuff. Tonight I found a dead cat. D'you want to see it?"

"A dead cat?"

"Yeah, it's been hung. It's Mrs. Grayson's cat, the housekeeper. It's always poking around. Not anymore, I guess. You see that pile of fire-wood? It's past that, over by those trees."

Hawthorne followed the boy across the grass toward a clump of pines. Scott was small for his age, barely over five feet tall. As he led the way, he lit another Gauloise and the strong smell drifted back to Hawthorne, who had an immediate recollection of sitting with Meg in Les Deux Magots and spending a great deal of money for a small cup of coffee.

The cat was fat, gray, and very furry. It had been hung from a low branch with a piece of yellow twine. Its pink tongue protruded from between its gray lips. Hawthorne touched it. The cat was stiff and must have been dead for quite a while. It swung slowly in a circle.

"Pretty fucked up to hang a cat," said Scott.

Hawthorne didn't disagree. He took out his Swiss Army knife to cut it down. "You have any idea who did it?"

"Nope, but I bet I'll find out."

3

Detective Leo Flynn had a cold. He had woken up with it that Monday morning and when his wife, Junie, had heard him snuffling she had been unsympathetic. "How many times do I have to tell you that you've got to quit the smoking." As if smoking caused colds, and not the hanging around with the lowlifes he came across working for the Boston homicide unit. Still, September was not yet over and this was his second cold of the month. He'd also had a cold in August, and in July he'd had two colds, though one was a holdover from June. He figured if he retired next year like Junie wanted, then he could make his money doing ads for Kleenex, because when Leo Flynn blew his nose there was nothing secret about it. The walls shook.

Despite the cold, Flynn was feeling more optimistic than usual—darkly optimistic. The sort of optimism that in a normal person would lead to severe depression. At the moment he was driving up to Revere, which he saw as a door leading out of a nightmare case he had been assigned to a week earlier, one of those jobs that could drag on and on and stay open in the files for years. He was hardly over the Tobin Bridge and already he had a small mountain of wet tissues on the seat beside him. It was hard to blow his nose while driving and hard to

smoke while blowing his nose. Even worse, the cold made his cigarettes taste like garbage. Like, it had become work just to smoke them.
Flynn had a heavy, meal-sack figure and was bald except for some tufts
of reddish hair on the sides and back of his head. Back in the early
fifties, while still in his teens, he'd been a lightweight Golden Gloves
champion in Boston for two years running, but now at sixty-three he
was more than twice the size, though he still had that bantam rooster
way about him, quick and cocky. His ears looked like a baby's closed
fists—tin ears, he called them—and they were the last remaining evidence of his years in the ring.

Flynn's professional problems had begun when his team had been
given a new homicide, and he'd known when they got it that it would
bust his balls. A guy had been ice-picked outside a dance club, the
Avalon on Lansdowne, and it had happened so fast that the lady he was
with had thought he was bending over to whoop his cookies. Then he
kept bending and tumbled flat on his belly. And he hadn't gotten up
again no matter how much the lady yelled.

All Flynn knew at first was that the corpse had a little bead of blood
at the base of his skull. But Flynn had expected the worst. Maybe his
twenty-five years in homicide had given him that kind of thinking. The
autopsy had showed the damage—entry through the foramen mag-
num of the occipital bone, then the cone-shaped depredation in the
brain, a quick swath through the gray porridge. And that's what had
upset him—not that Buddy Roussel was dead, which was only bad for-
tune for his friends and family, but that he had been iced so well.

Flynn and the three other members of his team had been at the
Avalon until four o'clock Sunday morning, then he and Kosta had
taken Buddy Roussel's girlfriend downtown. Her name was Bridget
Bonnelli and she couldn't stop crying. Flynn felt bad for her but he
had a job to do so he gave her the Kleenex. Flynn always had a few
boxes lying around his desk. Bridget and Roussel had been in the club
about two and a half hours. They had danced, talked with friends, and
seen about twenty people they knew. Flynn got their names, though
some were only first names and some were nicknames. Like Dick-nose,
how do you look for a guy named Dick-nose?

Roussel had neither quarreled with nor bad-mouthed anybody. He
and Bridget went to the Avalon about twice a month and the bouncers
never had a complaint against him. He'd been happy the whole evening

and when he'd left the club around twelve-thirty he was relatively sober. That's when he'd gotten ice-picked, just outside the club, walking beneath the trees with his arm around Bridget's shoulders on the way to his car.

Roussel was from Manchester, New Hampshire, but he'd worked for a restaurant-supply company in Boston for several years. He had a thousand friends. Bridget Bonnelli couldn't think why anyone would want to kill him. Just the thought of it made her start weeping again. She knew most of those friends. They were all friends together.

And had there been anyone that she hadn't known? She thought about this. After all, they'd seen many people that night. But maybe there was this one guy Buddy used to know and was surprised to see. He'd just come and gone. You know how it is standing at the bar— someone comes up and you say a couple of words. Buddy hadn't introduced her. He'd joked with the guy but it had only been for a few seconds. She couldn't remember what he looked like—just a young guy, regular-looking. Buddy had known him in Manchester. Did he have a name? Maybe it had been Fred, maybe it had been Frank. Had she seen this Fred or Frank outside? No. She didn't remember anything outside. For that matter, she wasn't even sure his name had been Fred or Frank.

Neither name had any special meaning for Flynn. Fred or Frank was just a name among twenty others. It would have meant nothing if it hadn't been for the break, the piece of news that made Flynn feel optimistic. All week he and his team had been talking to Roussel's buddies: four detectives knocking on doors and nobody could come up with a reason why Roussel had got himself iced. He was a good guy, worked hard, and his girlfriend loved him. No drugs, no debts, no bad habits. Buddy Roussel was an upstanding young man and now he was dead. It was a shame, and two hundred people had attended his funeral on Friday.

But this morning Leo Flynn had had a piece of good news. The state troopers in Revere had found themselves a two-bit hood who'd gotten killed the same way—a silver nail up through the occipital bone. They'd almost blown it because at first they thought the guy, Sal Procopio, was a floater, since he'd been dragged from the water at Revere Beach early Tuesday morning by a good citizen who had been making out with his girlfriend and happened to see Sal bobbing around in the surf. Sal had been tagged as a floater and stayed in the morgue all week because there was trouble finding his next of kin: parents dead, brothers and sisters spread out across the country.

Then on Friday the medical examiner in Boston had been using Sal to show his students what to look for in drowning victims and, lo and behold, it seemed Sal Procopio hadn't drowned after all. Further exploration turned up the mess in his brain—the cone-shaped slice an ice pick can make. They even found the hole at the base of the skull, nearly swollen shut by Sal's time in the water. By then the troopers were left with egg on their face, which was why they had gotten more active with the Revere cops than usual, tracking down Procopio's chums and bar pals. And this had led to the second detail that caught Flynn's attention and had him driving up to Revere. Procopio had been spending time with a guy named Frank—last name unknown—a French Canadian from Manchester who'd disappeared. Leastways, nobody could find him. But for Flynn this wasn't so terrible, because where there were two dead guys killed the same way, they'd probably find a third and maybe a fourth and already he'd had the M.O. sent throughout the East.

In the meantime, Leo Flynn wanted to talk to Procopio's pals. He wanted to find out what Frank looked like. And he even looked forward to walking along the beach to see where Sal had gotten himself iced. It was a sunny day and Flynn thought he would buy himself a cigar as a way to cut down smoking. He'd walk along the sand and think of the times he'd come to Revere as a kid with his parents and big sister. The salt air would be good for his cold.

The girl sat on the chrome counter, kicking the heels of her bare feet against the wooden door of the cabinet beneath her, making an iambic drumlike sound that echoed against the kitchen's metal surfaces. She was watching Frank LeBrun pummel a heap of bread dough about the size of a beer case, hitting it hard, then picking it up, spinning it around, and flinging it down on the countertop. He wore a white shirt, white apron, and a white cap. Afternoon light slanted through the kitchen windows from the southwest, a Technicolor brilliance from the vast lapis lazuli bowl that seemed to curve over the school. The light reflected from the hanging pots and pans, the aluminum doors of the three large refrigerators, and the chrome on the stoves so the whole kitchen flickered and gleamed. It was Wednesday of Jessica's second week, and while she was getting used to Bishop's Hill, she didn't like it any better.

"I don't see why you can't call me Misty," the girl said. Her peroxided hair was in two pigtails and her figure was hidden by an oversized University of New Hampshire sweatshirt.

The man laughed, keeping his back to her. "It's not your name."

"Maybe not legally, but it's still mine. It's the name of my soul."

"That's pretty dumb."

"Haven't you ever wanted to be called something other than Frank?"

"People call me all sorts of stuff. My grandmom called me François. My old lady called me Francis." He hit the mound of dough with his fist, then he took a quick look at the girl over his shoulder. He was grinning. "But I'm Frank."

"Well, I'm Misty."

"You ever hear what they call a Canuck with an IQ of 167?"

The girl gave an artificial yawn. "A village?"

"For Pete's sake." LeBrun gave the mound of dough another punch. "You know why a woman's got two holes so close together?"

"Why?"

"So you can carry 'em like a six-pack."

"That's disgusting." Jessica glanced out the window toward the trees. Then she looked down at her toenails, which were painted bright green. "Call me Misty."

"Your name's Jessica."

"That's what the jerks call me. I don't want you to call me that."

"Don't start that possessive shit. I don't even know you."

"Then why'd you talk to me the other day?"

"I talk to everybody, I'm a friendly guy." LeBrun stopped kneading the bread and turned toward the girl, wiping his hands on his apron. "You know how to catch a Canuck?"

"How?"

"Slam down the toilet seat when he's taking a drink."

"What do you have against Canucks?"

"My grandmom used to say they were New Hampshire's colored problem. So why'd she marry a guy named LaBrecque, I'd ask? What was she, Irish? Nah, her name was Gateau—a fucking Canuck as well. She was nuts, is all. She didn't know what the fuck she was. I'd visit her in the nursing home and I'd say, 'Hey, Grandmom, why'd Canucks wear hats?' And she'd say, 'So they don't flap themselves to death with their big ears.' And we'd laugh till the nurses complained. The lousy bitches, they fuckin' robbed her blind."

"You think I could hire you to do something?"

"You couldn't afford me." LeBrun turned back to the pile of bread dough.

"Maybe I could. There's something I need you to do."

LeBrun turned to face her. "Are we talking about real money?"

"Two thousand dollars."

LeBrun's face had become still as he watched Jessica. Then he said, "Aren't you going to be late to class?"

The girl glanced around at the clock on the wall behind her. She pursed her lips and jumped down from the counter. The bell must have rung without her hearing it. She scooped up her backpack from the floor. "Maybe we can talk after dinner," she said. Her bare feet made a faint slapping noise against the tiles.

LeBrun shrugged. "I won't hold my breath." As the door swung shut, he returned to his bread dough, right jab, left jab. He opened a drawer and removed a bag of chocolate chips. Taking one bit of chocolate, he inserted it deep into the bread dough. Then he reached in the drawer again and took out a silver-colored tack, which he buried as well.

He patted the dough. "Something nice, something nasty." LeBrun liked that. It made him laugh.

As Jessica hurried across the dining room, she looked at her watch. She had thirty seconds to get to her two o'clock Spanish class on the third floor and the other side of the building. Reaching the corridor, she broke into a trot. A few kids were still in the hall but most were in class. Above the wooden paneling of the walls hung rows of photographs dating back into the nineteenth century, showing formally posed groups of Bishop's Hill boys—graduating classes, baseball teams, chess club, debating club. All wore coats and ties, except for the athletes. She happened to notice the graduating class of 1950, the same year her father had been born. He was born in March in Portsmouth in the midst of a snowstorm; this graduating-class picture was probably taken in May or June. She didn't have time to study it, but she found herself calculating how old those boys probably were today—somewhere in their midsixties—and how they were probably alive while her father was dead.

Jessica began to run and her feet slapped the floor. The faces in the photographs became a blur as she ran past, as if they had been turned into a movie; but they weren't moving, she was moving, and she smiled at this. But then someone grabbed her arm, pulling her to a stop and wrenching her shoulder so it hurt.

"Why the hell are you running? You know there's no running."

A man's angry boiled-ham face rose above her. Jessica recognized him as one of the teachers, but she didn't know his name. She pulled herself free and swung her hand at him, meaning to push him away. The man blocked her arm and gave her a push so she fell back against the wall.

"You're not even wearing shoes. Jesus, you're in trouble—"

"Fuck you," said the girl. "Fuck you, fuck you!"

The man took a step toward her. His face looked swollen.

"Chip!" came a voice.

Both Jessica and the man looked up the hall and saw the new headmaster walking toward them. Behind him was Miss Sandler, her Spanish teacher. With some relief Jessica thought that, no matter what other trouble she was in, at least she wasn't late.

"He hurt me, he hurt my arm." Jessica held her shoulder. It didn't occur to her not to exaggerate. It seemed perfectly reasonable to get Chip in as much trouble as she could.

Chip became increasingly angry. "She was running. You heard what she said to me. She doesn't even have any shoes, for crying out loud."

By now the headmaster and Miss Sandler had joined them. Farther up the hall several students were watching and a teacher leaned out her open door to look in their direction.

"I should get a fuckin' lawyer and bust his ass," said Jessica. "What right's he got to touch me?" She continued rubbing her arm and wincing.

The headmaster turned to Miss Sandler. "Take care of her, will you?"

Kate put her arm lightly around Jessica's shoulder. "Come on, let's go to class."

"I don't feel like fuckin' Spanish anymore. He hurt me."

Kate smiled. "You know you were going to be late. Now we can walk together."

"And what about him?" said Jessica, jabbing her thumb toward Chip.

Kate began leading her away. "You're both upset. Let Dr. Hawthorne deal with it. We have a long hour ahead on the verb *to be*."

They walked slowly down the hall. Jessica glanced back with a sort of sneer, then put her arm around Kate's waist. "What a jerk," she said.

"You know," said Kate, "I happened to notice you right away the first day because we both wear ankle bracelets." She extended her foot so Jessica could see it.

Jessica looked down but didn't pause. "Yours is half the size of mine. You got a cheap one. Mine's worth a lot of money. My father gave it to me."

"You're a lucky girl," said Kate.

"Fat lot you know," said Jessica.

Hawthorne watched them walk down the corridor. He had to remind himself that the girl was fifteen. Dressed in her sweatshirt and jeans, she looked about twelve, slouching and scuffing her bare feet. Kate, on the other hand, was thin and erect.

Chip had turned away and was looking in the other direction. "You still need me?" The hall was now empty except for the two of them.

"Chip, these kids are used to abuse and to adults who push them around. We have to show them we're not like that. It's hard enough to teach them as it is. They shouldn't have the slightest fear that we might hurt them."

Chip turned slightly but he still wouldn't look at Hawthorne. He wore khakis and a tan crewneck sweater that gave him a slightly military appearance. "You know the difference between a kid with a learning disability and a juvenile delinquent?"

"Is that a serious question?"

"The difference is forty thousand a year. These are spoiled rich kids who've been kicked out of every place else and are used to doing what they want. Nobody has ever told them the difference between right and wrong and it's time somebody did."

Hawthorne stepped in front of him so Chip was forced to meet his eye. He was startled by Chip's anger, his dark red face, and he found himself thinking that Chip would be ripe for a stroke in about ten years. He tried to keep his voice calm. "Before that young woman came to Bishop's Hill, she spent ten weeks working as a stripper in Boston. Who knows what she experienced, but I don't expect it was anything nice. Our job is to convince her that Bishop's Hill is a place where she can be safe. If I ever see or hear of you laying a hand on a student again, I'll have to dismiss you. This is the only warning you'll get."

Chip's pale eyes widened, then relaxed. He made an ironical salute. "Noted," he said. Chip started to walk down the hall toward his classroom.

"One other matter," said Hawthorne.

Chip paused and half turned.

"You missed the first of the meetings yesterday to discuss the students. I'd like you to try and be there tomorrow."

"I've got a pretty busy schedule."

"We all do."

Hawthorne watched Chip continue along the hall. Had Chip's breath smelled of alcohol or had he just not brushed his teeth? Hawthorne wondered if his duties included telling the faculty and staff to floss. One advantage of working in treatment centers was that staff members were highly conscious of their physical impact on their surroundings. They were aware of how the kids looked at them, and they went out of their way to appear benign and harmless. That was even a talk that Hawthorne had given to child-care workers every year: the psychological effects of their body language and appearance.

Hawthorne also had to ask himself if he would have responded so sharply if Chip hadn't missed the meeting. In fact, half the faculty had failed to attend and the discussion had been desultory at best—more complaint than productive deliberation. He knew that they were testing his resolve, in which case they were making a mistake. But even in the best of circumstances, he would have spoken to Chip about his treatment of Jessica. There was no excuse for grabbing her like that. As for the girl, Hawthorne would talk to her when she calmed down. Although he would have preferred her to wear shoes, he expected that she would put them on soon enough as the weather got colder.

Hawthorne was on his way to see Clifford Evings, the school psychologist, whose office was near the dining hall. Although Evings had come to Tuesday's meeting, he hadn't spoken, and at one point Hawthorne had noticed that he was asleep. Then Evings had left before Hawthorne could speak with him, something that had also happened at the meeting the previous week when Hawthorne had been introduced to the staff. Indeed, he had begun to think that Evings was trying to avoid any serious conversation. A single man in his early sixties, Evings had an apartment in one of the dormitory cottages, where he was also expected to monitor the students. But the people who had described the arrangement to Hawthorne, including Fritz Skander, had made some slight gesture—a rolling of the eyes or tapping the nose—to indicate that only minimal monitoring went on. Evings was soft-spoken and his voice had an unfortunate nasal quality that reminded Hawthorne of a dentist's drill heard from far away. In addition, he was bald and thin to the point of being cadaverous. Hawthorne couldn't imagine how he was with the students. He had thought several times that, if Bishop's Hill managed to get through the year, he would encourage Evings in the direction of early retirement. In the meantime Evings was the only psychologist they had, though Hawthorne still hoped to hire another within the next few months.

Evings's office was an oversized closet with a single window, a wall of books, a desk, a file cabinet, and two wing chairs positioned on either side of a small coal-burning fireplace.

"Welcome to my lair," said Evings, looking up from his desk without enthusiasm.

"I've come to ask your advice about something." Hawthorne tried to be brisk and cheerful but in truth he found the little room oppressive.

Evings's hands were folded before him on a green blotter. His desk was empty and there was no sign of what he'd been doing before Hawthorne had knocked. Maybe he had slipped something into a drawer. The thought made Hawthorne feel slightly ashamed; there was nothing to say that Evings wasn't pursuing his duties to the best of his abilities. Evings wore a misshapen blue cardigan with leather patches at the elbows. The room was much too warm. A gentle hissing came from a radiator under the bookshelf.

"Let's sit by the fireplace, where it's more comfortable," said Evings, getting to his feet. "I could light a fire if you'd like."

"It seems quite warm enough," said Hawthorne.

"Ah, I'm always cold. I must have gotten it from my mother."

But Hawthorne was no longer paying attention. He was staring at the oil portrait hanging over the fireplace. It showed a cheerless white-haired man in a high collar and a thin white beard. His expression was severe, almost angry. With amazement, Hawthorne realized it was the same man he had seen staring down at him from a third-floor window of Adams Hall late Friday night. "Who's that?" he asked Evings.

"That's Ambrose Stark." Evings eyed Hawthorne with concern. "He was headmaster in the nineteenth century—oh, for about forty years. Are you all right?"

Hawthorne was astonished by the painting, and he couldn't take his eyes from it. After a moment, he asked, "He's the one they named the hall after?"

"That's right, and Stark Chapel. He died in the early 1890s. He's quite a figure here at Bishop's Hill. The spirit of the place, as it were."

"What do you mean, 'spirit'?"

"The fine old goals and traditions that we like to praise in our recruitment literature. Is anything wrong?"

Hawthorne made himself turn away. "He looked familiar, that's all."

"There are several other portraits here at the school. Perhaps you saw one."

"Very likely." Hawthorne tried to recall the figure he had seen. Had it moved or made any sign? Was it possible that someone had held up a similar portrait at the third-floor window? The alternatives were too absurd to consider. Evings was continuing to watch him warily. Hawthorne forced a smile and glanced around the office.

In another moment they were settled in the two armchairs beneath the portrait. Hawthorne had nearly regained his composure, though his mind was full of questions. Still, he had to turn the conversation away from Ambrose Stark and to the reason for his visit. Evings displayed a stiffness that Hawthorne couldn't explain, as if he were shy or had been caught doing something he shouldn't.

"I wondered if you had any thoughts on the meeting yesterday?" asked Hawthorne.

Evings looked mildly perplexed, as if he had already forgotten the meeting. "Seems the wisest approach—get matters out in the open. Of course, it would be a pity if it became no more than gossip. I've always been an enemy of gossip—feelings get hurt, people take dislikes to one another. Nobody would benefit, neither the students nor the faculty. In fact, it might be fair to say that gossip would be no improvement on silence. No, no, I'd hate to see it happen."

"As would I," said Hawthorne, somewhat tonelessly, "which is why I feel we could benefit from your psychological expertise."

Evings seemed both flattered and discouraged by the description. "I try to do what I can."

They discussed the meetings and what Evings might do. For instance, he might give the faculty some guidance on dealing with certain of the students who seemed especially troubled. Hawthorne mentioned several names but Evings didn't recognize them. The more Hawthorne said, the more uncertain Evings became. He agreed, however, to read the students' files and talk to Hawthorne about what might be done.

As Hawthorne stood up to leave, he thought of something else. "The other night I came on a cat hung from a branch of one of the pines near the playing fields. I gather it belonged to the housekeeper, Mrs. Grayson."

"Dear me," said Evings, "and who was responsible?"

"I've no idea, but I wanted to ask if anything like this ever occurred before or if any of the students might have had any trouble with . . ." Hawthorne let the sentence drift away. Evings was staring fixedly at his bookshelf to his right. Following his gaze, Hawthorne saw row after row of novels and tucked between them on the third shelf the bright yellow spine of a well-thumbed paperbound copy of the *Study Guide to the Diagnostic and Statistical Manual of Mental Disorders–IV*. Hawthorne wondered if Evings meant to take down the guide, turn to the index, and look up "cat" or "hanged cat." Then he realized the reason for Evings's stiffness—the man was frightened.

Evings cleared his throat—a sound rather like a bleat—and coughed. "I'm afraid this catches me by surprise. Hanged cat, you say? Absolutely nothing like that has happened here before, at least to my knowledge. Though it could have happened, I suppose, without my knowing about it. Now why should someone hang a cat? Of course, a few students have had difficulties with Mrs. Grayson, especially those she's reported for smoking in their rooms. Perhaps the motivation lay with Mrs. Grayson and not the cat. At least five or six have spoken ill of her to me. I could give you their names, though two have graduated, or at least haven't returned. But they might, of course, have returned to hang a cat, as strange as that may be. I'm sure there are stranger cases."

Again Evings glanced toward the *DSM* study guide as if he wished to search its pages. He took a handkerchief from the pocket of his cardigan and wiped his forehead.

"Are you all right?" asked Hawthorne quietly.

Evings gave Hawthorne a wide-eyed stare; he looked like someone who had tried to swallow something too big for his throat. Then he leaned forward and buried his face in his hands. "I know I'm terrible at my job. Nobody knows it better than I. Years ago, I think, I actually had something to offer." He rubbed his scalp and the pressure of his fingers made white marks on the pink flesh. "But now it gets worse and worse. The students who come here . . . I really have nothing to say to them. Of course it's simple for me to sit and remain silent. And for some, that's enough. But do you know that a few have sat there and laughed? I was afraid I'd burst into tears. I know I don't have much more time at Bishop's Hill. There's nothing surprising about that. The moment I laid eyes on you I knew you'd find me out, but I hoped I'd at least have a few months. Then that meeting yesterday—I felt unable to say a word. Others kept looking at me—what an awful humiliation! Believe me, no one feels guiltier than I about taking the school's money. I fully understand that you'd want me to resign."

Hawthorne experienced a sinking feeling. "Really, I only meant to ask you about the hanged cat."

"Well, I didn't do it," said Evings fussily, "that's the one thing I am absolutely positive about. I have never in my entire life hanged a cat." He laughed suddenly, a high barking noise. "Actually, I knew there would be changes. Can you deny that you're planning to hire a new psychologist?"

"I've already announced that fact, but I'm not getting someone to replace you."

"Yes, that's how it begins, a little innocuous levering. The new person settles in and suddenly I disappear."

"Has anyone told you that your position's in jeopardy?" asked Hawthorne. He felt a trifle guilty about his question, since he had been considering replacing Evings even before he had entered the stuffy office. He guessed that the temperature in the room was nearly ninety and he felt a drop of sweat roll down his rib cage until it was blotted by his shirt.

"I don't want to get anyone in trouble," said Evings. "I'm not that sort of person. By the way, I hope there really was a hanged cat and you're not just using this as a pretext to—"

"Oh, stop it, Clifford." Although Hawthorne had known he would have difficulties at Bishop's Hill, he hadn't expected people to be frightened of him. "You're the school psychologist and I thought you could help me with a problem that, after all, would seem to approach your area of expertise. Can't hanging a cat be considered aberrant behavior?"

"And I tell you I know nothing about it."

"Well," said Hawthorne, getting to his feet, "keep me informed. Perhaps you'll hear something from one of the students."

Evings was taller than Hawthorne by at least an inch. "I'll keep my antennae out."

The men shook hands. As Hawthorne left the office, he thought of the cluster of anxieties that at any moment filled a person's mind. How could objectivity be more than a dream? Most likely, Evings still doubted that a cat had been hung and thought it all a trick Hawthorne was playing. Now the sum of Evings's anxieties had been substantially increased to no purpose. But what did he do here? A little counseling and monitoring in his dormitory cottage. For the rest, he probably read novels all day long. Yet Hawthorne knew that his own objectivity was suspect. The portrait of Ambrose Stark had given him a shock and it surely affected the filter through which he had been trying to understand Clifford Evings. And what had been the degree of malice? The portrait and laughing teeth—had they been a practical joke or something more alarming?

Hawthorne glanced down the hall and saw the boy who had shown him the dead cat strolling toward him. Seeing the headmaster, the boy stopped and Hawthorne had the distinct impression that Scott was considering the possibility of flight.

"Don't you have class now?" Hawthorne asked. Over the weekend he had read the boy's file to make certain he had no record of torturing animals or something else that might suggest that he himself had killed the cat. Instead, he found a history of Scott's being shunted from one stepparent to another. Alcoholism, violence, sexual abuse—

whatever Bishop's Hill's failings, the school was a clear improvement over the so-called home environment of Scott's past.

"Mr. Campbell got a telephone call and I had to use the bathroom."

Approaching Scott, Hawthorne detected the odor of cigarettes. "And you thought it best to use a bathroom on the far side of the building. Have you learned anything about the cat?"

"I asked some kids but they didn't know anything. Mrs. Grayson thought a fisher caught it. She said it happens all the time. But a fisher wouldn't string it up."

"Was she upset?"

"Not particularly. She sighed a lot, though." A wing of hair fell across the boy's right eye and he tossed his head to resettle it back where it belonged.

"What class do you have with Mr. Campbell?"

"Ancient and medieval history. We're just finishing the Egyptians."

It was on the tip of Hawthorne's tongue to ask what Campbell was like as a teacher, but he didn't. Whatever Campbell was like, Hawthorne would find out soon enough.

"You'd better air out your sweater before you return to class. It will give you away."

"Thanks," said Scott, and he began hurrying down the hall.

"And no running," Hawthorne called after him, then grinned as the boy came to a sudden halt and proceeded to tiptoe forward.

Hawthorne opened the door to the dining hall; the kitchen, his destination, lay on the far side. The room had dark wainscoting under tall windows looking out on an expanse of lawn called the Common. The polished floorboards creaked as he walked across them. Twenty long oak tables stood in two rows with a twenty-first at the head of the room for the headmaster and his guests. So far Hawthorne had eaten at the students' tables, trying to engage them in conversation on subjects other than food. At the moment the chairs were up on the tabletops as two students mopped the floor. The ceiling had thick beams lined with plaques displaying the names of graduating seniors, going back year by year to the first class in 1854. Paintings hung on all the walls—old headmasters and chaplains. And there at the far end was another portrait of Ambrose Stark, sitting at a desk and looking censorious. Hawthorne couldn't remember seeing it before, but most likely he had let his eyes drift across it. Stark glared down as if he still had the school under his special protection. It gave Hawthorne a chill, but it seemed obvious that the thing at the window had been a picture. Presumably, one or two of the students had been trying to give him a scare.

Hawthorne pushed open the door to the kitchen. The only person in evidence was the new cook, who was in the process of looking inside the oven. The smell of baking bread filled the air.

LeBrun glanced up and saw Hawthorne. "The boss," he said.

"In a manner of speaking. I just wanted to say how much I appreciate the bread you've been making. A lot of people have been worrying about what changes might occur at the school and your bread has been a treat for everyone. It makes it easier to be here."

LeBrun shut the oven door. His face was narrow and his eyes close together, as if someone in the distant past had tried to squeeze his head. "Hey, I'm glad to do it. But thanks for the compliment. I've been getting a lot of visitors. A couple of kids tried to bum cigarettes, then Mr. Skander came in about the bread as well. He said he was glad there wasn't any mold on it. I guess the bread last year was mostly moldy." LeBrun laughed.

"Was Jessica Weaver in here by any chance?" It had occurred to Hawthorne that she'd been coming from this direction.

"That cute little kid with the pigtails? Yeah, she was."

"What did she want?"

"She wanted me to call her Misty."

"I beg your pardon?"

"Misty, she wants to be called Misty. You like jokes?"

"Some jokes. Why does she want to be called Misty?"

"I guess she thinks it's cooler than Jessica. She said it was the name of her soul." LeBrun chuckled. "If my soul had a name, it'd be Black Spot. You know what they call a female clone?"

"I have a feeling that's not the kind of joke I particularly like." Hawthorne was struck by the man's energy; he seemed to be moving all the time. Even when he stood still, his hands twitched at his sides.

"I guess it's too raw for a guy with a suit and tie. What would the teachers say if they heard the cook telling dirty jokes to the boss? You know what the bartender said to the horse that came into the bar?"

"Why the long face." Hawthorne grinned.

"You're quick," said LeBrun, grinning back, "you know all the answers."

"That's why I'm headmaster." Hawthorne couldn't calculate LeBrun's degree of seriousness. At least he didn't seem scared, like Evings. "How'd you get to know her?"

"We both got here the same day. You know, new kids on the block. And you too, you got here the day before us. We should form a club."

"Where were you before coming here?"

"I was doing odds and ends around Boston. Pizza, burgers, greasy French fries, the usual gut busters." LeBrun chuckled. "Being here is like reaching civilization."

"I'm glad you like it. You're a pretty jolly guy, aren't you?"

"Hey, if you can't laugh, you might as well put a bullet in your head."

Hawthorne considered pursuing that, then decided to ask about the cat instead. "You know anything about a cat that was hung on Friday night?"

"I heard some kids talking about it. Crazy days, you know what I'm saying?"

"How do you feel about cats?"

"Can't stand them. Remember what that guy used to say, that comic? 'Cats? I prefer rats.' That's me, all right. 'Cats? I prefer rats.' " LeBrun leaned back against a metal table and laughed. Hawthorne could see the fillings in his teeth. He began to laugh as well.

"You mind if I ask a favor?" said LeBrun, growing serious. "Can I look at that scar on your wrist? I caught a glimpse the other day but I couldn't see it very well. I don't mean to be rude."

There was something so childlike about the request that it didn't occur to Hawthorne to take offense. He took off his sport coat and pulled up the sleeve of his shirt.

LeBrun leaned over the scar. "That's a beaut. How far up does it go?"

"To the elbow."

LeBrun reached out and touched the skin. "Does it hurt?"

"Not anymore. The skin's a little tender in places."

"It must have been some fire." LeBrun gently turned the wrist to see the scar from all sides.

"It was."

"Anybody hurt other than yourself?"

Hawthorne had a momentary recollection of the screaming and the ceiling falling. "Yes, others were hurt."

LeBrun released the wrist. "Fuckin' great-lookin' scar." He laughed. "I got a bunch of them too, but they're all on the inside."

"Those are harder to treat."

"They don't bother me none. Leastways, not anymore."

The next day after her last class, Kate stopped by the main office to pick up some blue books for a quiz she was planning to give. Mrs. Hayes was on the phone but she waved Kate toward the supply closet. It occurred to Kate that Mrs. Hayes was the only person she knew who had mastered the art of smiling brusquely. The office was a large room with oak desks, oak file cabinets, and oak paneling on the walls, all of it somewhat yellow from the many layers of wax applied over a hundred years. In one corner of the room were a dozen large cardboard boxes with the name "IBM" printed on most and "Hewlett-Packard" on the others.

Behind Mrs. Hayes's desk the door to the headmaster's office stood open. As she got her blue books Kate could see Hawthorne sitting at his desk in his shirtsleeves. Two stacks of manila folders rose on either side of him. Kate hesitated, then tapped on the door frame. Hawthorne looked up and adjusted his glasses.

"Could I talk to you for a moment?"

"By all means." Hawthorne got to his feet as she entered and pointed to an armchair with a green leather seat. "Take that chair. It's the most comfortable."

Kate hadn't meant to sit down but she found herself doing so. The reason for her visit suddenly struck her as intrusive and politically unwise. Hawthorne sat on the edge of his desk, facing her. The sleeves of his white shirt were buttoned at the wrist. He looks tired, Kate thought. She heard a bell ring, then the sound of feet in the hall.

"Well, I'm not sure how to begin." Kate cursed herself for being foolish.

"At the beginning's always a good place." When Hawthorne smiled all his tiredness seemed to disappear. "I wanted to thank you for taking charge of Jessica yesterday. She was clearly upset and I wanted the opportunity to talk to Chip."

"Actually, that's what I wanted to talk to you about. Not Jessica but Chip . . ."

The girl had calmed down in class. Once they had begun their discussion of the verb *estar,* Jessica had asked the meaning of the word *chingada,* which had sidetracked the class for the rest of the hour. *Chingar*—to fuck. *Chingada*—one of the fucked or a child born as the result of rape.

"What about Chip?"

That morning Kate had heard several faculty members saying that Chip was in trouble and had already made an enemy of the headmaster. Seeing Hawthorne at his desk, Kate had decided to take the opportunity to say something in Chip's behalf. "I think he's under a lot of stress. You know, he's divorced and his wife has the two kids. They live in Littleton. Last week she told him that they were moving to Seattle. I know it doesn't excuse him, but it might explain why he's behaving so . . . abruptly."

Hawthorne scratched the back of his head. "Being new, I realize you all have histories I know nothing about. Is he a friend of yours?"

Kate felt herself blushing slightly. She recalled the thermos of martinis that Chip had taken to the movie theater. "We're friendly and he's been kind to me."

"You know I can't permit any physical aggressiveness toward the students. It's hard enough to gain their trust as it is. Chip's now lost all credibility with that girl. And she'll tell the other kids. I know very little about Chip Campbell, except that he seems to object to some of my changes and dislikes coming to meetings. I don't know if he's been physical with other students, but I mean to find out."

Kate put her hands on the arms of the chair, intending to stand up, then she relaxed again. "You must see that people are worried about you. Not the students so much as the faculty and staff. They're worried about their jobs and the security of their futures. For a while it will make them act rather oddly. They'll have to learn to trust you."

"Do you trust me?"

Kate wanted to smile but she didn't. "So far I have no feelings one way or the other. I'm new here and I'm not wedded to the place. I don't really want to look for another job, but I could easily enough. For many of the others, it would be much harder."

"It's certainly not my wish to dismiss anybody," said Hawthorne, lowering his voice and glancing toward the open door, "but the school needs to be changed. I'm sure you don't want to hear a whole philosophical discussion . . ."

This time Kate let herself smile. "I think I heard it last week."

Hawthorne smiled as well. "It's funny—before coming, everything seemed clear. But the longer I'm in here, the muddier it becomes. That's not a complaint, just a confession."

Kate got to her feet. "At least you're able to make it."

He walked her to the door. In the outer office, Skander was opening one of the boxes with the new computers. When he saw Kate, he gave her a smile that seemed to indicate such pleasure that she was almost startled.

"I'm glad you two are getting to know each other," said Skander, putting emphasis on the word *glad*. He wore a rumpled blue blazer and a blue-and-gold Bishop's Hill necktie.

"I hope to get to know all the faculty," said Hawthorne. "Give me a minute to put away some files. Then we can talk. We've got about a half hour before the meeting." He disappeared again into his office.

Skander continued to smile at Kate as he jingled the change in his pockets. "It's awfully good to see you. I'm sure your classes are going great guns."

It occurred to Kate, not for the first time, that all of Skander's actions and ways of speaking were somewhat inflated, as if he were talking to someone who was partially deaf or who only imperfectly grasped the English language. His gestures were all oversized. "They're going very well, thanks."

"And it was good of you to take that girl who so upset Chip yesterday."

"I like her. She's brash."

"Used to be a stripper, I gather. Too young, of course, to do it legally. Well, it takes all kinds. We used to have a boy here who augmented his allowance by selling stolen cattle."

As they spoke, Skander accompanied Kate to the door of the office with one hand resting on her shoulder and the other in his pocket.

"She looks awfully young to have been a stripper."

Skander patted Kate on the back. "It was apprentice work, surely."

Hawthorne was locking the file cabinet when Skander entered. "Tell me, who is this girl Gail Jensen who died a few years ago? It's not clear from her file what happened."

Skander sat down on the edge of the green armchair and his forehead wrinkled in distress. "A wonderful girl, one of our best. She had stomach pains that she was trying to ignore. It was at Thanksgiving. Turned out to be appendicitis. She died on the operating table, poor thing."

"She was fifteen?"

Skander nodded. "Old Pendergast was still headmaster and he had to call the girl's mother. It was awful for everyone concerned. We wanted to establish a scholarship in the girl's honor but the mother said no. It's odd how grief can affect some people."

As Skander had been talking, Hawthorne gathered some files remaining on his desk.

Skander raised his eyebrows. "Surely you're not taking all those home to read?"

"Some are for the meeting and others I'll take home," said Hawthorne, smiling. "It's got to be done."

Skander made a clucking noise. "I wish you'd get more rest. A shock such as you had in San Diego could take years to get over. I expect you still dream of them every night."

Hawthorne opened his mouth to speak, then said nothing.

"Don't worry about it, but I want you to feel free to talk if you wish. I'm glad you'll be coming over tomorrow night, if only to drop in. Hilda and I had such a good time when we had dinner together on Saturday."

Skander had invited the faculty to his house on Friday evening for coffee and apple cobbler around eight o'clock to give them the opportunity to socialize with the new headmaster. "With adult refreshment as well," he had said with a wink.

"Someone told you about the fire?" asked Hawthorne.

"Friends in San Diego happened to mention it. I can't tell you how upset I was. And Hilda, too. Of course you must torment yourself with questions. How could you not?"

"What do you mean?"

"You know, whether you did the right thing. What would have happened if you had done this instead of that. Letting that boy into your home."

Hawthorne moved to the door with the files under his arm. "It's hard not to think of it." He didn't want to talk about San Diego but the subject seemed always near at hand.

Skander followed Hawthorne to the door. "What if you'd never spoken to that boy? That's what I mean. Those thoughts must be very difficult. We've all done things that we've regretted afterward, but your experience is particularly awful."

"Time can do a lot. I suppose I try to move forward." Hawthorne despised the banalities he heard coming out of his mouth.

"How true, how true," said Skander, looking suddenly philosophical. "But you know, I was also impressed by your prominence. Certainly I knew from your curriculum vitae that you were an important figure in your field, but my friends' remarks . . . Well, they couldn't say enough. I can't tell you how fortunate I feel that you've decided to make Bishop's Hill your home. You're planning to write a book, I imagine."

"A book? You mean a sort of memoir?"

"No, no, an analysis of our little community. What was that book I read in college? *The Village in the Vaucluse,* something like that. Perhaps that's what you're intending for us. Bishop's Hill will be your very own Vaucluse."

Hawthorne stared at Skander, trying to determine if he was serious. "Believe me, nothing is farther from my thoughts."

"Oh, you say that now, but in five or ten years, who can say what you'll be up to. I only hope they spell my name right. You know how those editors can be."

Hawthorne made himself change the subject. "Fritz, I want you to check upstairs to see that everything is ready for the faculty meeting. I've asked the kitchen to bring refreshments of some kind, just so the occasion doesn't seem so onerous. But if you could make sure the room is set up . . ."

"I'd be delighted. Just let me have a word with Mrs. Hayes about those computers."

Five minutes later, Skander had opened one of the boxes containing a computer and was spreading the instruction booklets out on Mrs. Hayes's desk as the secretary sighed.

"What do you think?" he said. "Exciting, isn't it."

"I'll never be able to do it."

"Don't be silly. I'm sure it's very user-friendly." He opened three of the manuals and set them in front of Mrs. Hayes. "In six months, you'll be a regular champ, surfing the Internet with the best. Mind you stay away from the more lubricious Web sites. I'd hate to see you corrupted. My son is particularly fond of chat rooms. And games— really, his room is full of electronic explosions. By the way, has Dr. Hawthorne been quizzing you about Dr. Pendergast?"

Mrs. Hayes stared down at the manuals. "Not really, no."

Skander chuckled soothingly. "A wonderful old fellow in his way and sorely missed by quite a few. I suggest you take these books home and start getting into them. There's a computer class at Plymouth State that meets a couple of nights each week. The school will pay, of course."

"My bridge group meets tonight," said Mrs. Hayes, slightly embarrassed.

"Ah, I'm afraid you won't have much time for that anymore. Just promise you won't turn the machine on till you've fully mastered the manuals. It's expensive equipment and we'd hate to see it go up in smoke."

"I wouldn't dream of it."

"Much the wisest course. Oh yes, if you hear them make any noise in their boxes—you know, hum or click—just ignore it. These things have internal batteries, fans and suchlike. They can be unnerving if you don't know they're there. Mr. Dolittle has one in the library. He says the hard drive is always thinking even when the machine's been turned off for the night. The fans can be especially distracting. Ta-ta!"

Skander disappeared into the hall. Mrs. Hayes stared at the computer, waiting for it to do something. Its hindquarters seemed to require dozens of wires or connections, she wasn't sure what they were called. If she listened carefully she thought she could hear something from inside the machine, but she wasn't positive. From a classroom several doors away, she heard the Bishop's Hill cheerleaders practicing their cheers: "Bishop's Hill, we aim to kill! Bishop's Hill, we aim to kill!" Their high voices echoed down the empty hall.

Kate found the Xerox copies of the news clippings from the *San Diego Union-Tribune* in her mailbox just before she left for home Friday afternoon. She meant to look at them later but instead she read them while sitting in her small Honda in the lot behind Douglas Hall. By now she had heard that Hawthorne's wife and daughter had died in a fire and she had seen the scars on his wrist, though she didn't know any details. The articles described how Hawthorne, as director at Wyndham School, a San Diego residential treatment center, had befriended a boy who had grown jealous of Hawthorne's wife and daughter and had started the fire. Hawthorne had been out for the evening with a psychologist from Boston, a woman named Claire Sunderlin. They had had dinner and stayed for an hour at a jazz bar. When he returned, he found the building burning and his wife and daughter trapped inside.

A month after the fire, hearings were held by a panel that included representatives from the San Diego County Department of Social Services, the California Association of Services for Children, and the regional branch of the Child Welfare League. Much discussion focused on Hawthorne's theories that children at risk could benefit from being given increasing degrees of responsibility, tasks like tutoring other children, helping in the kitchen, and working with the grounds crew— even, in some cases, keeping pets. A woman from the Child Welfare League had especially criticized Hawthorne for giving the boy, Stanley Carpasso, privileges enabling him to move freely about the school. Although Hawthorne had not been faulted for being away from Wyndham the night of the fire, it had received a lot of attention, especially in the newspaper. There were pictures of the burning school and of Hawthorne's wife and daughter, as well as a picture of the psychologist from Boston, who was quite pretty. The hearings had exonerated Hawthorne of any responsibility. But the reporter's tone implied that the committee members had been swayed by their sympathy for Hawthorne's personal loss and the fact that he had been burned while attempting to rescue his family. And there was the suggestion that as psychologists investigating another psychologist the committee had been protecting one of their own. Because of the arson, the fire marshal had also conducted an investigation, but Hawthorne had been exonerated there as well.

Although Kate was distressed about the fire and Hawthorne's ordeal, she was far more distressed that someone had thought it necessary to put the news stories in her mailbox. The stories didn't discredit Hawthorne but they formed a slur, a black mark that could affect his connection with the men and women at Bishop's Hill. After all, he was trying to get them to trust him.

At the meeting the previous afternoon, there had been several more faculty members than on Tuesday but a number made it clear they were there under duress. Chip hadn't come and Clifford Evings had fallen asleep. Fritz Skander had forgotten to bring certain files. Roger Bennett had some complaint about having to return a television that he had borrowed from the school the previous year. One of the science teachers, Tom Hastings, had wanted to know "what all this fuss was about" Chip's stopping a girl who was running in the hall, which had led to a discussion of Jessica Weaver. Kate had defended the girl, saying that she did very well in Spanish even though she made a point of being rude to the other students. Bennett asked if that was the girl who had worked as a stripper and Mrs. Sherman had said, "Stripper? What stripper?" Afterward there had been limp crackers, hard cheese, and cider with too much fizz. It hadn't been a successful occasion.

Kate drove home along Antelope Road. It was almost dark and her headlights caught the flash of orange from the turning leaves of the maples. She picked Todd up at Shirley Hodges's, then took him home to make dinner. Todd was blond, and tall for a second grader. He was excited about some science project involving crickets, but Kate gave him only half an ear as she continued to think of the fire at Wyndham School and what Hawthorne had gone through. At eight o'clock, she planned to go to Skander's for a little while with the other faculty. She wondered if everyone had received the same news stories in their mailboxes and how that would affect the evening.

In the end, Kate almost didn't go. She knew it might be unpleasant, and there was no one she cared to talk to except perhaps for Hawthorne himself. But that very consideration led her to make the effort—not that she was so eager to talk to Hawthorne, but she felt hopeful about his arrival at Bishop's Hill. And because she was sure that hers was the minority point of view, she wanted to go to Skander's to express it. Consequently, when the baby-sitter arrived at seven-forty-five, she kissed Todd good night, reminded him to brush his teeth, and drove off into the dark.

Skander greeted Kate at the door and took her coat. He wore a bright red cardigan with gold buttons. "Punctuality," he said as he beamed at her, "is a wonderful gift." Then, before she could respond, he went on, "Did you receive those news clippings in your box? I'm afraid everybody did. I can't imagine who would have done such a thing. Everybody's talking about it. Jim will be terribly upset. He's quite shy, you know. We'll have to look out for him."

Skander lived with his wife and ten-year-old son at the far end of the Bishop's Hill campus, beyond the six dormitory cottages, in one of the five brown-shingled houses reserved for faculty. Some guests had arrived already but not Hawthorne. Chip Campbell was talking to Roger Bennett in front of the fireplace, where several logs were burning. Chip had a beer; Bennett had a handful of carrot sticks. Bennett's wife, the school chaplain, sat on the couch talking to Mrs. Sherman, the art teacher, who had the house next to the Skanders'. The chaplain was heavyset, serious, and slightly older than her husband. In fact, as Kate had thought before, she was the more masculine of the two. Not that Roger was especially effeminate, but he had a giddiness and a nervous laugh that at times struck Kate as girlish. The Reverend Bennett was definitely a no-nonsense woman—at least Kate had never seen her laugh—and she wore tweed skirts and thick, serious shoes.

Betty Sherman wore a dark blue skirt and a colorful peasant blouse. She looked distressed as she listened to Harriet Bennett. Betty was given to theatrical gestures and Kate had not been drawn to her until she had learned that she lived alone with her son, who was retarded in some way. Then Kate had thought how difficult her life must be. No one, as far as Kate could recall, had ever mentioned a husband.

Observing Chip and Roger Bennett, the chaplain and Mrs. Sherman, Kate realized they were all talking about what had happened in San Diego. She heard references to the fire and saw the earnestness of their faces. Mixed with it was a sort of charged inquisitiveness, the excitement of news that temporarily took them out of their daily routines. Hilda Skander came out of the kitchen followed by Bill Dolittle, the librarian, carrying a tray of cookies. Dolittle wore a white turtleneck that emphasized the roundness of his belly. He had been divorced years ago and had a son who was a sophomore at Plymouth State. Dolittle put the cookies on the dining room table and gave Kate a little wave. Hilda Skander smiled at her.

Hilda was like a smaller version of her husband, shapeless and bustling, but her face was pointier. She wore a denim jumper that nearly reached her ankles and had short graying hair. She said something to Bill Dolittle and they both returned to the kitchen.

Kate thought again how these people had been living in close proximity to one another for years. Although not a family, they were familylike. They shared a history. In fact, there were not many friendships among them and they often complained and gossiped about one another. But their joint interest in Bishop's Hill kept them from drifting too far apart. Kate had wondered, with a fear approaching dread, if she would become like them, and the thought made her determined to put a time limit on her position at the school. As long as George stayed difficult, however, it was doubtful that she could move from the area. In eleven years Todd would be eighteen and ready to go to college. But Kate swore she'd rather cut off her left foot than remain at Bishop's Hill for that length of time.

The doorbell rang and Skander bustled over to answer it. Kate joined Chip and Roger at the fireplace. It was a cozy living room with colonial-style furniture and horse-and-buggy patterns on the wallpaper. The air smelled of wood smoke and cinnamon. The fire crackled. Chip stood with his back to it, warming his legs. He wore a blue Bishop's Hill sweatshirt and matching sweatpants. Chip coached the swim team and tended to exaggerate his affiliation to sports, though he wasn't particularly athletic. He also ran the school football pool and was always collecting money from one person or another. Several times he had offered to explain the system to Kate and was surprised when she showed no interest, as if she had expressed no interest in daylight or breathing.

"So what do you think of our new headmaster," Chip asked her, "pursuing the fleshpots as his wife and daughter burned?"

Kate found herself stiffening. "I don't believe that's actually what happened."

Bennett offered her a carrot stick and she shook her head. "Certainly it was unfortunate for him to be away from the school," said Bennett, "whatever his motives."

"Why shouldn't he be away from the school for an evening? Anyway, perhaps it was entirely business," said Kate.

"She was too pretty for business," said Chip.

Bennett tittered, then said, "I must say that his credentials were rather impressive. I wonder what he's doing at Bishop's Hill."

Chip had his bottle of Budweiser raised to his lips and he arched his eyebrows. Wiping his mouth on the back of his hand, he said, "Fritz suggested that he might write a book about us."

"Oh my. Harriet will be pleased. So that's why he came here?"

"It's about the only thing that makes sense unless he's doing the dirty with that little ex-stripper."

"Our own Lolita."

Kate found their joking disagreeable. "Who do you think put the clippings in the mailboxes?"

"That's just what we've been wondering," said Bennett, lowering his voice.

"Some do-gooder, most likely," said Chip, giving Kate a wink.

"Did you do it?"

"Not me, but I don't mind that it was done. This stuff should be out in the open."

Kate began to ask what kind of stuff Chip meant, but it was too early to start an argument. Still, she couldn't keep herself from making a small jab of her own.

"And that's why you've missed those two meetings? To keep stuff out in the open?"

Roger laughed. "He probably wanted to be out in the open himself. You know, hunting or fishing."

Chip frowned. "I just don't have time for that bullshit."

Roger patted Chip's shoulder solicitously and raised an eyebrow. "I just hope you don't make our new headmaster too cross."

Kate moved away before she heard Chip's answer. She felt exasperated with both of them. Looking around, she saw Skander at the door with Gene Strauss, the admissions director, and his wife, Emily. Strauss also taught shop, automotive mechanics, and seventh-grade math. He, his wife, and teenage daughter lived in another of the faculty houses; he had been at the school for thirty years. Kate couldn't imagine how effective he was as a director of admissions since he always looked slightly dour.

In the next ten minutes, Kate spoke to nearly everyone in the room. Five more people arrived but not Hawthorne. Kate hoped he wouldn't come. Everyone had read the articles and held opinions about what had happened. A few were critical, a few were worried, though none appeared concerned about who had put the articles in the mailboxes. "Bound to come out sooner or later," Strauss had said. Several people mentioned being impressed by Hawthorne's reputation. Betty Sherman told Kate that she'd heard something about a book contract. "It would certainly put our little school on the map," she said.

Kate sipped a cup of mulled cider and listened to the conversations around her. At times someone's talk would shift to a student or the faculty meeting the previous day, but again and again the topic returned to the fire at Wyndham School. The news clippings had become part of the information they were using to determine what Hawthorne would do at Bishop's Hill. Nobody felt better because of what they knew, but some were more unnerved than others and several times Kate heard Chip Campbell repeat his remark about "fleshpots."

For Kate the dozen or so people in the living room were all extensions of Bishop's Hill and as much a part of the school as its architecture. It was the center of their lives, their home and place of confinement. It was safe and unsurprising even if they disliked it and wished to be elsewhere. Their only uncertainty was Hawthorne. Though it wasn't him they feared but change—Hawthorne was merely the instrument of change or potential change, because other than the Tuesday-Thursday faculty meetings and putting out litter baskets and making the faculty park behind Douglas Hall, little had happened. But that wasn't quite true. Hawthorne was also asking faculty members to return various articles they had borrowed, things like lawn mowers and sporting equipment. Ted Wrigley, the other language teacher, had been asked to return a pair of pruning shears that he had borrowed in May. Much had been hinted and more was expected. Everyone knew the school was in trouble and dire remedies were being explored. Kate could see how the clippings might fortify her colleagues. To resist Hawthorne because he was new and had ideas other than their own was hardly tenable, but if his credibility could be diminished, that was something else again.

It was eight-twenty before Hawthorne arrived, giving a rap on the door and ringing the doorbell. Then he entered without waiting for the door to be opened. His face was flushed from the cold and he wore khakis and a dark green sweater. His glasses steamed over as he shut the door behind him. He took them off and wiped them on a handkerchief, then rubbed his hands together as he approached Skander, who made his way toward him, beaming.

Kate was standing by the dining room table talking to Ted Wrigley, who taught German and French. Ted kept eating small spice cookies dusted in powdered sugar and the lapels of his sport coat were spotted with white. Ted was a little older than Kate and had a young wife who had remained home with the baby. Kate thought he must have been awfully ravaged by acne as an adolescent because his face was pockmarked with scars. He was very shy. The students complained they couldn't hear him in class and had nicknamed him the Phantom because of his whispering. Despite his timidity, he had objected to giving back the pruning shears, as if doing so acknowledged some offense on his part. "Certainly, I meant to return them," he repeated. Kate gathered that Hawthorne hadn't spoken to Wrigley himself but had asked the head of the grounds crew to round up missing equipment.

Kate was struck by Wrigley's expression as he watched Hawthorne enter. It wasn't hostile but there was a chill to it: Hawthorne was Other, the outsider. And as she looked around the room, she saw this expression again and again—on Chip Campbell and Roger Bennett, on practically everyone.

None of this showed in Skander, who was effusive as he welcomed Hawthorne and led him to the dining room table. "We have coffee—decaf and regular—as well as mulled cider." Then, lowering his voice: "Or something stronger, if you'd prefer. Beer, wine . . ."

"Regular coffee would be fine," said Hawthorne. "Black." He greeted Kate and Ted Wrigley, shaking hands with both.

"What a constitution you must have. It would keep me awake all night." At that moment Skander's wife signaled to him from the door to the kitchen. "Excuse me," he said, and hurried off.

Hawthorne turned toward Kate. "I was glad that you spoke up about Jessica Weaver in the meeting yesterday. She's been having difficulty with her roommate and a number of others in her dorm. She's got quite a tongue on her."

"I like her," said Kate, moving away from Ted. "She learns very quickly and I like her energy, but I can see that she's unpopular with the other students."

Hawthorne leaned toward her and said more quietly, "I'm sure she had no idea she'd be coming here till a few days before she actually arrived. The application didn't come in until after the first week in September. As Fritz said, 'It's not as if we didn't have plenty of room.' Her stepfather took her out of the strip club and gave her the choice of coming here or being turned over to the courts."

"Then no wonder she's angry. I'd be angry myself." Glancing around the room, Kate saw several of the faculty watching them. She realized that Hawthorne knew nothing about the news clippings. She wanted to tell him but the moment seemed awkward.

Fritz Skander came out of the kitchen and quickly rejoined Hawthorne. "Come and say hello to Hilda. She's eager to see you." Hawthorne smiled and shrugged his shoulders at Kate as Skander led him away.

In the next few minutes Hawthorne made his way around the room, shaking hands and greeting the teachers who were under his charge. Despite his courtesy, there was a coolness that Kate attributed to shyness. She found herself next to the nurse, Alice Beech, who had arrived just before Hawthorne.

Alice was watching Hawthorne talk to Gene Strauss. "He doesn't know those clippings were put in our mailboxes," she told Kate. "I'd like to shake whoever did it."

"What do you think's going to happen?" asked Kate.

The nurse crossed her arms over her chest. She wore jeans and an orange sweater. "I think somebody's going to tell him, but it's not going to be me."

"People are saying that he means to write a book about Bishop's Hill," said Kate, then blushed a little at finding herself repeating the current gossip.

"I wish him luck."

It seemed to Kate that the room had grown quieter, that the men and women, while continuing their conversations, were more intent on Hawthorne than on whomever they were talking to. They were watching him while pretending not to watch him. She wondered if he would notice and how long it would take. And she realized that whoever had put the clippings in the mailboxes was most likely somebody in the room at this moment.

As it turned out, it was the Reverend Bennett who told Hawthorne about the clippings. Kate didn't hear all that was said, but she heard Harriet say, "I think you should know . . ." It seemed that everyone in the room was trying to follow their conversation. A few more people had arrived and now some eighteen members of the Bishop's Hill community were gathered in the Skanders' living room and dining room. Kate stood with Alice Beech, who looked depressed.

"In everybody's mailbox?" asked Hawthorne.

The chaplain nodded brusquely. They stood by the fireplace. "That's what I gather."

Hawthorne pushed his glasses up his nose with the knuckle of his thumb. He was smiling slightly, or rather, thought Kate, in his surprise he had forgotten to unsmile. He stood very still and it occurred to Kate that he wanted to flee, that it was only with great effort that he was keeping his body motionless as he thought about what it meant that the articles had become common knowledge. Watching him, Kate felt drawn to him. Along with sympathy, she felt admiration.

"What an odd thing for someone to have done," said Hawthorne.

"In rather bad taste, I thought," said Harriet Bennett.

Skander came across the room to join them. "I'm terribly sorry about it, Jim. If I'd known about it in time, I would have put them in the trash. It's nobody's concern what happened in San Diego." Skander looked indignant and shook his head.

Standing next to Kate, Alice made a small, exasperated groan. "I wish he'd shut up. He's going to make it worse."

"It's public information," said Hawthorne quietly. "There's nothing to hide. And the articles, I expect, were accurate, for the most part . . ."

But not entirely, thought Kate. And she knew that Hawthorne wanted to tell the whole story of what had happened, to correct their misapprehensions, but she also knew he would say nothing. She realized that Hawthorne was now looking at them as a single group, that for him *they* had become Other. And Kate was surprised to find in herself a wish to tell him that she wasn't part of them, that she had only recently come to Bishop's Hill, that she wasn't allied with anybody.

"This is awful," Alice told Kate.

Hawthorne was asking Harriet Bennett which articles they had been and Harriet said they were four stories from the *Union-Tribune*. Chip Campbell made his way across the room. He still had a beer but Kate didn't think it was the same one he had had earlier. He was grinning.

"Tell me," said Chip, "who was that cute psychologist? What was her name? Claire something. Claire de Lune."

Somebody laughed. Alice Beech flushed deep red. "He's drunk."

"She was a former colleague in Boston." Hawthorne began to go on, then didn't. He turned back to the chaplain, looking for something else to say. Alice Beech was halfway to the fireplace before Kate realized that she had moved from her side. She was solid and business-like and people got out of her way.

"I wanted to ask about the Miller girl," Alice began. "You know she's in the infirmary . . ." Apparently Peggy Miller had the flu. Alice had talked to the girl's parents. She was wondering whether Peggy shouldn't be kept in a far room in the infirmary so that others who might come in wouldn't be infected, but that would require getting another bed out of the storage area in the attic of Emerson Hall. They discussed the logistics for a moment. Hawthorne said he would make sure that a bed was moved first thing in the morning.

People began to return to their conversations. Emily Strauss spilled her mulled cider and Hilda hurried to clean it up. Skander put a log on the fire. Bill Dolittle sought out Hawthorne with some pressing concern. Chip drank his beer and looked pleased with himself. Kate continued to watch Hawthorne, who had obviously been relieved by Alice's appearance. Kate envied her slightly. Why hadn't she herself been quick enough to change the topic of conversation? It always seemed that she had to think something through before she acted on it. She found herself drawn to Hawthorne's angularity and watched how his mouth moved and the quality of his smile. And she looked at his right hand, where it extended from the green sleeve of his sweater. The scar had a sort of plastic pinkness and the skin between the ridges seemed smooth. Kate imagined what it would be like to be touched by that hand.

On Sunday a wind blew in from the south and the day was unexpectedly warm for October. Hawthorne had spent much of the afternoon meeting with students, but late that evening he was again on the terrace outside his quarters. The night was clear and there were a million stars but the sky felt just as empty. It was odd picking out constellations that he had seen in fifty different places and to see them now at Bishop's Hill. The last time he had looked at the Big Dipper he had been walking along the beach in Coronado in early August listening to the surf. He had taken a woman out to dinner, which had been a mistake. Even though she was friendly, her presence made Hawthorne think of his dead wife and the times he had been with her in similar circumstances. Dinner at the Del, a walk along the beach. Men from the navy base jogging along the esplanade. Hawthorne had looked up at the Big Dipper, just as he was doing this evening, and wished he could be lost in the midst of its stars.

Now that Hawthorne was taking a break from his day's labor, thoughts of his wife and daughter returned to him, though their features were indistinct. Only in dreams did he see them exactly. His daughter had had light blond hair so bright that it sparkled, and when Hawthorne thought of her, it was the hair that he saw clearly, then a vagueness of face and features. He remembered combing her hair after her bath, easing the comb through the tangles so it wouldn't pull, and her clean smell and the apple fragrance of her favorite shampoo. Then her death once again swept over him and he felt lost.

Hawthorne's meetings during the day had been with the class officers and had dealt with setting up a buddy system between upper and lower classmen, getting juniors and seniors to volunteer as tutors and organizing student discussion groups. The president of the student body was a rather lummoxy football player by the name of Sherman "Tank" Donoso, who referred to his fellow students as "homeboys." Although the football team had yet to win a game, Tank maintained authority among his teammates and the students in his dormitory cottage by "dope slaps." "I just give them one across the back of the head," Tank explained.

Tank had gathered the other class officers and they had met in

Hawthorne's good-sized living room. Frank LeBrun had brought over a tray of freshly baked oatmeal cookies and a case of soft drinks. The students had been mildly interested in Hawthorne's plans, though several objected to Hawthorne's refusal to permit physical force.

"If you don't give 'em a knock," said Tank reasonably, "they don't shut up." Others had agreed, though Hawthorne had wondered if they hadn't worried that their disagreement might lead to getting dope slaps themselves.

"Then perhaps one of our discussion groups can be on the supposed necessity and the response to violence," Hawthorne had suggested.

The meeting had gone on until dinner. Afterward, Hawthorne had studied student files, learning that Tank was at Bishop's Hill after being shunted between stepparents who seemed to despise him. This had kept Hawthorne busy until late in the evening and he felt ready for bed. Yet once he stopped, he again felt alert as his mind filled with thoughts of Meg and Lily, as well as problems at the school.

Hawthorne had been stunned that someone had put the news clippings in the faculty mailboxes. He had hoped to remain a sort of blank slate whom the faculty could approach with little or no prejudice. As he thought about Skander's party, he again experienced the shame he had felt when he learned that everyone had read about what had happened in San Diego, or a version of it. Claire de Lune, Chip had said. How awful! Now they all had some fantasy of what Hawthorne had or hadn't done and he understood that his stock with the faculty—not very high to begin with—had fallen even lower. Hawthorne was certain that it hadn't been a student who had distributed the articles; students weren't that sophisticated. And he realized that the appearance of Ambrose Stark hadn't been the work of a student, either. Hawthorne had an enemy, someone who wanted to drive him away. This recognition upset him and also surprised him. And who knew how many of the faculty were on his enemy's side? Hawthorne wished he could convince them of his good intentions. Not even at the treatment centers where he worked had he been subjected to such scrutiny. Here even his smiles were looked at with mistrust.

And all this business about writing a book. Had Skander started that unfortunate rumor? The irony was that never in his life had Hawthorne felt so far from writing, from turning his professional eye toward a clinical analysis of his environment. But if the faculty felt that he was observing them as part of some peculiar experiment, then that was just as bad as seeing him as a villain.

But perhaps, Hawthorne thought, there was no way to avoid being a villain. He had told the faculty they could no longer park in front of Emerson Hall. And he had sent out memos on other new . . . he hated to call them rules. Faculty and staff were used to taking leftovers from the kitchen: desserts, cookies, fruit, pieces of fried chicken. Hawthorne had stopped that. About $2,400 was spent on food each day for 250 days, for a total of slightly more than $600,000. The pilfering probably added up to 1 percent of that, or $6,000. A few faculty were in the habit of using vehicles owned by the school; one teacher—Herb Frankfurter—actually kept one of the cars, admittedly an old one, in his garage at home. Hawthorne stopped that as well. And he asked faculty to return the lawn movers, hedge trimmers, weed cutters, even a chain saw that had been borrowed from the grounds crew. And talking to Mrs. Grayson about her cat, Hawthorne learned that towels, sheets, pillowcases, and blankets also had a way of disappearing into faculty homes.

These were the perks of teaching at Bishop's Hill, business as usual. Hawthorne couldn't bring it to a halt right away but he'd make a start. Perhaps I *am* a tyrant, he thought. But with the money spent on pilfered food, garden tools, and the whole business, he could hire a second psychologist. Was he simply going to look at Jessica and futilely wish to make her life better? How long before she went back to the strip clubs and eventual prostitution? If it was a choice between letting Frankfurter keep that old Chevy and helping Jessica, Frankfurter didn't have a prayer. It shocked Hawthorne that Skander had let these perks build up. But then Skander wasn't really an administrator; he had preferred being liked. And don't I wish that too? Hawthorne asked. To have the faculty, staff, even the students see me as a friend?

Hawthorne went back inside to the living room, where he had a stack of student files left to read. The room was twenty feet long, had three shabby couches, and was intended for entertaining. He should probably institute some social events—student discussions and faculty chats—but the furniture was falling apart and the wallpaper peeling. At least he would buy a new chair, something comfortable to read in. All the old chairs had broken springs or smelled of cat urine and the only good place to read was in bed.

Hawthorne opened the top file and tried to concentrate, but his mind wandered. After dinner, Bill Dolittle had asked if he could move into the empty apartment above the Bennetts in Stark Hall and give up being the faculty resident in Latham, one of the student cottages. Dolittle wanted to have a place where his son could stay when he came home from Plymouth State. The difficulty with Dolittle's request was that somebody else would have to move into Latham. Still, if he could help Dolittle, then he would.

But the students were Hawthorne's main concern. He had to keep repeating that to himself. At dinner he had sat with eight members of the Bishop's Hill football team, including Tank Donoso. Hawthorne was sure that two were stoned. Before he had come to Bishop's Hill there had been a rule that a student could speak only if he or she first asked permission of the faculty member or prefect who sat at the head of the table. Hawthorne changed that and the result was cacophony. At least it was happy cacophony.

Tank had asked Hawthorne if he liked professional wrestling and Hawthorne had to say that he had never seen any. Then Tank asked what Hawthorne thought about Stephen King's novels. Tank had written several reports on them for class. Hawthorne had to admit that he had never read any. The football players had been generally suspicious, as if Hawthorne meant to win them over in some unsportsmanlike manner. Tank and two others wanted to go into the armed forces after graduation and expressed a hope that the future might hold another Gulf War or trouble in Panama when the canal was turned over. Hawthorne was reminded of the alumni of residential treatment centers who often made their most successful adaptation to the adult world in the military service, where they never experienced insecurity or doubt and their every action was planned in advance.

Tank had kept glancing furtively at the scar on Hawthorne's wrist until Hawthorne wanted to roll back the sleeve and lay his arm down in the middle of the table for Tank's inspection. How refreshing had been the response of the cook, who had simply asked to see it and for whom the matter had become a closed issue. Across the room, Hawthorne had seen Scott arguing passionately with two other boys, and Jessica—her hair loose and hanging forward to obscure her face—sitting alone in her baggy sweatshirt and jeans. Her roommate, Helen Selkirk, had been at another table with several girls, all of whom were eating cottage cheese and ketchup and talking together in whispers. Once again there was fresh bread, a small thing for which Hawthorne felt grateful. There had been a smattering of jokes about the boy who a few days earlier had claimed to have found a tack in his slice. No one believed he hadn't supplied it himself, and the teacher at the head of his table had told him to stop making such a fuss.

Shortly before midnight the telephone rang. Hawthorne assumed that a friend in San Diego had forgotten the time difference. He put down his files and hurried to the phone.

"Hello?" He heard a deep breath, then a woman's voice speaking quickly.

"Mr. Hawthorne, Jim, this is Kate Sandler."

Hawthorne sat down on the chair next to the telephone. "Yes, how are you? Is something the matter?"

"I'm not sure. Well, yes, there might be. I guess I'm not sure how to talk about it."

Hawthorne leaned back. "Any way you'd like. Does this have to do with school?"

"Not exactly. You see, I'm divorced. I've been divorced now for about a year. My husband, or ex-husband, lives in Plymouth. He has a sporting goods store . . ."

Hawthorne couldn't guess what she was leading up to. He started to speak, then waited.

"The divorce was my idea," continued Kate. "He didn't want to. We have a son who's seven. George is still very bitter."

"Is that your son?"

"No, my son's name is Todd. George, George Peabody is the ex-husband." Kate laughed nervously. "George is very possessive. He keeps saying he wants us to get back together, though I can't believe he means it. But he's constantly afraid that I'll get involved with someone else. When I went out once last spring with Chip Campbell, George actually called him up and shouted at him."

"And what does this have to do with me?" Hawthorne asked, as gently as possible.

"I saw George late this afternoon in Plymouth when I was picking up our son. George sees him every week. Anyway, George said he was going to come over to the school and beat the shit out of you—those were his words. I didn't want to call, but . . ."

Hawthorne sat up. "Me? What in the world for?"

Kate spoke in a rush. "Someone put a note in his mailbox that he found this morning. It said we were sleeping together. I mean, you and me. I feel terrible about it."

"Why would somebody tell him that?" Hawthorne thought of how he had spoken to Kate briefly at Skander's. He'd regretted not having the opportunity to talk to her again.

"A prank, a malicious prank," said Kate. "But he was furious. He accused me of carrying on with Todd in the house. I thought of not bothering you, but George could easily come over, especially if he's been drinking."

It astonished Hawthorne to think that someone he'd never known about until this moment could harbor such anger against him.

"Do you have any idea who might have told him?" asked Hawthorne.

"Absolutely none. He showed me the letter. It was typed and unsigned."

4

The shouts and the sound of a basketball hitting a backboard drew Kate Sandler to her classroom window at the back of Emerson Hall. Half a dozen male students and several teachers were playing basketball in the small court between Douglas and the Common. Yellow leaves from a maple at the corner of Douglas floated through the sunlight and across the court, resembling gold doubloons drifting among the players. In the national forest to the north, Kate could see great bands of orange and red, with the color more fierce at higher elevations. The sky was intensely blue. The basketball players whistled and called to one another but Kate was too far away to hear more than the occasional word: a name or a shout of praise. The sound of the ball being dribbled across the blacktop echoed between the buildings.

With surprise, Kate saw that one of the adults was Jim Hawthorne. He had removed his coat and loosened his tie, which flapped over his shoulder as he ran. A second adult was Roger Bennett, whose pale blond hair would make him recognizable, Kate thought, from at least a mile. The third was Ted Wrigley, the other language teacher. It was shortly after three on Tuesday afternoon. Kate's last class had ended ten minutes earlier and she was washing her blackboard with a wet sponge, a chore that teachers were expected to do themselves. At three-thirty the third of the faculty meetings meant to discuss the students was due to begin.

The six boys were upper classmen, and though quicker than the adults, they were too hasty, more exuberant than efficient. Hawthorne was on one team, Bennett and Wrigley on the other. A boy passed the ball to Hawthorne, who dribbled in for a layup. People cheered. Another boy took the ball out, then passed it to Bennett, who dribbled it behind his back, then between his legs, laughing and showing off till Tank Donoso snatched it away, none too gently. In his shape and size, Kate thought, the boy was indeed tanklike, a tank with a square face and a fuzzy colorless crew cut.

From her third-story vantage point, Kate watched the players weave among one another, passing the ball, going in for a shot, competing for the rebound. One boy fell to the blacktop, lay still for a moment holding his stomach, then scrambled to his feet again. On a patch of the Common, about ten boys and girls sat watching. Several were students of Kate's, including Jessica Weaver, who sat to one side of the others with two yards between her and the nearest person, as if she was both in the group and pointedly not in the group. And she looked up into the maple tree instead of at the game, seemingly lost in the splendor of the leaves. Also standing to the side was Harriet Bennett, the chaplain, in a dark gray suit. She wasn't close enough for Kate to see her expression. Usually it was severe, which made her marriage to Roger a source of speculation, since he seemed to have the emotional makeup of an adolescent setter. Where she would walk stolidly, he bounced. Still, Roger had sometimes struck Kate as watchful and even guarded, as if his youthful fervor were no more than a convenient persona.

Kate leaned against the windowsill, holding the wet sponge. It seemed to her that Hawthorne was the best player, better even than the teenagers. At least Kate hadn't seen him miss a shot. His play had a seriousness that the others lacked. The court extended behind the far end of Douglas, which stood to the left of Emerson, so the two buildings made an L shape. Kate wondered what it meant for the school's headmaster to engage in a pastime that many would think beneath his dignity, but she was impressed by how Hawthorne was involving himself with so many aspects of the school. Not that he could do this unscathed. Two weeks earlier the gossip had concerned what he might do—jobs lost, positions changed, even turning the school into a home for the retarded. Now the gossip focused on his behavior—the people he liked and those he didn't, how he could be seen past midnight standing on the terrace behind his quarters, the speculation that he might be writing a book. Shortly the sexual gossip would begin. Indeed, given the anonymous letter that George had received and his subsequent anger, it had begun already. Was she the one whose name was going to be linked with Hawthorne's? It was a tiresome thought.

Hawthorne again had the ball and Bennett was trying to bat it out of his hands. Briefly the game shrank to a rivalry between them as Hawthorne hugged the ball to his body and Bennett tried to pull it away. Then Hawthorne passed the ball to a senior by the name of Rudy Schmidt, who shot from the foul line. The ball chimed against the rim and bounced into the grass. Wrigley took the ball out. In the bright sunlight his old acne scars gave his face a mottled appearance. He passed the ball to Bennett, who drove toward the hoop. Bennett's blond hair was perfectly straight and combed back over his head so it leapt up with every running step. It reminded Kate of English public school boys of the Evelyn Waugh era, or at least how such students were depicted on public television. Two boys ran in to block Bennett, waving their arms like passionate windmills, and he passed the ball back to someone behind him.

Kate hadn't spoken to Hawthorne since she had phoned late Sunday night, though she had seen him earlier in the day at lunch. He had smiled at her across the room. Just the smile had been a relief since Kate still felt embarrassed about the call. Her ex-husband hadn't contacted Hawthorne—not yet, at any rate—but she kept thinking of how George had accused her of having sex with another man while Todd was in the house.

"I bet he even heard you," George had said. "For all I know, he saw you. Don't you have a shred of self-respect?" He went on to tell Kate that his lawyer had been waiting for information like this. "Who knows what kind of damage it's caused Todd." His words had been slurred and Kate guessed that he had spent the earlier part of the afternoon watching football and drinking beer from his favorite mug—an elaborate German stein he had bought in Munich ten years earlier, as if drinking from it was not simply getting drunk but engaging in a culturally significant ritual. It had amazed Kate that he could talk like this and still claim to want her back, to make a life with her and have more children.

The faculty meeting at three-thirty would focus on the students in the lower school, grades seven through nine. Kate, like many other teachers, had students in both the upper and the lower schools and had to attend the meetings on Tuesdays and Thursdays. At lunch Chip had told her that he wouldn't be there, which meant missing his third meeting. Kate didn't know if he had prior business or was "taking a stand," as he might say. She wondered if others would cut the meeting and if Hawthorne would notice. But she knew he'd notice. He was making it his business to pay attention to everything that went on. Even now he was working with students who had been sent to the office because they had acted up or failed to do their class assignments. The previous day he had talked to an eighth grader in Kate's first-year Spanish class who refused to bring his book to class. Kate had spoken to the boy that morning to see if Hawthorne had scolded him.

"He wanted to help me study," said the boy, struck by the oddness of it. "We went over vocabulary after dinner. He wanted to make a game of it."

Kate was impressed by Hawthorne's willingness to devote all his waking hours to school business. Was this the man that George accused of going after his ex-wife? When would he have time? And in her question to herself Kate saw that becoming involved with Hawthorne didn't strike her as strange or inappropriate, which was followed by the feeling she sometimes got from too much caffeine or when her car swerved suddenly on wet leaves. It almost frightened her.

Tank and another boy were wrestling on the blacktop for the ball. Hawthorne knelt beside them with a hand on each and talking calmly, or at least his face appeared calm. Tank gave the other boy a shove as he stood up, and the ball rolled away. Grabbing it, Hawthorne tossed it to Rudy Schmidt and the game resumed. Several onlookers wandered off and others appeared, but Jessica was still among them, sitting with her arms around her knees and looking toward the mountains. Harriet Bennett also continued to watch with folded arms. Even from this distance Kate could see her big black shoes. On Sundays the Reverend Bennett preached about moderation and the need for equilibrium, as if her enemy were not Evil but Excess. In her vestments and with her bulk and wispy gray hair, she looked very eighteenth century. Kate had attended chapel a few times in the spring but had yet to go this fall. She wasn't a believer but it was expected of faculty to set an example for the students.

Kate happened to glance over at Douglas Hall, diagonally across the Common. There, at a second-story window, Fritz Skander stood with his hands in his pockets, watching the game. Kate recalled he had a geometry class that met in the afternoon. Skander had a faintly benign smile but there was a concentration about him, especially in the way he leaned forward as if listening for some delicate noise far in the distance. He was below Kate and to her left. For no reason she could think of, she moved back so he wouldn't notice her. To Kate, Skander's actions always seemed as if they were in fact reactions to the people around him, unspontaneous outbursts followed by small jokes and a sort of delayed ebullience. Now, framed by the window, he appeared unusually expectant, almost eager.

Bennett was trying to get the ball from Hawthorne, pressing him close and waving his hands in Hawthorne's face. Hawthorne passed the ball back between his legs to Tank, then dodged around Bennett, who turned quickly and stumbled. Tank passed it back to Hawthorne, who jumped and scored with a hook shot. Bennett got to his feet, then took the ball out again, his hair bouncing as he ran. Hawthorne's white shirt was pulled from his waist and the top buttons were undone. He wore black leather shoes that didn't seem to interfere with his game.

Kate noticed that a new person had sat down next to Jessica and was chatting with her. It was the assistant cook. Whatever he said, Jessica began to laugh. It made her look quite pretty. Kate recalled Chip Campbell's suggestion that Hawthorne was sexually involved with the girl—"doing the dirty with that little ex-stripper." Seeing Jessica laugh, Kate found it not quite so impossible. Jessica's roommate had continued to complain about Jessica whenever she and Kate happened to talk—how Jessica ignored her and refused to respond to the name Jessica, saying instead that her name was Misty. In Spanish, though, the girl was turning out to be the best in the class.

Hawthorne was running in for another layup and Bennett was trying to catch up, sprinting across the court as several students got out of his way. Hawthorne jumped and Bennett jumped after him, attempting to block the shot, but he was too late and the basket scored. But in jumping Bennett collided with Hawthorne in midair, knocking him sideways so he fell. Bennett landed on his feet but Hawthorne was twisting, trying to regain his balance. He went down, slid on the black-top, and rolled onto his back. Kate could see he was in pain, then she noticed that the fabric of his khaki pants was torn at the knees. He sat up, holding his legs. Bennett stood for a moment, watching, then he and Tank leaned in closer to him. The nurse, Alice Beech, was in the small crowd of onlookers and she ran onto the court, as did the assis-tant cook. Hawthorne was pulling up his pant leg and Kate thought she could see blood, but she was too far away to be sure. The game had stopped. The students were talking among one another and look-ing uncomfortable, as if they were afraid of being yelled at. Hawthorne's face was white. Gravel must have gotten embedded in the cut because he was picking at a spot on his left knee. Alice Beech knelt down beside him. The cook was saying something and helping him roll up his other pant leg. Bennett was talking to Ted Wrigley. His face was very earnest.

Kate glanced over to where Skander was standing. The afternoon sun reflecting against the windows of Emerson cast back its light to the windows of Douglas Hall, making them shine. Skander was chuckling. At first Kate thought she must be mistaken and she moved to the right, trying to see him more clearly. But he was grinning, she was sure of it. Kate looked down at the basketball court. Now both Hawthorne's pant legs were pulled up above his knees. The cook was helping him to his feet. Bennett was helping as well. When Hawthorne was standing, the two men each held one of his arms. Tank was arguing with one of Bennett's teammates. Then Hawthorne and the others began to hob-ble off the court. Judging by their direction, Kate guessed they were going to the infirmary. She looked again at Skander. There was a cheeriness to his grin, a lightheartedness, as if he had just heard a funny story. He was rubbing his chin and beaming. Then, as if he sensed he was being observed, he glanced up and saw Kate watching him. Kate stepped back, then waved, rather ineffectually. She felt she had to make some response. Skander didn't wave back.

Wednesday evening after dinner Frank LeBrun was hurrying out the back door of the kitchen to meet Jessica when his cousin called to him.

Frank slid on the tiles, stretched out his arms, and wobbled, making a little joke of it. Larry didn't seem amused. They stood by the back door looking out on the Common, which was dark except for the lights along the walkway. Frank had taken off his white jacket and wore his brown winter coat.

"Where you going?" asked Larry. His voice was quiet and serious.

"Out for a smoke. Why d'you want to know?"

"You're up to something. I can tell. What's going on?" Larry wore his white jacket. His anger made him especially red in the face. He was taller than his cousin and stood calmly while LeBrun always seemed agitated.

"Meaning what?" LeBrun leaned back against the doorjamb. He put a cigarette in his mouth but didn't light it. The cigarette waggled between his lips when he spoke.

"You called me looking for a job. I didn't mind helping you, even on short notice. And I didn't make a fuss when you wanted me to tell everyone that your name was LeBrun. I figured you needed the work and Skander came up with the money. Now I think it's something else. You didn't come here just for a job."

"Then what am I up to, smart guy?"

"Like why'd you put those tacks in the bread?"

LeBrun grinned. "What makes you think it was me?"

"You're the only one who touches it."

"Somebody could have snuck in." LeBrun took the unlit cigarette from his mouth and looked at it as if it didn't taste right. He put it back in his pocket.

"Don't give me that shit."

LeBrun's smile faded. "I put a tack in a chunk of dough and I put in a piece of chocolate. It was an experiment. You don't hear anyone bitching about the chocolate, do you? They find a tack, they let everybody know. They find some chocolate, they keep it to themselves. What's that say about human nature? It teaches you something, that's what I like about it."

"It could have hurt somebody."

LeBrun made a wry face, then winked. "Nah, a little prick, that's all, a little cut on the tongue. Nothing serious. You hear the joke about the Canuck who studied five days to pass his urine test? Sounds like you a little, doesn't it?"

Gaudette didn't respond. "Why're you hanging around that girl?"

"She's friendly, I'm friendly, we chat."

"I don't want you talking to her."

"I don't mean any harm by it. Come on, man, don't be so uptight."

"If one more tack shows up, I'm going to Dr. Hawthorne. As for that girl, stay away from her."

LeBrun pushed open the door. A cold breeze poured into the kitchen. "Hey, Larry, I'm just having a little fun. No more tacks, I swear." He put his hand on his cousin's shoulder but the other man pulled away. LeBrun turned and went out into the dark.

It was Chip Campbell's habit to check the rest rooms after lunch to see if he could find anyone smoking. It was a pleasure not far removed from gambling or playing cards. And this Thursday he was especially eager because lunch had been terrible—the first of Hawthorne's meat-less Thursdays, meant to save the school thousands each year, money Chip felt sure would wind up in Hawthorne's pocket. So they had all sat down to black beans and rice—peasant food. Chip would have complained but, having missed Tuesday's faculty meeting, he was try-ing to avoid the headmaster. In fact, he planned to cut today's meeting and all the meetings to come until Hawthorne forced him to attend or canceled them. He just didn't have time for that dipshit psychobabble. And hadn't Hawthorne nearly missed Tuesday's meeting, getting his knees bandaged by the nurse after having been tripped up playing bas-ketball? Chip laughed. Served him right, that was what Chip thought. He'd buy Bennett a beer for what he'd done. Not that he otherwise had much use for Bennett and he couldn't stand the chaplain. It was like they had gotten their masculine and feminine roles fucked up and didn't know who they were.

Chip had checked four boys' rest rooms without success but now he was up on the third floor of Emerson heading toward the toilet at the far end of the hall and therefore the one where some boys felt safest. But Chip didn't want to find just any boy; he wanted to find Scott McKinnon, who liked to cut up in history class. There was always the smell of cigarette smoke on the boy's sweater, not regular smoke but some foreign tobacco that was particularly strong and that Chip found particularly insulting, since its very obviousness was a taunt. Clearly, Scott was ducking out someplace. Today there was a cold autumn rain, and Chip knew that Scott wouldn't have made a run for the woods. And because Scott was lazy, he'd get caught.

It was ten minutes before one, the end of lunch hour. Soon the bell would ring and classes would resume. Maybe Scott had gone to another building for his cigarette, but Chip doubted he would take the trouble. If he caught him, well, smoking was against the rules and the law didn't permit smoking on school grounds. Even the faculty and staff couldn't smoke in the buildings, though some broke the law, like that fag Evings.

Chip stood by the door to the rest room and listened. He wore a brown tweed jacket over a blue school sweatshirt. The hall was empty and he heard a window rattling in the wind. Quietly, he pushed open the door and sniffed. He didn't quite smile but one side of his mouth rose a little. The pungent smell of the foreign tobacco seemed to fill the bathroom. How stupid, thought Chip, to smoke something so obvious. It made him feel justified in despising the boy. Gathering himself, Chip slammed open the door and ran forward. Before he'd gone five feet, he heard the flushing of the toilet. None of the four stalls had doors. Scott sat in the last stall with his pants at his ankles, smiling.

"Hi, coach," he said.

"You're smoking."

"Not me, coach, I'm just taking a dump."

"I can smell it."

"That's my dump you're smelling, coach. Pretty nasty, isn't it?"

"You're lying. And don't call me coach."

"Chip, is that what you want? Should I call you Chip, like 'Chip off the old block'?"

Chip reached forward, grabbed the boy's red sweater, yanked him up, and then let him go. Scott stumbled out of the stall with his pants around his ankles, trying to regain his balance, spinning around, then crashing against the sinks and falling to the tile floor.

"Where're the cigarettes?"

"Not me, Chipper. I don't smoke." Scott lay on his back, pulling up his pants.

Chip reached down and jerked him to his feet. He could smell the smoke on the boy's sweater. Quickly, he searched the boy's pockets. He found a pack of matches but no cigarettes. Scott must have had just one that he flushed down the toilet. He let the boy go roughly so he fell back to the floor, knocking his head against the tiles.

Scott finished pulling up his pants. He looked frightened but it didn't make him shut up. "You like feeling up boys in their underwear, Chipper?"

Chip grabbed hold of Scott's arm and took a swing at him with his open hand. Scott twisted away. Chip grabbed him again and shoved him toward the door. Scott crashed against it with a booming noise and bounced off—after all, Chip outweighed the boy by a hundred pounds. Chip opened the door and pushed Scott into the hall. The boy tripped, stumbling against the far wall, then fell again. Chip rushed out after him—and stopped abruptly. Standing in the hall with surprised faces were Hawthorne and Ruth Standish, one of the mental health counselors. Hawthorne was using a cane because of his injury on Tuesday. He went to Scott and helped him to his feet.

"He was smoking," said Chip, "and he was insulting me."

"I'm surprised you didn't just shoot him," said Hawthorne, holding the boy's arm.

Scott laughed.

"Do you have a class now?" Hawthorne asked. "You better get to it."

"Don't you want to hear my side of the story?"

"Just go to class." Hawthorne pushed his glasses up his nose.

Scott started to hurry down the hall, then he slowed down and began to walk with an exaggerated swagger. He glanced back over his shoulder and grinned.

"I've had trouble with him myself," said Ruth Standish somewhat nervously. "He's always talking back. He doesn't care what he says." She seemed undecided whether her allegiances lay with Hawthorne or Chip. She was a heavyset woman of about thirty-five, wearing a red checked dress that made her appear even heavier than she was.

"I want you to get your stuff and go home," said Hawthorne to Chip, matter of factly. "Didn't we talk about this? What in the world were you thinking of?"

"Are you firing me?" Chip stood with his fingers bunched into fists.

"I can only suspend you. But the board can fire you and I'm going to insist that they do. I don't want you here anymore."

"You're doing this because I won't come to those stupid faculty meetings." Chip's tone was scornful and defiant.

"I'm doing it because you don't know how to treat these kids."

"This is crazy. I've been here a dozen years."

"Surely you can give him another chance," said Ruth.

"He's had another chance." Hawthorne leaned on his cane and stared at the floor. Then he raised his voice. "How can I have a faculty member who physically abuses the students! Are you mad?" He caught hold of himself. "I'm sorry, but you make me angry. Get your stuff and go. I don't want you on school property."

"You son of a—" Chip clenched his jaw and stopped himself. He glanced furiously at Ruth, then walked down the hall, the rubber soles of his shoes squeaking.

After a moment, Ruth said, "Can't you make it a temporary suspension?"

"He abuses students. I've seen him do it twice and I've heard of him doing it other times. What signal would it send to the students if I didn't dismiss him? They'd see everything I've told them as being a lie. I'd be just one more adult they couldn't trust."

"Are you sure you're not firing Chip so they'll like you?"

"I'm firing him because that's my duty."

Ruth's expression was one of perplexity mixed with benevolent concern, as if she had come across a strain of mildly aberrant behavior that was new to her. "Do you think you'd be behaving like this if your knees weren't painful? You know it's probably affecting you. As for those meetings—"

"This has nothing to do with my knees and nothing to do with the meetings." Hawthorne gave each word the same emphasis, creating a staccato effect. "Now what were you saying about candles in the dormitory?"

Ruth was in charge of Smithfield, Jessica's cottage, and she had come to Hawthorne with a complaint from Helen Selkirk that her roommate was burning candles and using foul language. Because of the danger of fire in the wooden buildings, candles were not allowed. Ruth had already spoken to Jessica about this several times.

"Jessica keeps burning a candle in her lower bunk. Helen's been very worried. When I speak to Jessica, she's rude to me as well. We can't let students use candles. Smithfield would go up like a tinderbox." Ruth glanced at Hawthorne's right arm, then looked away.

Hawthorne, following Ruth's glance, looked at it as well. He flexed his fingers, then relaxed them. Hawthorne's eyes reminded Ruth of caves of blue water. She tried to see if there was sadness, even fear. But she could see no emotion at all, only resolution. Later, however, she would tell friends that she had seen not only sadness and fear but also something unstable, something that she couldn't really put a name to but that frightened her.

"Tell the girl to come and see me. Who was it again?"

"Jessica Weaver. She's new."

"Oh," said Hawthorne, "that one."

Clifford Evings tried not to smoke in his office but sometimes he really couldn't help it. "Do you mind?" he asked Ruth Standish as he reached into his coat pocket. Officially he was Ruth's superior, but he had always been a little afraid of her. Her very bigness was offputting and she seemed so sure of herself, while he had so many doubts.

"If you have to." She made a disapproving face.

"I have a little air purifier. Nobody will know."

Ruth didn't answer. It was Friday morning and she had come to Evings from the teachers' lounge, where everyone was talking about Chip's being fired.

"I must say I was shocked by how fast Jim acted. Most people are given more chances, especially someone with Chip's history at the school. I'm sure the boy provoked him."

"And he fired him just like that?" Evings was appalled. "Bennett said something about it at the faculty meeting, but I just didn't believe it."

"Technically he's suspended, but Jim said he'd insist that the board dismiss Chip."

"I had no idea he disliked him so much." Evings lit his cigarette, squinting a little and tilting his head to keep the smoke from his eyes. Then he blew the smoke up toward the ceiling. They sat in the two wing chairs before the fireplace. The portrait of Ambrose Stark stared down crossly.

"I don't believe he has anything against Chip in particular. He probably thought he had to set an example: emphasizing the principle over the person. And of course Chip has missed every single faculty meeting. But I can't help feeling that Jim's injury has something to do with it. I saw him go into the infirmary. You know how it is when you're hurt. Everything gets affected and you're in a bad mood. And now he has this cane."

"Roger did it on purpose?"

"No, no, Ted Wrigley swears it was an accident. He was simply clumsy." Ruth described what she had heard about the basketball game. Her tone suggested that if headmasters were going to play games with students, then they were asking for trouble. "Dr. Pendergast certainly wouldn't have played basketball," she concluded. "He wouldn't play anything. Not that he was perfect, of course."

"I'm told he's writing a book about us."

"That's what people are saying—he's doing one of those psychological dissections, the sort of thing I had to read in graduate school."

Evings thought of Hawthorne's visit the previous week with dismay. "He came in here last week with some wild story about a hanged cat. I couldn't make any sense of it. I thought of course that he came in to see what I was doing. And I wasn't doing anything. I mean, nothing he'd object to. Like smoking, though I'm not the only one. Who smokes, that is. I expect none of us are safe. He's already talking about hiring another psychologist."

"Certainly reevaluations will be in order."

Ruth's tone was slightly arch and Evings wondered what she meant by it. But even before she mentioned the other counselor, Evings knew it was coming.

"I know he's spoken to Bobby several times—purely about students, of course. I don't know if he's aware of your . . . relationship."

Evings gently gnawed the back of his thumb and then puffed on his cigarette without pleasure. He went behind his desk and turned on the air purifier. If he was fired, he wouldn't know what to do.

Robert Newland was the other mental health counselor and had been hired by Evings two years earlier. The men were a couple, although they didn't live together. Each was in charge of one of the dormitory cottages, where they had rooms. Mostly, however, they were together. Bobby was a tall, gangly man in his forties whose bland round face displayed a small mustache and goatee. He had a B.A. in psychology from Tufts but no graduate degree. Evings felt sure that if he was dismissed Ruth, who had been at the school longer than Bobby and had a master's, would take over as head of psychological services. This seemed to be her ambition.

Before Bobby came to the school there had been occasional rumors about a romantic connection between Evings and one gay student or another, although it was no more than speculation. He didn't think anything could be proven. He hadn't heard from the students for years, and now, obviously, they were adults. But he knew how things could turn up after you thought they were over and done with. He'd had that sort of experience before. And if anything was said against him and one of those old students suddenly reappeared, well, he could be in a difficult situation.

Evings regretted his confession to Hawthorne. Why on earth had he said he was bad at his job? He imagined Hawthorne scurrying back to his office and writing it all down. Perhaps he had a little tape recorder hidden in his pocket. Evings felt sure that his connection with Bishop's Hill was about to be severed. Roger Bennett had almost said as much, as had others. Certain reevaluations would be in order—what a nice way of putting it. And had it been entirely ethical for Evings to hire Bobby, who had never worked as a counselor before coming to Bishop's Hill? When Evings had met him on Martha's Vineyard, Bobby had been a waiter. Not even a headwaiter, at that. But the next summer Bobby had taken two classes at Plymouth State and then joined the staff. Skander had told them that Bobby's job was safe, but Skander wasn't in charge anymore.

"I knew this would happen as soon as I heard that Skander wasn't going to be named headmaster," said Evings, stubbing out his cigarette.

"Knew what would happen?" asked Ruth, still with her arch expression.

"Knew that our positions weren't secure. Wasn't that what people said? That man is going to turn the whole school upside down. I bet it won't even be a small book—I'll probably have a chapter all to myself, me and Bobby. With pictures."

Ruth patted her hair, which was a rich brown and fell to her shoulders in thick waves. "Well, I don't feel I'm at risk. I put in a full week and I'm busy on weekends as well. Nobody can make a complaint about me that I can't defend myself against and, unlike some, I don't fall asleep at faculty meetings." She gave a little laugh to show the remark was purely collegial.

In that moment, Evings hated Ruth Standish. She'd never been on his side; indeed, she hardly respected him. If Hawthorne learned about Evings's relationship with Bobby and if he talked to the wrong people—Ruth, for instance—then Evings would end up just like Chip. But Chip was a relatively young man and Evings was sixty-one. What job could he find at his age? Nothing as comfortable as Bishop's Hill. Nothing that carried any respect. Briefly, he saw himself working in the men's department of a large clothing store, but even that was doubtful. More likely he'd have to take a job at Dunkin' Donuts or McDonald's. And would Bobby stay with him then? Of course not. And how could he bear the humiliation?

Chip Campbell's suspension was discussed by many people at Bishop's Hill that Friday. Scott McKinnon described what had happened again and again—how Hawthorne had stood up for him and how Campbell had been given the boot. He liked being the center of attention. He showed the scarcely visible bruises on his arm to whoever would look at them and boldly smoked a cigarette in his room, even though Mr. Newland had already given him several warnings. But Scott felt he had a friend in high places. He could say and do what he wanted and Hawthorne would be there to look out for him. Consequently, he said a lot.

Throughout Friday the faculty continued to worry about what had happened. Roger Bennett, Ted Wrigley, and Tom Hastings sat in the Dugout drinking coffee and wondering if they themselves might be in danger. In the basement of Douglas Hall, the Dugout was a small snack bar run by students. It was shortly after three o'clock and classes had recently ended. About fifteen students were scattered at half a dozen tables, and the three teachers sat in a corner booth so they wouldn't be overheard. A video game of cars racing through a mountain landscape boomed and twittered against the wall.

"What amazes me," said Hastings, "is his p-power. He can fire anyone at any time. How long we've taught means nothing." Hastings taught general science and biology, and from time to time some of his students liked to tease him and provoke his stutter. He was small and dapper with light curly hair and delicate features. He liked to wear expensive boots and black silk shirts with black ties. On the little finger of his left hand was a silver ring with a large bluish amethyst.

"You think he'd do that?" asked Wrigley, ladling sugar into his cup. He had given a quiz in his first-year German class during the last period and had a stack of papers beside him.

"What's to stop him? P-plainly, he has big plans for Bishop's Hill. If we don't fit in, then we're out." And Hastings thought how foolish he had been to disagree with Hawthorne about the demerit system during the initial meeting.

"Pendergast never interfered with us in any way," said Bennett. "It's a real shame that Fritz wasn't named headmaster."

Wrigley blew on his coffee, then sipped it carefully. "Pendergast was hopeless and Fritz wasn't much better. Now the school's broke."

"According to Hawthorne, anyway," said Hastings. "And what's this business about a book? Are we just some kind of p-perverse experiment for him?"

"That's what Chip's been saying," said Wrigley. "Roger, too, for that matter."

Bennett leaned forward and lowered his voice. "I bet he fired Chip just to make his damn book a little more interesting. You know, conflict and confrontation."

"I don't believe it," said Wrigley. "It's too deceitful. He doesn't seem like that."

"Well, look at the t-trouble he had in San Diego," said Hastings, his stutter increasing. "How do you explain what happened there?"

"What's Dolittle been sucking up to him about?" asked Bennett.

Hastings picked a fleck of lint from his black silk tie. "D-D-Dolittle wants something. He always wants s-something."

"He's probably after a raise when no one else is getting one," suggested Wrigley.

They discussed the school's money problem and whether it was exaggerated. They complained about how they had had to return shovels and garden shears. They talked about the faculty meetings and the additional demands on their time. They wondered about Hawthorne's book. Bennett had been at Bishop's Hill for ten years,

Wrigley and Hastings for eight. The three were close acquaintances rather than friends. In fact, they had little respect for one another. Yet they formed a united front against these new changes.

"Those news articles were a shock for him," said Wrigley. "I wonder who put them in the mailboxes. When your wife told him, I thought he was going to bolt."

"You think he'll hold it against her?" Bennett looked worried.

"I'd love to have been there," said Hastings. "I can't imagine Chip mentioning that woman and how pretty she was." He began stuttering again. The others watched him, waiting for him to stop, already knowing what he would say. "W-w-was he sober?"

"Barely," said Wrigley. "Fritz says he's going to beard Hawthorne in his den and make him change his mind. But it was a dumb thing for Chip to do—that and missing those meetings. It was almost as dumb as Roger knocking Hawthorne down in the basketball game. Pretty clumsy, Rog. I hope he doesn't blame me because I was on your team. I was afraid Tank was going to tackle you."

Bennett set his coffee cup on the table, making a clinking noise. "I slipped."

When Hawthorne had gone up for the layup, Bennett hadn't meant to hit him so hard, but he'd been off balance and slipped. Had Hawthorne believed him? Bennett wasn't sure. If that damn cook had stayed out of it, he'd have been all right. Saying he had done it on purpose. "You must have been mad," the reverend had said. Even in bed, Bennett called his wife the reverend.

"It was an accident. Anyway, we were playing a game."

"Some game," she said. "You think he'll forget it? I know men like that."

Everyone was talking about what Hawthorne had done and what he might do next: the staff, the students, the housekeepers, people in the kitchen, even the night watchman.

Betty Sherman, the art teacher, had called Mrs. Hayes on the telephone.

"I'm not perfect," said Betty. "I've made mistakes. Look at that money that was missing from the budget for art supplies last June. I can't imagine what happened to it."

"It's awful, simply awful," said Mrs. Hayes. "I've been in a state all week."

For several hours each day Mrs. Hayes had been reading about computers and the Internet—*Windows 98, Excel, Netscape Communicator*. She had studied the books but hadn't yet turned on the machine. "These things can have internal monitors," Skander had told her. She had trouble sleeping and when she dozed off her dreams were full of flickering screens and hundreds of keys, buttons, obscure commands, cryptic terms—anchoring callouts and case-sensitive passwords, macros and spikes. And nothing she read stayed in her mind for over five minutes.

First thing Monday morning Skander had an appointment to see the headmaster.

"I just wish you'd reconsider." Skander stood with his hands folded in front of him. He wore a blue blazer flecked with light-colored dog hairs from Hilda's toy poodle and he spoke quietly, as if in church. "Really . . . for the good of the school."

Hawthorne leaned against his desk. He was no longer using a cane but his knees still hurt. And he felt uneasy; his anxiety was like a noise in his head and Hawthorne felt it interfering with what he regarded as his customary presence of mind. Now he was trying to understand Skander's mood but Skander seemed his usual self, at once businesslike and affable, a mixture of charm and artlessness. Even so, Hawthorne couldn't make out what lay behind Skander's words. It seemed more complicated than standing up for a colleague.

Hawthorne felt certain that he had been correct in dismissing Chip. He had done the same thing in residential treatment centers when a child-care worker had used too much force in subduing one of the kids. But, as he had told himself several times, Bishop's Hill wasn't a treatment center. He couldn't tolerate Chip's abuse of students, however, since it destroyed not only Chip's effectiveness but also his own. But over the weekend Hamilton Burke had called, asking him to reconsider, and now here was Fritz.

Hawthorne thought back to Ambrose Stark's appearance in the window of Adams Hall; he didn't believe he'd seen a ghost but he couldn't help feeling that the dead headmaster embodied all the anger of everyone whose life was being changed at the school. Then there were the news clippings that someone had put in the faculty mail-boxes and the anonymous letter to Kate's ex-husband. Surely the anger would surface again. Hawthorne hadn't discussed these incidents with anyone, for the reason that almost anyone could have done it. The unfortunate result was to further separate him from the people at Bishop's Hill. So even though Hawthorne trusted Skander, he listened to him with an extra ear, as it were, the ear of his suspicion.

"I'm afraid it can't be done," said Hawthorne. "If I changed my position, the students would feel betrayed. I know this is hard for you and the faculty, but the students must think this is their school. They must believe that they and their actions matter."

"Doesn't there need to be discipline?"

"What I object to is punishment. What does the victim learn except fear?"

"People say you were angry at Chip because he hasn't attended your meetings and also because he had made that remark at my little party." Skander looked embarrassed. "About that woman, I mean. Obviously, it was in bad taste."

"I would have reprimanded him about the meetings, but I wouldn't have dismissed him. As for his remark, it hardly registered." Not entirely true, Hawthorne reminded himself.

"Several people have also suggested that you overreacted because of your injury. I must say I'm surprised that you were out there playing a game with the students."

"Basketball. I used to coach it. Several other faculty were also playing."

"Yes, well, Roger Bennett." His tone indicated that nothing Bennett did would surprise him.

"My skinning my knees in no way affected my actions. Chip literally hurled the boy across the hall."

Skander's furrowed brow suggested that furious debate was being waged inside him. "Who's going to teach Chip's classes? And he was swimming coach. Who'll take that job?"

"There's a substitute there today. I'll take one of his classes. We can divide up the others. As for the swimming, I can do it if I can get someone to help me."

"You already have a job."

"It'll be all right. I'll find the time. After all, it'll only be temporary. I minored in history at Williams. I can do the ancient and medieval history. Where is he up to, the early Greeks? I can teach that, perhaps not as well as Chip, but I can do it."

Skander pursed his lips and looked worried. "You're pushing yourself too hard."

Hawthorne didn't answer.

"Is it this book you're writing?"

"Good grief, Fritz, I have no intention of writing any damn book!"

Skander tilted his head and looked vaguely skeptical. "Do you know how frightened people are? They think you'll fire us all."

"That's silly. I've talked to several teachers, and I think most will stand by me. I caught Chip physically abusing a student. Twice. That's why I suspended him. Are you saying they all hit students?"

"Of course not."

"Then they have nothing to worry about."

"Ruth Standish said you had words with a student on Friday. There was a quarrel."

"There was no quarrel. I spoke to a girl about burning candles in her room and the need to treat her roommate with courtesy. She yelled at me. We talked a long time. You know the girl. Jessica Weaver. She's the one who started the semester late."

"The stripper."

"Yes, she did that for several months. Anyway, I told her I meant nothing personal. Those cottages could go up in a second. I think she understood my position. We shouldn't even use the fireplaces. You've seen those insurance policies."

"I can imagine you're particularly sensitive about fire."

"Even apart from that," said Hawthorne more quickly than he had intended.

"I can tell it's something on your mind. That's only natural. That boy who set the fire at Wyndham School, what was his name?"

"Stanley Carpasso." There was no pause before Hawthorne's answer. It was as if he had the boy's name always on his lips.

Skander again looked as if he were undergoing some intense inner discussion. "You had no idea how this Carpasso might behave?"

"No."

"But he was, what do you say, emotionally disturbed? Aren't children like that especially dangerous? Of course, I'm no professional."

"It wasn't that simple. I'd worked with him for several years. He wasn't a fire starter. There was nothing like that in his record."

Skander spoke in a whisper. "And there was nothing you could do?"

"You mean once the fire started? I couldn't get back to them. The hallway was on fire. What do you mean? The whole place was burning."

"Weren't there ladders?"

"I expect in the garage. Certainly the grounds crew used ladders."

Skander shook his head. "I'm sorry, it must have been chaos. One can never know what such an event is like unless one lives though it. I once heard about a father who watched his son suffocate. An awful story. The boy was stung by a bee and had an allergic reaction. They were in their own backyard. The father tried to pry the boy's mouth open. After several minutes, he even cut into the boy's windpipe with a knife. Nothing worked. His throat had already swollen shut. Then, oh, at least a month after the funeral, the father woke up in the middle of the night. He had dreamed the whole thing again and realized that the garden sprinkler had been on. If he'd been quick, he could have cut a portion of the hose before his son's throat became blocked. He could have saved his life. It must have been like that for you, thinking about the ladders."

Hawthorne didn't speak for a moment, then said, "There was no time to get ladders. Anyway, they wouldn't have helped."

After Skander left, Hawthorne sat at his desk going over his notes for a talk he had to give at a Lions Club meeting in Plymouth later in the week. He had presented two other such talks to acquaint groups with changes at the school and to raise money. Several others were scheduled for later in the fall. All required a charm and enthusiasm that Hawthorne found difficult, a heartiness more appropriate to Fritz than to himself. As he tried to edit his remarks, he couldn't keep his mind on them. He kept thinking about the fire at Wyndham and Skander's questions. He knew that if he hadn't been pulled out of the burning hallway, he would have died as well. For months he'd been sorry that he hadn't died. Now he felt that way less often. Sitting at his desk, Hawthorne felt how he could reach out a hand and almost touch Lily's blond curls. He even knew how they would feel, their softness, how they would tickle his palm. It was as if his hand were separated from them by a fraction of an inch. He pushed and labored but he still couldn't cover the last, minuscule distance.

Later that morning Hawthorne had a shock. He had gone to the faculty lounge for a cup of coffee around eleven and when he returned to his office he discovered an eight-by-ten framed picture of his wife and daughter on his desk. The shock was that he had no such picture; it must have been put there within the past ten minutes. It showed Meg and Lily standing in front of a decorated Christmas tree. They wore matching green robes from L.L. Bean that Hawthorne had given them for Christmas six weeks before the fire. The picture had appeared in several of the San Diego papers. The frame was cheap—maroon plastic patterned to look like leather. It stood next to the telephone at the corner of the desk as if it had been there for months.

"Mrs. Hayes!" Hawthorne called.

There was no answer. Hawthorne got up to look in the outer office. Mrs. Hayes was not there. He returned to stare at the picture. Meg and Lily looked happy and loving; both had blond hair but Meg's was darker. Lily's curls, which Hawthorne had recently been thinking about, were now before him. Hawthorne had no idea how long he looked at the picture—perhaps ten minutes, perhaps thirty. He was interrupted when Mrs. Hayes came into his office.

Hawthorne spoke abruptly. "Where have you been?"

Mrs. Hayes looked startled. She wore a blue dress with a white sailor collar and put a hand to her throat as Hawthorne spoke. "I just carried something down to my car."

"Did you put this picture here?"

"Of course not. I haven't touched anything in your office."

Hawthorne wasn't sure he believed her. There was an oddness to her expression, but perhaps it was because he had raised his voice. "Did you see anyone else in here?"

"No, nobody. What's bothering you?"

Hawthorne sat down at his desk and began massaging his temples. "Somebody's playing tricks," he said. He looked at the picture of Meg and Lily. He had been avoiding old photographs ever since the fire. He didn't feel he was strong enough to see them.

"Well, it certainly wasn't me," said Mrs. Hayes. Her voice trembled.

Hawthorne saw that she had tears in her eyes. "Is something wrong? I'm sorry if I was abrupt."

"It's not that, it's just . . ." Mrs. Hayes stopped and looked bewildered. Then she suddenly thrust a white envelope across the desk toward Hawthorne. "I don't trust myself to say anything. Just take that and read it. I've thought of nothing else all week."

Hawthorne took the envelope. It was addressed to Dr. James Hawthorne. When he looked up again, Mrs. Hayes was hurrying from the office. He tore open the envelope.

"Dear Dr. Hawthorne," Mrs. Hayes had written. "As much as it upsets me to do so, I am afraid I must offer my resignation. I am not young anymore, and as much as I love Bishop's Hill, I realize that it must move forward. Your ways are not my ways, but if anyone can save the school, then you can. You are a brave man to come here. As for me, my training was in areas that seem obsolete: typing, dictation, file keeping, and payrolls. I understand you must have a modern office to go with your modern methods. I have thought about this for days but I knew it was coming. If I stayed at Bishop's Hill, I would just be in the way. Please do not try to talk me out of this. I know your intentions are well meant but you cannot turn back the clock, nor can you teach an old dog new tricks. Respectfully yours, Martha Hayes."

Hawthorne reread the letter, then folded it and returned it to the envelope. He looked at the photograph of Meg and Lily. His wife and daughter, the joy in their faces, their joy at being alive, formed the only subject in which he wanted to immerse himself. He felt angry with Mrs. Hayes for interfering with such sweet and terrible recollections. Then he thought: Someone's trying to drive me crazy. He got up, crossed the room to the front office. Mrs. Hayes was nowhere in sight.

He looked for some sign of the secretary—her coat or purse—but even the snapshots of her nieces and nephews were gone from her desk, even the little vase of plastic violets. In their place were the computer and software manuals neatly stacked. The other boxes, mostly unopened, stood along the wall. It occurred to Hawthorne that he might be able to convince the board to keep Mrs. Hayes as office manager; then he could hire someone else with computer skills. He hurried to the door to see if she was in the hall. As he moved, the scabs on his knees chafed against his pants, slowing him.

But Mrs. Hayes was gone. The only person nearby was the librarian, Bill Dolittle, who was just passing. In fact, Hawthorne almost bumped into him. He excused himself and stepped back. Dolittle wore a bright yellow V-neck sweater and a blue bow tie. He was balding and he combed his longish brown hair across his bare pink scalp in a way that Hawthorne had heard referred to as borrowing. His sweater was tight, as if he had bought it years earlier when he had been thinner.

They greeted each other in that surprised way people do when they have nearly collided. Dolittle said something about its being another glorious day.

Hawthorne nearly asked him about the photograph. Did Dolittle know who had put it on his desk? How foolish, he thought to himself. Must I distrust everybody?

"I was wondering," said Dolittle, "if you've had the opportunity to consider my proposal."

"You mean about moving over to Stark? I've thought about it but I haven't had the chance to discuss it with the board. I plan to talk to them next week."

Dolittle looked concerned. He had a distinct overbite, which he tried to correct by pushing his jaw forward, which made him appear pugnacious. "Why is this a matter for the board?"

"Because someone else would have to be assigned to Latham, which might mean another hiring. That probably couldn't be done until next year."

"I could live in Stark and still check on the boys in Latham."

"I'm sure you could but technically that would leave them unsupervised."

"I can't tell you how embarrassing it is to have my son visit me from college for a weekend and make him share a room with an eighth or ninth grader. I've been in Latham for eight years!"

"Then you deserve a change but I don't see how it can be done this semester."

Dolittle was one of the faculty members who had been supporting Hawthorne. Now Hawthorne wondered if it was only because Dolittle hoped to move from Latham to Stark.

Dolittle patted his hair, perhaps thinking it had been disarranged by the bad news. "How disappointing," he said.

———

Thursday afternoon, after the faculty meeting, Hawthorne took a walk with Kate on one of the many paths through the woods that bordered the school. He had noticed her in the parking lot and called to her. His intention had been to drive into Plymouth and do a few errands, like buying a new razor, but seeing Kate he decided his beard could wait. The faculty meeting had been frustrating and left Hawthorne in a bad mood. No one had been absent except Herb Frankfurter, who had attended only the first meeting, but people were upset about Chip and more interested in talking about him than about the students. Or more accurately, they were concerned not so much about Chip as about their own job security, until Hawthorne nearly lost his temper and said that as long as they didn't abuse the students and did what they were hired to do, then they needn't worry about being fired. All this took time. It was only after half an hour or so that Hawthorne was able to get on to the subject of the upper forms—discussing those students who seemed in immediate trouble, acted out in class, and refused to do their home-work. In the past few days two boys had been drunk in their room, about twenty had cut class, an equal number had been verbally abusive to faculty, Bill Dolittle had discovered marijuana spilled on the floor in the Latham bathroom, and Tank Donoso was still giving the other boys in Shepherd slaps on the back of the head. Hawthorne had also hoped to begin discussing the seniors one by one, listing their strengths and weaknesses, suggesting what might benefit them, but that hadn't been possible. At the end of an hour, they had only managed to talk about three students and at least ten faculty members hadn't said a word. Hawthorne tried not to show his irritation, but he wasn't sure how successful he had been.

Interfering with his ability to focus were his thoughts about the photograph of his wife and daughter—its mysterious appearance—as well as his concern about Mrs. Hayes's resignation. He had tried tele-phoning Mrs. Hayes, at last reaching her about ten minutes before the meeting. While not actually rude, she had been cool, telling him that she did not intend to reconsider her decision.

At lunch he had told Skander that the secretary had resigned.

Skander had sighed. "I was afraid this was coming. Well, perhaps it's for the best."

Stephen Dobyns

"I think we need her here. No one knows the school better than she does. Can't you talk to her?"

"I can try, but she's certainly a stubborn woman. Resiliency has never been one of her gifts. If I described some of the run-ins we've had in the past I'm not sure you'd be so eager to keep her. Not that she isn't a wonderful person."

At the faculty meeting Skander had been no help, sitting silently and appearing downcast. But a few teachers had contributed: Ted Wrigley and Kate, Bill Dolittle and Betty Sherman. Roger Bennett had been almost garrulous but he hadn't said anything substantive—that is, his purpose had been to show that he was still sorry for knocking Hawthorne down during the basketball game, which only made Hawthorne wonder if it had been an accident after all.

That was where Hawthorne was with his thinking when he saw Kate in the parking lot. Briefly, he wondered whether Kate had put the picture on his desk as a gift, but the very unlikelihood of that struck him as evidence of his distraction. Still, he believed he could benefit from her point of view. He also found her attractive. It made him realize that he wanted a face to insert between him and the faces of his wife and daughter, if only for an hour or so. And then he asked himself what right he had to rest. What right did he have to turn away from them?

Despite his uncertainty, Hawthorne called to Kate. She wore a red mackinaw, almost as if she wanted to be noticed. Soon they were walking along a path in the woods past the playing fields. Hawthorne spoke about the picture, how it showed his wife and daughter on Christmas day. He described coming back from the teachers' lounge and finding it on his desk. As he talked, he realized he had been badly frightened. Kate listened to him carefully as their feet scuffed through the fallen leaves. The muted sunlight through the trees made it seem they were walking within a vast Japanese lantern.

"And you thought I might have put it there?" she asked.

"I didn't know. But if it was meant as a friendly gesture, then it might have been done by—"

"By someone you've been friendly with," said Kate, laughing. "No, I didn't do it. Didn't anybody notice anything? There wasn't a note? What about Mrs. Hayes, did she see someone?"

"No, and that's another problem. She's resigned." Hawthorne

128

explained that she had been made anxious by the computers but he hoped to persuade her to come back.

"How difficult." Kate carried a backpack slung over one shoulder.

"She didn't give the computers a real chance. I'd meant to spend more time with her but what with one thing and another it wasn't possible, so I was going to help her this week."

"And what if she couldn't learn?" It was Kate's habit to look at a person out of the corner of her eye when she spoke, only half turning her head and not facing the other person directly.

"Then I'd hire someone to work under her. I told her that this afternoon on the phone but she wouldn't rethink her decision. She said the office was too small for two people. I'll write the board. If she won't change her mind, then perhaps they can give her a special tribute for her years of service as well as some improved retirement package, or at least a bonus."

"Who'll take her place?"

"Fritz says he knows of a person who might work out."

Half a dozen crows seemed engaged in an argument among the pines. The maple leaves under their feet were bright yellows and oranges. Occasionally, Kate would pick one up, study it, and carry it a while before letting it flutter back to the ground.

"Did you ask Fritz about the photograph?" asked Kate.

"If he'd put it there, he would have told me. To tell the truth, I find the whole business incredible." He was about to tell her about Ambrose Stark's appearance, then decided not to. It already struck him as too peculiar, as if it had been a hallucination.

"Do you think it's connected to whoever put those clippings in our mailboxes?"

"I don't know." Hawthorne took off his glasses and polished them on his tie. Without his glasses the colors of the trees became a spectacular blur.

"I felt bad calling you about George." Kate laughed abruptly. "Especially since nothing's happened."

"I was glad that you felt comfortable enough to alert me. You still think he'll call?"

"He could easily show up. If he's drinking, there's no telling what he might do. All of this should be terrific material for your book."

Hawthorne stopped and put a hand on her arm. "Believe me, there is no book. I came here to keep Bishop's Hill from going out of business, not to write anything."

"Everyone's talking about it. They think that's why you took the job, to write about dysfunctional education. I was looking forward to it."

Hawthorne began walking again. "Then you'll have to be disappointed. I don't belong to that world anymore." Hawthorne worried that his tone had been unnecessarily harsh, and he tried to soften it. "By the way, I've taken over the coaching of the swim team, but I may not be able to make all of the practices. Is that something you might help me with? I could probably take you off some other stuff—mail room and lunch duty."

Kate appeared to consider. "My son's home in the afternoon. It would probably mean more baby-sitting, but I think I could manage it. I used to swim a lot. That's where I met George. We both swam at UNH. He got booted off the team for drinking. I should have taken it as a warning." Kate began to talk about her marriage and George's jealousy. In part she wanted to show Hawthorne that she hadn't telephoned him out of foolishness, that George could easily make a scene. She described his temper and his drinking and how she was forced to stay in this area because of his visiting rights.

As they walked and Hawthorne listened, he knew that shortly they would talk about his own marriage and the death of his wife and daughter. Not only was it the place where his thoughts always went, it was the place where all conversations sooner or later arrived, as if anyone's pleasant remark or idle discussion of the weather was only a way of getting to what interested them most, the horrific deaths of Meg and Lily. It was like watching a ball roll down a hill: eventually this subject—the lowest part of all talk—would be reached. He could almost feel Meg and Lily waiting in the wings for their turn onstage. Yes, he too had been married. Yes, something awful had happened.

Yet, when he began to talk about Wyndham, it was almost with relief, as if his purpose in life was to tell that story over and over. To tell it until its last shard had been pulled from him. As he listened to himself, he realized that the story sounded practiced as it changed from event and recollection into language, as if each retelling were an attempt to scrub away the awfulness.

"The boy, Stanley Carpasso, had been at Wyndham for over three years. That may have been the problem. The usual stay at a treatment center is two. But he'd had a rough time. He was eleven when he came. He'd already been in four foster homes and was very destructive. He had no relatives and his father was unknown. His mother had been a prostitute and she'd died of AIDS. He became extremely fond of me. In fact, after the first six months or so, I was the only person who didn't become a victim of his tantrums. So it appeared I was doing him some good. That in itself seemed reason enough to keep him there longer. At first he was friendly with my wife and daughter and the affection he had for me extended to them as well. But with puberty he began to change. Not that he obviously came to dislike Meg and Lily, but he was jealous of them. He concealed this as best as he could, but when I was late to an appointment or when I was simply busy with my own family he resented it. And those feelings increased.

"Unfortunately, I wasn't sufficiently aware of them. I was busy, and when I saw him, he seemed the same as ever. No, that's not right; he'd sometimes complain about my family. He even asked why I didn't adopt him, why he couldn't live with us. His foster home experiences had been disasters, but he said that wouldn't happen if I took him in. He promised to be an angel. That was his word, an angel. However, I couldn't do it. Partly I was skeptical and partly it's bad practice to take in a favorite. I mean, all the kids wanted a home—perhaps not a real home but some ideal impossibility of their imagination. And if I'd taken Stanley in, it would have created a series of damaging expectations and disappointments for the others.

"So I tried to wean him from me, having him talk to other psychologists and seeing him less often. I probably should have had him transferred to another facility altogether, but his conduct with me didn't seem to change, at least on the surface. Because of his feelings for me, he couldn't let himself think the fault was mine. He couldn't believe that I had made a decision to reject him. So he blamed my wife and daughter. Not all at once, of course. But over a period of a few months he started believing that, without them in his path, I'd have no hesitation about adopting him. I see now it was a mistake to live at the school. I don't mean that ironically. By living there I wanted to present an example of what a home could be. I didn't realize it could make some of the children envious and bitter. With Stanley, it made him murderous. He thought he could set a fire that would kill Meg and Lily but that would also seem accidental, so he wouldn't be blamed."

"That's awful," said Kate.

"Yes," said Hawthorne. He thought how in his many retellings of this story he had simplified it until it was just the bare bones of what had really happened. He wondered if he would ever tell Kate the more complete version and he looked at her quickly, her cheeks flushed from their walk, her black hair damp along the scalp line, her red coat unzipped and fluttering in the breeze. He found her very pretty, and his response to this was guilt.

"And how were you burned?"

Again Hawthorne presented the censored account. "Our quarters were separated from the rest of the school by a hallway. The fire started around ten at night. I'd been at a dinner meeting . . ." He paused, recalling Chip's remark about "the cute psychologist." Claire de Lune. Certainly Kate would realize that Claire was missing from the story. "Stanley knew that, of course. When I got back, the building was on fire. The hallway was burning. I tried to get through and . . ." Hawthorne raised his arm as if gesturing with the scar tissue itself. "But I couldn't. Luckily, a fireman dragged me out."

"How terrible." They had stopped and Kate was staring at him.

For a moment it seemed that Hawthorne could see the flames, could even hear Meg's screams. No, it wasn't simply screaming, it was his name she was screaming.

"My wife and daughter died of smoke inhalation, mercifully, I expect."

Another lie. Hawthorne looked at the multicolored leaves at his feet and thought he would fall, tumble out of sanity into a deep and benign unconsciousness. He took hold of himself. But he thought, Wouldn't falling be better in the long run? Wouldn't it stop all this thinking? And suddenly in his recollection he saw Meg and Lily as they had appeared in the picture on his desk—standing before the Christmas tree in their matching green robes. Who had put it there?

They were at the edge of the parking lot and began walking again. It was approaching five-thirty.

"If something ever happened to Todd," said Kate, "I don't think I'd get over it."

Hawthorne nodded. Many people told him things like that.

"I don't expect I have, at least not yet. Now I'm in a different place, a different part of the country. And time, you know, makes a difference, just like they say. You think it never will, but things fade. Their faces aren't as clear to me now." Hawthorne stopped. It wouldn't do to weep. He watched two chipmunks pursuing each other around the base of an old oak. He heard chickadees. Ahead of him he saw the white bell tower on top of Emerson Hall. He had heard that the view from up there was breathtaking. They began passing between the parked cars. Hawthorne was still looking at the ground, while Kate was watching him, trying to read his expression. As a result, neither of them saw Chip Campbell until he was about six feet away. He wore an old leather jacket and he was swaying slightly.

"I forgot to give you something before I left," said Chip. "It's for your book."

Hawthorne had just time enough to see that the other man was drunk before Chip hit him in the jaw, knocking him against a parked car so he banged his head on the door.

"Chip, don't!" Kate screamed at the same time.

Hawthorne was on his hands and knees staring down at the asphalt. His glasses had fallen off. There was shouting that he couldn't understand. Looking up into the unfocused blur, he thought he saw not Chip but Frank LeBrun in his white jacket. LeBrun was holding someone. There was a loud grunt. Hawthorne felt around for his glasses, then found them and put them on. Looking up again, he saw that LeBrun had grabbed Chip around the neck and was holding him tight, choking him.

"Stop it!" said Kate.

Hawthorne, still dazed, got to his feet, pulling himself up by grabbing the back bumper of a pickup. He couldn't understand where LeBrun had come from.

LeBrun shook Chip, then, holding him with one hand, brought the other back in a fist.

"Stop it," said Kate. "Jim, make him stop."

Chip raised an arm to protect himself but LeBrun hit him in

the nose. Hawthorne swayed toward LeBrun, wiping the blood from his face.

"Frank, stop!" he called. Hawthorne grabbed LeBrun and dragged him back.

Ferociously, LeBrun turned on him. There were splotches of blood on LeBrun's white jacket.

"Are you going to beat me too, Frank?" Hawthorne managed to say, speaking as calmly as he could. He was close enough to smell the garlic on LeBrun's breath.

LeBrun's brow contorted with fierce intention. From somewhere out of sight, Chip was groaning.

"That's enough, don't you think, Frank?" asked Hawthorne.

LeBrun seemed about to say something, then abruptly turned away and stared off toward the woods with his back to them all.

Hawthorne put a hand on LeBrun's shoulder. "That's all right. You got excited."

LeBrun jerked away and Hawthorne again put his hand on the man's shoulder.

After a moment LeBrun said, "Dumb, you know? I just don't catch on."

"What do you mean?" asked Hawthorne. "You were trying to help. Don't be so hard on yourself."

"What d'you call a Canuck with an IQ of 167?"

Hawthorne didn't answer and LeBrun said nothing else but kept staring at the woods. Kate had given Chip a handkerchief. He knelt on the asphalt and wiped the blood from his nose. The sleeve of his leather jacket was torn. "Jesus, Jesus," he kept repeating.

Part Two

5

High against the sky the scaffolding of weathered two-by-fours around the bell tower of Emerson Hall formed a web of crisscrossing lines the same gray color as the overhanging clouds. At the corners of the rooftop, the crude alligatorlike gargoyles dribbled raindrops, and the scaffolding rose above the roof like a cage. Kevin Krueger, as he stood next to his State of New Hampshire Ford Taurus, found the scene oppressive. For Jim Hawthorne, however, the scaffolding was a source of celebration.

"I've spoken to groups from Plymouth down to Laconia," he was saying. "Kiwanis, Rotary, Lions. And I've written to alumni. I hadn't a hope of starting these repairs before spring, but then the gifts began to come in. Not a lot, but enough to get started."

"I'm impressed," said Krueger, trying to put enthusiasm into his voice.

"If we'd waited, there could have been water damage up in the attic rooms. Now it should be watertight before the snow starts, though we had flurries just the other day."

It was midmorning on Monday, November 9, and Kevin Krueger had just driven up from Concord. Officially, he was here to look at the school for the Department of Education, but he also wanted to see his ex-teacher and friend, from whom his only communication had been a phone call in September, then a postcard at the beginning of October making an obscure reference to the successes of Sisyphus. It was nearly seven weeks since he had last seen Hawthorne, and in that time Hawthorne appeared to have lost about ten pounds and aged five years. His face was even more angular and the hollows in his cheeks were small pockets of shadow.

"So, you've been successful," said Krueger, making it a statement.

"Not successful yet, I'm afraid. But we're moving along."

Hawthorne had come out to greet him when he saw Krueger get out of his car. Now they walked slowly toward the main entrance of Emerson Hall. It had been raining for nearly a week and the ground was muddy. This morning the rain had stopped but the sky remained slate-colored. Krueger stepped to avoid puddles. Everything seemed gray except for the gold spear points on the metal fence in front of the building. Krueger saw a few faces looking down at him from several windows, presumably students who were not paying attention to their teachers. The air was cold and raw. Hawthorne wore no coat but he didn't seem to notice the cold. Krueger wore a thick brown overcoat, tweed cap, and brown leather gloves, while his bushy mustache and eyebrows seemed to provide additional protection against the weather. He was a man who buffered himself against the world with his comforts, his optimism, and his intellect. He liked soft things and worried about Hawthorne—whether he ate enough or slept enough. There was a wariness about him that Krueger had never noticed before, an agitation and suspicion of his surroundings.

Krueger had heard about Bishop's Hill from a few other sources. For instance, he knew that Chip Campbell had been dismissed and that an injunction had been obtained against him to make sure he stayed off school property.

"And you remain hopeful?" he asked.

"Let's say I refuse to admit defeat. There've been changes and many have been successful. The problem is that each change is met with a lot of grumbling. If you only knew how tired I am of grumbling."

Most of the leaves had fallen and were heaped in sodden piles along the metal fence. The clouds were low enough that the hills seemed eaten up by them. Gray trees, gray clouds. A few crows were calling to one another—a rough, imperative squawking. It was the sort of day that always made Krueger tell himself that he was going to take his family south this winter for a week or two, though he never did.

They climbed the granite front steps of the building and Krueger held the door for Hawthorne. "I heard about that fellow Campbell. That must have been difficult for you."

"Did you know him?"

"I never had the pleasure. But his record indicated he'd been fired from a school in Connecticut in 1985." Krueger removed his cap and gloves and put them in his pockets.

"He has an unfortunate temper. It seemed simple, really—to have a rule that couldn't be broken. How many times do you have to say it? Students May Not Be Hit. You know he came back and tried to beat me up? He got more than he bargained for, from the cook of all people. He happened to see Chip knock me down. That's when I had an injunction taken out against him. Unfortunately, he's become a martyr for some of the faculty. And the whole business has made everyone anxious—as if I were going to go on a firing spree and get rid of them all. All my gestures get magnified. I say something quietly and it gets turned into a shout."

"That's what it's like to be boss."

"But it hasn't been that way at other places."

"Schools are different from treatment centers. They're more amateurish."

"You know, they had this idea that the only reason I'd come here was to write a book, and they resented it, as if they were no more than parts of an experiment. It's taken over a month to convince them that I'm not planning to write anything. Some of them still don't believe me."

"You spoke of writing a book when you went to Wyndham."

Hawthorne turned back to Krueger. "I'm not that person anymore. That was part of my ambition. If I hadn't been so ambitious, my wife and daughter would still be alive."

The Emerson Hall rotunda rose up three stories to a dome beneath the bell tower. In the center of its marble floor was a blue-and-gold crest with the letters *B* and *H* superimposed. Here, too, there was scaffolding, with two workmen in paint-spotted coveralls plastering the first-floor ceiling along the rim of the open space. Above him, Krueger saw chest-high railings surrounding the rotunda at the second and third floors. In a public school, the rotunda would be considered unsafe. The insurance companies would protest and the second and third floors would be extended across the opening. It was on the tip of Krueger's tongue to ask if they'd ever lost a student—some careless seventh grader tumbling down from the third floor—but he was trying to be upbeat.

Krueger wanted to argue with Hawthorne about Wyndham. He passionately believed that Hawthorne's ambitions had nothing to do with the death of his family, but he didn't feel ready to begin the discussion. "What's Campbell doing now?"

"He's got a lawyer. The school deals with him through Hamilton Burke, who's our lawyer and a member of the board of trustees. I expect he'll get some money and a noncommittal recommendation. Chip certainly won't be coming back here. I'd resign first."

"And his classes?"

"I hired a fellow to teach two. The others were picked up by people here. I'm teaching one in ancient and medieval history. We're well into the Romans now. What an ill-mannered bunch they were. And I coach the swimming team with another teacher."

"Where do you find the time?"

Hawthorne gave one of his sudden smiles. "It has to be found, that's all."

They were walking down the empty corridor. The floor was yellowish marble and the wainscoting rose to about four feet. Above the wainscoting were rows of photographs of Bishop's Hill students going back to the school's founding. Krueger felt they were an exceedingly glum lot.

"And what's the feeling of the board in general?"

"Optimistic, I think, although even there I have my enemies, one or two who feel the school should close. But we've done quite a bit. The faculty meets twice a week to discuss students and now they're mostly able to do that without carping at one another. The two mental health counselors are each in charge of four discussion sections—group therapy, basically—which have been a big hit. I go to two each week, as does the school psychologist, Mr. Evings. And other faculty go, too. It's a place where the students can say how much they hate us without getting into trouble. But recently they've begun talking about their feelings more. You know, their fears and why they have them. And the board has authorized a search for another psychologist—an entry-level position, I'm afraid, but better than nothing. I've had two Sunday teas to which different groups of students have been invited. There's a crisis hotline that the students try to operate eighteen hours a day. Mostly it works. We've put couches and chairs in one of the classrooms that was empty, and now it's used for time-outs. If a kid acts up in class, he or she can be sent there. A staff member monitors the room but doesn't interfere unless windows start getting broken, which has happened twice. Ten students have been enlisted as tutors in English, foreign languages, math, and science to help other students with their home-work. We've been able to set aside a special room in the library and even supply cider and doughnuts, which is a draw. And we're setting up a program to let students work with the grounds crew, in the kitchen, and in general cleanup. In return they get coupons they can redeem in the school store or at the Dugout, the student coffeehouse, or exchange for privileges like time in the gym or rides into town, even extra desserts."

"That sounds fantastic."

"Most of it's pretty basic stuff. I don't know why it hadn't been done before. But the students seem happy with the changes. I'm also setting up a buddy system where the upper classmen help out the younger kids and look out for them in general. And we're starting dis-cussion groups on things like homosexuality, anorexia, self-mutilation, even overeating."

"And the faculty, are they happy with the changes?"

"Less so, I'm afraid. One woman asked if I didn't understand that the more I gave the students, the more they'd want. She suggested I was setting dangerous precedents. For years they've seen the stu-dents as the enemy and the students have reacted by being adversarial. Being bad has been the only power they've had. It will take time to change that."

"What about the psychologist, Mr. Evings?

141

"He's something of a disappointment. I've spoken to him a few times—really, only trying to help—but I seem to frighten him. At least he attends the meetings. Unfortunately, he tends to fall asleep. The students, well, he doesn't have much credibility with them. Some are quite rude. Evings is gay, which is neither here nor there, but he feels that's why he's unpopular and it increases his anxiety. And of course some people *do* object to his gayness, which is one reason we've started these discussion groups. But the school nurse has helped a lot, as well as some of the faculty. The admissions office is perking up. And Bill Dolittle, the librarian, has been supportive."

"Isn't there a chaplain?" From the half-closed doors of a classroom, Krueger could hear talking and occasional laughter.

"Reverend Bennett, a woman. She rather disapproves of me. Early on she asked if I'd please refrain from engaging in athletic events with the students. I'd been playing basketball and scraped my knees. Actually, her husband knocked me down. He teaches math and is known for never flunking a student no matter how much the kid deserves it. He's considered a character—very bouncy, for the most part. Anyway, the chaplain does her job well enough, giving sermons about vice and abstinence, though I don't think many students would attend chapel if it weren't required. Her husband was very apologetic when he hit me. It wasn't on purpose. At least, I don't think so."

Krueger had taken off his overcoat and held it folded over one arm. "And what about Fritz Skander?"

"He's been a big help, but it worries him that he's had to mediate between me and the faculty. He's always asking if I don't think we're moving ahead too quickly and he talks vaguely about 'repercussions.' But he means well, I believe. When I came here I thought of the faculty as a sort of unit—people who had been living and working together for years—but they've got all sort of dislikes and rivalries, even hatreds. Two teachers who in public strongly objected to Chip's dismissal came to me privately to assure me that I'd done the right thing."

"Certainly there are rivalries in treatment centers."

"There they're part of the fabric, basically superficial; here they're part of the foundation. Sustaining timbers. In some cases, it's all these people think about, as if the hatred were preexisting. And now a certain amount of their hatred has been redirected at me." Hawthorne laughed. "But it's hardly personal. They would have hated any headmaster."

"You've been very active."

"Yes. For many that's a decided fault."

A bell rang and within seconds the hall was filled with students moving from one class to the next. They seemed mostly congenial— noisy and good-natured, with backpacks and Walkmans. Two boys carried skateboards. A girl had a hockey stick. Krueger tried to look at them in the way that he expected the review board would look at them when its members visited in the spring to decide on accreditation. Krueger had visited schools all over the state. He had seen sullen schools and angry schools, even dangerous schools, but here the students seemed cordial, though there was a tension that Krueger couldn't identify. A sort of vigilance. Quite a few greeted Hawthorne. In their dress, they seemed rather ragtag, as if their clothes had been obtained from a local thrift shop. Several had dyed their hair orange or scarlet, and one young man wore a Mohawk with three-inch purple spikes.

Hawthorne pointed him out to Krueger. "He's sporting Bishop's Hill's first Mohawk and he's terribly proud of it. Only conventional haircuts were allowed before this year. It seemed a pointless rule so I got rid of it. When I arrived, there was also a dress code. Boys were expected to wear coats and ties, girls had to wear skirts. It wasn't very popular. So we had a vote and the coats and ties lost, nearly unanimously. Many of the faculty disliked the change. The fact that students wore coats and ties seemed proof that what the teachers were saying in class was important. Anyway, now the students are going to opposite extremes. When the rule was first dropped, one boy insisted on wearing a loincloth. So I said everyone had to be completely dressed— no bathing suits or leopard skins. It eventually got straightened out. When they come back after Christmas break, I expect they'll be dressed more conventionally. Christmas is a good time for new clothes."

The faculty weren't so spirited. Some were friendly, others were cool or indifferent. They nodded to Hawthorne or said hello. They regarded Krueger with suspicion. Hawthorne introduced him to several, beginning with Herb Frankfurter and Tom Hastings, the two science teachers. Though Frankfurter was only in his forties, he walked with a cane; Hastings was younger and sharply dressed in a black shirt and a black tie. Hastings seemed cheerful enough but Frankfurter clearly objected to being stopped and introduced to strangers.

After they departed, Hawthorne said, "Mr. Frankfurter's mad

because I made him return an old Chevy he borrowed from the school last year. Since no one was using it, he didn't see what the problem was. But the school was insuring the car and he was getting gas at the school pump some of the time. He's one of those whose hatred seems preexisting. It's what he does, like a hobby: hatred and football, hatred and hunting."

"So what will you do with him?" asked Krueger.

"He'll either come around or he won't. The thing is, he feels ill-used. He still thinks he should be able to take the car."

Next Hawthorne introduced him to Bill Dolittle, who had paused to speak to Hawthorne. After absentmindedly shaking Krueger's hand, he asked Hawthorne, "Have you heard anything yet?"

"Nothing yet, I'm afraid. It's unlikely that I'll know anything before Christmas."

"The waiting's hard."

"I know, I regret that, but as I told you before, it's a matter of money."

After Dolittle left, Hawthorne said, "He hopes to move to an apartment on campus. He asks about it twice a week. But he supports me in meetings—a loyal but vexing soldier."

Next Krueger met Kate Sandler, who taught Italian and Spanish, an attractive woman with a white streak in her thick black hair that reached back from her left temple. Krueger could see she was fond of Hawthorne and he felt a twinge of jealousy. She had large dark eyes and looked at him quite candidly, as if to determine whether Krueger would be a supporter or a rival in her affection for Hawthorne.

"Kate's also been helping me coach the swim team," said Hawthorne as they walked away. "She's a great swimmer."

"She clearly likes you."

"We're friends, I think. There's been a lot of gossip about us. Entirely without reason, I'm afraid. It's made her ex-husband quite upset."

A bulky student dressed in a blue sweatshirt and sweatpants jogged up, gave Hawthorne a high five, said, "Yo, boss!" and hurried down the corridor.

"That's the president of the student body," said Hawthorne. "His name's Tank. He's a little rough, but without his support I would have had a much harder time."

Then Krueger met the art teacher, Betty Sherman, a theatrical middle-aged woman dressed all in black. And there were others—a music teacher, a history teacher, math, civics. Krueger felt they all had certain similarities: they seemed needy and lacking in confidence. And they had a watchful quality that disturbed him.

Hawthorne pointed up the hall. "See the man talking to the fellow in the white jacket? That's Fritz Skander. The other's the assistant cook, who's also new. He's the one who held off Campbell."

There were fewer people in the halls as classes got ready to begin. Students were hurrying. Skander was smiling kindly at the cook, one hand resting on the other man's shoulder, nodding and shaking his head as the cook talked to him rapidly, with a great amount of gesticulation. When Skander saw Hawthorne, he broke off his conversation and came toward them. The cook waved to Hawthorne, then rushed off in the opposite direction. Krueger noticed that even his walk was jerky, as if his legs came with several extra sets of joints.

"This must be your friend from Concord," said Skander, reaching out his hand to Krueger. "I'm afraid I've forgotten his name."

"Kevin Krueger." Krueger shook Skander's hand. He found himself staring at Skander's necktie, which had the phrase "What, me worry?" printed over and over.

"This is a wonderful treat to have you here. I gather you're having lunch with us."

Krueger had heard nothing about this but he smiled nonetheless.

"Is everything okay with Frank?" asked Hawthorne.

"Yes, yes, he has plans for a new casserole. Something with winter squash. Really, he's an absolute treat." Skander started to move off, walking backward as he spoke. "I must dash, I'm afraid. Duty calls. Good to know that Concord really cares. Sometimes we've felt terribly isolated. Not anymore, of course." At last he turned and ducked into a classroom.

Krueger watched him go. "Friendly fellow."

"He's been a great help."

"Have you learned anything about the previous headmaster?"

"Pendergast, or Old Pendergast, as Skander calls him? He evidently saw which way the school was heading and resigned so he wouldn't have the failure on his résumé."

They had reached a large door with the word "Administration" printed on the oak panel in gold letters. "Here we are," said Hawthorne. "I don't know if I told you that the previous secretary left in October. I began to computerize the office and she panicked." Hawthorne put his hand on the knob. "Skander again came to the rescue. His wife, Hilda, knows all about computers—pretty much, at any rate. So I gave her the job."

Hawthorne pushed open the door. Krueger's first glimpse of Hilda Skander was to see her start in surprise, then she gave a welcoming smile. She looked about forty, with short graying hair parted in the middle. There was something pointy about her face and Krueger had the sense of a somewhat pointy nose in the exact center of the circle. As he approached her, he became aware of the distinct smell of peppermint.

"You must be Kevin Krueger," she said, getting up from her desk. "We've heard so much about you. When Dr. Hawthorne saw your car, he dashed out just like a racehorse."

"I told them a special friend of mine was coming," said Hawthorne.

Krueger tried to be hearty but he couldn't quite manage it. Hilda Skander had bright little dark eyes that reminded him vaguely of an animal's. He shook her hand and for several minutes they chatted about his first impressions of the school and what his drive up from Concord had been like. Krueger still smelled peppermint but he couldn't imagine where it was coming from.

"Dr. Hawthorne is making a big impact on our little school," said Hilda pleasantly, keeping her eyes on Krueger. "He's our own campus radical. He loves to change things."

Shortly, Hawthorne said something about keeping Hilda from her work and took Krueger into his office and shut the door.

"Whew," he said, then grinned. "I think of her as my pet mole."

"Mole?" said Krueger, misunderstanding.

"She looks a little like a mole, don't you think? Those small dark eyes. It's meant affectionately. She's wonderfully energetic."

"You seem surrounded by Skanders. Do you have any more of them employed?"

"You mean brothers and sisters? No. There's a ten-year-old boy, but he has yet to engage himself with the school except to shoot baskets in the gym. But with Hilda's help I've been able to put all the students' files on disk. Faculty, staff—now it's easy to look up anything."

On the desk, Krueger saw a framed photograph of Hawthorne's wife and daughter standing before a Christmas tree with unwrapped presents heaped around their feet. He thought again how pretty Meg had been. Although he hadn't meant to say anything, he realized that Hawthorne was watching him look at the picture.

"It's a nice photograph," said Krueger, uncertain whether to say anything else.

Hawthorne opened his mouth, then, unaccountably, said nothing.

They sat down on the couch. Krueger kept trying to square Hawthorne's optimism with the fact that he looked thinner and tired. He glanced quickly at Hawthorne's wrist but it looked the same as ever, white and pink splotches of scar tissue protruding from his white cuff.

"And what's that peppermint smell?" Krueger asked.

"Hilda has asthma. She claims the smell of peppermint helps her, so she sprinkles peppermint drops on her handkerchief. Often the whole office reeks of it."

"Doesn't it bother you?"

Hawthorne laughed. "It's more aggressive than I'd like, but I'm getting used to it."

Krueger sat back and looked around the office. It still appeared rather generic—a framed print of the school seal and two photographs of winter landscapes—as if Hawthorne had yet to put his stamp on it apart from the photograph of Meg and Lily.

"So tell me more about the people here."

Hawthorne took off his glasses, held them up to the light, looking for smudges, then put them on again as he spoke. "At first they were suspicious, but that was only natural, especially considering all the talk about a book. Some wouldn't come to my meetings and that was annoying. I had to tell myself it was reasonable for them to worry about their job security and for their worry to translate into ill will. The cook you saw talking to Skander troubled me to such an extent that I made some calls to see if he had any kind of record . . ."

"Prison?"

"Yes, but also mental institutions, treatment centers. He was too impulsive for my taste. Too hyperactive. And when he went at Chip, it was a scary sight. But there was nothing, so I felt I'd been overreacting. I'm glad nothing came of it, because he's really a great cook."

In the hour left before lunch, Hawthorne and Krueger continued to discuss the school, following up various points that one or the other had raised earlier. All the evidence suggested that Bishop's Hill was improving, even if the endeavor was rather like raising the *Titanic*. Still, Krueger wasn't entirely happy. Hawthorne didn't look well, as if he were draining his own blood for the school's transfusion. And Krueger knew Hawthorne well enough to believe that the deaths of Meg and Lily remained in the forefront of his thinking. But Hawthorne was also passionate about succeeding and that was fueled by his sense that he had failed at Wyndham.

Nor was Krueger happy with what he saw as the mood of the place, although he tried to tell himself that the raw autumn day made him overly pessimistic—those evil-looking gargoyles. It seemed clear that Hawthorne was being thorough. As far as the students were concerned, he was clearly achieving success. And when Krueger asked about funding and budget questions, here too Hawthorne's answers were positive. Money was being raised. Applications and inquiries, while not streaming in, were a steady trickle. Although Krueger was here as a friend, he would also have to write a report that would eventually find its way to the accreditation board and, as he wrote that report in his mind, he was not displeased with what he saw. Then what bothered him?

Shortly before twelve o'clock the telephone rang, the first call to interrupt them. Hawthorne went to the telephone slowly and Krueger was struck by the hesitancy in his friend's movements. When Hawthorne picked up the receiver and said hello, it was almost with fear. As he listened to whoever was on the other end of the line, his expression changed to dismay, then anger.

"Stop calling me! Who are you? Why are you doing this?" Then Hawthorne caught Krueger's eye and hung up the receiver. He stood beside his desk, rubbing his forehead.

Before Krueger could speak, Hilda knocked quickly, then opened the door wide enough to stick her head through. "Is everything all right? I heard shouting."

"Yes, yes, everything's fine. Did you put that call through to me?"

"I was out of the office. It must have gone through automatically."

"You're sure about that?"

"Of course, of course." She looked at Hawthorne with motherly concern, then withdrew, quietly shutting the door.

"What in the world was that?" asked Krueger.

Hawthorne stood by the desk, half-turned from his friend. "Nothing important."

Krueger hesitated, reluctant to push too deeply. But he had to push. "It frightened you. What was it?"

The expression on Hawthorne's face shifted between anger and relief. "A woman keeps calling me; it's happened five times. She tells me how much she loves me, how much she misses me. She says how she wants me to join her. She says it's Meg, that it's Meg calling me."

"Good grief."

"But it's not Meg, it's not her voice. The woman's called twice in the middle of the night. Every time the phone rings I'm afraid it might be her."

Frank LeBrun leaned back on the pumpkin-colored broken-down couch that, other than his bed, was the only half-comfortable place to sit in his studio apartment above the garage. In his left hand he held a small glass of tequila. He held it toward Jessica Weaver and she clinked her glass against his. They both drank. LeBrun swirled the tequila around in his mouth and smiled.

"We could cut his balls off," he said conversationally, sticking his legs out in front of him and crossing his black cowboy boots. "Just cut them off and shove them in his mouth. I've read books where guys did that."

Jessica coughed as the tequila burned her throat. "Wouldn't he still be alive?"

"Bleeding pretty bad would be my guess. I don't know if it'd kill him or not."

"We wouldn't have a lot of time." Jessica took a little sip, then set her glass on the arm of the couch, where tufts of white stuffing pushed through the frayed fabric. She didn't particularly like tequila but she didn't want to offend LeBrun.

"Hey, he just about ate you up. Fucking babies—you don't fuck babies. You hear what I'm saying? He deserves something with a lot of pain. It'd be a waste to kill him too quick." For a moment LeBrun's face grew still, then he wrinkled his brow and said. "Did I tell you what kind of sheep make virgin wool?"

"Yeah, ugly sheep. I didn't like it."

"Picky, picky, picky."

LeBrun reached for the bottle of tequila and poured them both another shot. It was lunchtime, but he and his cousin Larry alternated lunch duty, and Jessica hadn't felt like going to the dining room. She wanted to sort out some stuff with LeBrun—her business deal, she called it. His studio apartment had windows on three sides, but the shades were drawn and the overhead light made everything look yellow. LeBrun's bed was unmade and dirty dishes were stacked on the table. There was a sweaty smell and a whiff of oranges gone bad.

"And we've got to work out when we do it. I mean, I can't just take off anytime. It wouldn't be responsible. I got friends here. Like, I got talents people want. I can't just let them down." LeBrun chuckled contentedly. "Besides, the money's too good."

"I don't know about killing Tremblay," said Jessica. "I just want to grab Jason and get out of there. If he gets killed and Jason is missing, the cops will be right after me."

"Hey, two thousand bucks, basically you're paying me to ice a guy whether you want an ice job or not. Maybe you could take your brother, then I could come back and finish up. Or maybe I could do Tremblay someplace else. Like a golf course, I never did a guy on a golf course."

"It'll be December," said Jessica. Her eyes were running from the tequila and she wiped them with the back of her hand. "Guys don't play golf in December."

"They do in Florida."

"Yeah, smarty, but this is Exeter, New Hampshire. There'll be snow."

LeBrun dropped his glass, spilling tequila on the sofa. His hand shot out and he grabbed the girl's chin between his thumb and forefinger, squeezing it. "Don't make fun of me, Misty. You just don't know how mean I can get." He held her briefly, then let go.

Jessica rubbed her jaw. "I was only joking . . ."

"Don't talk to me about it."

LeBrun picked up his glass from the cushion and poured himself more tequila. He stared straight ahead at the opposite wall. A thirteen-year-old calendar hung above his bed. It had a photograph of a covered bridge with snow on the roof and birch trees in the foreground and a blue sky. He had hung it there himself. He liked the picture; it looked like the sort of place he wanted to visit. He didn't care about the year. What the fuck did he care what year it was?

"Then I'll just pop him," said LeBrun perfectly calmly, as if he had never gotten angry. "I'll just come back the next day and put a nail in his head. Did I tell you why women have legs?"

Jessica had moved to the other end of the couch. She leaned forward, holding her tequila in both hands. Her glass was a jelly jar decorated with two purple dinosaurs. "Yes, you did. I didn't like that one, either."

"Come on, tell me. What's the answer?"

Jessica didn't look at him. "So they won't leave snail tracks on the linoleum floor."

LeBrun threw himself back and laughed. "Jesus, I love it. Can't you just see it?" His laughter had a grating sound. "I could hear that joke again and again."

Jessica watched him laughing. "I don't think we should kill Tremblay," she said, raising her voice to get LeBrun's attention.

He turned to face her, surprised. "Why the fuck not? Doesn't he deserve it?"

"I want to get away. I want to get Jason and disappear. I don't want cops after me."

LeBrun lit a cigarette. He offered one to Jessica but she shook her head. "Well, fuck, then the job's not worth two grand. Maybe one, sure, but not two. You don't want to pay me that much. You'll be just throwing your money away."

Jessica was uncertain whether he was serious. Sometimes she couldn't tell with LeBrun. It was one of the things that had come to frighten her about him. You wouldn't know whether he was serious or joking until it was too late. "That would be a help. I'd need money to live for a while."

"That doesn't mean there isn't some other kind of payment I want." LeBrun leaned forward and poured her more tequila. She looked up at him quickly and a few drops of the tequila spilled on the couch. "Hey, watch it," he said, "that's valuable stuff."

"What kind of payment?" Jessica told herself this always happened sooner or later.

"How come you wear those baggy sweatshirts all the time? They make you look like a rag doll. You don't look like a girl, you don't look like nothing."

"Maybe I like wearing them. What kind of payment are you talking about?"

"I don't know, maybe it's not worth the trouble." He stubbed his cigarette out in a saucer. "It's another job I'm doing for a guy. One of my buddies." He laughed again.

"What kind of payment?"

"Stand up and turn around."

Jessica set her glass on the floor and stood up. She wasn't sure whether to make a joke of it or to be serious. She turned slowly, trying to imagine all the things she would do to get LeBrun to help her. She wondered who the other person was and what he wanted.

"Jesus, you're a klutz. I can't see a thing. Don't you have a body? Take off the sweatshirt."

Jessica removed the sweatshirt. She wore nothing underneath. It was cool in the room and her white flesh got goose pimples.

"Keep turning, Misty. Hold your arms out. Not much to you, is there?"

Jessica turned with her arms outstretched. She remembered how men had shouted to her in the club—banana body, tiny tits. She began to feel angry but she tried to give no sign of it.

"Turn faster," said LeBrun.

Jessica began to turn faster, keeping her eyes focused on one spot so she wouldn't get dizzy. She could feel her two peroxided braids bouncing on the skin of her shoulders.

"Faster, Misty. Come on. Pretend you're a merry-go-round. Let's go!"

Jessica turned faster, trying not to stumble. She didn't want LeBrun to get mad. The rug seemed to drag at her sneakers. The muscles of her outstretched arms were already sore.

"Okay, stop!" LeBrun clapped his hands once.

Jessica stopped. The room was spinning a little. She bent over with her hands on her knees, trying to catch her breath. She could see her small breasts hanging down. "So you want to fuck me, don't you? Are you going to do it now?"

LeBrun made a grunting noise. "You don't fuck babies, didn't you hear what I said? Wait till you're grown. There's something else I want you to do."

"Like what? You mean I have to fuck somebody else?" She grabbed her sweatshirt from the floor. She felt furious and humiliated.

LeBrun lit another cigarette. "You'll find out soon enough."

At noon, Hawthorne led Krueger to the dining hall. They were late, and by the time they arrived everyone else was seated. Work-study students in white jackets carried large silver trays of food. The dark oak tables, dark wainscoting, and dark beams on the ceiling made the room appear dim. On the walls, the dark portraits of past headmasters seemed devoid of humor or benevolence: men in stiff suits with white hair and, here and there, a beard. The globe lights hanging from the ceiling were on because the day was so gray. Hawthorne took his place at the head table with Krueger on his right. Skander sat across from them. Three students and two adults were seated in the other places. Krueger shook hands and tried to focus on their names. There was Gene Strauss, who ran the admissions office, and Ruth Standish, one of the two mental health counselors; the students were Scott McKinnon and the two girls in charge of the yearbook. People looked at Krueger from the other tables. There was a lot of talking and general noise, and the smell of furniture polish mixed with the aromas of spices, tomato sauce, and fresh bread. Krueger still felt stunned, even horrified, by the phone call that Hawthorne had received less than fifteen minutes before. What sort of insanity would lead a person to pretend to be Hawthorne's dead wife?

Unfolding his napkin, Krueger grew aware that Skander was speaking to him.

"I asked," Skander repeated, "how you found our little school." He held a slice of bread in one hand and a knife in the other, as if he couldn't butter it until he had an answer.

"It seems quite lively."

Skander beamed. "We have Jim to thank for that. He's made

changes that I'd never have dared to make, but then mine was no more than a caretaker government. Keeping the ship afloat was the most I could manage. But I tell my colleagues we haven't sunk yet. There's still hope."

Krueger hardly heard him. He kept remembering the fear on Hawthorne's face as he had listened to the woman on the phone. Now, however, Hawthorne seemed relaxed and was joking with Scott McKinnon. But Krueger felt certain he could see evidence of tension in how straight he was sitting and how he kept glancing around.

"What else has been going on?" Krueger had asked. "What aren't you telling me?"

"Practical jokes, that's all. Nothing important."

Hawthorne had looked away.

Krueger took a slice of bread and buttered it. The waiter began passing down plates of lasagna and green beans from one end of the table.

"You asked about Clifford Evings," said Hawthorne, leaning toward Krueger and lowering his voice. "That's him sitting at the head of that first table on the right."

Evings appeared elderly and cadaverous in a rumpled brown suit. He ate very delicately, cutting his green beans with a knife and fork, and bringing them up carefully to his small, puckered mouth. Next to him was a man in his forties who was also thin and balding, though he had a mustache and small goatee. He wore a bright yellow shirt and a green necktie. A tan jacket hung on the back of his chair.

"That fellow on his left looks enough like him to be his son," said Krueger.

"That's Bobby Newland; he's the other counselor." Hawthorne lowered his voice a little more. "He and Evings are a couple. But he's good in the group discussions and the kids like him."

Krueger was struck by the evident composure he saw around him: everyone civilized and on their best behavior—Skander chatted affably with Ruth Standish, Gene Strauss spoke to the two girls about the yearbook. Outside it had begun to rain again and gray streaks scarred the tall windows. Practical jokes, Hawthorne had said. To pretend to be Hawthorne's dead wife, to urge him to join her—surely that went beyond practical joking. It was raw malice. Krueger thought of what

Hawthorne had endured in San Diego. Just what reserves of strength did he have left?

"I gather you were a student of Jim's," said Ruth Standish, leaning forward over her plate. She was a large woman and wore a dress with a pattern of pink peonies against a bed of leaves, which, to Krueger's mind, made her seem upholstered like a couch.

With some relief he moved into the neutral topic and spoke about his time at Boston University. That had been less than six years ago, but it seemed that a century had gone by. As he talked, other images from that time returned to him. Hawthorne holding forth from the head of a seminar table, raising his voice above the sound of traffic on Storrow Drive. Hawthorne discussing his plans for books and articles. Hawthorne, Meg, and Krueger crowded onto the T, making their way to the North End in search of the perfect lasagna. He and Hawthorne driving through the Berkshires in a snowstorm to Ingram House, where Hawthorne had a surprise birthday party planned for Krueger. Although Krueger knew these times were past, it amazed him they had gone so completely. Krueger was married with children of his own. Meg and Lily were dead. And Hawthorne was working at a place that Krueger in his wildest dreams could never have imagined.

Hawthorne kept glancing around the room. For a moment he would watch Evings, then turn his attention to someone else. It was hardly more than a fluttering of the eye and he did it while discussing the need for new promotional material with Strauss or talking to Skander about putting someone in charge of alumni relations. It made Krueger more attentive and, as he looked around, he was astonished at how many mistrustful looks were aimed in their direction. If the student body seemed content, the faculty and staff were not. Not only were they unhappy with Hawthorne, they seemed fairly glum with one another.

At one point, Ruth Standish leaned across the table and remarked to Hawthorne, "I wish you'd say something to Alice Beech about her behavior in the group discussions. She's far too direct. I doubt we need a nurse there anyway."

"How do you find her 'too direct'?" asked Hawthorne.

"A young woman—I won't mention her name—was saying how she liked to purge herself, that was the word she used, after every meal except breakfast and Alice interrupted to say, 'I find that a completely stupid thing to do.' "

Instead of agreeing, Hawthorne abruptly laughed. Then he stopped himself and took a drink of water. "I'm sorry, I shouldn't have done that, but it sounded just like her."

"So you see my point?"

"I can see it could create a complicated group discussion."

"I don't like it," said Ruth, pursing her lips.

"I'd be patient. The students like her. Ask if anyone thinks she's right or wants to say what's wrong with her point of view. But it would be best to see her comments as a legitimate addition."

Ruth Standish nodded but Krueger could see that she didn't agree; now she was irritated with Hawthorne as well, though she said nothing more.

"So you have a family, Mr. Krueger?" asked Skander as the plates were being cleared. He sat back in his chair and unbuttoned his blue blazer.

Krueger nodded. "We have a son and a daughter."

This information appeared to make Skander very pleased. "Children are such a happy addition, I find. What are their ages?"

"The girl is six and the boy is four. Actually, the boy—" Krueger was about to say that the boy had been named after Hawthorne, but Skander interrupted him.

"My wife and I have a ten-year-old boy. He loves to play the guitar. As a matter of fact, we'd hoped for a large family, five or six youngsters around the table, but that just wasn't to be. Not that we're not delighted with what we've got." He turned to the boy beside him. "Tell me, Scott, do you have siblings?"

"I've got four sisters and they all suck."

Skander erupted in laughter. "Isn't that typical? Nobody ever likes what he has." He then proceeded to ask about Gene Strauss's children.

Krueger found himself wondering if Skander knew that Hawthorne had lost his wife and daughter. But he must have known. Hawthorne seemed to be listening attentively to Strauss's answer about a boy who'd just started as a freshman in Durham and a daughter at home. But again Krueger felt he detected some strain in Hawthorne's face, an inner sadness that he tried to conceal.

After lunch, Hawthorne gave him a tour of the rest of the school.

The rain had decreased to a drizzle that showed no sign of stopping. Krueger's least-favorite period of the year was between the time the clocks were set back and December 21, when the days started to get longer again. Now, though it was only a little after one, it seemed closer to four o'clock. They walked along the driveway, past Krueger's car, to the chapel in Stark Hall. The bricks were streaked with water, which made shadowy designs on the building.

Stark Chapel was a severe horseshoe-shaped room with dark pews raked so that those in the back were at least twenty feet above those in the front, as if the pews had been placed to make certain that all students could be seen at all times. There was an aisle down the middle and aisles on both sides. Three golden chandeliers, each with some twenty candlelike bulbs, hung from the arched wooden ceiling, which was painted white and resembled the hull of a schooner. On both sides of the chapel, stained-glass windows depicted biblical scenes. One showed Abraham holding a knife to Isaac's throat before the angel interrupted the sacrifice. Krueger asked himself what sort of message that had been designed to send to the students of Bishop's Hill.

"The organ's quite good," said Hawthorne. "Rosalind Langdon, the music teacher, plays it every Thursday evening. She doesn't like to call them recitals but they feel like recitals. They're really one of the nicest things that happen here. Mostly she does transcriptions of popular songs—you know, 'Ruby Tuesday' and 'Eleanor Rigby,' but once she did Bach. I try to make it every week, though sometimes I can't. Too many people wanting to see me with a new complaint."

The front of the chapel was very plain, with a wooden altar and wooden cross. On the right side were pews for the choir and on the left was a pulpit flanked by two large oak chairs. Above the pulpit hung a painting of a slender, dour man dressed in black. He had a thin white beard covering little more than his jawbone and colorless lips like twin sticks.

Hawthorne pointed to it. "That painting of Ambrose Stark is one of at least four. He was headmaster for forty years and clearly spent a lot of time getting his portrait painted. Given the prominence of his picture, you'd think he was the object of worship."

"Not what I'd call a fun-loving man." Approaching the painting, Krueger saw that the frame was bolted to the wall. The bolts looked new. "What's this?" he asked.

"I had the paintings of Stark tied down, as it were. A few of the faculty see it as a serious eccentricity on my part, but they had a way of wandering. I saw one staring at me from a window."

"Good Lord, are you serious?"

"After it happened a second time, I had the paintings bolted to the walls, which was probably a mistake. But I was angry. You have no idea how frightening it was."

"I can imagine. Was this another practical joke?"

"Not a very funny one. I assume someone was holding it up for me to see. I couldn't be sure it was a painting at first, but it had to be. Anyway, the Reverend Bennett fits in quite well here—everything serious and repentant."

"You get calls from someone pretending to be Meg and pictures of this old geezer keep popping out at you—what's going on?"

Hawthorne began to walk back up the steps of the aisle. "Most simply, it's someone unhappy with the changes I've been making."

Krueger hurried after him. "And what are you going to do about it?"

"Well, I bolted down the paintings and have taken to prowling around the buildings late at night. I've become so watchful that my eyes ache. Otherwise, I'm trying to wait it out. Maybe I'll catch the person."

Once outside, Hawthorne pointed to the two faculty apartments at the back of Stark Hall. "The Reverend Bennett and her husband live in the biggest one. That fellow you met earlier, Bill Dolittle, wants to move into the one above it."

They walked around the drive in front of Emerson toward the library in Hamilton Hall, directly across from Stark. It began to rain harder.

"What do you mean, someone's unhappy with the changes you're making?" asked Krueger. "Is this one person or several?"

Hawthorne stopped by the steps of the library. Raindrops glistened in his hair. "I told you that Mrs. Hayes resigned. Half the faculty thinks I fired her, just as I fired Chip. Even though a lot's been done, the school's barely hanging together. There's endless gossip, and the rumor that I was writing a book didn't help. One group is certain I'm fucking the language teacher, another thinks I'm messing around with the nurse, though she was purportedly a lesbian before I came. There's probably a third group that believes I'm fucking them both, and a fourth is sure I'm having an affair with someone else entirely. Nearly forty people work here: faculty, staff, housekeepers, kitchen help. Half can't stand me. They're angry that I've taken away their perks, they're angry I've given them more work, they're angry I'm trying to get them to do what they've been hired to do."

Hawthorne paused to wipe the rain off his face with the back of his hand. Splotches of water dotted the front of his white shirt.

"At least a dozen people think I'm getting rich on the place. Never in my life have I been so distrusted. I don't really believe there's a conspiracy against me, but at times it seems that way. As I say, there are people here I trust but then they become the focus of gossip. Beyond that, things turn up missing. A snow blower disappeared. Someone stole one of the new computers. Several telephones have been vandalized. Supplies vanish. Some of it can probably be blamed on students, but the rest, the vicious part, seems too sophisticated for students. Those telephone calls—I can't believe a student would do such a thing."

"Could it be Chip Campbell?"

"I doubt it. I'm sure he hates me, but he's got other things on his mind—his ex-wife is in the process of moving to Seattle and taking their two kids, and he's doing substitute teaching in several schools. Believe me, when this began to get worse, he was the first person I thought of, but he just doesn't have the time. I even drove over to his house, though I didn't go in. I could see him through the picture window with a six-pack of beer, staring at the ceiling. I felt sorry for him."

"Have you called the police?"

"I reported the theft and vandalism for insurance purposes. There's a policeman in Brewster who's come out several times, a sort of local character but very intelligent. He's talked to the night watchman and some students, but he doesn't have the time to mount a full investigation and the business is too small for the state troopers. As for the gossip, I don't know who's behind it. Maybe they're friends of Chip, maybe it's someone else." Instead of going into the library, they kept walking along a path that circled Hamilton Hall.

"Let me show you where I live," said Hawthorne. "I'll give you a cup of coffee."

Krueger could smell the wet wool of his overcoat. He turned up the collar. They hurried toward the terrace that extended out behind

Adams Hall. Beyond the playing fields, only the first trees were visible. Past that, everything was gray.

"The trouble is," said Hawthorne, "whenever I hear something unpleasant is going on, I think there must be even more to it. I hear Ruth Standish criticizing Alice Beech and I wonder, Who put that in her head? When you first meet a person, he or she's mostly on their best behavior, kind, smart, well-meaning. But the longer you know the person, the more appearances get stripped away. You see the person get angry or act selfishly. Is someone saying something because that's what he feels, or because he wants to present you with this particular deception for devious reasons of his own? At times in faculty meetings there'll be so much double-talk I'll think that Irony should be given a classification as a legitimate language. I should ask Kate to teach it: Irony 101, Irony 201. It lets a person talk without being held responsible for what's being said."

By now they had reached Hawthorne's quarters. Krueger was the first to see a white plastic bag hanging from the doorknob of the French windows. In the unrelenting grayness, it seemed the focus of all available light. Then Hawthorne saw it and ran forward.

"Damn it to hell!" Hawthorne took the bag from the knob and unlocked the door.

"What is it?" asked Krueger, catching up to him.

"Someone keeps leaving me gifts of food."

"And?"

"It's rotten. Look at this." Hawthorne opened the bag.

Krueger leaned forward. Even before he saw anything he caught the smell of spoiled milk. Then he saw moldy bread and some kind of moldy meat.

"Don't you get it?" said Hawthorne, pushing open the door. "It's a food offering but it's dead. Just like Meg and Lily are dead. This is the third time it's happened. The first time, there was a note: 'Dead lunch.' Funny, isn't it?" He forced himself to speak more calmly. "I'm sorry. Fritz upset me. Asking everyone about their children. What about me? I think. I had a child too."

He crossed the living room to the kitchen to put the plastic bag in the garbage.

Krueger followed him, removing his cap and hitting it against his leg. Then he took off his wet overcoat. "Actually, I couldn't imagine why Skander brought up the subject." The living room was shabby, with one brand-new oversized brown leather armchair.

Hawthorne busied himself in the kitchen, measuring coffee into a filter. "He's dense, that's all. What's the saying? He'd mention rope in a house where a man had been hung. He's fascinated with what happened at Wyndham. The fire, the reasons for the fire, why Meg and Lily couldn't get out. I listen to him and I want to shout, Shut up! But I don't. He's a good man, he's just tactless. After all, he didn't spend a dozen years studying psychology. He's a mathematician. Do you know that someone put news clippings from San Diego in all the faculty mailboxes? From the *Trib*—about four stories in all. They contained practically my entire history—that I played basketball, that I like jazz, that I read John Le Carré. Then everybody had this skewed idea of what happened—the fire and the hearings afterward. God, I swear I almost went back to California."

Krueger stood in the doorway of the kitchen wiping his face with a paper towel. He wished Hawthorne *had* given up Bishop's Hill and gone someplace else.

Hawthorne talked about the school as he made the coffee. Everything positive that he had mentioned in the morning was being countered that afternoon by a negative. A few minutes later, they were sitting in the living room. Hawthorne insisted that Krueger take the leather chair, which he had bought several weeks before.

"I'm sure people believe I bought it with the money saved from my meatless Thursdays."

"Why don't you call the police about these pranks?"

"And say what, that someone's leaving me bags of rotten food?" Hawthorne stood up and walked to the rain-streaked window. "I'm the prime example of someone ready to embrace every foolish conspiracy theory under the sun. I've even skulked around trying to catch whoever's leaving the food, but the actual running of the school takes every moment. I can't spend half the day hiding behind a tree and watching my back door."

"It's bound to get worse."

"How much worse can it get?"

"I hate to think."

They sat in silence for a while. Neither man drank his coffee.

"Come on," said Hawthorne, "I want to show you where Kate and

I coach swimming. Balboni Natatorium. I don't know who Balboni was. Some gloomy fellow."

They put their coats back on and went outside. Crossing the Common, they walked around to the gymnasium. There was no sign of the forest, just a foggy wall reaching past the playing fields. Hawthorne unlocked a set of green doors leading into a short, dark hall that smelled of chlorine and dampness. There was a door on either side, one labeled "Boys" and the other "Girls."

"I won't show you the locker rooms. They're too depressing unless you like mildew."

They continued down the hall to a door marked "Pool."

"Let me get the lights," said Hawthorne, unlocking the door and going inside. Krueger stood in the doorway. The air was warm and humid and reeked of chlorine. There was a sharp clank as twenty fluorescent panels began to flicker. A few came on directly; most blinked on and off.

Krueger took in the light green cinder-block walls, the sagging bleachers, the cracked tiles. There were no windows. Half the acoustic tiles were missing from the ceiling. The water in the five-lane twenty-five-yard pool was the color and opacity of pea soup, the painted lines at the bottom nearly invisible. Clumsily written in black letters on the far wall were the words "Bishop's Hill, we aim to kill!"

"Nice," said Krueger.

"I'm told there's something wrong with the filtering system or perhaps the chlorine. The phys ed teacher keeps talking about the 'pH.' Don't get me started on the pH."

The fluorescent lights had turned their skin greenish yellow. At the deep end of the pool, two diving boards had been tilted up and leaned vertically against the far wall.

"This is my humble place of work," said Hawthorne, "where Kate and I strive to make the Bishop's Hill swim team a league competitor. Strauss's school brochures claim that we have an Olympic-size pool, though prospective students never actually get to see it. I've often thought we could grow things in here, like mushrooms."

Curlicues of mist rose from the water.

"When I get depressed, I start seeing the pool as a metaphor for Bishop's Hill," Hawthorne continued. "You ask yourself, How could one make it better? The only answer is to tear it down and start over."

Krueger attempted to laugh. "That's rather drastic."

"Well, we won one of our meets this fall and that's a positive sign. Kate's a good coach and I swam in college, so I know what you're supposed to do. But if the school doesn't close, I hope to hire someone to do this so I can go back to simple administration."

"Simple administration," said Krueger.

"It sounds almost restful."

There was a crash as the outside door was flung open, followed by the sound of feet running in the hall. Hawthorne and Krueger turned toward the door. Almost immediately Scott McKinnon slid through it and stumbled to a stop. His wet red hair hung in strings across his forehead.

"Mr. Skander wants you. You better hurry. Someone ripped apart Mr. Evings's office. I didn't get a good look, but they say it's a wreck."

One whole wall of Clifford Evings's small office had been a bookcase. Now the books were on the floor and many were torn—pages ripped out, covers pulled off. Hundreds of loose pages were scattered across the room, or cubby, as Evings liked to call it. One of the wing chairs by the fireplace was tipped over, and Evings was perched on its side with his head in his hands. He wore a green cardigan so threadbare at the elbows that the fabric of his white shirt was visible. The second chair was slashed and its stuffing had been pulled out. The desk lay on its side; the desk lamp was by the door with its glass shade smashed. The frame that had held the painting of Ambrose Stark had been partially pried from the wall. The painting itself was missing.

Bobby Newland stood behind Evings with his hand on Evings's shoulder. "I've called the Brewster police and the state police."

Krueger was again struck by how alike the two men looked: bald and gangling. He imagined that Newland had grown his mustache and goatee just to make a clear distinction between Evings and himself.

"Most assuredly everything will be done," said Skander. He stood by the fireplace and looked around in dismay. "Of course, if the culprit is a student and a juvenile . . . but we'll see, we'll see. Unquestionably an expulsion would be called for. Nothing like this has ever taken place in all my time at Bishop's Hill. And how dreadful for it to happen while a representative of the Department of Education is visiting us."

Krueger remained with Hawthorne by the door, which was shut to prevent the students from peering in. Krueger found the room warm to the point of stifling. Was Skander saying that the vandalism was particularly awful because he, Krueger, was here to witness what had happened? It seemed an odd position. When Hawthorne told him that the empty frame had held the portrait of Ambrose Stark, Krueger found himself thinking that Stark had broken loose, as if the former headmaster himself had caused the wreckage.

"When did this happen?" asked Hawthorne.

"We don't know," said Bobby. "Possibly during lunch. Clifford and I came back about one-thirty and found it like this."

"Of course it happened during lunch," said Skander. "We'll have to make a list of all the people who weren't there. That would be a good start."

Krueger couldn't help staring at Skander's necktie and its message, "What, me worry?" "And nobody saw anything?" he asked.

"Believe me," said Bobby, "if I knew who did it, that person would be here *right* this instant."

"Do you have any ideas, Clifford?" asked Hawthorne gently.

Evings shook his head but neither spoke nor removed his hands from his face.

"It *had* to be students," said Bobby. "They've been making fun of Clifford all fall. Those damn discussion groups, talking about gayness and diversity and whatnot. Nobody ever cared that Clifford was gay until it became a matter of discussion."

"Of course we don't know for certain that students did this," said Skander. "It could be an adult. Try to imagine a parent with a grudge against the school, someone who felt his child had been unduly punished." He raised an index finger and looked at it thoughtfully.

"And I suppose you're going to say that someone might have just happened to stroll by the school—some stranger who came in here and just on a *whim*—"

"Stop it, Bobby," said Evings quietly.

"I think I'll wait for the police outside," said Skander. "And if I were you, Robert, I'd watch my tongue. We all understand that you're angry, but that's no reason to be unpleasant."

Skander left. Krueger briefly got a glimpse of several students standing in the hall.

Hawthorne knelt down beside Evings, putting a hand on Evings's knee. "I'm terribly sorry this happened, Clifford. We'll find out who did it and make sure it doesn't happen again."

Evings shook his head but didn't speak.

"There are many people," said Bobby somewhat primly, "who don't believe you've done this school any good at all."

Evings raised his head and put a finger to his lips. "Hush, Bobby, let's not talk about it. You know as well as I do that I haven't done all I could."

"Given the situation," said Bobby, "how could you?" He kicked at some papers on the floor. "A disaster waiting to happen, that's Bishop's Hill in a nutshell."

Krueger began to feel annoyed but kept his thoughts to himself. Newland and Evings had good reason to be upset and this wasn't the time to engage in a discussion about Hawthorne's merits. Yet what had happened was horrible. All day Krueger had felt that the school was about to burst apart, as if the display of decorum were the thinnest of veneers covering a mass of hostility, resentment, and fear.

"Is this a practical joke too?" he asked Hawthorne.

There was a knocking on the door.

It was Skander with a policeman from Brewster, a heavyset middle-aged man with a red face. When he saw the state of the office, he took off his cap and massaged his brow. "My, my, hasn't someone been making a mess." He introduced himself as Chief Moulton.

Hawthorne told him what had happened, though it was clear that Skander had already passed on the basic facts. Before he finished, a state police sergeant arrived from the barracks in Plymouth, so Hawthorne had to begin all over again. Not that there was a lot to tell. The incident had apparently happened during lunch and no one had seen anything. Krueger kept thinking of the missing painting and Stark's harsh expression. Seven men were now in the office and whenever Krueger moved he either stepped on something or bumped into someone. He began to make his way toward the door. He had a two-hour drive ahead of him and felt he should leave the police to their work.

Hawthorne walked Krueger to the entrance of Emerson Hall. Classes were in session and the corridors were empty. Outside it had resumed raining hard. Krueger buttoned up his coat and drew on his gloves.

"Don't worry," Hawthorne kept saying, "I'll be perfectly fine."

"Do you really think students wrecked the office?"

"I don't know."

Krueger wanted to urge Hawthorne to leave Bishop's Hill, to quit his job and walk away. He felt dismayed by his own inadequacy, that he couldn't take Hawthorne's arm and say how worried he was. He wanted to tell his friend that he was afraid for him, but he lacked the courage. Still, there was more he wanted to learn about the school and he believed he could do it best from his office in Concord. He took Hawthorne's hand and his eyes scanned his friend's face.

"I'll be in touch," he said.

Away from home Detective Leo Flynn didn't have a natural smile, no matter how much he tried. He needed to be in his own chair in his own living room—preferably with Junie, to whom he had been married for forty-one years, or with one of the kids—before he could let himself go. Even when one of his colleagues in the homicide unit told a joke he liked, Flynn's smile had a watchful, self-observed quality. Now, as he directed his smile at Jerry Sweeney, a bush-league miscreant with two larceny convictions and a half-dozen years in Walpole, Flynn could see Sweeney fight off a desire to hurry from the room.

"Of course," said Leo Flynn, widening his smile, "we could discuss this downtown."

They were sitting in Sweeney's small apartment in Dorchester. It was Monday afternoon, November 9, and Flynn had happened upon Sweeney after several weeks of hanging around sleazy bars in Revere, Dorchester, and South Boston looking for friends of Sal Procopio. Sweeney was a freckled, florid Irishman of about forty, already thin on top, with hands like slabs of meat. From the kitchen came a banging and clattering, as if Sweeney's wife were engaged in throwing pots and pans on the floor.

"I don't want to get anybody in trouble," said Sweeney virtuously.

"You mean you don't want to get yourself in trouble."

Jerry Sweeney cradled his jaw with a fleshy hand. "That too."

Leo Flynn leaned back on the couch, stuck out his legs, and tried to look inoffensive. "What interests me is Sal Procopio's murder and this guy Frank. The larceny and general thievery, that's not my department."

"Sal and Frank," said Sweeney, lowering his voice and taking a quick glance toward the kitchen, "they'd been knocking off some liquor stores."

"I already know that. Where can I find Frank?"

"He left town."

"I know that as well. Where'd he go?"

"No place around here. Someplace out of state. He said he was going back to school, he made a joke about it."

"Yeah? And what was he planning to study?"

Sweeney looked at Flynn with surprise. "Hey, that's just what I asked him."

"And?"

"He made it clear he was going to do a number, at least that's what I took him to be saying. But it'd be different from the others. He said it'd be something new for him. Like that was what he was going to school to learn."

"What'd he mean by that?"

"Beats me. I told you, he gave me the willies. He'd get mad and you couldn't figure how it happened. Like one moment he'd be laughing and the next he'd be all over you."

"So what do you *think* he might have meant?"

"I figured he'd been hired to ice someone but it was going to be different from his other jobs. Jesus, what do you expect me to say? Just different, that's all. Maybe he'd iced a bunch a short people and now he was going to do a tall guy."

Leo Flynn refitted his uncomfortable smile onto his thin lips. "That's a joke, right?"

"I'm just telling you I don't know."

Flynn watched Sweeney's round face, waiting to see if anything twitched. Sweeney was the fourth of Procopio's friends that Flynn had managed to find. Of the others, only one had known about Frank and the liquor stores—a discovery that had led the friend, a cardplayer named Exley, to cut all connection with Procopio. But Exley had claimed to know nothing about Frank except that he was a Canuck. Flynn thought that if he had been blessed with friends like these, he'd prefer to buy a dog, which, if things turned sour, could only bite him.

"Who hired him?"

"No one around here. Least that was my impression."

"Was it somebody from Portsmouth?" Flynn had learned that Frank LeBlanc or LeBon, whatever his name was, had been working as a short-order cook in Portsmouth prior to coming to Boston and, if all went well, Flynn meant to drive up there in a week or so.

"If it was, he didn't share it with me." Sweeney widened his eyes in mock innocence.

"We could still go downtown," said Flynn conversationally. "But you know how it is, all that red tape. And you still on parole—no telling when you'd get home."

A drop of perspiration appeared on Jerry Sweeney's puffy brow and Flynn felt gratified to see it. "I tell you, I got no idea," Sweeny insisted. "You didn't ask him questions. If he said something, then you nodded and smiled and let it go. He was touchy."

"Murderous."

"Yeah, that too." Sweeney wiped his face with the back of his hand.

"How well'd you know him?"

"I'd see him in the bar with Sal. Even Sal was scared of him."

"You're lying to me again."

Another drop of sweat seemed to emerge from nowhere. "Okay, okay, he wanted me to drive for him. I didn't like it. I said I was busy. He started to get pissed off and I told him about Sal. That Sal was a good bet."

"So you introduced them and now Sal's dead."

"Yeah, well, at least it's not me. But before that I'd see him in the bar. We shot pool a few times. Like we'd be partners. He bet the dogs; he even won some."

"And he talked about doing a number now and then."

"Not directly, but, yeah, it'd come up."

"You never thought of giving us a call? An anonymous tip?"

"Hey," said Sweeney, looking offended, "I got my reputation to consider."

Flynn drew an old Kleenex from the side pocket of his jacket and blew his nose. The next time Sweeney was brought in for questioning, Flynn decided, he'd have a friendly word with the assistant prosecutor, maybe get Sweeney some extra time in Walpole. "So, tell me, what's so special about this number that Frank's planning to do?"

"Different, that's all. Frank didn't confide in me. But it worried him. I don't mean it scared him, I don't think anything scared him. It was just something he had trouble making jokes about. And it was connected to the school, like the thing that worried him was something he had to get over. You know, like a defect of character."

Scott McKinnon had piled his textbooks on his desk and was using them as a pillow, but he was listening. He made sure of that because every so often Dr. Hawthorne would ask him a question to check and he always got the answer right. If Scott was asked why he didn't sit up like the other students, he'd say he didn't feel like it or he was tired or it wasn't any of your business. But he liked Dr. Hawthorne and he saw himself as the headmaster's special pet and so he did things like putting his head down on his desk just to show he could get away with it. Dr. Hawthorne treated him different. Like the two times they'd gone for a drive and Hawthorne had let him smoke. Scott felt good about that and he'd talked to him about the school and what the kids were like, although, of course, most of them were pretty dumb. It wasn't like being a snitch. He was Dr. Hawthorne's agent.

There were eleven kids seated in a semicircle and Dr. Hawthorne was up at the blackboard, drawing several lines indicating the northern boundary of the Roman Empire in what was now Austria, Hungary, and Romania. He had gotten chalk on his jacket but he didn't seem to care. He was talking about the Second Marcomannic War between AD 169 and 175, when Marcus Aurelius and his legions fought the German tribes—the Iazyges, the Marcomanni, the Quadi, the Sarmatians—defeating them and pushing them north into the Carpathian Mountains. For these victories a triumphal column was raised to Marcus Aurelius that still stood in Rome's Piazza Colonna.

It was last period on Monday and getting dark. All afternoon Scott had been thinking about Mr. Evings's office being wrecked. While not exactly exciting, it was more interesting than most of the stuff at Bishop's Hill. Scott had caught a glimpse of the room before he got shooed away: a great pile of busted books. And Scott had seen the police arrive in two different cars. A little later Dr. Hawthorne had taken the cops into his office. Scott felt frustrated because he knew nothing about who might have done it, nor did he know who might be suspected. Usually he knew stuff, but today he hadn't heard anything and nobody looked guilty. Scott looked forward to prowling around the dorms after dinner to see if he could learn anything. He was sure some kids had done it, or almost sure. On the other hand, if kids weren't to blame, then Scott couldn't figure it out, unless it was evil spirits. He liked the idea of evil spirits. Or maybe it had been gay bashers from off campus. Scott had never talked to Mr. Evings, though he knew Mr. Newland. When Scott had entered seventh grade some kids had told him to watch out for Evings, that he would try to grab your pecker, but Scott didn't know if that was true or just a story. Anyway, he hadn't tried to find out.

As for history, Scott enjoyed the battles best and Mr. Campbell had made them exciting. The Greek and Persian wars had been absolutely great. Dr. Hawthorne wasn't as good at battles as Mr. Campbell. And Scott didn't really get stuff like Stoicism. "Everything that happens, happens justly." What kind of sense did that make? "For a thrown stone there is no more evil in falling than there is good in rising." Not only did Scott not understand it, he didn't care about the riddle it posed except to stay friendly with Dr. Hawthorne. "The business of the healthy eye is to see everything that is visible." Now, that made sense, because Scott prided himself on trying to see everything there was to be seen. Secret agents had to be on the alert.

Dr. Hawthorne spoke of Marcus Aurelius in his tent by the River Gran writing his meditations at night while during the day he and his legions fought the German tribesmen, who, Marcus believed, would someday break through the frontier and conquer Rome. All Marcus was doing was giving his people a respite, a breathing space before they were beaten. When the class had studied the Celts, Scott had learned that they'd attacked the Romans naked, just ripping off their clothes and jumping up and down and shouting. He couldn't imagine it, though in his history book there was a picture of the *Dying Gaul* and he was pretty naked as well. Scott had asked Dr. Hawthorne whether the German tribesman had fought naked. "Get your mind outta the gutter," Jimmy Lucas had told him.

" 'As a spider is proud of catching a fly, so is one man of trapping a hare, or another of netting a herring, or a third of capturing boars or bears or Sarmatians. If you investigate the question of principles, are these anything but thieves one and all?' "

Dr. Hawthorne explained that the Sarmatians were one of the tribes along the Danube that Marcus was fighting. Then he asked what

Marcus meant by saying that the spider capturing the fly was no better than a thief. What was he saying about human behavior? Scott had no idea, so he kept his head down. He wanted Dr. Hawthorne to get past Marcus Aurelius and talk about his son Commodus, who was a real butcher and once killed a hundred tigers with a hundred arrows. Surely that was more interesting. From the corner of his eye he watched Dr. Hawthorne walk back and forth at the front of the room.

"Maybe he likes flies better than spiders," said Jimmy Lucas.

"All right, we'll try another one," said Dr. Hawthorne, walking over toward Scott.

" 'When men are inhuman, take care not to feel toward them as they do toward other humans.' Can anyone tell me what that means?" Nobody answered. Dr. Hawthorne tapped Scott on the shoulder and he snorted, pretending to be asleep. "All right, Scott, we'll start with you. And don't mumble into your armpit, if you please."

6

Kate Sandler and Jim Hawthorne stood in the bell tower on the roof of Emerson Hall, looking out across the playing fields to the north. It was the Thursday afternoon following Krueger's visit and Kate had a free period after lunch. The sky had cleared in the night, but a few clouds still lay far to the east over the mountains, where the treetops were dusted with snow. The bark of the leafless birches gleamed in the sunlight. The only greens were the pines scattered on the hillside. In the distance a red-tailed hawk rode the air currents in wide circles above the trees.

Kate and Hawthorne had just made the climb up the circular staircase that rose from the building's fourth-floor attic. As they leaned their elbows on the wall, their breath made cottony shapes in the cold air. Both wore coats. The supports holding the roof formed an open square window, actually four joined windows facing in four directions. A dozen feet below was the wooden scaffolding where workmen were repairing the slate on the dormers, though no workmen had been seen for several days. Two fat gray pigeons paraded across the weathered lumber and cooed impatiently. All around was a vastness—to the north and east spread the national forest, and more forest lay to the west; to the south lay the tree-lined road to Brewster, and farther on—just a smoky blur on the horizon—was the small city of Plymouth.

Hawthorne turned to take in the entire panorama, stepping around the bell, which hung from a double chain. From the brace supporting the bell, a rope descended through a hole in the floor. "Incredible," he said. Sunlight glittered on the lenses of his glasses.

"Too bad you weren't up here during the height of color." said Kate. "I felt like a smudge on a painter's palette." She wore a blue scarf with her red mackinaw and her black hair was gathered in a ponytail.

A white laundry truck with red lettering made its way up the driveway to the school. Dead leaves blew across the lawns. Three miniature students were throwing a football over by the gymnasium. Then, from far in the distance, Hawthorne began to make out the faint barking of dogs—a high chatter off to the west. They both looked.

"They're over there in the woods," said Kate, pointing. At first they saw only the empty playing fields and distant trees.

The barking got closer, a blended yapping that gradually began to separate itself into individual sounds, a baying and shrill yelps. The barking had a breathlessness, almost a hysteria. Then Kate stretched out an arm. "Look there."

A deer burst from the trees on the western side of the playing fields. Trailing after it were eight dogs—so small from this distance that it was impossible to identify their breed or even color. One dog after another kept leaping at the deer, jumping at its belly. The deer would swerve and the dog fall back. If there was blood, they were too far away to see it.

Neither Hawthorne nor Kate said anything. The deer and the dogs raced along the edge of the field, weaving between the sunlight and shadow, becoming bright, then dark again. Away from the trees, the deer was able to draw ahead, its shape becoming increasingly horizontal as it picked up speed. The dogs were falling back. Hawthorne could almost see their pink tongues lolling from the sides of their mouths. Then the deer plunged again into the trees with the dogs in pursuit. In a moment it was as if they had never been. The distant barking grew fainter.

"They catch the deer in the trees," said Kate matter-of-factly.

"Does it ever get away?"

"Very rarely. At least that's what George says. He was always eager to have me go hunting with him. Anyway, the dogs can keep it up longer. They try to rip the deer's stomach and get its intestines. Sometimes twenty or thirty feet will be dragging behind the deer. Eventually it collapses. Often the dogs eat the intestines even before they kill the deer."

"They show no mercy?" asked Hawthorne, half seriously.

Kate smiled. "It doesn't exist in that world."

Hawthorne continued to look at the spot where the deer and the dogs had disappeared into the trees. "Destructivity is the result of an unlived life," he said, mostly to himself.

"What's that?"

"It's a quote from Erich Fromm. 'Destructivity is the result of an unlived life.' It's applicable to human beings but not to dogs."

"What does he mean by 'unlived'?"

Hawthorne leaned back against the wall, facing south, as if he felt more comfortable looking in that direction. "Let's say someone has experienced a violent trauma or betrayal: a child has been raped by a parent or has witnessed the destruction of someone he loves or has been so traumatized by the possibility of beatings and punishments that he's afraid to act. If the trauma is great enough, that person's life may become frozen, emotionally frozen, even though he still gets up in the morning, is busy all day, and goes to bed at night. But there's this empty space that begins to fill with rage, rage toward everyone— the perpetrator, the people in the world who haven't suffered, even toward himself. Then he just wants to destroy, hurt others the way he was hurt. The rape victim becomes a person who rapes, the victim becomes a brutalizer."

"Do all rape victims become rapists?"

"Of course not, but in many cases it happens, especially if the victim's young enough. It's far more common with boys than girls. I know of a serial killer who killed at least fifteen young women. He was young, handsome, and intelligent. His mother had been a high-class specialty prostitute catering to sadists and masochists. Some of her clients paid extra to have her son witness the beatings and abuse that she gave and sometimes received. This didn't turn the boy into a killer of young women, but it was an influence, a bias, that pushed him in that direction. The awfulness in his past created this vacancy, an unlived life, a space where nothing could exist except violence."

"Do you think that might have been the reason for Chip's violence?" Kate took off her blue scarf, folded it, and put it in the pocket of her mackinaw.

"I really know nothing about him. There are many reasons for violence. This is just something that sometimes happen. We'd see it in treatment centers—the child who'd suffered something awful. Even in the best recovery there'd be a fear that everything would fall apart and they'd become victims again. And their final loyalty was to themselves. They couldn't be forced. They preferred to wreck everything, preferred self-destruction to surrender."

Kate and Hawthorne stood side by side, leaning against the wall of the bell tower. "Was this true of the boy who started the fire?" asked Kate.

"Stanley Carpasso? I'm not sure. I was too close to him and I've probably lost all objectivity. But he'd been sexually abused repeatedly—some boyfriend of his mother's. And such a trauma could have created that frozen space. Stanley actually saw his way out of it. I was to be his savior. He could be very loving, very affectionate, stopping by my office to ask if there was anything he could do for me. Sometimes he brought me flowers. Then he began to save food at mealtimes—cookies and fruit and cake, a drumstick. He'd wrap it up and leave it for me in a bag hanging on my doorknob. It was both gruesome and touching."

"I think they mentioned that in one of those articles."

"He got a lot of attention—boy victim, boy aggressor. One article tried to show him as evil and another as innocent. It seemed impossible to believe that he was neither, that he was simply a damaged human being. As I told you, he wanted me to adopt him. The only trouble was that I already had a family."

"So he started the fire . . ." Kate buried her hands in her coat pockets.

"It was more cunning than that." Far to the south a plume of smoke rose up from the trees. The smoke rose straight upward, then the wind caught it and blew it eastward. At that moment Hawthorne realized he was going to tell Kate more of the story, part of what he had left out during their walk earlier in the woods.

"Our apartment at Wyndham was on the second floor, above the offices," he began. "It had a heavy oak door. Presumably so nobody could easily break through it. And there were grates on the windows. I had meant to take them off but several people who'd been at Wyndham longer than I had urged me to keep them. Kids used to break in before the grates went up. The apartment was a temptation. Certainly other windows had grates as well. So I kept the grates and the keys were in my office.

"One day I came back to the apartment after work and found these heavy rings screwed to the doorjamb. I asked Meg about them but she had been out as well and knew nothing. I called a few people but no one could tell me anything. And of course it was the end of the day and people were scattered. I assumed the rings were there for a good reason. It was something I meant to find out about the next morning. I mean, it didn't seem terribly important at the time. Lily was asking me to help her with her homework. I remember she had just begun to study fractions . . ."

Hawthorne paused. Beneath them half a dozen students ran down the steps of the library and along the driveway toward Emerson Hall, their excited voices drifting upward. Hawthorne leaned back against the wall, unbuttoning the top of his blue overcoat.

"That evening," he continued, "I had to meet with a psychologist who had flown in from Boston to give a lecture at UCSD—a young woman I had known before moving to San Diego. She'd been a student in several of my graduate classes at BU. We were going to have dinner. Meg had meant to come, but she said she was getting a sore throat and decided to stay home. We went to a restaurant downtown run by Jim Croce's widow that has a jazz bar. We had dinner and talked about Boston. She told me about her lecture, which I hadn't been able to attend, then about nine o'clock we decided to stay for the first set."

Hawthorne paused. In his many retellings he had always left out the part about Claire, so it was almost as if it had never taken place. He asked himself if he could forget it completely, erase that hour and the guilt that stayed with him—Claire's face, her short dark hair, the scooped blue silk blouse showing the deep shadow between her breasts and the red stone hanging from a silver chain around her neck: all of it had become a fixed part of his interior landscape.

"That's what I remember of this dinner," continued Hawthorne, "I stayed an extra twenty minutes to hear this jazz quartet playing old standards. There was a young woman on the clarinet who was very good. When I got back to Wyndham, the main building was already burning. They were getting the kids out but the fire department hadn't arrived. I didn't see Meg or Lily. There was tremendous confusion.

"I ran inside and up the stairs. There was smoke in the second-floor hall but no fire. I reached our door. There was a chain across it. Someone had put a thick chain through the two rings and locked it with a padlock. The door couldn't be opened. Meg and Lily were on the other side. Meg kept throwing herself against the door. There was a gap of about four inches and I could see part of her face. We could talk. I was afraid, but it seemed obvious they could still get out. Already we could hear the sirens of the fire trucks. Meg and I were able to clasp our hands through the narrow space. Lily kept asking me to open the door. I stroked her hair with one hand and held Meg's hand with the other. As I say, the grates on the windows were locked and the keys were in my desk. Meg had opened the windows but couldn't do anything about the grates.

"Downstairs, in the administration office, was a fire ax set into the wall in a little locked cabinet. I'd passed it a thousand times. Meg urged me to get it and to get the keys for the grates. I don't know, I stayed too long holding her hand. But maybe it was only a minute. Not even that. Maybe it was ten seconds, no more. Then I ran down the hall. The smoke was thicker. I could hear sirens and men shouting. When I got to the office, the cabinet was empty. The glass was broken and the ax was gone. It was never determined whether Carpasso had taken it or if someone else had.

"My own office was on the other side of the administration office. I ran to my desk to get the keys to the grates. By now the electricity had gone out and the only light came from the window—emergency lights and the lights of the fire trucks. And it was smoky. I couldn't find the keys right away. I ripped out the drawer and overturned it on the top of the desk. You know the junk you can accumulate—paper clips, pencils. All this took time. But the keys were there. I grabbed them and ran back to the stairs. The emergency lights up by the ceiling had come on but the smoke was worse. I ran back down the hall toward our door. If I could get the keys to Meg, she could open one of the grates and jump. What I didn't know was that the fire was already inside the apartment.

"By now the hall ceiling was on fire and I could see flames through

177

the smoke. I could hear Meg calling my name but it seemed very far away over all the noise. And I could hear Lily. Then the ceiling began to collapse, great segments of flaming acoustic tile were falling around me and the ceiling itself was sagging. I tried to keep running, jumping over stuff. Then I don't know. Something hit me. I tried to keep moving. I could hear people shouting behind me as well. I knew I had to get her the keys. It was difficult to breathe. I don't even remember being burned. I just remember Meg's voice, how her calling changed to screaming. I only wanted to reach her, to grasp her hand. I don't know if I thought we would all die. I'm sure I still thought I'd be successful. Then that was all. That's all I remember. When I woke in the hospital and found they were dead, I felt I had been the most awful of traitors."

Hawthorne stopped and looked around, almost surprised to find himself at Bishop's Hill. Kate touched his shoulder, letting her hand rest there briefly before removing it. Hawthorne looked out across the front lawns toward the glistening water of the Baker River and beyond. He tried to focus on something but there was only the distance, the vastness. Again, he had left out part of the story.

"For weeks I could hear Meg calling my name. Other people spoke to me, of course, but her voice was loudest. And Lily too, I heard her voice. If I hadn't waited so long. If I hadn't stood holding her hand. If I hadn't stayed to hear that jazz group. They played 'Satin Doll,' an Ellington-Strayhorn tune. Do you know it? It's very sweet, and the woman on the clarinet played it beautifully. When I hear the song now, I feel horror. I'm amazed by its ugliness. After a while Meg's and Lily's voices became softer and my arm began to heal. I was almost angry that it was healing. I wanted it to stay raw and painful. But all that went away. At times I still hear their voices. I don't mean that I remember them, I actually hear them. I hallucinate them. If I'm very tired or distraught or very sad. Or if something frightens me. But it's softer, just a whisper. They were the only ones killed in the fire, which was Carpasso's intention: to lock them up as he had been locked up. Most of the school was saved and I gather it's been rebuilt or they're working on it. I didn't want to see it again."

Hawthorne stretched out and touched the cold metal of the bell, let his hand slide down it to the rope. He had a sudden desire to ring it, swing it with all his strength so the clapper banged and banged. He was surprised by the violence of his emotion. Kate stepped away to the other side of the tower. She reached back and freed her hair from its ponytail, then shook her hair loose. From far away came the sound of a chain saw.

"Part of me was sorry that the whole place didn't burn to the ground."

"Is that why you didn't want to work at a similar sort of place?" said Kate after a moment.

Tapping the bell with one knuckle, Hawthorne listened to its faint ringing. It was nearly as inaudible as the voices of Meg and Lily had become—nearly inaudible but not yet silent. Then he hit the bell harder, hurting his knuckle. Kate looked up at the sound.

"I failed at Wyndham Hill. I should have paid more attention to Carpasso, and maybe it was wrong to give the kids so much freedom, maybe they weren't ready for it. I don't know anymore. It's as if I no longer have any credibility with myself. It's as if I let my abstraction of the place—all my ideas and theories—take precedence over the physical reality. I came here to get back to that physical reality. Beyond that, there's trouble in the whole field. Treatment centers are hugely expensive. Kids needing serious psychiatric care can be charged a thousand dollars a day—most of which comes from insurance companies, though they're increasingly reluctant to cough up the money. More and more centers are being run privately, governed by the bottom line and the stockholders. For-profits, they're called, as opposed to non-profits. Some do good work, but a lot of the places exist only to milk the insurance companies. They talk about milieu therapy so everything that happens to the patient can be considered treatment and given a price. People do jobs they aren't trained to do, and it's far more profitable to hire two half-time or four quarter-time employees than one full-time. Dog groomers make more than child-care workers in this country. Emotionally disturbed children, retarded children, psychotic children—it's a big business. There's less public money and the funds available can only be used on the treatment itself. In Massachusetts, for instance, there's no way to tell if a kid was helped or hurt by the treatment centers, no way to know what he's doing a year after he's left, five, ten, twenty years after. That's considered research, and there's no money for research. A large percentage end up in prison, but there's no money to confirm the connection.

"I could get a job in a for-profit tomorrow and make four times what I'm making here. But it would mean betraying everything I believe in, at least everything I *thought* I believed in."

"You sound angry."

"I *was* angry. Maybe I'm still angry."

"Why'd you come to Bishop's Hill?"

"At best, I hoped I could do some good. At worst, I could hide and lick my wounds. It didn't occur to me that I'd become public enemy number one."

They continued to talk about the school: faculty who were difficult to work with, students who were troublesome. They walked from one side of the bell tower to the other, looking out across the playing fields or the Common or the front lawns. They could see sections of the Baker River, a glimmer of silver through the leafless trees. Now and then a car drove up to the school or another drove away. They saw students on their way to the gym or coming back. Several of the grounds crew were replacing a window in one of the dormitory cottages. Kate and Hawthorne were aware of the hundred and seventy or so students, teachers, and staff pursuing their various occupations far below, but they were separated from that. Perhaps they could have been seen from the ground or another building had someone looked carefully: one figure in a blue overcoat, one figure in a red mackinaw. They were careful not to get too close or touch each other.

Kate spoke about her ongoing difficulties with her ex-husband. George had called Hawthorne twice and accused him of sleeping with Kate. The second time he had been drunk and could hardly speak. Hawthorne had had a difficult day and was brusque. "One, I'm not having sex with her," he said. "Two, if I did it'd be none of your business." And the next morning, he asked Hamilton Burke to call George and remind him that his actions could have legal consequences. George hadn't called again. As for who had sent George the anonymous note, that remained one of Bishop's Hill's little mysteries.

They talked about Evings and speculated about who had wrecked his office. Chief Moulton from Brewster had returned to ask more questions but Hawthorne had no idea whether he had learned anything. Hawthorne said nothing about the phone calls, the bags of rotten food hung from his doorknob, the reappearing image of Ambrose Stark. He wasn't sure why he didn't tell Kate, but it seemed part of his sense of isolation. He had even thought it was meant to happen, that these calls and bags of food and practical jokes were an aspect of his punishment. He linked them to his failure with Stanley Carpasso and Wyndham School. They were a result of the time he had spent with Claire in Croce's and after. Sometimes he even wished these taunts would get worse, like a noise turned higher and higher till it became a scream, just so he would know how much he could take. And sometimes he wished he could strip away his emotional self, that part that still heard the voices of Meg and Lily, the part that was human.

Still, after one of the phone calls from the woman calling herself Meg, Hawthorne had dialed *69. Once he had the number, he called his caller back. The phone had rung and rung. Then a man answered, a postman in West Brewster—the phone was a public telephone outside the Brewster post office. And three times Hawthorne had hidden within sight of his door leading out to the terrace just to see if he could catch someone leaving a bag of food. He had waited about ten minutes and each time had felt like a fool.

These events were taking a toll. Hawthorne's nerves were suffering; he had become jumpy—phobic, was how he described it to himself. And he knew that Kevin Krueger had looked at him with concern. Staring out over the fields, Hawthorne thought of Krueger's suggestion that these pranks were bound to get worse. But how bad could they get, and wouldn't they stop after people saw that the school was actually improving?

After Hawthorne and Kate had been up in the bell tower for nearly an hour, he opened the trap door and they descended the spiral staircase to the fourth-floor attic, going around and around in the dim light that filtered through louvers on the tower windows. At the bottom was the door separating the staircase from the attic. It had two dead-bolt locks so students couldn't go into the tower and "fool around," as Skander said. Hawthorne had locked one of the bolts behind them before going up into the tower, he was certain of it, but now as he inserted the key he found the door was open.

"What's wrong?" asked Kate.

"I thought I had locked this. I must have been mistaken."

"Who has keys?"

"I thought I had the only set. Maybe there are others in the office."

They ducked through the low door. Hawthorne locked it and they descended to the third floor, where they stood for a moment at the low wall of the rotunda, looking down. Hawthorne wondered again about the unlocked door and what it might mean. A student hurried across the open space with a backpack slung over his shoulder, carefully stepping around the blue-and-gold crest with the letters *B* and *H*. Then the bell rang, signaling the end of fifth period. Doors began opening and voices rose toward them. Hawthorne and Kate continued down to the first floor to resume the business of their day.

When Hawthorne got back to his office he found Hilda Skander standing at the door waiting for him. She put a finger to her lips and pointed toward his inner office. "Reverend Bennett would like a word with you," she said. "I told her to go in. I hope you don't mind." Hilda wore a denim skirt and a green sweater. The air around her reeked of peppermint.

"Of course not." Hawthorne took off his overcoat, which Hilda hung in the closet.

"She seems very businesslike," said Hilda. "You know, on a mission."

Entering his office, Hawthorne found the chaplain studying the photograph of Meg and Lily posed in front of the Christmas tree.

"They were very pretty," she said somewhat stiffly, as if annoyed to be caught snooping. She put the photograph back on the desk.

"Yes," said Hawthorne, "they were." He couldn't think of more to say beyond that. "You have something you want to talk to me about?"

The chaplain sat down in the chair by the desk. She wore a gray blouse with a clerical collar and a voluminous skirt of a darker gray. She took off her rimless glasses and polished them on a handkerchief as Hawthorne sat down at his desk.

"It's this business about Clifford. The students are quite worked up about it. And that policeman from Brewster has been asking questions. I can't help but think that Clifford brought this on himself." She tucked her handkerchief back in her breast pocket, then fussed with it for a moment to make sure that the point stuck up in the exact center.

"In what way?" asked Hawthorne, watching her straighten her handkerchief.

The chaplain gave him a forced smile. She spoke slowly, as if she felt that Hawthorne would otherwise have difficulty understanding. "Well, certainly he's unpopular and there have been stories in the past about him being involved with students, though quite a few years ago. True or not, these get handed on. And you have to admit that he's ineffectual: from what I hear he regularly falls asleep in your group therapy sessions. Then there's his homosexuality."

"What about his homosexuality?" Hawthorne had had few dealings with the chaplain. Her wish to control whatever came within her circle of influence, her air of disapproval—Hawthorne felt his task would be easier if he stayed out of her path. He knew she worked hard and was popular with some students. She taught a class in biblical history and another in comparative religion. And she led a weekly Bible study group that was attended not only by students but also by a few faculty and staff.

The chaplain touched her hair. Its wispy gray strands reminded Hawthorne of smoke and he observed the pinkness of her scalp beneath it. She wore no makeup and her face had a claylike pallor. On her left wrist was a gold Omega watch.

"It gets in the way of his effectiveness. Of course, Clifford makes no secret of being gay. That seems to be the current fashion. But unfortunately the students think of him as a homosexual before they think of him as a psychologist. And his manner is so . . . unattractive. Believe me, you've done very well at Bishop's Hill, but now we have prospective students visiting with their parents. And this business of his office being vandalized is simply the last straw. Who knows what he did to cause some student to react so violently? I think it would be wise if you did for him what you did for Mrs. Hayes."

"I'm afraid I don't follow you."

"I think you should let him go."

"I didn't fire Mrs. Hayes, she resigned."

"I know that's what you've been saying . . ."

Hawthorne nearly lost his temper. Reaching into the drawer of his desk, he withdrew a copy of Mrs. Hayes's resignation letter and handed it to the chaplain.

The Reverend Bennett glanced at the letter and returned it. "You must know, of course, that copies of this have been circulating. Some people say that she wrote it after she had been promised a retirement package."

Hawthorne hadn't realized the letter had become public. "Good grief, Reverend, if I say she resigned, she resigned. Why do you insist on thinking I'm not telling the truth?"

The chaplain became red in the face. "Do you deny you fired Chip Campbell?"

"That's very different. He gave me cause. I twice caught him being violent to students. And I've since learned of other incidents."

"It can easily be argued that Clifford's ineffectuality is cause. He doesn't do his job. The students have no respect for him—he's a joke to them. As for the vandalism of his office, many think he deserved it."

It occurred to Hawthorne that the chaplain had no belief in psychology. She believed in morality alone—right and wrong without gray areas or gradations. The God that occupied her heaven was a harsh divinity who toted up a person's sins and after a certain number booted the unfortunate sinner down to hell.

When he spoke again, Hawthorne tried to soften his voice. "I can't fire Clifford and I have no wish to. The board of trustees makes the ultimate decision on all firings, just as it did with Chip. We're going through a difficult transitional period. This requires patience. Right now Clifford has a great deal of anxiety and the gossip doesn't help. But soon I hope he'll settle down. The person who deserves punishment is whoever wrecked his office. Not Clifford."

"You know, of course, the vandalism could occur again."

"We'll be on the lookout. And if the person is caught, then he'll be punished."

But when the chaplain finally left, Hawthorne knew she hadn't believed him. She took it for granted that he had unlimited power. And Hawthorne knew that if she herself had unlimited power, Evings would be gone in a shot. She would have no qualms about dismissing him. Mercy wasn't a quality that the Reverend Bennett valued. And me too, thought Hawthorne, I'd be gone as well. But he felt troubled about Evings. He didn't much like the man and Evings was doing a bad job. On the other hand, he was also suffering—both from his guilt at his failure as school psychologist and his anxiety about being fired. Then there was the destruction of his office.

Hawthorne looked forward to hiring a second psychologist, someone who could take over the burden of the work. Already ads had been placed. Once the new person arrived, Evings could be left to drowse in his overheated office with his novels. Next fall, if the school was still open, Hawthorne would talk to him about early retirement. In the meantime, Hawthorne again had to reassure Evings that his job was safe. He had to reduce the man's panic.

In the fifteen minutes before his history class, Hawthorne signed papers and took care of immediate business. He had the sense of playing catch-up, that he was always behind in his work. When he left his office, he was late for class and had to remind himself not to run in the hall. Entering after the bell, Hawthorne caught Scott throwing an eraser at another student. But the students were livelier than earlier in the week. They preferred the vicious emperors to the sane ones, whereas Hawthorne could easily have spent a few more days with Marcus Aurelius.

After class, Hawthorne had an appointment with Skander to go over a few bookkeeping details, but he was delayed by several students with questions. When he got back to his office shortly before three o'clock, he found Skander sitting on the edge of his wife's desk chatting with Hilda.

"Busy, busy, busy," said Skander with an affable smile. "I don't see how you do it."

"You know," Hilda told her husband, "he's always in here when I get here at eight."

Both Skander and his wife beamed at him as if they found Hawthorne's hard work endearing. He wanted to shout, Don't you realize we're all that's keeping the ship from sinking? But he imagined there was something innocent to their cheer—like the blind flutist playing his dance along the cliff's edge.

In another minute, Hawthorne and Skander were settled on the couch in Hawthorne's office. Hawthorne had several pages of figures that he had gotten from the bookkeeper. Skander began talking about Clifford Evings as soon as they sat down.

"I saw him after lunch hurrying back to his apartment." Skander said. "He's still awfully upset. Canceled all his conferences, I'm told. I remember years ago Old Pendergast bragging that he had gotten Clifford so cheaply. These things unquestionably come back to haunt you. Of course I've tried to have a friendly word with Clifford. He's been avoiding his office altogether. We certainly can't have that."

Hawthorne looked up from his papers. "I don't blame him for feeling disturbed." They talked about Evings for a moment and

Hawthorne said he would speak to him. Then Hawthorne tried to turn Skander's attention to the business at hand. "You know that leather chair I bought . . ."

"That wonderfully comfortable one. I was terribly envious." Skander had his arms stretched out on the back of the couch and reached over to pat Hawthorne's shoulder.

Hawthorne laughed. "You can come over and sit in it anytime you want. Anyway, I ordered it through the school so that I could obtain our discount, but I paid for it myself. You remember, I gave you the check. Going over the records, I find that not only was the chair billed to the school but we seem to have paid for it."

"My Lord," said Skander. He sat up and took the papers from Hawthorne. Studying them, he raised the thumb and fingers of his right hand as he counted. "I do believe you're right. I'll have to talk to Strokowski about this." Midge Strokowski was the bookkeeper who worked under Skander. She also taught a computer course and an elective on modern economics.

"I wish you'd fix it and get the money back. I mean, if the store was paid twice . . ."

"Of course, of course. How embarrassing."

They discussed how the mistake might have happened. Possibly Hawthorne's check had been put in another account. Skander had a pocket full of hard grape candies. He offered one to Hawthorne, who refused. Skander popped a candy in his mouth, then chewed it, making a noise like radio static.

"By the way," said Skander, "I saw you and Kate coming down from the bell tower. I'm so glad that you two have become friends. It's good to see that you're putting San Diego behind you. Obviously you've both had losses and so it's a pleasure for me to see you take such enjoyment in each other's company. Not that George Peabody hasn't been unhappy as well. I quite liked him the several times I met him. But people have to move on. I, for one, never blamed Kate for the divorce. And if he's angry now, I'm sure he'll get over it."

Skander had heard that Peabody had called Hawthorne and threatened him. Peabody had also called several of the faculty members to complain.

"I believe he'd been hoping to get back together with Kate," continued Skander. "Up until now, of course. Gets a little too friendly with the bottle, or so I hear, but he keeps it in the privacy of his home. Not a bad man, by all accounts. Who knows who got him going, but I wouldn't be surprised if it was Chip Campbell. He always had a malicious streak. Chip was another of Pendergast's little economies."

Hawthorne tried to make appropriate responses, though he was unsure what those responses should be. All he knew about Peabody he knew from Kate, and he wasn't disposed to think well of the man. He was also annoyed that Fritz kept harping on the subject, just the way he'd harped on children during Kevin Krueger's visit. Maybe it was time to speak to him about his tactlessness. Yet Hawthorne felt the fault was his, that he was being oversensitive. After another moment, he was able to turn to the papers that he still held in his lap.

"Another matter I wanted to discuss . . ." Hawthorne began. "I don't follow the accounting about Chip's salary. Four thousand should be going to Ted Phillips, the substitute we hired for two of his classes. Then our faculty who took over classes should each get a thousand per class, except me, of course. But I don't see what happened to the remaining eight thousand or so. It should be going toward the repairs on the roof of Emerson Hall and for the new psychologist we bring in."

Again Skander took the pages. "Surely it's right there. You must be overlooking it."

"Show me."

Skander ran his finger down the page, then pointed to a figure. "Here, where it says 'Miscellaneous.' "

Hawthorne leaned forward to see. "But it's not miscellaneous. It had a specific purpose. And this doesn't seem like the right amount. It's far too low."

"But we gave Chip an extra two months. You approved that. He was paid through the end of December." Skander unwrapped another hard candy.

"Even still, Fritz."

"Yes, yes, I see you may be right."

They remained huddled over the papers for another ten minutes. Skander admitted that there had to be a mistake. He telephoned Midge Strokowski, asking her not to leave until he had seen her and speaking more sharply than was usual for him.

"Try and get this cleared up," said Hawthorne. "It may be that we'll have to have an audit before the end of the calendar year." They were both standing by the door.

"That would keep Midge on her toes." Then Skander laughed and scratched the back of his head. "And me too, I expect."

When Skander left, Hawthorne meant to go down to the Dugout and chat with students, which he often liked to do, but when he went to the door he found Bobby Newland pacing back and forth in the outer office.

"I'd like to talk to you about Clifford," he said brusquely.

Hawthorne invited him in. Bobby didn't want to sit on the couch but preferred the visitor's chair. He turned down Hawthorne's offer of a cup of coffee. He wore black jeans and a black turtleneck under a gray sport coat. His dark goatee was like a furry drop suspended from his moon-shaped face. Bobby appeared tense and kept his hands bunched in the pockets of his coat. Glancing around the office with disapproval, he slowly eased himself into the chair as if it might swallow him.

After Hawthorne sat down at his desk, Bobby glared at him for several moments. "I hope you realize that Clifford is *absolutely* terrified."

"I know he's upset. I'm very sorry."

"It's more than being upset. He's very frightened. Not only is he terrified of being fired, but now he has to worry about his personal safety."

"I have no intention of firing him. As for whoever wrecked his office, the police are investigating and the board knows of the situation. I asked Clifford if he wanted me to hire someone, a private investigator, but he said he didn't want anyone."

"Of course he said that. He's terrified of making you even more angry."

Hawthorne leaned forward with his elbows on the desk. "Look, Bobby, where are you getting this idea that I'm angry? I've no idea who wrecked his office but we're doing what we can. If you feel we need additional security, then I'll make the call right now. Ease up on me, will you."

"That's very simple for you to say," said Bobby, "but what about Mrs. Hayes and Chip Campbell? And Chip was even beaten up. Why shouldn't Clifford be frightened?"

Hawthorne considered showing Bobby the letter from Mrs. Hayes that he'd shown to the Reverend Bennett. Had he no credibility at all?

He looked down at his desk and rubbed the wrist of his right hand. There was the picture of Meg and Lily smiling at him. He thought that if the phone rang at that moment and a woman's voice said how much she loved him, that it was Meg and she wanted him to join her, then he would surely begin to scream.

"Mrs. Hayes wasn't fired. If you want proof, there's plenty of proof, but right now I'm sick to death of the whole subject. As for Chip, he was fired for a specific reason and don't tell me you know nothing about it. I count on you to do your work as a mental health counselor. The students like you and I've been impressed by how you handle yourself in the group sessions. But you're continuing to spread gossip and it's going to wreck us if we're not careful. Who told you that Clifford was going to be fired?"

"It appears to be a general topic of conversation."

"But who's saying it in particular?"

"I'd prefer not to name names."

"I insist."

Bobby stood up and walked back across the office. At first Hawthorne thought that he meant to leave, but then he turned around again. "Roger Bennett, Ruth Standish, Tom Hastings, Ted Wrigley, Herb Frankfurter, and others as well. One says one thing, one says another. Herb keeps talking about Clifford's involvement with some senior years ago that created such a scandal that the boy's parents removed him from school. Then that Standish woman tells everyone that Clifford secretly smokes in his office, which sets a bad example for the students. And Roger was saying down in the Dugout just this morning that his wife was going to make sure that Clifford was gone by Thanksgiving."

"Do they say who wrecked Clifford's office?"

"They assume it was students."

"I'll talk to Clifford again. I don't know what else I can do."

Abruptly Bobby seemed on the edge of tears. "I feel frightened as well. I talk to this person and that. I've no idea who to believe. I'm sure you've got the students' best interests at heart. Compared to last year, their morale is almost exciting. But everything else is on the very edge of collapse. It's like watching a building fall down."

After Bobby left, Hawthorne considered ordering Roger Bennett into his office and demanding that he explain his part in the gossip. Or he could call a faculty meeting and threaten the lot of them. The temptation was always to use force—he was busy, he had a hundred things to do, and force seemed the easy shortcut. But although threatening Bennett might shut him up, it wouldn't solve the problem.

Hawthorne wasn't able to see Evings until five-thirty. By then it was dark and the empty hall was illuminated by the globe lights suspended from the ceiling.

The psychologist was sitting on the floor of his office with glue and tape, trying to patch his books back together. Hawthorne had knocked and a cheery voice had told him to enter. Evings looked up at the headmaster with a heartiness that Hawthorne found unnerving. His cardigan had been buttoned incorrectly and formed a zigzag down his narrow chest. Hawthorne sat down on the arm of the wing chair. The other chair was missing; presumably it had been taken off to be repaired. Next to Evings towered a stack of books still to be patched.

"And what sort of psychosis do you call this, if you please?" asked Evings, holding up the glue. "Was I scared by a pot of glue as a small child? Or perhaps my mother wouldn't let me play with paper dolls. I hope you haven't come to lock me up." When Evings grinned, his bald head became skull-like. The room was warm and the radiator hissed quietly.

"I wanted to say again how sorry I am and see if there's anything I can do to help."

"Try shooting me," said Evings cheerily. "If not that, you can send me to Cape Cod. I like Provincetown in the winter. Traffic is never a problem and there's no wait at the better restaurants. Oops, too many gay men. I'd better keep my mouth shut—you homophobes hate that kind of talk." Evings patted one of the books he had finished mending and returned it to the shelf.

"Have I ever done anything to suggest that I'm homophobic?" Hawthorne wanted to lay out his credentials and take credit for establishing the gay and lesbian discussion group, then he grew exasperated by this new impulse to defend himself.

"Not directly, but the Reverend Bennett certainly hasn't concealed her feelings. Others too. Herb Frankfurter's always muttering under his breath."

"Bobby came to see me a little while ago," said Hawthorne. "He told me that you think that I intend to fire you. I just want—"

"What a sneak he is. Going behind my back. He should have his fanny paddled."

Hawthorne kept his face expressionless. "Stop it, Clifford. I want to talk seriously."

"I have no wish to be serious. It gets you in trouble. All my life I've been serious and look where I am today." He gestured around his office. "You know, I really would have preferred to be beaten up like poor Chip than to have my books destroyed. They aren't even very *good* books." He raised one over his head without looking at Hawthorne. "Did you ever read *Goodbye, Mr. Chips?* An old favorite of mine." He held up two more. "*Tom Brown's School Days. Stalky and Co.* Perhaps you see a disturbing motif. Where in the world is my *Study Guide to the Diagnostic and Statistical Manual of Mental Disorders–IV?* Oh, oh. Shall I tell you a secret? I threw it out. I've always hated it. It was the one book that wasn't even damaged and I threw it in the trash. How's that for being sick?"

"And why do you think you're sick?" asked Hawthorne.

"I must be. Look what's happened to my office. Isn't that a sign of sickness? Someone thinks it's time for me to go. And now you're here to fire me. Why would you fire me if I weren't sick?"

"Clifford, I am not here to fire you."

"Aha, you say that now, but I know the drill. Hit the road, you'll say. And there I'll be with Chip and poor Mrs. Hayes, just like checker pieces shoved to the side of the board. Then Bobby and Roger Bennett and Ted Hastings will get the ax. Roger thinks you'll fire him because he knocked you down in basketball. Poor boy. Tell me this, Dr. Hawthorne, what will you do when you're all alone? When you've nobody left except your dear Kate and that cook? Really, if I had any standing with the Department of Education, I'd have to report you."

That night Hawthorne worked in his office till ten o'clock, then he shut down his computer, returned some papers to the file cabinet, and made his way out of the building. Early in the evening he had spoken again to Bobby, then phoned Hamilton Burke in Laconia to describe Evings's continued anxiety after the vandalism of his office. He suggested to the lawyer that Evings be given a paid leave of absence— let him go someplace warm so he could knit himself back together.

Hawthorne and Bobby had felt it would be best if the offer came from Burke, as a member of the board, and carried the board's assurance that Evings's job was safe. Hawthorne was worried; Evings was clearly unwell. But Burke had taken much persuading, saying that he was afraid of intervening in what appeared to be an internal matter. At last, however, he agreed to call Evings and visit the school, if need be. He even grew mildly enthusiastic and offered the opinion that a short vacation might be just the ticket to set Evings to rights again.

Hawthorne walked back around the outside of Emerson Hall to Adams. It was a clear night and cold, with a half-moon revealing the outline of the mountains. He wore no hat and the tips of his ears seemed to prickle with frost. From across the lawns he could hear muted rock music from one of the dormitory cottages. There had been no phone calls that day, no little packages of food. And as he looked up at the darkened windows, he was relieved to see that each was empty. Yet he felt tense, as if ready to fend off an attack that might come from any direction. To counter this, he meant to sit in his new chair, have a beer, and relax. Kick back, as Scott McKinnon said. He would listen to NPR and read nothing more taxing than the *Boston Globe*.

But once Hawthorne was settled in his chair, he left the *Globe* folded in his lap. The large living room was dim, the only light coming from a shaded floor lamp behind his right shoulder and the glow of the moon through the French windows. Hawthorne had almost decided to schedule a faculty meeting to which he would invite Burke and other members of the board. He had to stop these rumors. The issues would be discussed frankly, and if the faculty wanted him to act differently, then that would be discussed as well. It seemed absurd that they couldn't manage to join forces. If that wasn't possible, then Hawthorne's job was hopeless.

Hawthorne hated the prospect of defeat. The thought was almost intolerable. But what had he been beaten by? Could it be no more than stubbornness and a spirited defense of the status quo? Even if Chip Campbell had sent the note to Kate's ex-husband, could he be blamed for everything? Perhaps he had put the news clippings in the faculty mailboxes, but the painting, the phone calls, and the bags of rotten food—he couldn't have done all that. Surely others were involved.

Hawthorne had again begun to think of Wyndham and his wife and daughter, when he slowly grew aware of a squeaking noise over by the French windows. Glancing up, he saw a light shape, then he realized it was a woman's body. With a shock, Hawthorne saw she was half naked. He stood up and took a few steps toward the window. A woman was rubbing her naked breasts against the glass, rubbing them in a circle. Hawthorne clearly saw her dark red nipples, then the pale skin and behind that an indistinct head with blond hair, saw the small breasts pressed nearly flat and the nipples like coins, saw even her ribs as the woman rubbed herself across the strips of wood separating the panes, bending her knees, then pushing herself up again so her breasts were dragged across the glass.

Hawthorne walked quickly across the living room, almost expecting the woman to vanish before he reached the door. He pushed opened the French window. The woman stumbled back. It was a girl: Jessica Weaver. She stretched out her arms and began to turn in a circle, drifting like some weightless thing picked up by the wind. Her feet were bare. Around one ankle was a gold chain with a heart, which glittered in the moonlight.

Jessica lurched back against the balustrade and stopped. "Would you like me to dance for you?" she asked. Her voice was slurred.

Hawthorne could see the goose bumps on her white flesh. He took her arm and pulled her across the terrace and into the living room. Then, before shutting the door, he glanced around. Was someone watching? But he couldn't tell; it was too dark.

Jessica continued to turn in circles and bumped up against the arm of Hawthorne's new leather chair. "I'm a good dancer," she said. "Shall I take off my jeans?" She began undoing her silver belt buckle. Her toenails were painted bright green.

Hawthorne realized she was drunk. "Stop turning like that or you'll throw up."

Jessica pushed herself away from the chair and, as she turned, she tilted back her head and stared at the ceiling. "The trick is not to get dizzy. If I focus on one special spot, it's okay." Her peroxided hair hung down across her shoulders.

Hawthorne tried not to look at her breasts but he found it impossible not to. His overcoat was draped over the arm of the couch. He took it and put it around her shoulders, trying to be careful not to touch her skin. "Keep this on."

She was still turning but more slowly. "Would you like to fuck me?"

"No, thanks." Hawthorne walked to the telephone.

"Don't you think I'm pretty?"

"It has nothing to do with prettiness." Hawthorne dialed the nurse. It rang five times and the answering machine picked up. "This is Alice Beech. I'm away from my desk right now . . ."

Hawthorne waited for the message to finish. "Alice, this is Jim Hawthorne. It's about eleven o'clock. Could you get over here as soon as possible. I've got an emergency." He hung up.

The overcoat had fallen to the floor and, as Jessica continued to twirl, her feet got tangled in it, causing her to stumble. "I think my feelings should be hurt. Lots of men would like to fuck me."

Hawthorne picked up the coat and put it back over her. She turned and his knuckles slid across her bare back. "Keep this on," he said, dropping the coat onto her shoulders.

He returned to the telephone and called Kate. She picked up after the third ring.

"Hi, this is Jim. Could you come over here right away. I need your help."

She paused, as if considering the concern in his voice. "It'll take about fifteen minutes. I just have to make sure that Todd is settled."

"Make it as soon as you can." Hawthorne hung up. Seeing that Jessica had again dumped his coat on the floor, he picked it up and held it out to her. "I told you to keep this on," he said, more roughly than he intended. He saw that she had unbuckled her belt; the two ends hung loose.

"You're not very nice," said Jessica, still turning in front of him.

Hawthorne again put the coat over her shoulders, then took her arm and led her over to the couch.

"Who've you been drinking with?"

"A friend." Jessica took little baby steps as Hawthorne urged her forward.

"What friend?"

"It's none of your business." She looked up at him. "Do you like margaritas?"

"I don't think I've had one for about a dozen years." Hawthorne settled her in a corner of the couch. He began to sit down at the other end, then he got up and went to his new leather chair instead. "So to what do I owe the honor of your visit?"

"I thought you'd like to see me dance." Jessica began to get to her feet.

"Stay where you are and keep that coat over your shoulders. Aren't you cold?"

Jessica put her little finger in her mouth and sucked on it, staring at Hawthorne with her head tilted. "Tequila's very warming. Would you like to see me do a somersault?" The coat had slipped down, exposing her right breast.

"I want you to stay right where you are."

Jessica took her finger out of her mouth and looked at it. The finger was wet and shiny. "You're not very fun."

"It's not my job to be fun. Who gave you the tequila?"

"I don't want to say."

"And why did you come over here?"

"Your light was on. I thought you'd like to see me dance."

"Are you sure someone didn't tell you to come over here?"

"What a silly idea." She abruptly stood up and the overcoat fell back onto the couch. "Watch this!" She took two running steps and did a cartwheel, then another.

Hawthorne stood up as well. "If you don't go back to the couch and put that coat over your shoulders, I'll have to ask you to leave." He knew it wasn't much of a threat, but perhaps in her present condition it would work. He glanced at his watch. Hardly five minutes had passed since he had called Kate.

Jessica was now standing by the kitchen door. Her jeans were unfastened and partly unzipped. She seemed to be wearing nothing underneath. Looking at Hawthorne, she put her finger back in her mouth. "Call me Misty."

"I'd be glad to call you George Washington if you'd just put that damn coat over your shoulders." Hawthorne picked the coat up off the floor.

Jessica walked back to the couch, swaying slightly. "Just Misty is good enough."

"So, who gave you the tequila?"

Jessica turned and threw back her shoulders so her breasts jutted out at him. "There's just no way that I'm going to tell you that, so you'd better stop asking."

"Then put the coat on and I'll stop, for the time being at least."

Jessica took the coat and slid her arms into the sleeves, which hid her hands. The coat nearly reached her ankles. "Do I have to button it up?"

"Yes."

Jessica began buttoning the coat but had trouble focusing on the buttons and so she stopped. "You're very difficult. I'd thought you'd be nicer."

"You caught me at a bad moment."

Jessica sat down in a corner of the couch. She raised her left leg. "See this?" She shook her leg so the anklet jiggled.

"The chain? What about it?"

"My father gave it to me six years ago. You know where Mount Monadnock is?"

"More or less."

"My father flew his plane into it. That was also six years ago. Ka-boom! All they found was scraps. Did you ever have a father?" Jessica lowered her leg.

"Of course."

"Did you ever have a stepfather?"

"No."

"You're lucky. When my father died, I thought I'd die too."

Hawthorne nodded. "I thought that when my wife and daughter died."

"They died in a fire, didn't they? That's a shame."

"Would you like a cup of tea or coffee?"

"Wouldn't it be awful to have a stepwife and a stepdaughter? I mean, like having a stepfather? I have a brother but he's my whole brother. His name's Jason. He's sweet."

"You're lucky you have someone you love, Jessica."

"Yes," she said seriously, "I think that's true . . . You're not calling me Misty."

"Would you like some tea, Misty?"

"No, thanks. I'm afraid I'd puke. You ever seen girls puke?" As Jessica spoke, she wrapped a strand of blond hair around one finger, released it, then began to wind it around her finger again.

"A few times."

"There're girls over in the dorm that puke just about every time they eat. Why would someone do that?"

"Maybe they're sick."

"My stepfather's sick. You wouldn't believe some of the stuff he's done. If I told you, you'd be so angry you'd want to hurt him. And you'd be right, too." Jessica pulled her knees up on the couch and rested her chin on them. Her toes with their green polish stuck out from beneath the hem of the blue overcoat. "I have a friend who'd like to kill him, but that'd get me in trouble. It's a temptation, though. Just shoot him dead, that's what I'd like. I wish you could tell me why my dad flew his plane into a mountain. You think it was on purpose?"

"Of course not."

"That's what I thought too, but Tremblay said he did it on purpose. He said my dad flew his plane into the mountain because he knew he was fucking my mother. Tremblay, I mean. I asked Dolly—that's my mother—but she just got angry. Tremblay doesn't even like Dolly; he just likes her money. He's turned her into a zombie."

"It sounds like an awful story," said Hawthorne.

"It *is* an awful story. That's why I got to get Jason outta there."

There was a knocking at the French window. Hawthorne stood up. Kate entered and saw Jessica sitting on the couch. "So this is your problem," she said.

"I'm nobody's problem 'cept my own," said Jessica. "I don't see what you're doing here. I've already done my homework for tomorrow." Jessica giggled.

"Dr. Hawthorne invited me." Kate removed her ski cap and shook out her dark hair.

"I was dancing for him," said Jessica, standing up and letting the coat slip from her shoulders. "I bet you couldn't dance if you practiced a hundred years."

"Leave the coat on," said Hawthorne, taking a step toward her.

But the coat was already puddled at her feet. Jessica turned with her arms outstretched. "See how good I am? And I don't even have music. Watch this." She ran several steps, then did three cartwheels, landing on her feet by the door to the kitchen. "You couldn't do that, no matter how much you practiced." She suddenly looked thoughtful. "I think I'm going to be sick."

The French window opened again and Alice Beech entered. She looked at Jessica, half naked and swaying a little with her hand to her mouth. "Good grief," she said.

Jessica glanced around and nodded her head as if agreeing with something important. "I think I've got to throw up right now."

Alice ran toward her. "Oh no, you don't. You wait till you get to the toilet." She took the girl's arm and hurried her out of the room. After a moment there came the sound of retching.

Kate and Hawthorne looked toward the bathroom door. "I don't know where she got drunk," said Hawthorne. "She's been drinking tequila but she won't say with whom."

"And why did she come here?"

"She said she wanted to dance for me." He heard how foolish it sounded.

"Do you think someone put her up to it?"

"I just can't imagine her doing it on her own."

Hawthorne walked to the French windows. He looked though the glass, then pushed open the door and stepped out onto the terrace. Kate followed him. The wind was blowing.

"Aren't you cold?" she asked.

Hawthorne shook his head. He looked up at the windows but they were empty. He turned back to Kate. "I'm glad you were able to come over. Alice wasn't home. I'd left a message on her machine."

They looked at each other as they stood by the balustrade. The moonlight made their faces pale and dark at the same time. "You sounded upset," said Kate.

Through the French windows, Hawthorne saw the nurse lead Jessica back across the living room to the couch. "Maybe I'm losing my sense of perspective," said Hawthorne. "When she showed up, I wanted to get someone here right away. You know, a witness."

"I don't blame you." Kate looked out across the moonlit playing fields. "I was glad we talked today and that you told me about Wyndham. It made me feel I knew you better."

Hawthorne thought of what he hadn't said and the deception it created. He felt guilty about increasing the degree of their intimacy. The wind rustled the dead ivy on the wall above him. The moon, hanging above the roofline, shone on the gargoyles.

"I was glad to spend that time with you," he said at last.

"It's awful to think of you carrying those memories inside."

Hawthorne wasn't sure how to respond. "Yes," he said at last. Through the window, he saw that Alice had gotten blankets and a pillow for the girl.

"What happened to the boy . . . Carpasso?"

Hawthorne didn't speak. Carpasso's adolescent face seemed to float in the air.

"Jim?"

"He died. He hung himself." He heard Kate's intake of breath. "He sent word to me in the hospital that he had to see me. By that time it was clear he'd set the fire. He was being held in a juvenile detention center. I said that I didn't want to see him, that I never wanted to see him again. I had no sympathy left. He phoned me. I said I didn't care what happened to him. The next day I was told that he was dead. He had taken sheets and hung himself from the door. When I heard he was dead, I felt glad. I hoped he'd suffered. Then, I don't know, later at any rate, I felt terrible. I felt responsible for all three deaths. It was as if I had murdered him."

Kate had turned to face him. "But that's not true. You were full of grief."

"At times part of me still feels glad that he's dead. I can't forgive myself for that."

"Kate, come here a minute." Alice was calling to her. Jessica had gotten to her feet. Alice held her arm and Jessica was trying to pull free. They stood by the couch, staggering a little. Kate hurried through the French windows as Hawthorne watched.

The two women made Jessica lie back down on the couch. Hawthorne could barely make out their voices. Alice again covered her with a blanket as Kate stroked her hair.

Hawthorne looked up at the windows above him. They were empty but he still had the sense that something was there.

Then, gradually, a shape materialized in a third-floor window—the dark coat, white hair, and thin white beard outlining the jaw. Ambrose Stark again stared down at him. But this time it was different. A great malicious smirk distorted the lower half of his face. The lips were bright red. Hawthorne dug his fingernails into his palms. He stared back at the specter above him, forcing himself not to turn away. He told himself it was a portrait that someone was holding up at the window. But that grin—surely that wasn't on any portrait. Stark's eyes were bright with malevolent humor.

"What are you staring at?" Kate was coming back out to the terrace.

Hawthorne looked up toward the third floor. The image of Ambrose Stark was gone. He tried to calm his breathing. "Nothing," he said.

"You look awful." Kate joined him, then looked up at the empty windows.

"It's nothing. How's Jessica?"

"She's better. Alice will take her over to the infirmary. What did you see up there?"

"Nothing. Just shadows."

"How spooky those gargoyles look in the moonlight."

"Yes," said Hawthorne.

Alice joined them on the terrace with Jessica, who had a blanket wrapped around her shoulders.

"When you walked over here," Hawthorne asked Alice, "did you see anyone?"

"I don't think so. Well, I think I saw the night watchman."

"Think?" said Hawthorne.

"I didn't see his face and he wasn't nearby."

Then, strangely, came the liquid notes of a clarinet. They all stood unmoving, struck by the oddness of hearing the single instrument.

"Do you hear that?" asked Hawthorne, almost fearing that they didn't.

"Of course," said Kate. "How pretty it is."

It was a jazz tune of almost unbearable sweetness. The music seemed to be coming from someplace above them.

Jessica raised her head. "I could dance to this," she said. "Really, let me try."

Alice gripped the girl's arm to keep her from throwing off the blanket. "What is it?" she asked. "I know I've heard that song before."

Hawthorne was afraid he wouldn't be able to keep his voice steady. "Someone is playing 'Satin Doll,' " he said.

7

Detective Leo Flynn was sucking on a big Dominican cigar, inhaling so deeply that he could feel the smoke banging against his lungs' air sacs and infundibula—as the medical examiner liked to say. The smoke felt good. Even the fact that it was bad for him felt good. Flynn was sitting on the bench of a picnic table behind a small house on the outskirts of Portsmouth. It was early Monday afternoon and raining but Flynn was sitting under an umbrella poked up through a round hole in the redwood table, and only a few drops blew against his face. The umbrella had green and white stripes. Through an L-shaped tear in one green panel a stream of water cascaded into a blue coffee cup with the words "Irving's Caddy Shack" in white letters around the side. Seated across from Flynn, Irving Porter, a detective with the Portsmouth police department and the owner of the house, also sucked on a cigar. In fact, the cigars had come from Porter and the backyard was the only place where Porter's wife would let him smoke. She didn't even like him smoking in the garage because she said the smoke snuck into the cars. Flynn didn't know anything about that. He was glad to have a good cigar, even though it was cold and the trees were bare. And he liked Porter, who was a man about his own age and who shared his own bad habits.

Beyond that, they were talking about floaters and bodies that washed up on shore, because Porter had a body that had been tagged a simple drowning till Flynn nagged and nagged, calling twice a day from Boston—a car mechanic named Mike Ritchie who'd been pulled out of the bay in June. So Porter had the body exhumed and it turned out the guy had been killed just like Buddy Roussel and Sal Procopio: an ice pick jammed into the brain. By now Flynn had no doubt he was looking for a Canuck named Frank, a guy in his late twenties with dark brown hair and a thin face like somebody had given it a squeeze. And Frank was a joker, or at least he told jokes. Flynn even had one repeated to him. What's the sign say over the urinals in the Canuck bar? Please don't eat the big mints.

"Sure you don't want a Bud?" asked Porter, blowing a cloud of smoke up into the umbrella.

"Too early for me. I'd hafta take a nap later. I'll come back after I talk to a couple of people."

"You want lunch?" Porter was wearing a heavy overcoat and a red hunting cap with the flaps pulled down over his ears, which made him look like an old hound.

"The cigar's enough."

"You ever smoke any Cubans?" Porter's voice had grown wistful.

"Sometimes. I mean, if they get confiscated."

"Never see any Cubans up here. Had one in Mexico once. Least they said it was a Cuban." Porter poked at the ash on his cigar with a fingernail. "You know, I never felt good about Ritchie turning up in the bay. The guy didn't fish, didn't swim. I must of asked myself a thousand times what he was doing there."

"Now you know."

"Fuckin' ice pick—only an autopsy would pick it up after that time in the water. I figure the tide carried him a ways. Shit, he could of been dumped off a dock right here in town. My kid brother was in high school with him. Even went to his funeral."

"What kind of guy was he?"

"Ritchie? Shortcuts, he was a great believer in shortcuts. It never works."

"Quick money," said Flynn. Then he thought, What the fuck do I know about it?

"Ritchie wasn't greedy. He was just trying to get by. But he was sloppy, drank too much, made a lot of mistakes. He kept trying to figure the angle, like the right number, the right piece of information would solve his problems. I figure somebody got tired of dealing with him and decided to clear the decks. A guy like Ritchie, who drinks like he did, you can't trust his mouth."

"Why didn't you do an autopsy back in June?"

Porter looked off across his wet backyard as if unhappy with the question. "No marks. No sign of foul play. He could have been drunk and taken a tumble. And maybe we had a full plate at the time, I don't recall."

Flynn sucked on his cigar and looked out at the wet brown grass. It wasn't much of a yard except for the picnic table. A seagull was flapping along above the rooflines. Flynn watched it for a moment and wondered what it was like to have no thoughts, no morality, no worries, just belly rumblings.

Flynn pushed himself to his feet. His head bumped the umbrella and a thin stream of water trickled down his neck, causing him to bite deeply into the cigar. Then he took it out of his mouth and spat into the dead grass.

"I'll go talk to the girlfriend," said Flynn. "Thanks for the smoke."

"Not too many people to share it with anymore. The wife won't even let me smoke in the car. I mean regular cigarettes. Filters, even. Makes me feel like a crook."

Flynn walked around the side of the house. Pausing, he bent over to pick up a twig, wiped the twig on the sleeve of his raincoat, and popped off the smoldering tip of the cigar. There was almost enough left to last him down to Boston that afternoon. The department's unmarked Dodge was parked in Porter's driveway. Flynn unlocked the door, started it up, then drove across town.

The woman's name was Letta Smothers and she worked afternoons at Shaw's supermarket as a cashier. She was single with two kids, neither of whom were Ritchie's. Irving had drawn him a map to where she lived, but still Flynn missed the apartment twice and had to double back. He kept thinking of what he knew about Frank the Ice Pick

Man. Not a lot. On the other hand, everything he knew was in the computer and Flynn had no doubt that Frank's full name would turn up in Manchester or Concord. Surely the guy had a record and when Flynn popped in one or two more pieces of information—even Frank's shoe size, for crying out loud—then the whole story would fall into his lap. Chapter and verse.

Letta Smothers's apartment house was one of those buildings that Flynn called pregentrified. The developers hadn't got their hooks into it yet. It was a rectangular three-story building from the mid–nineteenth century, with flaking white paint. Rusted tricycles formed an obstacle course up the front steps. The door was unlocked and the buzzer system was broken. The woman's apartment was on the third floor. A dump like this wouldn't have an elevator and Leo Flynn wouldn't have trusted it anyway. By the time he reached the third-floor landing, he was out of breath. The hall looked like it hadn't been swept since Vietnam. Flynn found the woman's door and knocked.

Letta Smothers was a big, blowsy woman with multicolored hair—blond streaks, auburn streaks, and gray roots. She wore blue jeans that were too small for her and a sweatshirt that was too big. A cigarette was stuck in the corner of her mouth.

"I don't normally like cops," she told Flynn, leaning in her doorway, "but seeing it's about Ritchie, it's okay." She pronounced the name "Witchie."

"I appreciate that," said Leo Flynn. Over the woman's shoulder, he could see some tattered furniture and two hefty preschoolers watching cartoons on television. As Flynn glanced at the TV, a black cartoon cat got blown to smithereens.

"Didn't make any sense for Ritchie to be out in the bay anyway," Letta said. "He hated water. I even had to tell him to wash regular. He said water was for plants and fish."

"I'm more curious about this friend of his—Frank something."

"They weren't friends, not like real friends." Letta dropped the cigarette on the floor of the hall and ground it out with her slipper, which was fluffy and orange. "Frank just showed up one day. I don't think Ritchie knew him before. They had some business deal—I don't know what it was unless it was car parts. You know, buying and selling. You want to come in and sit on the couch?"

Flynn again looked at the television. Now a hyenalike creature was getting blown up—turning into a mass of stars.

"That's okay. It's probably more private here in the hall," said Flynn. "Can you tell me anything about Frank?"

"Not much. He looked kind of strange, with this thin face all squeezed together like it had gotten caught in a press. He had a lot of energy, always moving. More'n once I had to tell him to take a load off his feet just to keep him from walking back and forth in front of the TV. And he liked jokes, he knew lots of jokes. He couldn't shut up with them."

"You remember any?"

"You hear the one about the queer nail? Laid in the road and blew a tire."

Flynn nodded. "Any others?"

"You know what you get when you cross a donkey with an onion? A piece of ass that makes your eyes water."

"Any about Canucks?"

"You know what you call four Canucks in a Mercedes? Grand theft auto."

"He must have been a lot of fun."

Letta Smothers scratched her hair, then looked at her fingernails. "I don't know, it got a little tiresome. Even Ritchie got sick of it, and he liked jokes. Poor Ritchie. And I had to tell Frank to watch his mouth in front of the kids. Like he couldn't shut up."

"This guy have any good points?"

A dreamy expression came over Letta's wide face. "Bread. He'd make this fantastic bread. Muffins, cookies, cakes. Bread with fruit in it. Bread with chocolate chips. He liked doing it. Sometimes I thought he didn't come over here to see Ritchie and me. He came to use the oven. He'd done baking in a vocational school someplace. It was a real gift."

Jim Hawthorne got the call at six-thirty Tuesday morning. Clifford Evings was dead. Hawthorne had been shaving, and as he listened to the nurse's voice he got shaving cream on the telephone's black receiver. Alice spoke calmly but with a slight tremor. A breeze from the open bedroom window blew across Hawthorne's bare skin as he stood in the living room dressed only in his pajama pants.

"The body's cool. He must have died in the night."

"Who else have you called?"

"The doctor, the Brewster police, the state police."

"Why the police?"

"There's an empty bottle of pills on the night table."

"I'll be right over."

Hanging up, Hawthorne returned to the bathroom. The tile floor was cold on his bare feet. A faint gray light came in through the window. He finished shaving, then looked at his face in the mirror—his tired eyes, his drawn expression, his wet and uncombed hair. He took no comfort in what he saw, and in the lines on his forehead and at the corners of his eyes he felt he was witnessing the effect of his horror from the week before. His face looked tighter, bonier. Even as he stared at his reflection it seemed he could hear the notes of "Satin Doll." Then he went to get dressed.

Clifford Evings was dead. Hawthorne would hear his nasal whine no more. Evings's thinness and great height, his bald head and ragged cardigan sweater would never again be seen making their way through the halls of Bishop's Hill. Hawthorne felt a thickness inside him. Wasn't there more he could have done? He remembered the red scratches that Evings had sometimes left on his scalp as if they were symbols of the greatest fragility. He regretted that he hadn't liked him more. Yet everything had been set for Evings to take a leave. The board had agreed. Money had been provided. Hamilton Burke himself had driven up to the school the previous day to assure Evings that all was well. He didn't have to be back until classes resumed in January, almost two months. Instead, he had killed himself.

There was frost on the grass when Hawthorne let himself out the French windows onto the terrace behind Adams Hall. The sun had yet to crest the eastern mountains and Hawthorne couldn't tell if the day would be cloudy or clear. The sky and ground had an equal grayness; the distant trees formed a leaden curtain. Crows were calling. Hawthorne hurried toward the row of dormitory cottages. Shepherd, where Evings had his studio apartment, was the third, and all the lights were burning. Half a dozen kids in puffy down jackets stood on the grass looking up at Evings's windows. Scott McKinnon was one of them. He took a few steps toward Hawthorne. "Old Evings scragged himself," he said. He looked both pleased and horrified. His blue base-ball cap was turned around so the bill pointed down his back.

Hawthorne couldn't bring himself to answer. Five boys and two girls looked at him with an excitement that seemed devoid of grief. Yet there was distress nonetheless. Hawthorne hurried past them up the front steps and opened the door. To the right of the hallway was the student lounge, where about twelve junior and senior boys were talking quietly. They looked at Hawthorne as if he might do something—erase their sadness or return Evings to life. Two were weeping.

Hawthorne greeted them, then used the house phone to call the kitchen. Breakfast wouldn't be served for another forty-five minutes, but he didn't want the boys to remain in the dorm. Gaudette answered and Hawthorne explained what had happened.

"I want to send about a dozen kids over to the dining hall. Give them some hot chocolate and juice or something, maybe get them to help you set up. Don't let Frank tell them any jokes."

"That's fine. I got some muffins."

Hawthorne told the boys to get their coats and go over to the kitchen. He tried to think what else he could do, but only the impossi-ble came to mind—like removing those parts of their memories that hurt them.

Upstairs he found Alice Beech and Bobby in Evings's apartment, a long room with a sloping ceiling and two dormers under the roof. Piles of books lined the wall across from the windows. Evings lay on his back in his single bed, fully dressed but with his shoes off. A pair of polished black wing tips stood side by side on the floor by the foot of the bed. Evings wore threadbare black socks and Hawthorne could see his long toes through the fabric. He wore a dark suit, white shirt, and blue striped tie, as if he had already dressed himself for his funeral and meant to cause as little trouble as possible. His hands were folded across his stomach. His eyes were slightly open, as if he were furtively watching the people in the room. There was a faint gleam from his teeth. The air smelled sweet. Hawthorne thought the smell was com-ing from Evings, then he realized that Evings had been burning incense.

Both Alice Beech and Bobby were wearing bathrobes. Bobby's eyes were red from weeping. He kept rubbing them. Alice and Bobby stood at the foot of the bed and watched Hawthorne.

"Who found him?" asked Hawthorne.

"His door was open and the light was on," said Bobby. Mixed with his grief, Hawthorne also heard anger. "A student who was going to the john saw him. He tried to wake him to see if he was all right. That was a little after six."

"I'm sure he's been dead four or five hours," said Alice.

As Hawthorne looked at the dead man, he grew aware of several students in the hall behind him. He turned and shut the door. But he felt sorry for them. Even if they hadn't liked Evings, they had spent a substantial amount of time in his company. Evings had become a three-dimensional presence and surely they felt guilt, as if by acting differently they could have kept him alive.

Hawthorne was increasingly aware of Bobby's anger. Alice took his arm, trying to calm him.

"I don't care," said Bobby, shrugging her off. "I don't care what he thinks."

"What are you talking about?" asked Hawthorne. It was hot in the room and he unbuttoned his overcoat.

"I'm talking about what you promised," said Bobby. "You said everything would be all right, that he'd be safe. Is this what you meant, damn you? He's dead. Is that what you call safe?"

"Bobby, stop it," said the nurse. There were tears in her eyes as well.

Hawthorne put a hand out toward Bobby but the other man brushed it aside. "The leave had been approved," said Hawthorne. "I don't know what went wrong."

Bobby pulled his blue terry cloth robe around himself tighter. "He called me last night, did you know that? He said everything was over. And I misunderstood. He sounded happy. Or relieved, he sounded relieved. I thought he was glad he'd be going. Instead he was glad he was going to die. I even asked if he wanted me to come over and he said no, no, he wanted some time by himself. He meant to kill himself even then. Damn it, what did you do to him?"

There was a rapping at the door, and Chief Moulton entered, breathing heavily from his climb up the stairs. The Brewster policeman was wearing khaki pants, with a dark green jacket and hunting boots. In one hand he held a cap and in the other a blue bandanna with which he wiped his forehead then shoved in his back pocket. His cracked leather holster flopped against his hip as he walked.

"What a shame," he said, looking at Evings. "I passed the doctor on the road. He should be here any minute." Moulton glanced around the room, then his eyes settled again on Evings. "Not much he can do, of course. Everything as you found it?" Moulton had a low, raspy voice and his northern accent turned his *a*s into dipthongs.

"That's right," said Bobby. "I've been here the whole time."

Moulton walked to the bed and clumsily knelt down by Evings's head. Hawthorne could hear the older man's knees creak. He thought the policeman was going to touch the dead man but Moulton only stared at him. "Rescue squad will take him into Plymouth. An unhappy man," said the policeman. "I'll give them a call."

There was the sound of hurried footsteps on the stairs and the doctor entered. He was a young man in a dark ski jacket. He paused at the threshold to take in the assembled group, walked to the bed, and put the backs of two fingers against the dead man's neck. He straightened up and pushed a hand through his dark hair, then he pursed his lips.

"Sorry," he said.

Hawthorne was aware that Bobby was still staring at him angrily. He looked back, not knowing what else to do.

"If you knew how much I hate you," said Bobby. "I hope they destroy you here."

"Bobby, stop it," said Alice. "He didn't do anything."

"If it weren't for him, Clifford wouldn't be dead."

"You're wrong," said Hawthorne.

Bobby took several steps toward Hawthorne, until he was almost touching him. His wispy goatee seemed to quiver with rage. "You promised him a leave of absence but you never meant it. You found something easier than firing him. You made him kill himself."

The doctor looked embarrassed. Chief Moulton shut the door, which had been left open. Then he hitched his pants up over his belly. "I'd watch your tongue, young fellow. That kind of talk makes no sense, specially with kids listening on the stairs."

Late that morning Hawthorne was hurrying down the corridor of Emerson Hall when Frank LeBrun called to him from the door of the dining hall. Hawthorne stopped, even though he had seen Hamilton Burke's red Saab coming up the driveway, splashing through the puddles. LeBrun wore his white jacket and there was a smudge of flour across the bridge of his nose. He kept shrugging his shoulders and stretching his back, as if it were an exercise. He had a grin on his face, but his eyes were pinched so that it seemed more of a grimace. Perhaps that was why Hawthorne stopped, because of the agitation in his eyes.

"Those kids were pretty upset this morning."

Hawthorne stood still as Frank came up to him. "I'm sure they were."

"Why d'you think he did it?"

Oddly, it didn't occur to Hawthorne to think that Evings's death was no business of LeBrun's. Again, it was the uncertainty in the man's eyes.

"He was unhappy and he was frightened."

"Shit, I been both of those." LeBrun noticed the flour on his hands and he wiped them on his jeans. "He should of just taken off, that's what I would have done. Unhappy here, happy someplace else. That's how it works."

"You're stronger than he is."

"Was," said LeBrun. "He's now a was. Nobody shot him or stuck a knife in him or pushed him in the drink. You hear what I'm saying? It was his own choice. These things that frightened him, why didn't he just say, Fuck it?"

Hawthorne wanted to tell LeBrun to lower his voice but he thought it better to let him talk.

"Poor old fag," LeBrun continued. "It's not good to do it to yourself—you got to stick it to the other guy right to the end."

"I guess he couldn't do that. He didn't want to do anything anymore."

LeBrun rubbed his nose with the back of his hand. "You ever had something you couldn't do?"

Hawthorne wasn't sure if they were still talking about Evings. "You mean something I couldn't face?"

"No, something you couldn't do. Like you knew that you had to do it but you kept dragging your feet."

"We all have to do things we don't like."

"So if you can't do it, then what happens?"

"I try to figure out what's holding me back. Or perhaps it's something I shouldn't do in the first place. You have something that's bothering you?" Not for the first time, Hawthorne wondered what bad stories existed in the other man's life.

"Nah, I'm fine. Maybe I'm just pissed about Evings. You think it was having his office busted up that made him do it? That's a real shame. It's too bad he couldn't find one fucking reason to keep going." LeBrun shrugged his shoulders twice and snapped his fingers, then he pointed up the hall. "There's a guy waiting for you."

Hawthorne saw Hamilton Burke standing in the rotunda, unbuttoning his dark overcoat. When Hawthorne glanced back, LeBrun was already walking toward the kitchen. He had a jerky stride, as if he weren't comfortable in his skin. And he was still shrugging his shoulders. Hawthorne felt there had been something childlike about LeBrun's concern, as if his main worry was his own survival and Evings's decision to commit suicide had somehow put that survival in jeopardy. As Hawthorne approached Burke, he was struck by the deep crease between Burke's eyebrows; the lawyer looked like a man who had heard bad news that made him think even less of the human race than before. Burke was stout rather than simply overweight, as though the excess were due to wealth and good living, the result of real estate investments and commercial takeovers, not overeating. He wore a three-piece blue suit under his overcoat. On his feet were rubber galoshes. He pulled off his leather gloves and put them in his overcoat pockets as Hawthorne came up to him.

"You heard about Clifford Evings?" asked Hawthorne.

Burke's eyebrows went up. "No. What happened?"

"He's dead. He took pills. They found him this morning. Everyone's very upset."

Burke shook his head, then patted his silver hair with one hand, smoothing it down. "What a shame." He continued to regard Hawthorne with his pale blue eyes.

Hawthorne wondered what accounted for Burke's expression if it hadn't been Evings's death. "The police were here. We'll have a memorial service later in the week."

"My office can deal with the police." The lawyer's mellifluous baritone had a practiced sound to it. He spoke as if the problem had already been solved.

"Didn't you see Clifford yesterday?"

"I did. Everything seemed fine. He was delighted about the leave."

"Had you meant to see him again?" Hawthorne didn't understand why Burke had driven back up to Bishop's Hill. They stood in the rotunda looking at each other

"Actually I wanted to talk to you about some other business."

The lawyer's response to Evings's death seemed so detached that Hawthorne wondered if Burke truly understood that he was dead. Then Hawthorne found himself thinking about finances and building repairs. "What did you want to talk to me about?"

Burke lowered his voice. "I heard that you had a girl in your room Thursday night."

Now it was Hawthorne's turn to be surprised. Their voices echoed slightly in the open space.

"A girl came to my apartment late in the evening. She was drunk. I called the nurse and another faculty member. Surely you don't believe there was any impropriety?"

"I also heard she was naked."

"Topless," said Hawthorne. The word came out almost as a bark.

Burke looked at him skeptically. "Perhaps we'd better talk about this in your office."

They turned down the hall. Burke's rubber boots squeaked on the marble floor. A few times Hawthorne began to speak, then he remained silent. He was surprised by how he felt, as if he had been caught doing something that he shouldn't. When they reached the administration office, he held the door open for the other man.

Hilda Skander was watering the plants along the windowsill. Hawthorne wondered how many people had some garbled idea about Thursday night—a naked girl in the headmaster's rooms.

"Has anyone phoned?" he asked.

Hilda kept her back to him. "Chief Moulton would like you to call him."

When Hawthorne shut the door of his office, he didn't even give Burke a chance to sit down. "So what are you accusing me of?"

"I'd rather hear your explanation."

"There is no explanation. Jessica Weaver came to my apartment. She was drunk and wasn't wearing a top. She said she wanted to dance for me. I called the nurse and left her a message. Then I called Kate Sandler."

BOY IN THE WATER

"Why didn't you send the girl away?" Burke stood by a table on which there was a stack of brochures about the school.

"As I say, she was drunk. She was unwell. I wanted to find out what'd happened."

"You should never have let her into your apartment."

"I suppose I should have called the police."

"Don't be ironic with me. This is a serious matter. Lots of people know about it. If it gets to the ears of the county prosecutor, we could be looking at a grand jury investigation."

Hawthorne walked to his desk. Because of Evings's death, he had temporarily forgotten about Jessica. Even at the time, Ambrose Stark and the sweet tones of the clarinet playing "Satin Doll" had diminished the shock of her appearance. Alice had taken Jessica to the infirmary and stayed with her. The girl remained there all Friday, hungover and unhappy. Alice asked where she had gotten the tequila but Jessica refused to say. Saturday afternoon Jessica returned to her room. Hawthorne had seen her in the dining hall over the weekend but hadn't spoken to her. Several times he had noticed her looking at him, but when he looked back, the girl had turned away. As for the fact that the incident had become general knowledge, Hawthorne wondered who it had come from. He was almost positive that none of the people involved would have spoken of it.

"You're mistaken," said Hawthorne, leaning back against his desk, "this is not a serious matter. A girl got drunk and came to my room. I called the nurse and another faculty member. The girl was then taken to the infirmary."

"People say you had sex with her." Burke spoke slowly, as if weighing each word.

"That's preposterous."

"They say you called the nurse after the girl had already been with you for an hour or more, after you had already had sex with her." Burke began to remove his overcoat.

"Who says that?"

"The night watchman saw the girl before ten o'clock, an hour before you called the nurse. The Reverend Bennett also saw her going toward your quarters around that time."

"Then why didn't she do something?"

"She didn't realize that the girl was going to you."

"Even if she was naked?"

"She wasn't naked then." Burke held his coat over his arm.

"What does the girl herself say?"

"I'm told she can't remember."

"Can't remember having sex?"

"That's what I gather." Burke spoke less certainly.

"Who else has been making accusations?"

Burke laid his overcoat on the arm of the couch and sat down. "They're worried about their jobs. They feel if they accuse you, then you'll fire them."

Hawthorne approached the couch. "Good grief, Burke, you're a lawyer, how can you keep up this slander? If there's the slightest chance of this being taken seriously, then I want a hearing immediately. If people have charges, they must be brought into the open. If you refuse, I'll have to get a lawyer of my own. But I suggest you talk to Alice Beech and Kate Sandler before you take this any further. And you'll have to talk to the girl as well."

Burke no longer looked as sure of himself as he had a few minutes before. "Of course I'll talk to them. Perhaps I've been hasty. You know that woman's ex-husband has called my office four or five times—George Peabody? He objects to your involvement with his wife. It's certainly not my concern, but it's no pleasure to have to interfere and frighten him away."

"There is no affair," said Hawthorne, "but if I were seeing Kate, then it would be nobody's business but our own."

The sides of Burke's mouth turned downward as his look of disapproval returned. "There's always been a tacit rule at Bishop's Hill that people's friendships should be no more than platonic."

Hawthorne walked back to his desk. It wouldn't do to lose his temper. He sat down in his chair and looked at Burke over a stack of papers. "There's no way the school can regulate relationships among consenting adults. What about Evings and Bobby Newland, for Pete's sake? And there're others. Midge Strokowski has been having an affair with Jennings on the grounds crew for years. Just what did you tell Evings yesterday?"

"I obviously said nothing about his relationship with Newland. I told him the board had given him a two-month paid leave of absence, that he could leave as soon as he wanted."

"And you told him that his position was safe?"

"I said that he could come back in January and pick up where he left off."

"You're certain that he had no doubt about what you were saying?"

Burke stared back at Hawthorne with his pale eyes. "Completely."

Hawthorne frowned. "And what was his reaction?"

"He seemed grateful. We talked about the details of money and benefits. He spoke of going to Florida until January."

"That far away?" Had Evings ever said anything about Florida?

"It was only a possibility."

"And he didn't seem depressed?"

Burke spoke without a trace of doubt. "Not at all."

"Then I don't understand it."

The telephone rang. As he picked up the receiver, Hawthorne assumed the call was from Chief Moulton or had something to do with Evings. Instead it was a woman's voice.

"Jim, you know who this is. You know I still love you. Lily loves you too—"

"Who is this?" demanded Hawthorne. The woman's voice wasn't Meg's. It was higher than Meg's voice. He was sure of it.

"Jim, why are you fucking that girl? Don't you see that you belong to me—"

"Who are you?" demanded Hawthorne. He saw Hamilton Burke attentively leaning forward. Hawthorne realized he had shouted into the phone. Slowly, he returned the receiver to its cradle. As if from very far away, he heard the woman's voice still talking.

The kitten was orange-colored and sleeping on a folded blue towel on Jessica's lower bunk after having drunk half a small container of cream. Its stomach was puffed out and it purred quietly. Jessica stroked it very gently in order not to wake it. She wasn't sure if it was a boy or girl and so she was thinking of a name that would do for either. Already she had rejected Candy Stripe and Tiger and at the moment she was leaning toward Lucky since, after all, she had saved it from being run over by a car or worse. Jessica had been walking along the side of the road and there it had been—mewing and unhappy, no more than a foot from the pavement. She had saved the kitten's life, she was positive.

And so she thought Lucky would be a good name. After all, every marmalade cat in the world was named Tiger. Jessica had picked it up and
carried it back to school. At the Dugout she had bought the cream,
and the rest, she thought, was history. Now it was shortly past noon on
Tuesday—lunchtime, but Jessica didn't plan to go to lunch. She had
better things to do.

Earlier that morning Jessica had been running away. She had had
enough of Bishop's Hill and these crazy people. Had she really fucked
that old headmaster? She didn't think so. On the other hand, the
whole evening after drinking tequila with LeBrun was pretty vague.
Maybe she *had* fucked him. But she was pretty sure it hadn't happened, even though the sweatshirt she had been wearing had completely vanished. And it was no secret that she'd had a shitload of
tequila—its aches and pains still seemed to be elbowing their way
around her gut, nothing at all like the kitten's stomach, which was still
pure. The kitten wasn't old enough to fuck up yet, and in any case, cats
were just cats. For instance, you couldn't blame Lucky for drinking so
much heavy cream that he looked ready to explode.

No, Jessica didn't think she had fucked anybody, although the
other kids were all talking about it and so were the teachers. Even
LeBrun. "Got some, right?" he'd said to her. "Cleaned the old guy's
clock. Ha, ha, ha." Not a real laugh but a sarcastic noise. The pig. So
Jessica had a perfectly good reason to be upset—then she got the call
from Tremblay that sent her right over the top. He wanted her not to
come home for Thanksgiving but to stay at Bishop's Hill with the
other kids whom nobody cared shit about, kids whose parents didn't
want to see them.

"I just think it would be a bad idea," Tremblay had said over
the phone.

"But why? I want to see Jason."

"I don't want to deal with it, that's all. Your mother's not well and
it's hard for Jason to get settled down."

"Is Dolly drinking?"

Tremblay didn't respond, which answered Jessica's question well
enough. She could almost see him leaning back in his black leather
chair in the den, staring up at his golf trophies. "I just don't want you
here. I don't think I can trust you . . ."

"Please, Tremblay, you said I'd be able to come . . ."

"I've already made up my mind."

"Then let me talk to Jason for a minute."

"No."

"Why not?"

"Our deal was for you to stay away and not bother anybody."

"But you said Thanksgiving would be all right."

"I said maybe. It's just not convenient at this time."

"Have you been messing with Jason? Let me talk to him."

"He's perfectly all right. And if I were you, I'd watch my tongue."

After hanging up, Jessica had broken three windows, but she was careful not to let anybody know who had broken them and she hadn't cut herself. Then she'd heard that that old guy—Evings—had killed himself; she didn't really know him, but once he had asked her if she was happy and she'd told him that what the hell, she was okay, and Evings had said, "Well, we can't ask for much more than that, can we?" Jessica neither liked him nor disliked him but she didn't want him dead. She didn't want anybody dead except Tremblay. And she almost felt hurt by Evings's death. She almost took it personally, as if he had done it to make her feel even worse. So she had decided it was time to clear out, plans or no plans.

As for LeBrun, he frightened her, making her drink the tequila and dance and go over to the headmaster's, where she did God knows what. She didn't see why he had made such a big thing of doing it, like it was more than a joke. He still said he would help her rescue Jason. Actually, he seemed eager, but even his eagerness frightened her. So she had put some stuff into her backpack and left. She still had her money and maybe she could rescue Jason by herself. But every step she took down the road made her increasingly nervous. That chubby cop from Brewster had passed twice, and the state cops had gone by and the rescue squad's ambulance, and she knew very well that every single one had stared at her and wondered what she was doing walking along the side of the road. She didn't have the nerve to stick out her thumb and hitchhike. She realized that she would never be able to get away from Bishop's Hill by herself, that she needed LeBrun's help after all. It was then that she found the kitten. If she had ignored it, if she had just kept on going, the kitten would have been killed for sure. And so Jessica had come back.

Now she was getting ready to write to Jason and tell him about the kitten, how it seemed to love her already and purred extra loud when she scratched its neck. And she would tell him that she wouldn't be able to come at Thanksgiving, that Tremblay wouldn't let her, but that didn't mean the rescue was off, because one day in the next four weeks it would happen. LeBrun had promised. When Jessica had come back to her dorm room a little after eleven, some kids had seen her and they might have seen the kitten, although she had tucked it under her coat. Students weren't allowed to have pets. She'd already been told this ten times. And so Jessica was half expecting a visit from Mrs. Grayson, the housekeeper, or Ruth Standish, who was in charge of Jessica's cottage. And if either one of them tried to take Lucky away from her, she would scream holy hell.

It was only ten minutes after that, when Jessica was already writing her letter to Jason, that there was a heavy knock on the door. Jessica ignored the noise, of course, but the kitten stirred in its sleep. Carefully, she drew a corner of her blanket up over its marmalade body. Then she heard a key in the lock. Jessica hated passkeys, unless she had them—they were a total violation.

The door opened and there stood pudgy Ruth Standish with her face arranged in an annoyed pout. Jessica tried to imagine her dancing topless and the thought made her laugh. Behind Miss Standish were several students, probably the ones who had told her about the kitten and who now were feeling virtuous.

"Why didn't you open the door?"

"I didn't feel like it."

"Do you have a cat in here?"

"It's none of your business." Jessica remained on her bunk with her knees up and her sweatshirt pulled down over them to her ankles.

"Of course it's my business. Having a pet violates school regulations. Give it to me this instant."

It was then that Jessica began to scream. She didn't care that she woke the kitten. She didn't care if she woke everybody alive.

Downstairs in the common room, Scott McKinnon was sitting with some other students in the ten minutes between the end of lunch and the beginning of classes. Scott would have liked to be someplace smoking a cigarette but he had no cigarettes and no money and no one would lend him a cigarette, even though he almost always paid them back. Scott was talking about Evings's suicide with Ron French, Adam

Voigt, and Helen Selkirk, Jessica's roommate. The others tried to talk about it as if it were nothing out of the ordinary but Scott knew they were shocked. Even Scott was pretty shocked, though he'd had an uncle who had committed suicide because he had cancer. Offed himself—Uncle Bob had offed himself. But there had been nothing wrong with Evings that anybody could see, except that he was old and ugly, and that didn't seem like a good enough reason. Ron French didn't see how a person could just back out, as he put it, just call it quits. And Adam thought it might have had something to do with Jessica and how she had been caught in the headmaster's rooms and maybe she'd been involved with Evings as well, even though Evings was a fag, because it surprised you what some people would do. And Helen Selkirk had no opinions at all but she thought the whole business was a shame.

That was when Jessica began screaming. Scott knew it was about the kitten, since he had seen her bring it into the dorm but hadn't told anyone.

"She's got a cat," he said, "and old Standish doesn't want her to keep it." He enjoyed being the person with all the answers.

"A cat?" said Helen, who knew nothing about it.

"Well, a kitten, sort of tiger-striped."

"How cute," said Helen, getting interested.

"She won't be able to keep it," said Ron French.

"If they're going to kick her out of school," said Adam, "then they should let her keep it. I mean, she can take it with her."

"You think they'll really kick her out?" said Helen. She didn't like Jessica—she was scared of her—but she also didn't want her to get in trouble, not too much, anyway.

Ron French made a scornful noise. "Getting drunk and fucking the headmaster or whatever she did. She'll be lucky to stay out of jail."

Scott disliked the way the conversation was drifting out of his control. "The main trouble with having a cat is that someone might kill it. Look what happened to Mrs. Grayson's cat. When I saw it hanging from the branch, I knew we had a crazy person right here at Bishop's Hill. Somebody who liked torturing animals. You don't think that kitten's safe, do you? It'll get hanged as well. As for Dr. Hawthorne, he never fucked her. She was drunk, that's all, and Hawthorne called the nurse."

"Do you think Evings fucked her?" asked Adam.

"No way," said Ron French.

"No way," said Scott.

"Personally," said Helen, "I hope they let Jessica keep the kitten. I love cats."

When Hawthorne heard about Jessica's kitten later in the afternoon, he decided not to take it away from her, at least for the time being. Having the kitten might be good for her. Jessica would have to take care of it and she needed to have the consent of her roommate. But if those details were worked out, then Hawthorne didn't see the harm.

Fritz Skander felt differently. Pets, he said, were nothing but trouble. They were dirty, they carried fleas, and they made the students quarrel with one another. Skander and Hawthorne were in the headmaster's office and it was shortly after three o'clock. In less than thirty minutes the faculty meeting to discuss the students in the lower school would begin, but Hawthorne and Skander had other business first. They had been going over Evings's memorial service. Skander thought it should be very modest. In fact, he would have been happier with no service at all.

"We can't just pretend that Clifford never existed," Hawthorne had said.

And while Skander had agreed, he hadn't agreed entirely. He was distressed by Evings's suicide—he truly felt sorry for the man—but one couldn't deny that it had been, at least to a relative degree, a solution to their problem, although a deplorable solution.

Hawthorne had been shocked. "Are you saying we're fortunate he's dead?"

They were interrupted by a telephone call from Ruth Standish about the cat. Both Jessica and the kitten were now in the infirmary, where Alice Beech said they would remain until the matter was resolved. And she made it clear that she herself stood firmly on the side of Jessica's keeping the cat.

"We've always had clear rules about pets at Bishop's Hill," said Skander after Hawthorne got off the phone.

Skander sat on the couch picking lint from the sleeve of his blue blazer. Hawthorne was pacing back and forth on the rug. He was still upset by Skander's suggestion that Evings's death was somehow convenient. It reminded him of how insensitive Skander could be, as if his world were made up of numbers and not people. Hawthorne himself had begun to see the death, among other things, as a personal failure—he'd been unable to convince Evings that his job was safe.

"I think it would be good for her to have the kitten," said Hawthorne, "as long as she takes care of it and her roommate agrees."

"Then they'll all want pets."

"I don't think so. But a few pets, what's the harm?"

Skander leaned forward with his elbows on his knees and rubbed his hands together as if washing them. He looked worried and his thick gray hair trembled slightly as he shook his head. "The trouble with your giving Jessica permission to keep the kitten is that some people—perhaps more than some—will think you're granting her permission to break an established rule because you had relations with her."

Hawthorne paused in his pacing. "I can't believe they'd think such a thing."

"It's how people's minds work. You can't deny human nature."

Hawthorne and Skander had already spent some time discussing the events of Thursday evening—Jessica's appearance, Hawthorne's phone calls to the nurse and Kate Sandler. The issue seemed to be that Jessica had been observed going to Hawthorne's quarters at least an hour before he had phoned Alice Beech. The night watchman swore to it and the Reverend Bennett had seen Jessica walking in that direction. All Hawthorne could do was to deny that it had happened. But soon, Burke had said, the county prosecutor would learn of it, and then it could easily be turned over to the grand jury. Hawthorne had told Skander he would welcome an investigation.

"I'm certainly not going to take away the kitten because I'm afraid of gossip."

"I'm sure you'll do what you think best," said Skander. "I'm just thinking of what's best for the school itself. Even that girl's staying in the infirmary will cause unpleasant talk."

"What do you mean?"

Skander shifted his position, as if the couch were uncomfortable. "Naturally Alice Beech is one of my favorite people and she does a wonderful job, but what if she has some other sort of interest in Jessica?"

"What are you suggesting?"

"There are her own personal preferences to consider," said Skander stuffily.

Hawthorne could hardly believe that Skander was serious. "Are you saying that she might have a sexual interest in Jessica?"

"Of course not, of course not, but I'm just trying to show you how people's minds operate. Jessica spent Friday and most of Saturday in the infirmary and now she's gone back again—and she's not even sick. You know how people are. They see an action and they think it exists simply to hide another action. They'll think Alice has a less than professional interest in the girl." Skander gave a resigned smile.

Hawthorne looked at Skander angrily. "The girl doesn't have to stay in the infirmary. She can return to her room and she can take the kitten with her."

"Then they'll all be getting kittens. There'll be fleas and cat messes in the closets and the cats will be dragging in dead birds and rabbits. I really wish you would rethink your position. The wisest course, I believe, would be to expel the girl from school for that unfortunate business with the tequila, et cetera. Then all this talk about the two of you having a relationship would disappear. We certainly don't want a police investigation."

Hawthorne sat down on the edge of his desk. He told himself that he was mistaken to feel anger. What Skander was expressing was no doubt the common view, and the only effective way to deal with it was to stay calm. And it occurred to him that if there was an investigation, then he could tell the police about the portrait and the phone calls and the bags of food. But why should they believe him? Why wouldn't they just think he was crazy?

"I've told you what happened on Thursday night. The more important question is where the girl got the tequila, but she refuses to talk about that. If the police get involved, then so be it. I'd certainly prefer that to the alternative of expelling Jessica from school. Surely you can see she needs our help."

Skander finally agreed, but Hawthorne realized that he hadn't been convinced and was just dropping the subject for the time being. Later that day or the next he would bring it up again. Hawthorne could see he was bothered by loose talk, how it might affect enrollment and the school's reputation. Skander wanted to stop the gossip as quickly as possible by whatever method was most expedient. But Hawthorne doubted that silence and truth could ever be reconciled, that drawing a zipper across one's lips was better than talking about what had happened. Hilda rapped on the door. It was nearly three-thirty and they had to get to their meeting.

It was held in a second-floor classroom and about a dozen teachers were already seated at the small wooden desks when Hawthorne and Skander entered. Hilda was at a table in front with the files of the twenty or so students to be discussed. She wheezed quietly. Hawthorne nodded to Kate and a few others. Bobby Newland and Ruth Standish, as mental health counselors, also had files. They sat together by the window but they didn't appear to have been talking. Hawthorne didn't know if they were friendly and he wondered if that was the sort of thing he should pay attention to. Betty Sherman, the art teacher, was filing her nails. Tom Hastings, Herb Frankfurter, and Ted Wrigley sat in back—there was a gravity to their appearance, even a disapproval, that Hawthorne couldn't help noticing. The afternoon was dark and the fluorescent lights gave everyone an unhealthy pallor.

Hawthorne sat down on the edge of the teacher's desk at the front of the room. Looking at the faculty, he couldn't help but compare them to the students in his history class, except this bunch was more recalcitrant. Skander joined his wife, making a groaning noise as he lowered himself into his chair. Hawthorne tried to count the friendly faces. Kate, certainly, and perhaps Bill Dolittle. Then there was indifference, distrust, and dislike. Roger Bennett had his hand raised.

"I know this isn't what we're here to discuss," said Bennett, pushing back his hair, "but I'd like to know how I'm supposed to teach algebra when all the class wants to talk about is whether the headmaster is having sex with one of the students?"

The silence that followed had a palpability that seemed to give it physical shape.

"That's rather out of line, Roger," said Dolittle, somewhat apprehensively.

Kate begin to speak, then stopped herself. After all, she too was the subject of gossip. Usually when the faculty meetings strayed from their purpose Skander was the one who spoke up. Now he sat quietly and watched Hawthorne.

"Is this what you want to talk about?" asked Hawthorne. "Gossip and slander?"

"I just want to know what to tell my students," said Bennett.

"You can tell them that it's not true," said Hawthorne.

There was a silence of several seconds. Bennett glanced around at his colleagues.

Ted Wrigley raised his hand. "Perhaps it'd be best to know what the official line on this is supposed to be."

"You can tell them the truth," said Hawthorne. "A girl was drunk, she came to my rooms and I called the nurse and Kate Sandler."

Bennett spoke up again. "My wife said she saw the girl going to your quarters an hour before you called the nurse."

"Perhaps she was mistaken," said Dolittle.

"My wife is never mistaken, Mr. *Do* . . . little. Are you accusing her of falsehood?" Bennett's expression was almost joyful. "In any case, the night watchman saw the same."

Kate got to her feet, facing Roger Bennett. "That's not true. I talked to Jessica. She had just gotten there."

"Did you see her enter?" Bennett surveyed his colleagues again, this time with a smile.

"No, but it was clear that she had just arrived." Kate sat back down.

"From what I've heard," said Herb Frankfurter, "there are quite a few rumors about Miss Sandler as well. She can say what she wants but many people will argue that she's just looking out for her job."

Frankfurter stroked his beard and leaned back in his chair. Hawthorne wondered if Frankfurter would have attacked Kate if he hadn't been forced to return the car he had taken—seemingly on permanent loan—from the school. Hastings, Wrigley, Bennett—they had all had their perks that Hawthorne had removed. Larry Gaudette had told Hawthorne that Roger Bennett had taken a pie from the kitchen every week. Looking at these men's faces, Hawthorne saw that what had happened with Jessica on Thursday night was less important than the offense of making them stop seeing the school as a natural resource available for them to plunder. Surely everyone felt this to different degrees, but Herb Frankfurter was practically bursting with indignation—not that Hawthorne might have misbehaved, but that he himself had had to return the car. And so if he could blame Hawthorne now, then he was only getting even.

Betty Sherman raised a hand. "Shouldn't we be getting on about the students?"

There was another pause as several of the faculty glanced at one another.

"Who's first?" asked Hawthorne.

Hilda Skander opened the top file on her stack. "Julie Petrowski. She's fourteen and in eighth grade."

"I've been working with her," said Ruth Standish, getting to her feet. "Julie's not been handing in her homework in any of her classes and recently, in the past month, she's been trying to subsist only on cantaloupe and cottage cheese . . ."

Sluggishly, like an old car grinding its way out of a ditch, the meeting got back on track. Herb Frankfurter was looking out the window. Roger Bennett drew circles on a pad of paper. Fritz Skander sat next to his wife and stared down at his hands. Hawthorne could feel his disapproval. It surprised him that Skander hadn't spoken up to get the meeting started. He tried to catch Kate's eye, but she was looking down at the top of her school desk.

By five o'clock the meeting was over. Eight students had been discussed but few teachers had participated and the ones who remained silent made it clear they were there under protest. Naturally, Hawthorne also spoke about Clifford Evings and the shock of his death. He said that a memorial service would be held for Evings during first period on Thursday morning. Bennett said he had scheduled a test for that time and Hawthorne suggested he reschedule it. Several people expressed their remorse about Evings, but Hawthorne could tell they had already talked about it and his death had immediately become old news. Others didn't seemed to care. Herb Frankfurter, oddly, confessed that he hadn't spoken to Evings in the past five years. After the meeting Hawthorne wanted a chance to talk to Kate, but she left while he was talking to Bennett about rescheduling the algebra exam. Then Bill Dolittle again inquired about his anticipated move to the apartment in Stark Hall.

"Do you think someone on the board dislikes me?" asked Dolittle nervously. He wore a white sweater that was too small for him. In fact, for some weeks Hawthorne had been thinking that all of Dolittle's clothes seemed too small for him, as if he had experienced a sudden growth spurt during the summer, even though he was over forty.

"I'm sure it's not that," said Hawthorne almost impatiently. "As I think I said before, the board would have to hire a new faculty or staff member before you could make the move. And there's no point in hiring new faculty until it's certain that the school will remain open." He wondered if Dolittle had any sense of the school's problems.

"I looked in there the other day. The night watchman let me in. It was quite dusty."

"I expect it is. No one's lived there for several years."

"Do you think it would be all right if I did a little light housekeeping? You know, just touched up a few places with a wet sponge?"

Hawthorne had to remind himself that Dolittle was one of his allies among the faculty. "If it would give you pleasure, then do it by all means."

When Hawthorne at last shut off the light, he found Bobby Newland waiting in the hall.

"I'm sorry I lost my temper this morning." Bobby leaned back against a locker and folded his arms. He wore jeans and a black turtleneck. Despite his apology, he seemed full of skepticism and dislike. Hawthorne thought of Kevin Krueger's remark that Bobby looked like a younger version of Evings himself.

"That's all right," said Hawthorne. "You had reason to be upset."

"I keep thinking how Clifford said everything was over and I misunderstood."

Hawthorne tried to persuade Bobby not to feel guilty and repeated Hamilton Burke's assurances that Evings had understood about the leave of absence, even that he was looking forward to it.

"And you believe him?"

Hawthorne was surprised. "Why should he lie?"

Then Bobby said, "You might find out more about Gail Jensen."

At first Hawthorne couldn't place the name.

"She was the student who died several years ago. They said it was appendicitis."

"And wasn't it?" asked Hawthorne.

"I'm not sure."

"Then what was it?"

Bobby smiled humorlessly. "That's what you need to find out." He pushed himself away from the locker. "I appreciate your having a memorial service for Clifford. I look forward to it."

A few minutes later, Hawthorne was on his way to the infirmary in Douglas Hall. Dinner was at six and he still had forty-five minutes.

Although he could have avoided going outside, Hawthorne wanted a breath of fresh air. The faculty meeting had shaken the last of his composure—the attacks on his credibility, the reluctance of the faculty to engage with the subject, the gossip. It made him miss the residential treatment centers he'd worked in. Six weeks ago it had struck Hawthorne as ridiculous that some teachers would prefer to see Bishop's Hill shut down than change. Now he saw that point of view as one of his greatest obstacles.

Jessica Weaver was still in the infirmary with her kitten. Hawthorne had learned that Jessica's roommate would be happy to have the kitten in the room.

"You'll have to take care of it," said Hawthorne, "make sure the kitten eats properly and that it has a cat box and the litter's changed regularly. And if you're going to keep it, I expect you to fulfill your obligations as a student at Bishop's Hill. No drinking, no smoking, no cutting classes, and you have to go to meals."

There was more of this. Hawthorne felt foolish saying things that struck him as obvious, but they had to be said. The girl wore an oversized sweatshirt but Hawthorne kept remembering how she had looked that night. He couldn't erase the image from his mind. He asked himself if there was truth to the accusations, if he wanted to have sex with her, but he only had to raise the question to see its absurdity. Jessica was a child. Even if he had seen the girl dancing in that Boston club, he wouldn't have been attracted. He was sure of it.

The girl sat cross-legged on the floor, teasing the kitten with a long strand of her hair as she listened to Hawthorne.

"So it's agreed?" asked Hawthorne at last.

Jessica gathered up the kitten in her arms. "I guess so."

"And you'll take care of it?"

"Sure. I mean, I love it."

"And are you going to tell me where you got the tequila the other night?"

"I can't." She raised her chin defiantly.

He was tempted to blackmail her. If she didn't tell about the tequila, she couldn't keep the kitten. The idea made him dislike himself. "Then you better get to dinner," he said.

Hawthorne stayed a few more minutes to talk to Alice Beech.

"Certainly I remember Gail Jensen," said Alice. "But I wasn't here when she was taken to the hospital. It was just three years ago at Thanksgiving break. I'd gone to Boston to see some friends. The girl had stayed at school. She went into the hospital on the Friday after Thanksgiving. When I got back on Sunday night, I heard she'd died." They were sitting in Alice's office. On the walls were photographs of Alice kayaking with a number of friends, all women.

"And it was appendicitis?"

"That's what I was told. I had no reason to doubt it."

"Had the girl been sick?"

"No. It was very sudden."

"What was she like?"

"The girl? Very quiet, a little plain, not a particularly good student."

"Did she have friends?"

"Not many, maybe none at all. She had a job in the office helping Mrs. Hayes—photocopying and answering the phone. That was really the only time I saw her."

Hawthorne thanked Alice again for taking care of Jessica, yet even as he spoke he recalled Skander's absurd suggestion that Alice had a sexual interest. The thought made him feel even more isolated. He considered the good or bad construction that could be put on any action and asked himself why the faculty at Bishop's Hill seemed so relentlessly determined to imagine the bad.

After dinner Hawthorne went down to the Dugout to spend an hour or so with the students. Many were upset about Evings's death and he wanted to give them the chance to vent their feelings. He found about twenty at tables scattered around the room, talking, listening to the jukebox, and playing video games. Often during the fall he had joined a table of students, and they had come to see nothing out of the ordinary about his presence. Now they seemed more distant and he suspected it was because of the rumors about him and Jessica.

Still, half a dozen settled around him to talk about Evings, although they tried to mask their shock behind an affected composure.

"What I don't see," said a sophomore named Riley, "is why he couldn't of split. I mean, go to California."

His girlfriend disagreed. "He was too old to go to California." She combed her fingers through her long black hair.

"Hey, he had a big problem," said Tank Donoso. Tank wore a

T-shirt that showed off his muscular bulk. "And who could he talk to? Like, who's the psychologist for the psychologist? It's a problem—"

A thin blond girl by the name of Ashley interrupted him. "He could have talked to Dr. Hawthorne."

"Yo," said Tank, "Dr. Hawthorne's his boss. You don't go to the boss and say how you're fucking up, even if the boss is a shrink."

And Rudy Schmidt, with whom Hawthorne still sometimes shot baskets, asked the question that the others may not have had the nerve to ask. "You think the school's going to make it to the end of the year?"

"Why shouldn't it?" said Hawthorne, feigning more surprise than he felt.

"Well, you know, money and stuff."

"I just want to make sure I'll graduate," said Tank.

"I promise that you'll both graduate," said Hawthorne, "as long as your grades don't take a nosedive."

The small joke hardly raised a smile.

"What about next year?" asked the girl with the long black hair. Hawthorne thought her name was Sara.

"I'm doing everything I can to make sure we'll be here in the fall." Hawthorne realized, not for the first time, that no matter how much the students complained about Bishop's Hill and fantasized about an ideal home, the school was still a place of security, even of comfort; for some of them, it was the only real home they had.

"That doesn't mean you'll make it," said Riley.

"We'll make it," Hawthorne told him, trying to put absolute certainty into his voice.

After the others drifted away, Hawthorne told Tank that he wanted to talk to him. He had the idea of asking Tank to help him catch whoever had been leaving the bags of food.

"Homeboy," said Tank, straddling a chair and folding his beefy hands on the table.

"How've you been?" asked Hawthorne. The dark wooden surface of the table was scarred with students' names and initials and dates going back as far as the fifties.

Tank shrugged. Then he said, "Hey, I got something I got to show you." He raised his hands, putting one on his forehead and the other on the back of his head against his short blond hair. He tilted his head toward Hawthorne and pushed both hands upward, squeezing his scalp and creating a number of furrows across the top that looked like rumble strips. Tank relaxed his hands, squeezed, then relaxed his hands again so the rumble strips came and went. "Cool, huh?" asked Tank.

"Cool," said Hawthorne, and he considered the incredible desperation he must be feeling in order to imagine that Tank might make a suitable accomplice.

It was Hawthorne's sense of his increasing isolation that led him to call Kate Sandler that evening.

"I wonder if I could come over," he asked Kate around eight-thirty. He had spent a good half hour building up his nerve to call and he worried that his voice might show his nervousness. "I don't have anything in particular to talk about. I'd just like the company."

Kate hesitated and Hawthorne could imagine her thinking about her ex-husband and how her name had been linked with Hawthorne's. He was sure she would say it was a bad idea.

"Come over anytime," said Kate. "I'll make some coffee."

Kate lived in a small Cape Cod on a dirt road about three miles from the school. Hawthorne got there about nine. Her son, Todd, was just on his way to bed. He was a tall seven-year-old who shook hands with Hawthorne but looked at him a little distrustfully. Hawthorne remembered how the boy had been grilled by his father as to whether Kate had been seeing other men. And what would the boy say about Hawthorne?

The living room had a stone fireplace and gray plank paneling on one wall. A pile of books was heaped on the coffee table. Kate took Hawthorne into the kitchen. He sat at a round oak table and drank black coffee from a blue mug. At first he didn't know what to say, then without making any conscious decision, he began telling her about the pictures of Ambrose Stark and the calls from the woman who purported to be Meg. He almost laughed at himself, so needy was he to tell another person about what had been happening. And he was afraid of Kate's disbelief, that she would think he was crazy.

"But that's terrible," Kate kept saying. "I can't believe you've been keeping this to yourself."

He told her of the mutilated Stark painting that had stared down at him the night she had helped with Jessica. As he told her about the gifts of spoiled food, his coffee grew cold by his elbow. He found himself thinking of Kevin Krueger and what Krueger had said about the school's malice and rancor.

"But who do you think's doing it?" Kate sat across from him at the table, her dark hair framing her brow. She stared at his face as if she meant to draw it.

"For a while, I thought it was Chip Campbell. Then I thought it might be Roger Bennett or Herb Frankfurter. So many of them are angry at the changes. My friend Krueger says I should call the police. It's so stupid—if I bring in the police, I'll never get the school on my side. And why would the police believe me? That policeman from Brewster is still poking around because of the vandalism of Clifford's office. Maybe I could talk to him. And certainly there'll be an investigation into Clifford's suicide. If I tell him, then this stuff about Ambrose Stark and the phone calls is bound to come out. People will think I'm nuts. I mean, I don't have any witnesses. I'm the only one who's seen that damn picture."

"They want to force you to resign."

"Yes."

However, it was more than that. Hawthorne had wanted Bishop's Hill to be his punishment—his great Sisyphean task—but he had wanted it to be a punishment under his control. He had meant to be prisoner and jailer both. Now he thought how ridiculous that had been. Not only was he being punished, he was worried that he would fail at keeping the school from going under. But of these thoughts he said nothing.

"You must tell the police," Kate said. "Tell Chief Moulton. Surely, whoever is doing it is the same person who wrecked Clifford's office."

Kate urged him to tell some of the other faculty, those who seemed sympathetic—Alice Beech and Bill Dolittle, even Betty Sherman and Gene Strauss in admissions. And there were several more who were friendly, Kate was sure of it. Hawthorne listened but wasn't convinced. Every time he heard a car pass he thought of his car in Kate's driveway and how people would notice it.

It was past eleven when Hawthorne stood up to leave. Kate walked him to the door, then stood by as he put on his coat.

"I'm glad you told me," she said. "That you trusted me that much."

Glancing into her face, Hawthorne thought how pretty she looked. Her eyes seemed to shine as she watched him. Without thinking, he reached out and touched her cheek. She took his wrist, then turned his hand, kissing his palm. They stood like this for a moment. Gently, he pulled himself free.

"Let me," she said, taking his hand again.

Once more Hawthorne gently pulled himself free. "When I touch your cheek, I feel my wife's cheek," he said. "When you kiss me, it's Meg's kiss that I feel."

All at once Hawthorne turned and walked into the living room, standing with his back to Kate. She watched him without moving from the door.

"There's something else I need to tell you about San Diego," he began. "That psychologist, my former student, I knew her better than I said. Her name was Claire Sunderlin. I'd seen her a few times in Boston. Nothing had ever happened between us but it could have. We liked each other. We'd flirt. In San Diego, we'd had a good time during dinner, talking about Boston and other places. Afterward, listening to this jazz quartet, we were flirting again—making what-if kinds of jokes and laughing. Then we left the club and I walked her to my car. She was staying at a downtown hotel; it was only a couple of blocks. But I told her I would drive her. The car was in a parking lot and it was dark. We got in the front seat. We were still joking, then we began touching each other. I kissed her. We didn't stop. We'd had a few drinks but I can't even say I was drunk. It was like there was nothing outside my car, nothing outside in the world. She unzipped my pants. She made love to me with her mouth. My hands were buried in her hair and I held her over me. That's what I was doing when Stanley was setting the fire."

8

The chapel was full and the three golden chandeliers were blazing with light. Most of the faculty and staff were sitting in the two front rows, but Roger Bennett and Bill Dolittle stayed in the back in order to watch the doors and keep an eye on the students who occupied the pews behind their teachers. Also standing in back was Chief Moulton, the Brewster policeman. As headmaster, Hawthorne sat to the right of the altar, facing the school. On the other side of the altar was Harriet Bennett in her ecclesiastical robes. It was eight-thirty Thursday morning. Through the stained-glass windows, the November sun sent multicolored rays across the faces of faculty and students alike. Rosalind Langdon had just finished playing a Bach fugue on the organ and Tank Donoso, who lived in Shepherd, was climbing into the pulpit and looking somewhat truculently out at the chapel. As president of the student body he had been chosen to speak for the other students in Shepherd about their feelings for Evings, feelings that had probably ranged from the critical to the indifferent until death had increased Evings's importance. Tank wore a dark blue suit that seemed too tight and he must have run his electric clippers across his scalp that morning, because he was nearly bald. Hawthorne glanced away and saw the door in back open. Frank LeBrun entered. He hesitated, then remained by the exit.

The service had begun shortly after eight with the Reverend Bennett talking about "Clifford Evings the man," as she had called him. Her eulogy had been a mixture of homily and reminiscence but so generalized that she could have been taking about anybody. Hawthorne wondered what she truly thought, since she had urged him to dismiss Evings or at least force him into early retirement just the previous week. Instead she had spoken about the luminescence of his soul and the weight of his mortal burden. She said the light of his presence had been dimmed in this world only. Hawthorne imagined accusing her of hypocrisy, which he would never do. But possibly, now that Evings was dead, she could feel charity and even remorse. Possibly the prayers with which she concluded her remarks had been heartfelt.

Others had spoken. Skander told how he and Evings had both come to Bishop's Hill exactly twenty years earlier. He had little to say beyond that numerical fact except that Evings had become a "fixture" and "one of those quiet people upon whom I had come to depend." Tom Hastings, stuttering only a little, had spoken of a weekly chess game that he and Clifford played for years. Bill Dolittle had spoken of Evings's love of books. But in none of these descriptions did Hawthorne see the frightened and desperate man he had come to know in the past two months. There was no mention of someone's trashing his office only a week earlier or of Evings's having taken his own life. And Hawthorne asked himself what the students thought of such a veneer of praise or if these pieties were just something they had come to expect.

Tank cleared his throat. "I can't say that I knew Mr. Evings very well," he began. He stuck a finger under the collar of his white shirt and pulled. "But he was certainly Shepherd's main man. Like, he was in charge and he was a pretty good guy and if any of us wanted something, Mr. Evings was usually there to help or he could tell us who to see. And he never got angry. If someone broke something or if there was too much noise, he would come downstairs in his slippers and say, 'Gentlemen, if you please.' Then he would go back upstairs. And once when I was wrestling around with Charlie Penrose, he came downstairs and asked us to cool it. Then he sat with us until we'd settled down and asked if we wanted a cup of tea. I don't know, it's pretty lousy that he's dead."

Although Tank never described Evings as ineffectual, that was the idea that came across: Evings was a nice man who did as little as possible and let the students run Shepherd as they wished so long as they weren't troublesome and there was no fuss. It seemed clear to Hawthorne and perhaps others that whatever discipline existed in Shepherd came from Tank Donoso and his dope slaps. Hawthorne noticed that several of the faculty were dozing, while a number of students were using the occasion to finish their homework. Scott McKinnon was staring up at the stained-glass image of Isaac and Abraham. Jessica Weaver seemed to be writing something. Then Hawthorne's eyes came to rest on Kate just a few feet away in the front row. She wore a dark blue dress with a string of lapis lazuli beads around her neck. Her dark hair hung loose and the strip of white shone in the light of the morning sun. Her legs were crossed and as she watched Tank her right foot twitched nervously. Hawthorne thought how attractive she looked and of what he had told her on Tuesday night. His face burned at the memory. He hadn't spoken to her since and he felt the awful vulnerability of someone who has at last revealed all his secrets. He felt certain she must despise him.

For another five minutes Tank ground on, trying to pick his words and avoid his dated rap-singer slang. He described how Evings had once helped him with an English paper, how he had introduced Evings to his parents. Hawthorne was touched by Tank's efforts to achieve some level of decorum. A cloud briefly obscured the sun and the light shining through the windows faded, darkening the faces of the faculty and students. Then the light returned as Tank reached the end of his talk and hurried down the stairs out of the pulpit, obviously glad that his ordeal was over. Bobby Newland was waiting at the bottom. His round face expressed an eagerness that caught Hawthorne's attention.

Bobby wore a dark suit and bright red tie. As soon as Tank was out of the way, he quickly climbed the steps. Then he stood with his hands gripping the lectern as he looked out at the audience with his head slightly tilted back so his goatee seemed aimed at the men and women in front of him. He didn't speak. Hawthorne began to count the seconds. Slowly, he saw faculty and students alike stop what they were doing and look up. Frank LeBrun was sitting on the top step by the door with his elbows on his knees and his chin cupped in his hands.

After another minute Bobby began to speak, raising his voice and precisely articulating each word. "Clifford was my lover. We met nearly three years ago in Edgartown, where I was working in a restaurant. He brought me to Bishop's Hill and had me hired as a psychological counselor. He was the kindest man I've ever known and you killed him."

There was an immediate stirring. A few faculty members called out some words of protest. Hawthorne saw LeBrun get to his feet. The Reverend Bennett leaned forward and gasped.

"Whoever wrecked Clifford's office as good as murdered him," Bobby continued above the noise, "but that wasn't the beginning. Ever since September people have been telling Clifford that he was about to be fired. These were men and women who pretended to be his friends. At first I thought it was true, that Dr. Hawthorne meant to get rid of Clifford as soon as possible. Isn't that what you told me? You, Hastings and Bennett and Chip Campbell? And there were others. You know who you are. I even heard it from students. 'Old Evings is about to be shit-canned,' one boy told me. Why did you do it? He deserved better than to be stuck here at this shitheap, but this was the only place he had. You tormented him and terrified him till he couldn't stand it anymore. Wrecking his office was the last straw. Can't you see your crime? Can't you see that you killed him?"

By now Bobby was weeping and Hawthorne was standing below the pulpit. In the back, Bennett was holding onto LeBrun's arm, as if LeBrun meant to rush down to the altar. Students were on their feet. Chief Moulton seemed calm, leaning against the back wall with his arms crossed.

"G-get him out of there," shouted Hastings from the front row.

The Reverend Bennett crossed in front of the altar to Hawthorne. "Make him stop."

Hawthorne looked at Skander, who was bent over with one hand across his eyes.

"Bobby," said Hawthorne, "come down from there."

Bobby looked down at Hawthorne with surprise. He glanced quickly out into the chapel. "Damn you," he shouted, "damn each one of you!" Then he hurried down the steps, half stumbling so Hawthorne had to catch his arm. They stood facing each other with Hawthorne still supporting the other man. Bobby's face was wet with tears. A small door was positioned to the side of the altar under the painting of Ambrose Stark. Bobby pulled away from Hawthorne and left the chapel.

Hawthorne climbed the steps of the pulpit. Looking out, he noticed a range of emotions, from anger to grief, surprise to remorse. Somebody whistled and students banged the pews. Prayer books and hymnals fell to the floor. Several of the faculty were trying to speak; most of them were standing.

Hawthorne held up his hand for silence. He saw LeBrun talking angrily to Bennett. Slowly the noise lessened. "Please sit down," said Hawthorne. Beneath him the chaplain moved back to her chair, her white robes billowing around her in the breeze from the small choir door that Bobby had left open.

Hawthorne waited a moment, then began to speak. "I don't know why Clifford Evings committed suicide," he said. "He left no note. He was about to begin a two-month paid leave of absence. Instead, he chose to kill himself. It's true he was frightened and his fear had become a sickness. And it's also true that, intentionally or not, certain people had scared him, and the vandalizing of his office absolutely terrified him. I don't know who did that, but the police are investigating and whoever is responsible will be prosecuted to the full extent of the law."

Hawthorne paused again. He could feel the attention of the students and faculty fixed upon him. "I didn't know Clifford very well. He wasn't particularly effective at his job and he felt guilt about taking the school's money and giving little in return. Eventually, I would have urged him to retire, but I wouldn't have fired him. Whatever his failings, the school had a certain responsibility. I don't know why people told him he was about to be fired, except that it was one more example of the malice and gossip that I have seen since I arrived at Bishop's Hill. Most assuredly, Clifford was its victim.

"But we are here now to say good-bye to him and to praise what we can praise. He was kind, he meant well, he had no meanness in him. How many can say that of themselves? He had the same mixture of qualities and failings found in all human beings. His greatest pleasures were in his friendships and in books, the novels that filled his spare moments. He was a gentle man, and in saying good-bye to him we should remember that and say good-bye with as much goodwill as we can muster. I want to close with two quotes that I came upon this fall in my history class. Both are from the emperor Marcus Aurelius. 'An empty pageant; a stage play; flocks of sheep, herds of cattle; a brawl of spearmen; a bone flung among a pack of dogs; a crumb tossed into a pond of fish; ants, loaded and laboring; mice, scared and scampering; puppets, jerking on their strings—that is life. In the midst of it all you must take your stand, good-temperedly and without disdain.' "

As he paused, Hawthorne thought of yet another quote from Marcus Aurelius that had stayed with him over the weeks: "You may break your heart, but men will still go on as before." He had first thought of it in relation to his wife and daughter, but now it had become one of his truths, as if Aurelius's role were to fill the agnostic's empty heaven. Aurelius offered consolation when there seemed none other to be had. Glancing up, he saw Kate watching him from the second row. He tried to smile and felt his awkwardness as a clumsy twisting of his lips.

"And here is the second quotation that gives me guidance and may be of help to you as well. 'Be like the headland against which the waves break and break: it stands firm, until presently the watery tumult around it subsides once more to rest.' "

Leafing through an issue of *Boston* magazine, Detective Leo Flynn thought how it reflected a Boston he knew nothing about, or at least very little—the newly prosperous and yuppie Boston, the online Boston. The city was full of people without history, or whose histories were elsewhere. Was there anything in the magazine about Somerville, where Flynn had grown up and gone to school? Not likely—Somerville wasn't upscale enough. Bean sprouts and exotic mushrooms were absent from its supermarkets. But even that was changing. The yuppie sprawl from Cambridge was making inroads. And soon there would be no one to remember Scollay Square and Mayor Curley or even Ted Williams. Flynn closed the magazine and tossed it back on the table.

It was Thursday morning and Flynn was in Concord waiting to see Otto Renfrew of the Division of Children, Youth, and Families of the New Hampshire Department of Social Services. Fourteen years earlier, Renfrew had been associate director of the Bass Vocational

School for troubled boys in Derry. One of the boys had been Francis LaBrecque, who had trained as a baker. Flynn wanted to talk to LaBrecque but so far he had found no trace of him. But he knew that LaBrecque was who he was looking for. He knew LaBrecque was the Ice Pick Man.

The door to the inner office opened and a round bald head stuck itself through the widening crack. "We've got to make this as short as possible," said Renfrew. "I have a lunch meeting."

Leo Flynn smiled affably and pushed himself up out of his chair. The trouble with New Hampshire was that he had no clout. In Boston he could make Otto Renfrew come to police headquarters any time of the day or night. He could keep Renfrew waiting for an hour or two without even an old magazine to help pass the time.

"I'd be grateful for just a minute," he said. "I'll make it quick."

But ten minutes later Flynn was still asking questions while Renfrew scratched his bald head and furtively looked at his watch.

"I wouldn't say he was especially bad," said Renfrew. "He was emotionally damaged and educationally handicapped. He was certainly angry but there was no evidence of bipolarity. Perhaps overactive would be a better word, at times even hyperactive."

"So you wouldn't say he was fucked up," said Flynn, checking Renfrew's reaction.

"Well, he'd been mandated to the school by the court, presumably because the public schools couldn't control him—he had a ferocious temper—but I don't remember any instances of criminal behavior. He was disorganized and sometimes violent, though not to the other boys. But he might break up furniture or smash windows. Once he saw that we'd take away his privileges, though, he tried harder to fit in. Many of the boys at Bass were there for sexual-behavior modification, but that wasn't entirely true in LaBrecque's case, although he'd been sexually abused. Basically, he seemed friendly, but his anger and then his secretiveness made him completely untrustworthy. I wasn't sure we could do anything for him, apart from giving him meds, until he got caught up in baking."

"Did he have friends?"

"Frank was very much a loner. He was always eager to help out and he did favors for the older boys, but if given the choice he preferred his own company. When I first met him, he did lots of little favors for me—helping me clean my office, wash my car. And I thought it would lead to a friendship of sorts but it never did. His sociability was just a way of keeping a close eye on what was going on. It existed to mask his fear."

"Was he ever sexually abused at the school?"

Renfrew's brow wrinkled. "There was an older boy who bullied him constantly, always giving him orders, making him run errands, knocking him around. Looking back on it, there probably was a sexual aspect. Once I caught him snapping LaBrecque with a wet towel in the showers, aiming for the genital area. I put a stop to it and reprimanded him. He accused LaBrecque of coming on to him, although LaBrecque denied it. LaBrecque was somewhat peculiar-looking, thin and with an extremely narrow face. He was teased a lot. In all likelihood that was one reason he tried to ingratiate himself with the other boys, just so he wouldn't be picked on."

"What happened to the boy who'd been bullying him?"

Renfrew moved his tongue across his upper teeth. His discomfort seemed to increase. "He was nearly killed."

"By LaBrecque?"

"I don't know, but I rather think so. The boy was attacked one night as he was leaving the gym. He was beaten with a two-by-four. He didn't see who did it and lost consciousness. His shoulder and arm were broken. Some other boys came running up and the attacker fled. The police became involved and all the boys were questioned. But suspicion didn't fall on LaBrecque. He denied any involvement, and there was nothing of the fighter about him. All his violence had been directed at inanimate objects. He even seemed to be improving—he was calmer and making an effort in his classes. I remember he came to my room to say what a shame it was that the boy had been attacked and offered to make him a cake. I saw no harm in it. LaBrecque had done so well in the kitchen that he had a few special privileges. The boy had been in the hospital but after a week he was brought back to the infirmary. So LaBrecque made his cake and delivered it to him. It had bright red frosting. Actually, I should have been more careful."

"What about?"

"The cake was full of tacks. The boy got several in his mouth and got a scratch on his tongue. I went to find LaBrecque but he was gone.

No one saw him leave. There was a fence around the property but it wasn't high; we didn't want the place to look like a jail. The police searched for him for weeks. Obviously, his disappearance suggested that he had attacked the boy. And the business with the tacks was disturbing. In any case, the police lost track of him. They found a man who'd given him a ride to Boston—but nothing after that."

"What about his family?"

"They seemed pretty indifferent."

"Didn't they visit him?"

"Never, as far as I remember, and LaBrecque himself never spoke of them. His mother was dead. There was a younger sister he was close to, but she was hardly more than a child. And there was a brother but no one really took an interest. Actually, I have to take that back. There was a cousin who visited him a couple of times, quite a young man."

"Do you remember his name?"

"No, except that it was French and it wasn't LaBrecque. And he was a cook."

Flynn figured he could get the name of the cousin when he talked to LaBrecque's brother that afternoon. He still lived in Manchester. The father was dead.

"Do you think LaBrecque is capable of killing someone?"

Again Renfrew looked uncomfortable, seeming to study the fluorescent light fixture. "I don't know," he said, looking back at Flynn. "At first I was absolutely certain he hadn't been responsible for the attack on the other boy. He seemed so shocked by it. He even wanted to help question the other students and he talked to me several times about what might lead a person to do something so awful. I was touched by his concern, especially since he'd often been this other boy's victim. But let's say he did it. Then the lies he told afterward are amazing, because he didn't simply deny that he'd attacked the boy. He went to great lengths to act shocked and play the detective. And there was that business about the cake." Renfrew shifted in his chair. "It suggested that he saw it all as an elaborate game. His ego has to be immense. Behind his apparent concern there must have been a complete lack of feeling, which makes me think he might easily be capable of taking another person's life. He'd be able to explain it in a hundred ways, and his first justification would be that he himself had been a victim."

———•———

Frank LeBrun was waiting outside Emerson Hall. It was getting dark, though it was only a little after four o'clock, but the day had turned cloudy. Snow was forecast. The TV had been showing footage of winter storms in Colorado and Montana. LeBrun had only a sweater. He paced back and forth in front of the iron fence posts, rubbing his arms and talking angrily to himself. He had been upset since the memorial service. Bobby Newland had made him mad. He didn't like being at Bishop's Hill anymore and he wouldn't have stayed if there hadn't been special work to do. The whole business had become disagreeable and he was getting that boxed-in feeling that he hated.

When he heard the front door open, LeBrun pressed back against the fence. Soon Roger Bennett hurried past. LeBrun wasn't sure that Bennett had seen him—his sweater was dark and the sun had already set. And Bennett was in a hurry—but he always seemed in a hurry. He was always running somewhere and never had time to talk. But it wasn't going to be like that this time.

LeBrun sprang after him and grabbed Bennett's arm. "I got a question."

"Let go of me," said Bennett, pulling free, then stumbling a little.

"Why didn't you tell me that old guy was going to kill himself?"

"How in the world could I have known?"

"You knew him better than me. You all knew him."

Bennett stood facing LeBrun in the driveway. He wore a black leather coat that reached his thighs. Although his face was in shadow, his blond hair shone in the light from the windows. "I thought he'd quit. You know, resign."

LeBrun stepped forward and took hold of the lapels of Bennett's coat. "Don't fuck with me. I had nothing against that old fart."

Bennett didn't try to shake him off. "You should watch how you behave. You could be in big trouble. The police want to know who destroyed Clifford's office and they also want to know where that girl got the tequila. They could probably charge you with quite a few things—corrupting a minor, breaking and entering, vandalism. Maybe Clifford made a pass and you got mad. Why should the police think anyone else was involved?"

LeBrun pulled Bennett toward him, until their faces were almost touching.

"I'm not the only one who knows about this," continued Bennett. "You've been paid and you need to keep quiet. Do you actually care whether Evings is alive or dead?"

LeBrun let go of Bennett's coat. "I didn't mean for him to off himself."

"A little late for that, isn't it?"

"You know, Bennett, you don't smile anymore. You used to smile all the time when there was stuff you wanted me to do. How come you quit smiling? Is it because you think you've got me in your pocket?"

For the first time Bennett looked uneasy. "Perhaps I see nothing to smile about."

"Hey, there's always jokes. You hear about the Canuck who stole the Thanksgiving turkey?"

Instead of answering, Bennett turned abruptly and hurried up the driveway to his apartment behind the chapel.

LeBrun angrily kicked the metal fence. Then he sat down on the ground and massaged his bruised toes. In the beginning it had seemed easy: a little money for this, a little money for that. As for that stuff with the girl, it was a joke. But now Bennett had something on him. And so did others.

For a moment, LeBrun considered running, going out to California, where he had lived before. His sister was in Riverside and he hadn't seen her for years. But he was almost broke. He had to stay at Bishop's Hill until he got his money, which would be a bundle, a double bundle. After that he'd have all the freedom he could want. But to get the money he had to finish the job he'd been sent to do. No more fucking around. No more indecision. That fat policeman had come sniffing around the kitchen. LeBrun had talked to lots of cops in his lifetime. They never got shit. But LeBrun hated to see him hanging around the school. And the state trooper had come back as well.

LeBrun got up off the ground. His butt was cold and his foot hurt. Maybe he'd busted a toe, like he'd once busted a finger when he punched a wall. He had to talk to the girl and get the dates straight. Fucking Misty. When he was younger, girls like that wouldn't give him the time of day. You had to get a hold on a person, otherwise you were nothing. And wasn't that what Bennett had? A hold? LeBrun hated them all. But he didn't hate Hawthorne, not yet. On the other hand, he didn't doubt that if Hawthorne knew more about him, then he'd become an enemy, too. Hawthorne liked him now, but that was because he didn't know anything. The more a person knew, the sooner they'd turn against you. It had always been like that. Even when he'd been a kid, even before he'd actually done anything. It was a fact of life.

LeBrun walked around the outside of Emerson, rubbing his arms and deep in conversation with himself. He wanted to talk to the girl. It was past four-thirty and she was probably in her room. He'd never been there but he knew it was on the second floor of Smithfield. LeBrun always made a point of finding out where things were. There was no telling when it might come in useful. And keys, he always liked to have a lot of keys.

He rounded Emerson by Stark Hall, into which Bennett had disappeared, then he continued toward the row of dormitory cottages. LeBrun liked how the days were getting shorter. He could never see why people complained about the decreasing daylight. He liked the dark. Maybe he should live in Alaska, where there was lots of night. Or he could go to Quebec and live with the rest of the Canucks. He'd picked up a little French from his grandmom, maybe twenty or thirty words. It would be a start.

There was a back door to Smithfield and LeBrun unlocked it. He stepped inside and listened. He could hear girls' voices and laughter from the living room. And there was music. LeBrun didn't like music, not even rock and roll. It made him jittery. He couldn't imagine listening to music to relax. There was lots of stuff he didn't like. LeBrun paused on the back stairs and thought about it. He didn't like people fucking with his space, and to tell the truth, a whole lot of people fucked with his space.

LeBrun paused again at the second-floor landing. A girl was walking down the hall from the bathroom with a towel wrapped around her and he waited for her to get out of the way. Jessica's door was the second one down on the left. He would surprise her. It would help to make her think he was invincible. But he wouldn't touch her. On the whole, he didn't like to touch anyone, except for business purposes.

LeBrun made his move, counting the seconds off to himself. Five steps to her door, two seconds to get the key in the lock and he was inside. The girl was on the lower bunk fussing with something. The only light came from a lamp on the desk, and the room was dim. LeBrun looked again. It was a fucking cat.

"Hey," said Jessica.

"Get rid of that cat." LeBrun stayed by the door.

"You're not supposed to be in here." Jessica sat up on the bed and put her bare feet on the floor. The kitten crawled behind her.

"I said, get rid of the cat."

"It's not a cat, it's a kitten. Its name is Lucky."

Now that LeBrun couldn't see the cat, it wasn't so bad, but just thinking about it made him disgusted. Even kittens were filthy with fleas and mites crawling over their skin and feeding on their blood. And they ate filthy things—mice and birds—and played with them as they died. That was as bad as the filthiness. If you had to kill something, you killed it quick. You didn't fuck around. You only teased something if you hated it and wanted to punish it everlastingly, if its suffering excited you.

"How'd you get a key?" asked Jessica, more curious than frightened.

LeBrun ignored her question. "This business with your brother, I want to do it right away. We can do it this weekend."

"Nothing's ready yet. I don't even know if they'll be home. I have to tell Jason and the only way I can do that is by writing him."

"What the fuck's Jason need to know for? We can just go down and snatch him."

"Then they'll call the police. We need time to get away."

LeBrun kept an eye on the bed behind Jessica to make sure the cat stayed put. If it came sneaking out, then he'd have to twist it. He'd hardly be able to help himself. And if he twisted it, all hell would break loose. Beyond that, he didn't like being in the room. It smelled of girl things and girl perfumes. There was underwear on the chair—black panties and a little bra—and a box of Tampax on the desk right next to the computer. There were posters of young men stuck up on the wall—that kid who had been in *Titanic* with a swan curling over his naked shoulder and that singer who'd killed himself, offed himself for no reason that LeBrun could see. Killing yourself was what you did last, and LeBrun laughed because it was a joke and he hadn't meant it as a joke.

"What's so funny?" asked Jessica.

"Hey, Misty, what's the last thing a Canuck does?"

"What?"

"He dies."

"I don't find that very funny."

LeBrun thought about it for a moment. "I guess you had to be there."

"I don't like you being in my room. I'm already in trouble and if they see you in here, they'll guess where I got the tequila."

The girl had her hand behind her back and LeBrun understood that she was keeping the cat out of his sight, which meant she was touching it. "I want to know exactly when we're going to get your brother. You're just fucking with me, promising me that money."

"No, really, we'll do it. We have to do it."

"Next week then."

"That's Thanksgiving. There'll be too many people."

"Then right after that. On Monday, that's the thirtieth. We'll do it on the thirtieth."

"Won't there be school that day?"

"You nuts? You plan to come back? You take him and you'll be gone."

"Okay, the thirtieth. We'll do it on that Monday. I'll write to Jason." Jessica stuck out her hand. "You want to shake on it?"

"You fucking kidding? You been playing with that cat. I wouldn't touch your hand unless you boiled it."

LeBrun had been leaning against the door. Suddenly it pushed against him. He half stumbled forward as Helen Selkirk entered. Seeing him she stopped, leaving the door open.

"What're you doing in here? You're not supposed to be here."

LeBrun felt himself getting angry. "I'm checking the pipes. You wouldn't want the pipes to burst now, would you? They'd cause one unholy fucking mess." Then he left, darting down the hall to the back stairs and making no sound.

The Saturday before Thanksgiving there was sleet. Despite the weather, Hawthorne drove in to Plymouth in the morning, telling himself that he had errands, but in fact he wanted to get away from Bishop's Hill.

He had bought a used Subaru station wagon early in the fall and he felt some self-satisfaction that he had had the foresight to buy a vehicle with four-wheel drive. He would have lunch by himself and wouldn't think that people were talking about him and conspiring against him. He would rest his mind. His subjective and objective selves seemed hopelessly entangled and he wasn't thinking clearly. His guilt about the fire at Wyndham School, the deaths of his wife and daughter, the phone calls, Evings's suicide, and all the other business kept rattling through his brain.

Hawthorne now realized that he had accepted the phone calls and the rest as his due, as a criminal might accept lashes of a whip. No punishment, he had felt, would be too awful, if it could expunge those moments with Claire in his parked car. How many thousands of times had he begun the sentence "If that hadn't happened . . ."? It seemed that before that evening with Claire his life had been utterly in his control. He was a success, he was loved, he could do no wrong. And so he had let her unzip his pants. And although he knew with all the logic at his command that the one event had not caused the other—Stanley Carpasso would have started the fire regardless—he did not believe it. Part of him was certain that the moment with Claire had made the fire inevitable. As a result, he deserved punishment, and if the world wouldn't mete it out, then he would do so himself.

Now he was truly being punished but he wasn't the one doing it. He wasn't the one holding the whip, and the irony of this made him smile: How could he have ever thought that he would be able to choose the time and nature of punishment? Hawthorne's attempts in that direction were nothing but hubris. The truth was that Hawthorne felt that he could do nothing but hold on and endure what he had to endure. But he worried that he didn't have enough strength and in his worst moments he feared that he might collapse entirely, retreat to a corner and weep until an ambulance came to take him away. Maybe he'd be sent down to McLean's, where he had friends on the staff and they would see how far he had fallen. Later in the week, on Thanksgiving, he would drive to Concord and tell Krueger all that he had gone through.

Clifford Evings's suicide meant that the punishment was no longer Hawthorne's alone. The stories that Evings had been told about being fired, and the trashing of his office—these had been part of Hawthorne's burden, part of the gossip, the malice, the Sisyphean boulder of Bishop's Hill. Hawthorne had tried to bear that burden, but he had done little to discover who was responsible for Evings's torment, since surely he himself was the real target. And then Evings had died. As Hawthorne drove the gray, sleet-covered road to Plymouth, his hands clenched the wheel so tightly that the car swerved. Was he responsible for Evings's death as well? He had allowed Evings to become a shareholder in his punishment. He had done nothing to stop it. And who would be next? Kate? Jessica Weaver? Skander? Alice Beech? He had to do more than foolishly peering around a tree at the door of his apartment. He had to involve others—and others more capable than Tank Donoso.

At first, he had been tempted to talk to Chief Moulton, but he was afraid of not being believed. In his years as a clinical psychologist he had heard dozens of delusional confessions, ranging from intimate acquaintance with space invaders to the boast that the speaker was Jesus of Nazareth. He remembered hearing these confessions and trying to keep his face immobile, to maintain a certain smoothness of tone as he rid his speech of all trace of emotion or doubt. How awful it would be to see these responses in Moulton, for of course he would see them. How awful to hear Moulton say, "How interesting," and "Tell me more," as his eyes glazed over. No, he couldn't talk to Moulton, as least not yet.

What were his alternatives? Solicit help from the people who were on his side? Who were they? Kate? Bill Dolittle? Fritz Skander? Mrs. Sherman, Rosalind Langdon, and Alice Beech? Gene Strauss, Larry Gaudette, even Frank LeBrun? But what did he know about Strauss except that they had both rooted for the Yankees during the World Series and had watched two games together on Strauss's mammoth TV? As for Dolittle, his loyalty depended on whether he got the apartment in Stark Hall. And what did Hawthorne know about Skander, the eternal backer of conservative measures who disliked rocking the boat? Though he was tactless and insensitive, Skander had worked with these people a long time. If not his friends, they were at least friendly. Skander hadn't minded that they borrowed cars and lawn mowers and chain saws and took food from the kitchen.

Briefly Hawthorne considered hiring a private detective but the idea struck him as ridiculous. He imagined a Sherlock Holmes type creeping around Bishop's Hill with a magnifying glass. Besides, good detectives were expensive and who would pay? Would the money come out of his pocket or would he ask Hamilton Burke? And what did he know about Burke? What exactly had he said to Evings the day before Evings died? Had he really told him that he could take a leave?

It seemed that the only person available to investigate these matters was himself, but that seemed as foolish as hiring a private detective. His job as headmaster took at least sixty hours a week, so when would he find the time? And what did he know about investigation? He was an academic and a clinical psychologist. All his investigations had occurred in the decorous environment of the conference room and the therapist's office. Could he really snoop? Moreover, there was the likelihood of violence. Obviously the destruction of Evings's office had been violent.

Should he leave Bishop's Hill? Or do nothing, work hard, and hope that the people who disliked him would be won over? These choices were equally impossible because each was a failure, a surrender. Then why was he hesitating? Was he afraid? The mere possibility shocked him. And without the least hesitation, his mind moved to Wyndham School and the fire. When he had found the key to the window grate and had run back toward his apartment, to what degree had fear dragged at his footsteps? Flames were sweeping across the ceiling and up ahead the fire was worse. Later he told himself that, if he had left Claire just one minute earlier, Meg and Lily would have lived. But though that might be true, it didn't address the question of his fear. Had he run as fast as he could? Wasn't he using those minutes with Claire as an excuse? He had been afraid. He had not run his fastest. There were two crimes for which he deserved punishment, not one. And again Hawthorne nearly swerved off the road as he took his hands from the wheel and pressed them to his face.

When he arrived in Plymouth ten minutes later, he felt dazed, as if he had just awoken after a binge. The cars on the streets, the people on the sidewalks—he hardly saw them. His mind was full of the possibility of his fear. Although it was lunchtime, Hawthorne no longer felt hungry. He stopped at the drugstore to buy shampoo, deodorant, and aspirin, then realized he could easily have bought them at the supermarket where he would be going in any case. He walked aimlessly up Main Street despite the cold and intermittent sleet, looking into shops and staring into people's faces. He bought a *New York Times,* then went into a coffee shop and read it for an hour, letting his coffee get cold. When he was done, he could hardly remember anything— difficulties in Israel and Iraq, drug problems in Mexico. Below the level of consciousness, his mind was furiously engaged in argument with itself. He left the coffee shop, retrieved his car, and drove to the supermarket behind a great orange truck that was scattering salt on the pavement ahead.

Although Hawthorne took his meals in the dining hall, he liked to keep his small kitchen stocked with coffee, soft drinks, and an occasional six-pack of Beck's. And he usually kept crackers and cheese, nothing too elaborate. His Sunday teas for the students were catered by the dining hall, and the only items he might add were a box or two of chocolates, Jordan almonds, or something mildly exotic like a few tins of smoked oysters.

He was pushing his cart down one aisle after another with his mind hardly focused on his surroundings when he saw Mrs. Hayes standing in the checkout line. She wore a knee-length brown coat that swelled out over her full figure and a matching rain hat made of canvas. A man's black umbrella hung over her left forearm. Hawthorne knew that she lived in Plymouth but he couldn't remember where. He hadn't spoken to her since just after her resignation, and in truth she had nearly slipped from his memory.

Hawthorne watched her pay for her groceries then push her cart loaded with bags through the automatic door. She moved slowly, as if conscious of her fragility, and once outside she put up her black umbrella to protect herself from the sleet. Somewhat clumsily she maneuvered her cart while holding the umbrella. Abandoning his own cart, Hawthorne moved to the front of the store so he could observe Mrs. Hayes cross the parking lot to a green Ford Escort dotted with circles of rust. Hawthorne forgot about his shopping. He left the supermarket and hurried to his car, staying out of Mrs. Hayes's line of vision. Once in his car, he waited for her to finish loading her groceries through the rusty hatch of the Escort.

Mrs. Hayes drove out of the parking lot and turned left. Hawthorne followed. She drove slowly through the center of town and past the college, with its red brick buildings. She turned right down a residential street, then after three blocks she turned left. The streets were lined with small white Victorian houses. There was nobody else in sight. Hawthorne's windshield wipers made a steady whap-whap. The day was dim and he began to switch on his lights, then he decided against it.

When Mrs. Hayes turned right into a driveway, Hawthorne pulled to the curb. He knew she lived alone. Her house was small with a gable over the front porch and green shutters. He watched her carry her groceries up the steps and through the front door, turning on the porch light and making several trips. Sleet and wet snow accumulated on his windshield. After Mrs. Hayes closed the door, Hawthorne waited five more minutes to give her a chance to start putting away the groceries. The street was deserted. Not even any dogs were out.

Hawthorne left his car and hurried across the street and up Mrs. Hayes's front steps. For some reason he decided to knock rather than ring the doorbell. It seemed less intrusive. The storm door had two panels of glass at the top and bottom and the front door itself had a large glass pane. Through it, Hawthorne could see down a short hall to the kitchen, where a light burned.

Mrs. Hayes came out of the kitchen into the hall. She held a dish-cloth and was wiping her hands. When she saw who was at the door, she stopped and her face took on a worried look. She stared at Hawthorne from the hallway without moving. Her tight gray curls covered her head like a bonnet. Hawthorne made himself smile and felt intensely foolish. After at least ten seconds, Mrs. Hayes moved forward, still wiping her hands with the dishcloth. She looked at Hawthorne, and with her concern there was also a suggestion of anger. She opened the front door a few inches, leaving the storm door closed.

"What do you want?" she asked.

Hawthorne had nearly forgotten her voice, which was high and elderly. A creaky voice, he had once called it. "I need to talk to you."

"We have nothing to talk about."

"I think we do. Did you hear that Clifford Evings was dead?"

Mrs. Hayes's expression softened. "Yes, the poor man."

"I need to talk to you about what's going on at the school."

Mrs. Hayes unlatched the door, pulling it open. "I don't like you coming here."

"I'm sorry to bother you but I'm afraid it can't be helped." Hawthorne wiped his feet on the mat and entered the hall.

"I guess you'd better come in and sit down. Please excuse the mess."

The living room was as neat as a pin—an old woman's room with antimacassars and photographs of people who had probably died long ago. On the coffee table were several copies of *Reader's Digest* and *Yankee* magazine. Mrs. Hayes motioned to a worn armchair. "That was my husband's chair. You can sit in that."

Hawthorne sat down. He knew nothing of Mrs. Hayes's husband, whether he had died or had simply gone away. On a side table was a photograph of a beefy middle-aged man standing in a stream and holding a fishing pole above his head. He was grinning.

"I'd like to have you tell me again about the reasons for your resignation."

Mrs. Hayes sat down on the couch, perching at the very edge of the cushion. "That's all over and done with."

"Did someone say you would be fired?"

She didn't speak and looked down at the coffee table. Her gray hair had a bluish tint, as if she had recently been to the beauty parlor.

"I'd no intention of letting you go. Therefore you must have heard it from other people."

Mrs. Hayes straightened up as if she had come to a decision. "Roger Bennett told me you meant to fire me. He said he heard it directly from you and that he'd argued on my behalf. He said you were rude, that you called me 'old baggage.' "

"Anyone else?"

"Chip Campbell said you'd told him the same, that I was too dumb to learn about computers and the sooner I was out of there the better. People talked. They said they were sorry, they offered their sympathy—Herb Frankfurter, Tom Hastings, Ruth Standish. Ruth offered to help but I felt confused. Of course I was angry, but part of me couldn't help thinking you were right. I couldn't make any sense of those manuals."

"Did you talk to Mr. Skander?"

"He tried to help as well. I asked if you meant to fire me and he said that he didn't know. He told me we were going through difficult times and some changes were necessary. But Mr. Bennett warned me several times and Mr. Campbell, after he'd been dismissed, called me at home to say he'd talked to the board about my pension, that it was secure. I didn't feel I had any choice, and Mr. Bennett said that if I made a fuss it could jeopardize whatever I received. Really, my pension was small enough as it was. I was quite frightened." Mrs. Hayes still held the dishcloth, which she twisted in her hands.

"What about the Reverend Bennett?"

"She never spoke to me at all. Cold, I found her. She never even said hello when I passed her in the hall."

"And were there others?"

"I can't remember. Many people were sympathetic. Really, I'd no idea who to believe. I can't think Mr. Bennett meant me harm. He was always friendly, nothing at all like his wife. And Chip Campbell gave me little gifts at Christmas and would always stick his head into the office to say hello."

"Did you ever have anything to do with the finances of the school?"

"No, never. Mr. Skander handled all that as bursar—him and the bookkeeper. I ordered supplies but I never knew anything about the billing."

"Tell me about Mr. Pendergast."

Mrs. Hayes sat a little straighter and pursed her lips. After a moment she said, "He wasn't a nice man, especially after his wife died."

"You mean he had a temper?"

"No, nothing like that."

"Then what was it?"

"I'd rather not talk about it."

"Were you surprised when he resigned?"

"He'd said nothing about it to me. He made the announcement in early December that he'd leave at the end of the semester. Yes, I suppose I was surprised. He was only in his midfifties or so, and I suppose I thought he was going to stay until he retired."

"Can you give me any more sense of how he was?"

Mrs. Hayes gave a slight smile, half mocking. "He was very vain. Once he asked me if I thought he was losing his hair. Then he began to tint it. And he worried about his figure. When it was somebody's birthday and there was cake, he never ate any."

"Was he good-humored?"

"He had a big, booming laugh and I'd hear it when he was talking on the telephone."

"Did he have any close friends at the school?"

"He was friendly with everyone, but he was headmaster. He felt he should keep a certain distance. He was friends with Mr. Skander and perhaps one or two others. He also had friends here in Plymouth and Laconia."

"When did his wife die?"

"About two years before he resigned. In the spring. He was quite distraught, although she'd been sick for some time. It was cancer. After she died, he was barely able to finish the semester."

"And when he came back in the fall he was different?"

"Yes."

"How?"

"I said I'd rather not talk about it."

"But he wasn't nice?"

Mrs. Hayes pursed her lips and said nothing.

"Tell me," said Hawthorne after a moment, "has he ever been back to visit the school?"

"Never. He's never been back."

When he left Mrs. Hayes, Hawthorne drove directly to Brewster. He'd forgotten that he hadn't had lunch and that there was shopping he meant to do. He thought of the basketball game when Roger Bennett knocked him to the ground. He thought of the Reverend Bennett's insistence that Mrs. Hayes had been fired. And he thought about Pendergast, old Pendergast, as Skander had called him. The sleet was now mixed with snow. Cars were traveling slowly with their lights on.

Hawthorne found Chief Moulton in his office in a small building next to Steve's Diner. Yellowing Wanted flyers were stuck to a bulletin board with colored tacks. Against a wall were three wooden file cabinets. Moulton was unwrapping two bologna sandwiches from wax paper on the green blotter of his oak desk. He was in his shirt sleeves, and a can of Diet Coke stood between his left elbow and the telephone. A chunky, balding man, he had an oblong face as smooth as a toddler's knee. He looked up at Hawthorne and raised his eyebrows.

"You caught me eating my lunch," he said. Yellow mustard had soaked through the white bread of the sandwiches. Moulton folded the wax paper and slipped it into a small brown paper bag.

"I can wait outside."

"That's okay. I guess you've seen somebody have lunch before."

He bit into a sandwich and chewed slowly as he looked at Hawthorne without speaking. After a moment, he took a drink of Coke and swallowed. "You can sit down if you want."

Hawthorne took the chair on the other side of Moulton's desk. The smell of the bologna and mustard made him recall that he had missed lunch.

"If you tell me what's on your mind," said Moulton, "that'll give me time to chew."

"I wondered if you knew any more about who had vandalized Mr. Evings's office."

"You came all the way from Bishop's Hill to ask that or were you just driving by?" Moulton's tone indicated that he was making a joke. As he chewed, he continued to watch Hawthorne.

"It was a contributing factor in Evings's suicide. I wanted to know if you thought the person who did it was someone at the school or from outside."

"It was someone at the school."

"How do you know?"

"Firstly, because Evings hardly knew anyone outside of Bishop's Hill. He didn't seem to have friends *or* enemies. Secondly, because whoever did it knew the layout of the buildings and had a key. The lock wasn't picked or forced. And why'd the fellow steal that picture from the frame?"

"Do you think it could have been a student?"

"There was too much cunning in it. It was too worked out."

"Did you ever know Pendergast," asked Hawthorne, "the previous headmaster?"

"I met him several times over the years." Moulton had stopped eating but continued to watch Hawthorne closely.

"What did you think of him?"

"I can't say I'd formed an opinion. He seemed friendly enough. Hail fellow well met. I was sorry when he lost his wife."

"Were you surprised when he resigned?"

"I expect I was surprised that I hadn't heard anything about it before it happened."

"Do you know anyone very well at the school?"

"I can't say I know anyone well. The head housekeeper, Mrs. Grayson, and I were in school together. And I've known Mrs. Hayes for many years. The local people at the school, I pretty much know all of them. And a number of the teachers I've seen around."

"And you talked to them?"

"You mean about the vandalism? I expect I've talked to them all." Chief Moulton sipped his Coke, then patted his lips with the back of his hand.

"One more thing. There was a girl, Gail Jensen, who died over the Thanksgiving break three years ago. Do you know the cause of her death? She probably died in Plymouth, but I'm not sure."

Moulton pushed his sandwich away, got to his feet, and hitched up his belt. "I can find out." He walked to the file cabinet, limping slightly, and pulled out the top drawer. Then he drew out a sheaf of papers that had been stapled together and began to read.

"Well?" asked Hawthorne.

Moulton went to his desk and lowered himself into his chair. He seemed to be pondering something. "She died of a hemorrhage."

"Due to appendicitis?"

Moulton dug at one of his front teeth with a thumbnail, then he plucked something off the tip of his tongue. "She died due to a botched abortion," he said.

It was Monday night and Scott McKinnon was playing detective. He liked it. There was nothing at Bishop's Hill that escaped his notice, or almost nothing, since he still had to find out who'd trashed Evings's office. For that matter, he still hadn't worked out who had hung Mrs. Grayson's cat. But he hadn't given up. Persistence, that's what he had. Indefatigability.

Like tonight, for instance, he had been outside by the garage smoking a cigarette when he heard shouting from the kitchen, then LeBrun slammed out of the back door, followed immediately by the cook, who was angry and shouting at his cousin, and now Scott was hurrying behind them, eager to hear what the fuss was about.

It was cold and no stars were visible, just a glow from the hidden moon. It was supposed to start snowing in the night and snow all the next day and maybe the day after, and Scott liked to think they'd be marooned and the kids who hoped to go home on Wednesday for

Thanksgiving would get stuck and wouldn't be able to go anywhere, because Scott wasn't going anywhere either. His father was in L.A. and his mother was in Boston and both said they didn't have time for Thanksgiving. "Maybe I'll grab a turkey sandwich," his father had told him over the phone, then he had laughed. It would snow so much there would be a great mountain of snow covering the first-floor windows and all the kids who had homes to go to for Thanksgiving and couldn't go anywhere would feel like shit.

LeBrun hurried along the edge of the playing fields with Gaudette about ten feet behind him. Gaudette wore a white jacket that made him glow in the light of the distant security lights. LeBrun wore a dark sweater. Scott thought they must be freezing, because he was wearing a down jacket and he was still cold and his feet in their basketball shoes were chunks of ice as he jogged forward to catch up. But he didn't get too close, only close enough to hear. So far the only word he'd made out was *tequila,* which didn't seem like much, though he guessed it had to do with Jessica's getting drunk in the headmaster's house and dancing wildly with her clothes off, which was a scene that Scott would have liked to see.

"Stop!" called Gaudette. "I'm warning you! I'll go to Hawthorne!"

Abruptly, LeBrun turned to face his cousin and Scott had to fling himself down so he wouldn't be seen. Then he wriggled toward the trees in order to soak up some shadow.

"Fuck you," said LeBrun.

Gaudette stopped a few feet from LeBrun. "What's wrong with you? I thought you liked Hawthorne. Who paid you to wreck that old guy's office? Was it Bennett? Jesus, you make a mess wherever you go."

"Just stay out of it, do you hear? You got work, I got work. That's just how it is."

"How come your work always brings in the cops? And you're fucking that girl, right? She's a kid."

"I'm not fucking anybody."

"Who paid you to wreck that office?"

"I don't want to talk about it."

Gaudette took a pack of cigarettes from under his cook's jacket. He popped one out and lit it. The glow from the lighter briefly illuminated his face, making it seem redder than usual.

"Give me one of those, will you?"

Gaudette stepped forward and handed his cousin the pack. Now LeBrun's face was quickly visible and disappeared again. Scott thought it looked twisted, but that was just a result of the shadows. He wished he too had a cigarette but there was no way he was going to ask them.

Gaudette and LeBrun stood smoking and not saying anything. The tips of their cigarettes made red arcs as they moved them up to their mouths and away.

"You want to hear a joke?" said LeBrun.

"I'm sick to death of your jokes."

"What does an elephant use for tampons?"

"I said I'm sick to death of your jokes. When you called me about this job, I thought I was doing you a favor. And you promised to stay out of trouble, right? What else have you been doing? You wrecked that office and you're fucking that girl and getting her drunk . . ."

"I said I'm not fucking anybody." LeBrun flicked away his cigarette and Scott watched where it went because there had to be a lot left and maybe he could find it after they had gone.

"Somebody must have paid you. If it wasn't Bennett, then it was probably Campbell. Why else would you have done it unless someone paid you? You caused that old guy's death just as much as if you'd shot him. I don't know what I was thinking, bringing you up here. You're as wacko as ever."

LeBrun took a step toward his cousin, then stopped. "I don't like being talked to like that. You needed someone to help with the cooking and I done it. I been making good bread."

"I want you out of here," said Gaudette. "I'll drive you to Plymouth and you can get a bus in the morning. If you need cash, I'll lend it to you. You can pay me back when you get your check."

"No way, man, I got stuff I got to do."

"You don't have a choice. If you don't go tonight, I'll talk to Hawthorne. Don't you see that me knowing this stuff makes me an accomplice? I got a good job here and I don't want to lose it."

"Come on, man, I need two more weeks. We're brothers."

"Two more weeks to get in even worse trouble? Look what's happened because you gave the girl tequila. Shit, you said you liked Hawthorne."

"I was having some fun. It didn't hurt anybody. A girl dancing, what's the trouble with it?"

"She's fifteen." Gaudette flicked away his cigarette. "And Hawthorne could lose his job. Believe me, I don't want Skander in charge again."

"I did a lot worse when I was fifteen. I got dicked and no tears were shed. As far as I know, she's still got her cherry. Leastways I didn't take it, that much I know for sure." LeBrun laughed.

"I'm tired of your troubles. Pack your bag and I'll drive you down to Plymouth." Gaudette began to turn away.

"I don't want to hurt you, bro."

Gaudette turned back again, furious. "Hurt me, you wacko little shit, you want me to bust up your face? You got one last chance—take it or you'll go to jail."

LeBrun laughed again. "Okay, okay. Don't get so serious." He began to walk back. "I'll pack my stuff. I was getting pretty sick of this place anyway. Fucking cold just about tears you apart. You hear about the Canuck who died while getting a drink of water?"

The two men began walking toward the garage. Although Scott wasn't directly behind them, he was closer than he cared to be, lying flat on his belly. He rolled over, moving nearer to the trees. As a result, he didn't see exactly what happened.

"Some fucker slammed the toilet seat down on his head," said LeBrun.

And as Scott looked, it seemed that LeBrun had his arm around his cousin's shoulder, except that Gaudette fell forward. LeBrun made no attempt to catch him and Gaudette fell onto his face, jerking a little, then lying still, a white mound on the grass.

LeBrun kicked his cousin lightly with his foot. "Wacko, wacko, wacko—you got to watch out what you call a person."

It was only Scott's terror that kept him from leaping up and running back toward the school. He lay on the ground and pressed his hands to his face.

LeBrun chuckled a little. He bent over and grabbed Gaudette's arm, pulling him up. "We got to do one more trip together, bro, one more little journey and that will be that." He yanked Gaudette upward, then ducked down and pulled his cousin onto his shoulder. Scott had no doubt that the man was dead. He just didn't see how it had happened so fast. It felt like screaming was going on inside his head, huge amounts of loud noise.

Still, when LeBrun set off across the playing field, Scott followed, staying some distance behind so that, if it hadn't been for Gaudette's white jacket, he couldn't have seen them. LeBrun moved quickly across the grass, then around the gym, at times even jogging forward a few steps as the dead man jostled on his shoulder. He crossed the lawn in front of the school till he joined the driveway, then he quickened his pace, passing between the gates and up the road. Scott couldn't guess where he was going but he kept after him, sometimes losing sight of him, sometimes catching the glint of Gaudette's jacket as it lurched on LeBrun's shoulder.

A quarter mile up the road was the bridge over the Baker River. All weekend there had been rain and sleet and Scott could hear the water flowing noisily. LeBrun stopped and Scott crept forward. He could make out LeBrun standing on the bridge with Gaudette's white shape up in the air as if it were floating. Then the dead man seemed to fly, because the whiteness rose up and disappeared. Seconds later Scott heard the splash and again he felt horror, as if he too had been splashed by frigid water. But he had no time for horror. LeBrun was coming back.

Scott ducked down in the bushes by the side of the road. He heard LeBrun approaching—not the man's footsteps but his heavy breathing getting louder. It was all Scott could do to stay motionless. Now he heard LeBrun's hurrying footsteps heading back to the school and he knew that LeBrun would pass only a few feet from him. LeBrun got closer and stopped. He stood in the road breathing heavily and looking around him, a darker shadow in the darkness. Suddenly there was a flame of light as LeBrun lit one of his cousin's cigarettes, but at first Scott didn't understand and he jerked and the leaves around him rustled.

LeBrun stood still, breathing heavily, invisible except for the glow of his cigarette. Seconds passed. LeBrun's breathing grew quieter. "Are you out there, little rabbits?" he said at last. "You watch out the hawk doesn't get you. They'll eat you up, little rabbits."

LeBrun moved forward again and Scott waited until the sound of LeBrun's footsteps had almost disappeared, before he followed. As he and LeBrun approached the school, Scott could see LeBrun's silhouette. Again LeBrun cut across the lawns, passing the gym and veering across the playing fields. Scott stayed back, at times losing him, at times catching sight of him in the glow of the security lights. Scott's body felt weak, as if he were exhausted. He followed LeBrun to the garage where Gaudette's car was parked. LeBrun got into the car, started the engine, and backed out of the garage. In the light of the headlights, great fat snowflakes began to appear.

Then Scott made a mistake. He thought that LeBrun would try to escape, that he'd turn right and follow the driveway around to the front of the school. Instead, he turned left, driving back toward the old dilapidated barn, which was never used and which the students were told to stay away from because the floor was weak. Scott flung himself down by a bush. He could feel the snowflakes falling upon his neck and face, onto the back of his hands. The car's headlights moved across him.

Part Three

9

The black lines on the floor of the swimming pool seemed to shiver and bend—five black streaks at the bottom of the iridescent turquoise. The natatorium itself was dark, with only an eerie glow coming from the underwater lights. Somewhere a kitten was mewing, frantic and unceasing, like a squeaking wheel going round and round. Hawthorne stood beside Floyd Purvis, the night watchman. Along with the smell of the chlorine, Hawthorne could smell the whiskey on Purvis's breath as the older man gently swayed on his heels with his hands in his hip pockets. It was late afternoon on the Saturday after Thanksgiving and Hawthorne had just returned to Bishop's Hill, having spent the holiday with Kevin Krueger and his family in Concord.

A shadow was floating on the surface of the pool and Hawthorne realized it was the body of the boy, a dark shape on the brightness of the water.

"Turn on the lights," said Hawthorne.

Unsteadily, the night watchman made his way to the switch. There was a loud clank and the banks of fluorescent ceiling lights began to flicker and hum. The green cinder-block walls blossomed out of the dark.

Scott McKinnon floated face down in the center of the pool. He was naked except for a pair of Jockey shorts. The orange-striped kitten, wet and bedraggled, was perched on Scott's shoulder. It mewed and kept lifting its paws one after the other out of the inch or so of water across Scott's back and shaking them. Scott's arms were outspread as if he were gliding over the surface.

"I found him just ten minutes ago," said Purvis. His voice was cracked. He started to reach for a cigarette, then stopped himself. He was a red-faced, soft-looking man of about sixty who wore an orange camouflage hunting jacket and dark blue shirt and pants. "The cops'll be here anytime."

Hawthorne didn't answer. He felt sick in his stomach. A pole with a hook hung on the far wall but Hawthorne didn't think it was long enough to reach the boy. The lights flickered, giving the two men's faces a greenish tint. Hawthorne took off his glasses, then kicked off his shoes and began removing his pants.

"You're supposed to wait for the police," said Purvis. "I know that much. You're not supposed to touch the body." Purvis moved back as if to disassociate himself from Hawthorne.

Again Hawthorne ignored him. Once he was down to his underwear, he stepped to the edge of the pool and dove, gliding under the water with his eyes shut till he rose to the surface. He thought of the hours he had spent in this ugly space coaching the swim team with Kate and how he had never imagined it could get any uglier. Using a breaststroke and keeping his head above water, he swam toward the dead boy, who bobbed gently, as if there were still life in him. When the kitten saw Hawthorne approaching, it began to mew loudly in terror and anticipation, arching its back and bristling its orange fur. Hawthorne tried not to disturb the water, so as not to jostle the boy's body and further frighten the kitten. Reaching Scott, he began pushing him to the side of the pool. When he'd gone halfway, Hawthorne felt a sudden pain on his right shoulder. The kitten had jumped onto him and dug in its claws. Hawthorne sucked in his breath, trying not to move abruptly. He nudged the body forward. The boy's skin was the same temperature as the water and felt like rubber. Long strands of Scott's hair floated on the surface and brushed against Hawthorne's face.

When Hawthorne had pushed Scott up against the gutter, he called to Purvis, who still stood by the door watching.

"Grab his arm!"

The pain from the kitten's claws made Hawthorne feel dizzy. Purvis walked part way around the pool, then said something that Hawthorne couldn't make out because the kitten kept mewing just a few inches from his ear.

"Say that again?" Hawthorne kept kicking his feet to stay afloat.

Purvis took a few more steps along the side of the pool and shouted. "I said I don't want to touch him. I mean, you're not supposed to touch the body. I know that much."

Hawthorne felt so angry that it scared him. "Then take the cat. And for Pete's sake, hurry!"

Hawthorne had an arm under Scott's neck and was holding on to the gutter along the side of the pool. With his other hand he held the body against the tiles. This close and without his glasses, Hawthorne took in Scott's face as a chalky blur—the bump of his nose, the curved horizon of forehead. He tried to lift himself in the water so that Scott's hair wouldn't touch his face. The kitten mewed and clung to him anxiously.

Purvis knelt down on the side and reached over Scott's body to the kitten, which began to hiss and spit. Then he grabbed the kitten, but the kitten wouldn't let go. Bending forward, Purvis yanked the kitten loose, then fell back into a sitting position.

"Jesus!" said Hawthorne.

Purvis groaned and got to his feet, holding the kitten away from his body with both hands so its legs dangled down. "You're bleeding," he said. He seemed surprised

Hawthorne didn't answer. He tried to roll Scott's body up onto the side but the water was over his head and he couldn't get sufficient purchase. He let go of the boy and scrambled out of the water. Then he grabbed Scott's arm and pulled him onto the tiles. The boy's skin was puckered and wattled. He looked swollen. There was a black-and-blue mark on the upper part of his right arm. He lay on his back and the water ran off him, forming rivulets that ran back into the pool. Scott's eyes were slightly open but there was only grayness behind them. Hawthorne stared at him. It was worse than seeing Evings dead. Hawthorne's grief made him breathless.

"He must of been fooling around and got drowned," said Purvis matter-of-factly, still holding the kitten away from his body. The kitten squirmed and tried to scratch him but couldn't.

Hawthorne walked toward his clothes, keeping his back to Purvis. "Then how did he get in? The door was locked." He picked up his glasses and put them on.

"He must of had a key."

Hawthorne said nothing to that. He went into the pool office and called Alice Beech and after another moment he called Kate because he wanted to hear the voice of someone he felt close to. Although he had only spoken a dozen words to her alone since Evings's funeral, Hawthorne couldn't get her out of his mind and he kept worrying about what she thought. He felt convinced that she despised him.

"Scott McKinnon drowned in the pool." He described how the watchman had found him and explained that he was calling from the pool office.

At first Kate couldn't believe it and began to ask questions. Then she said, "I'll be right over."

Hawthorne started to say that she didn't need to come and then he said nothing.

After he hung up, he looked at his shoulder in the mirror. It was still bleeding and drops of blood had rolled down to the waistband of his wet underwear. There was a first aid kit in a rusty white cabinet with a red cross attached to the wall and Hawthorne took out some bandages. Purvis stood in the doorway of the office still holding the kitten, which had stopped mewing and was dangling from his hands and looking around as if trying to accommodate itself to a difficult situation. Purvis held it out as if offering a gift.

"Can you wipe off this blood and put a bandage on my shoulder?" asked Hawthorne. The scratches and cuts were on his shoulder blade below where he could easily reach. Through the window of the office he saw Scott lying by the side of the pool. Very briefly Hawthorne felt surprise that the boy was still there, that he hadn't gotten up.

Purvis looked at the scratches on Hawthorne's shoulder, squinting his eyes. "I'd rather not," he said. "My hands aren't steady."

Hawthorne had taken a towel from the coach's locker and was drying himself. He paused to glance at Purvis but didn't speak. Alice could put on the bandage. The scratches still stung but not as badly. Hawthorne took off his wet underwear, then went to get his pants. Purvis seemed uncomfortable with Hawthorne's nakedness and looked away.

"What do you want me to do with this here cat?" asked Purvis.

Hawthorne finished putting on his pants, then reached out to take the kitten, holding it close to his naked chest and scratching its ears. He knew it was Jessica's kitten and wondered how it had gotten in the pool. He thought about the cat that had been hung in September, but beyond summoning up the recollection, he didn't know what to do with it. He took the kitten into the office and dried it off on the towel, then he got another towel and made a little nest on the desk. The kitten began to purr. He put the kitten into the nest and stood back.

"It'll get away," said Purvis. He was still swaying a little.

The kitten stretched and began sniffing its way around the desk.

"It might fall in the pool again."

Hawthorne made no answer and went to put on his shoes.

When Alice showed up a few minutes later, she was out of breath. Her square, chunky face was red with cold. She knelt down by Scott's body and smoothed back his hair, touching him with great tenderness. She wore jeans and a gray sweater under her down jacket and her short dark hair looked bristly.

"But how'd he get in the water?" she said at last. "Couldn't he swim?"

"I don't know," said Hawthorne.

"He's been in the water quite a while."

"The door was locked," said Hawthorne. "I don't know how he got in here. And I don't know where his clothes are. Maybe in the locker room."

"Where're the police?"

"Supposedly on their way."

Alice stood up and moved behind Hawthorne, then lightly touched his back with one finger. "Let me fix up your shoulder. It must hurt."

They walked back to the pool office. Purvis had gone outside to smoke a cigarette and wait for Chief Moulton. The kitten was nosing around the office, sniffing what there was to be sniffed.

Alice unwrapped the bandage, then took a bottle of alcohol from the cabinet. "This is going to sting a bit."

Chief Moulton and Kate arrived at the same time about five minutes later. It was snowing and they brushed snow from their jackets and stamped their feet, leaving small puddles of water on the tiles.

Purvis ushered them in somewhat officiously, as if he were personally responsible for their arrival. The shoulders of his orange hunting coat were white with snow and there was snow in his gray hair.

"I told Dr. Hawthorne to leave the body where he found it," he said. "But he insisted on dragging it out." He looked disappointed and disapproving. He wheezed when he breathed.

Purvis and Moulton knew each other but there seemed no love lost between them. The policeman acted as if Purvis were invisible, hardly looking at him when he spoke. Both he and Kate went over to the boy's body. Moulton bent down, taking hold of Scott's arm and moving it a little. Kate stood behind him, staring down with one hand pressed to her mouth and the other pressed across her stomach.

"I called the troopers and the rescue squad," said Moulton, standing up, then bending over and rubbing his knees. "Not much to be done, but the troopers like to stay abreast of things. Who's the kitten belong to?"

"A girl at the school," said Hawthorne.

"It's a wonder it didn't get drowned as well," said Moulton. "It must of fallen into the water after the boy had already been dead a while."

"Why do you say that?"

"If he drowned, then he'd sink down and some time later he'd come up again. The kitten couldn't have been paddling all that time, leastways I don't think so."

Scott's clothes were found behind the bleachers, where they had apparently fallen. There were no keys in his pockets to let him into the gymnasium. Hawthorne remembered the boy's green parka and wondered where it was.

"Little cold to be wandering around without a coat," said Moulton.

They stood just outside the pool office. Kate hadn't said anything. She held the kitten in her arms, stroking it. "Scott called me Thursday evening. Thanksgiving." She nodded toward Hawthorne. "He was looking for you. He sounded excited and scared. I told him you were down in Concord but would be back on Friday or Saturday. I asked if anything was wrong and he said nothing was wrong. But he was almost whispering over the phone and talking fast. I asked if he wanted to come over to my house and even offered to pick him up. But he said no, he could handle it himself, that it wasn't important. Then I gave him your friend's name. I told him I didn't have the number but he could probably get it from information. I don't know, I should have gone over to the school right away. It was past eight o'clock and Todd's bedtime." She turned away and didn't say anymore. Alice Beech put her hand on Kate's arm.

"He didn't call," said Hawthorne uncertainly. "What happened on Thanksgiving? Did Larry Gaudette come back?"

Gaudette had turned up missing on Tuesday. His car was gone and he seemed to have taken a small suitcase of clothes. LeBrun said he had no idea where his cousin had disappeared to. "Maybe he's got family problems," he had suggested. "That whole family's messed up."

LeBrun had declared that he could handle the cooking by himself. He seemed eager. It would be a challenge. Tuesday had been the last day of classes and many of the students had left for Thanksgiving, but twenty students had remained, including Scott and Jessica. LeBrun cooked four large turkeys, making a Thanksgiving dinner with the fixings, including fresh biscuits. Alice Beech had eaten with the students, as had some of the faculty members. She said the meal had been wonderful.

"Frank LeBrun was a real impresario," she said. The Reverend Bennett had said grace and led them in a few Thanksgiving hymns, accompanied by Rosalind Langdon on an electric keyboard. LeBrun had sung as well, louder than anyone. Alice couldn't remember if Scott had been there, but she thought he had. She just wasn't sure.

Moulton asked a few questions about Gaudette, where he was from and how long he had been at the school. Then he made several phone calls from the office. The rescue squad arrived and a few minutes later Fritz Skander came hurrying into the natatorium. He had seen the flashing lights on the rescue truck and asked why no one had called him.

"What a pity, what a pity," he kept saying. His dark overcoat was dusted with snow. About ten students had gathered outside and Purvis kept them from entering the building. Skander stood by the pool office and watched the men from the rescue squad lift Scott onto the stretcher. He kept wringing his hands as if they were wet. "Jim, could you have possibly left the pool open? After all, you'd been coaching the team—"

"Of course not. Everything was locked. Purvis had to unlock the door."

"I don't understand it," said Skander. "What a tragedy."

"Did you see Scott on Thursday or Friday? Did he talk to you?"

Skander seemed to consider this. "I don't think I saw him since *before* Thanksgiving. We had a quiet turkey at home with a few friends. I don't believe I came over to the school all day."

The men from the rescue squad covered Scott with a red blanket. As they carried him past the group standing by the office, Kate began to weep. Hawthorne wished he could weep as well.

"This is awful, simply awful," said Skander. "Jim, you'll have to call the boy's parents right away. Poor things. And goodness knows what the newspapers will make of this. What a pariah we'll become." His thick gray hair sparkled with melting snow. He ran his hands through his hair, wiped them on his overcoat, then studied them.

The rescue squad carried the boy out of the building and drove off, taking the body down to Plymouth. Moulton was waiting for someone from the state police. He went outside to talk to Purvis about when he had found the body, when he had last looked in on the pool, and whether he had seen Scott on the grounds either Thursday or Friday.

Skander decided to leave, saying that he felt obliged to tell the other staff and faculty members—those who hadn't left for the Thanksgiving break. The students were bound to be terribly upset. "Ruth Standish has gone down to Boston and poor Clifford is dead. We've no counselors, no one who's been properly trained, except you, of course." He nodded toward Hawthorne. "I wouldn't be surprised if we didn't have to engage grief counselors. Who knows where the money will come from?" He buttoned his coat. "I'll call Hamilton Burke; perhaps he can make a suggestion. And perhaps he can also deal with the press. Poor man, as if he didn't have enough to do."

As Skander walked toward the door, Jessica Weaver came hurrying in. She had tried to get in earlier but Purvis had kept her out. Now Purvis was engaged with Chief Moulton.

"Where's Lucky?" she said anxiously. "They said outside my kitten was here." She wore a red down jacket. It was speckled with snow and snow was caught in her hair. Seeing her kitten in Kate's arms, she ran to it and took it gently. "Oh, I thought it was dead." She hugged the kitten to her face, kissing it, and the kitten squeaked. "It must be starved."

"How did it get out?" asked Hawthorne.

Jessica unzipped her jacket and slipped the kitten under it. "I don't know. I went to Thanksgiving dinner and when I came back it was gone. I thought it was a trick. I mean, my door was locked. I've been looking everywhere. Scott once told me that someone would probably try to hang it and I was scared. I was even looking at tree branches. But now she's safe, or he, I'm still not sure."

"Did you see Scott at Thanksgiving dinner?"

"I don't know. I don't think so. Everything is so awful. Poor Scott" The kitten's orange head was sticking out from the crack in Jessica's jacket. It kept mewing over and over. "You see how hungry it is? It wants me to feed it."

Hawthorne told her to go back to her room and take care of the cat. Kate and Alice Beech were talking together, then Kate said, "Scott must have taken the kitten. He must have been going to play some trick."

"Perhaps," said Hawthorne.

"But he certainly wouldn't hurt it," said the nurse.

At every pause in the conversation, Hawthorne could once again feel the rubbery coldness of the boy's skin. Early in the fall he had asked Scott if he wanted to join the swim team.

"I don't like getting wet," Scott had said.

But that didn't answer the question of whether or not the boy could swim.

Shortly, Hawthorne left the gym and headed back to Emerson Hall, meaning to talk to Frank LeBrun. It was a little before six and he assumed Frank would be in the kitchen. It was dark and the snow fell heavily, a mass of white flakes caught in the security lights, swirling yellow and white, a vortex of shiny particles. Away from the light the snow became a shadow in the air between Hawthorne and the looming shapes of Adams and Emerson Halls, where most of the windows were dark. Hawthorne buried his hands in the pockets of his coat. He wore no hat. The snow from earlier in the week had been plowed from the paths, but now several more inches had fallen and it shifted and blew around his feet as he scuffed through it. At least a foot covered the ground. He wondered how much more could fall. He had heard that in some winters, the really bad ones, there had been three hundred inches, though surely that wasn't all at once. But three feet of standing snow wasn't unusual, and a few times each winter the school would be cut off for a day or two—no phone, no electricity—before the snow-plows could get around to clearing the road. Once, two years earlier—so he'd been told—it had snowed so hard that not even jeeps and cars with four-wheel drive could get through, although usually such conditions didn't last long, no more than a day.

When Purvis had come to fetch Hawthorne with a garbled story about a boy in the water, Hawthorne had run out without his hat or scarf, even without putting on his boots. Now snow got into his shoes and his socks were wet. More snow got down the collar of his overcoat and fell onto his hair. His ears stung with cold. Having come east from San Diego, he hadn't seen snow in over three years. Often at Ingram House in the Berkshires there was snow, but never as much as in northern New Hampshire—there were not the great drifts, the roads indistinguishable from the fields around them, the trees under their white cloaks. Hawthorne felt a shiver of claustrophobia as he imagined being unable to get away from Bishop's Hill, the snow heaped halfway up the windows and the wind pushing its way through the cracks. Then he slipped on the walkway and lost his balance. As he twisted to regain his footing, the bandages pulled on his shoulder and he felt a stab of pain.

Hawthorne had liked Scott. More than liked. He had admired Scott's energy and rebellion, even when the boy exasperated him. Hawthorne had taken pleasure in the wiry intensity of his body, his tireless curiosity. It seemed impossible that he wouldn't see Scott in class on Monday or see him in the halls. Three times in the fall Scott had come to Hawthorne to take him up on his offer to go for a drive so Scott could smoke a cigarette. Hawthorne would take one of the dirt roads along the edge of the mountain—the trees changing and full of color the first time, then the leaves brown and falling, then the trees bare and skeletal. Through the trees were the bluffs and cliff faces that attracted climbers from all over New England. Scott would crack jokes and tell Hawthorne the harmless gossip, the gossip that wouldn't get anyone in trouble: boys and girls with crushes on one another, not who had been drinking or smoking dope. After forty-five minutes or so, Hawthorne would drive back to the school, feeling more content than before he had left, feeling that his work at Bishop's Hill wasn't so terrible after all. Now he would have to call Scott's parents and tell them the boy was dead.

The dishes of food for dinner already stood on the heated serving tables—turkey casserole, green beans and mounds of mashed potatoes, small white pitchers of gravy and, of course, bread. Shiny aluminum pitchers of water stood on a shelf by the entrance to the dining hall and two students were carrying baskets of bread through the swinging doors. The kitchen was warm and smelled of apples and cinnamon from the pies that LeBrun was taking from the oven.

"Only thirty-five tonight," he called as he saw Hawthorne come through the back door and pause to stamp his feet on the mat and brush the snow from his coat. "A piece of cake. You going to be eating as well? There's a place set."

Hawthorne took off his coat and hung it from a hook. The two older women who worked part-time in the kitchen were putting dishes into the dishwasher and scrubbing the pots. There was a small white plastic radio in the corner but it was unplugged.

LeBrun had baked eight apple pies and was setting them on the counter to cool. Hawthorne walked up to him. "Any news about your cousin? Do you have any idea where Larry could have gone?"

LeBrun looked bewildered and his eyebrows went up. "It took me by complete surprise. He'd gotten a call, I don't know who from, right here in the kitchen on Monday night. It upset him. He said he had problems, but he didn't say what they were. Hell, I didn't know he meant to take off. I didn't even know he was gone till I came in the next morning to make breakfast. I figured he'd overslept. I ran over to his apartment. His drawers were pulled out and there were clothes on the floor. He'd packed a bag and split."

"And his door was unlocked?"

"Larry never locks anything. He'd even leave the kitchen wide open if I didn't remind him. Tell you the truth, my feelings were hurt. I thought we were close enough that he'd let me know if anything was bothering him. I don't know, I'm still feeling down about it."

"Did you hear that a boy drowned in the pool?" asked Hawthorne.

Now LeBrun appeared shocked. He took a step backward and

his eyes widened. "Shit, you're kidding me. I didn't even know it was open."

"It wasn't. I don't know how he got in."

"Who was it?"

"Scott McKinnon. Did you know him?"

LeBrun's narrow brow wrinkled. "Wasn't he a tall kid?"

"No, he was quite small." He described Scott—small for his age, an eighth grader, thirteen years old, red hair, freckles. As he described the boy, Scott's face came vividly to mind. A nice kid, he thought, a kid who shouldn't be dead.

"I don't know," said LeBrun, "sounds familiar. I'm not sure I can place him. Was he in the chorus?"

"I don't believe so." Hawthorne went on to describe what had happened, how Purvis had come running to find him about two hours earlier, and how Scott appeared to have been in the pool for quite a while. He didn't mention the kitten.

LeBrun's thin face continued to express dismay. "And you just got back from seeing your friend, right? Damn, what a shame." He wiped his hands on his white apron.

"Anyway," said Hawthorne, "the police are here and they'll probably talk to you. They'll want to talk to everyone." It occurred to him that LeBrun had been more upset when Evings had died.

"I don't know if I want them in here," said LeBrun, beginning to fidget.

"I expect there'll be only one man. You can talk to him anywhere you want. The police will probably ask about Larry as well, about his family. They live in Manchester?"

"Sure, I can give them all that stuff. I don't mind talking to them unless they get rude. I don't like rude."

"You need to be patient, in any case."

"Yeah, well, maybe."

Hawthorne glanced at the apple pies. They made him hungry. "I'm sorry you've got this extra burden. You work hard enough without doing Larry's job as well. I'll make some calls tonight and try to get someone to help you."

"Nah, it's fine. I just have to move faster, that's all." LeBrun appeared pleased. He looked down at the floor and shifted his weight from one foot to the other. Then he grinned.

Hawthorne had driven down to Concord early on Thanksgiving. It had been a bright, sunny morning but cold, and the sunlight reflecting off the fresh snow sparkled so fiercely that Hawthorne needed his dark glasses. There were few cars on the interstate and no trucks, but the people he passed or who passed him seemed unusually cheerful. One little girl waved and waved to him from the rear window of a red Volvo station wagon. The closer he got to Concord, the less snow there seemed to be.

Driving to see Krueger, Hawthorne found it impossible not to think of other Thanksgivings they had shared in Boston when Meg and Lily were alive. And it was for this reason that Hawthorne had almost refused the invitation. But he told himself that he had to force his life forward even if he didn't wish to. He knew that part of him wanted to make himself suffer, the part that kept reminding him of how he had been late that night coming back to Wyndham, how he might have run faster down the burning hallway, if only he had been less afraid.

Against this was the memory of putting his hand against Kate's cheek, just that, the night he'd gone over to her house—he could feel its soft coolness under his palm even still. And Kate had taken his hand and kissed it. As he drove down to Concord the memory gave him a little thrill of pleasure. He knew that if he was going to move beyond the events in his past, then Kate might be able to help him.

Yet how could she not despise him? Here he professed to love his wife and daughter and yet he'd had sex with another woman in a parked car. Looking back, Hawthorne felt amazed by his hubris. He had been director of one of the most prestigious treatment centers in the country. His articles were taught in clinical psychology classes in dozens of universities. Specialists from around the world had come to Wyndham to see how well the school worked. Give the kids responsibility, he had said, give them things to care about. Let them earn their independence. Help them feel connected to their surroundings, feel a sense of belonging, obligation, and love. And it worked. Kids left Wyndham to lead successful lives. And when Claire had turned to him in the car, she was just one more gift that the world was giving him. Then came the fire that would destroy Hawthorne's theories and end his life.

Kevin Krueger and his wife lived in a small white Victorian with a wraparound front porch, the corner house on a quiet street a mile west of the capitol building. Hawthorne had arrived around eleven and already the house smelled rich with spices and cooking. Although Hawthorne wanted to ask Krueger's advice about Bishop's Hill and describe what had happened, he didn't wish to burden Krueger's Thanksgiving. And he told himself that he needed to live entirely within this day, with no grieving over the past and no worrying about the future. He knew he wouldn't succeed, or not completely—after all, he had brooded about Wyndham all the way down from Bishop's Hill—but he had to try, if only out of courtesy to his friend. Krueger's daughter, Betsy, was six and his son, James, was four. Hawthorne wanted to engage himself with these children, to be close to them without also thinking of Lily and how much he had loved her and how responsible he felt for her death.

Hawthorne managed not to talk to Krueger and his wife, Deborah, about the past and he said little about Bishop's Hill. He helped his namesake build a snowman in the backyard and duly admired the daughter's collection of Barbie dolls. Yet the past tugged at him ferociously and he kept having to jerk his mind away from its grip. Two other couples with whom Krueger worked in the Department of Education came to dinner in the afternoon and one brought their ten-year-old daughter, who Hawthorne couldn't stop looking at, her hair was so blond. As they ate they discussed education and psychology, even movies, staying away from sensitive subjects. Hawthorne realized that Krueger had warned them—don't talk about California or Bishop's Hill, remain in the plain vanilla of conversational material. They were careful not to look at the scar on his hand. Even the girl tried not to look at it, although she wasn't as successful as her parents. Partly everyone's efforts made Hawthorne feel like a cripple and partly he felt grateful.

The only difficult moment was when they were discussing people they knew in common. "Claire Sunderlin is a friend of ours," the man named Beatty said to Hawthorne. "I gather she used to be a student of yours."

"Yes, long ago at BU. She was very smart, very energetic. I haven't seen her for some time."

Twice during dinner Hawthorne caught Krueger glancing at him with concern. Krueger's wife kept urging him to eat more and he realized they both thought he was too thin. And his nerves were bad. When Krueger's small son overturned his milk, Hawthorne jumped and pushed back his chair. Even the Beattys looked at him curiously. He retired early to the upstairs guest room, then read until past midnight—an Agatha Christie mystery with Miss Marple that he had found on his bedside table. He envied a world where simple reasoning and analysis could bring about such successes.

The next morning after breakfast Krueger and Hawthorne retired to Krueger's study off the sunporch with a pot of black coffee. Hawthorne told him all that had happened since Krueger's visit— Jessica's drunken visit, the clarinet playing "Satin Doll," the grinning portrait of Ambrose Stark, the continued phone calls. Krueger already knew about Evings's suicide, but Hawthorne described the memorial service and how Bobby Newland had accused the school of murder. He recounted his conversation with Mrs. Hayes and how Bennett and Chip Campbell and others had convinced her that she was about to be fired. He talked about the girl, Gail Jensen, who had hemorrhaged to death after an abortion. And he talked about Lloyd Pendergast and what Mrs. Hayes had said about him. Deborah brought in a fresh pot of coffee. In the backyard, Krueger's children played in their red and blue snowsuits, throwing snowballs and sledding down a small hill. Their shouts were muted through the picture window.

Then Hawthorne talked about Wyndham, telling Krueger that he felt he was making himself accept these events at Bishop's Hill because he considered them a just punishment for what had occurred in San Diego—the hubris that had led him to be inattentive. He responded to the gossip and attacks by trying to endure them, doing little to stop them, and part of him wanted the attacks to get worse until they destroyed him. But Hawthorne didn't mention Claire and his adultery. He was afraid Krueger would hate him and he didn't think he could survive Krueger's hate. Through it all Krueger listened without interruption, drinking cup after cup of coffee, hardly changing his position on the couch as the morning sun moved across the snow-covered backyard.

At the end, Krueger said, "You've got to get out of there."

"That's what they want me to do."

"It doesn't matter. Your life and sanity are more important."

Hawthorne sat in a sprawling brown armchair that he had turned to face Krueger. "There are good people there. And there are the students. Nothing would be gained by forcing the school to close. Because that's what would happen. If I quit, the school will shut down. They might not even make it to May."

"I thought you said you were there to punish yourself, not to make the place work."

"I'm there for both."

"It's a piece of property. The board of trustees would most likely sell it to pay off the debts." Krueger drank the last of his cold coffee and made a face. He wiped his mustache. "It's private. It's got a physical plant. It's in a beautiful location."

"Who'd buy it?"

"Lots of people. A religious group, for instance. Didn't the Moonies buy a chunk of Farrington College? Or it could be turned into another sort of institution. Think of the money in for-profits. At least a dozen companies have bought up schools or hospitals around the country. The Galileo Corporation, Health International, even Holiday Inn and Sheraton have gotten into nursing homes and care for the elderly."

Hawthorne pictured Bishop's Hill full of the dazed and semi-comatose, the classrooms turned into bedrooms or wards, the library sold, the marble panels with the names of young men from Bishop's Hill who had fought in half a dozen wars taken to the dump. Then a fence would be erected around the property—high, but not so high that the place looked like a prison.

"I know some people in that industry," said Krueger, returning to the couch. "Let's say Bishop's Hill became a home for the elderly or for men and women with Down's syndrome, or a detox for alcoholics and addicts, or even a residential treatment center—the place would still need personnel: ward attendants, secretaries, kitchen and grounds people, housekeepers. I bet a bunch of people now at the school could find jobs. And at higher pay."

"But they wouldn't be teaching," said Hawthorne.

"Why should they care? You're looking in the wrong direction. The people spreading gossip and holding up the painting and playing the clarinet, they probably have nothing against you. You're simply in their way. My guess is that they want to sell off the school. They're greedy, that's all. It's too bad about Evings, but whoever wrecked his office can blame it on the kids. Wasn't he gay? They can say he was hitting on someone, that certain students objected to his homosexuality. The fact that he committed suicide—it was all for the best. The same thing with Mrs. Hayes quitting. Each of these things weakens the school, and if you resign, then that will be that. The place will open next year as a subsidiary of Holiday Inn and this guy Bennett will be a director or manager and making twice the money. You really think he's going to miss teaching algebra?"

Hawthorne laughed. "So it's all just progress."

"Bigger and better into the millennium. Fat profits, that's what life is all about. You should feel ashamed for standing in their way."

"But the vandalism and getting that girl drunk . . ." Hawthorne walked to the window. Krueger's children were making a snow fort, rolling balls of snow and stacking them on top of one another. "I want to talk to Lloyd Pendergast but I've no idea where he is. Do you think you can find out?"

"I expect so. What do you intend to do?"

Hawthorne continued to look out at the snow. "I don't want the school to close."

"And what if it gets more violent?"

"Then I'll have to deal with it. I like that policeman in Brewster who's investigating the vandalism. Perhaps I can count on him if things get bad."

"I still think you should leave."

Hawthorne turned around. "I can't."

"If you fail, will you take responsibility for that as well? Because, believe me, you're setting yourself up to fail. Will you go to some new place to seek a new punishment?"

Hawthorne had thought of nothing past Bishop's Hill. "I don't know."

Krueger cleared his throat and looked embarrassed. "I've got a pistol. I wish you'd take it."

The thought of packing a gun struck Hawthorne as immensely funny. He began to laugh. "The only guns I've ever fired have been in penny arcades."

"I'm serious. I'll show you how it works."

"I'm not that kind of person. I'm a talker. What would I do with a gun?" He paused, then asked, "Do you think a specific company is interested in Bishop's Hill?"

They went on to discuss possible interested parties. Krueger didn't mention Wyndham and Hawthorne didn't bring it up again. Nor did Krueger say anything else about Hawthorne's need for punishment. But Hawthorne felt better for having told his friend about Bishop's Hill. Krueger now knew what Hawthorne knew. He had become a witness and it made Hawthorne feel less isolated.

Around noon Krueger's wife had knocked on the door of the sun porch and brought in a plate of turkey sandwiches. The rest of the day was relaxed. They helped the kids with their snow fort, read, and went for a walk. At times Krueger would ask a question about one or another of the faculty—Herb Frankfurter, Ted Wrigley, Fritz Skander. Hawthorne talked somewhat vaguely about his friendship with Kate. That Friday evening they went to a movie. It was about a couple, each with their own children, trying to begin a romance. Hawthorne thought of Kate and tried not to think of Meg and Lily. He and Krueger were comfortable with each other, almost as they had been years before. Saturday morning they went to the YMCA and shot baskets for several hours. After lunch Hawthorne had driven back up to Bishop's Hill. The closer he had gotten, the more he had felt the old chill settling around him. Where things had seemed clear, they now began to seem confused again.

It was nearly dark when Hawthorne got back to his quarters in Adams Hall. The lights were out. He paused to stamp the snow from his feet and suddenly, inexplicably, he heard the frantic flapping of wings. Turning on the light, he saw that two birds had gotten into his living room: a mourning dove and a chickadee. The rug was spotted with feathers and bird droppings. At first he wondered how they had gotten in. All the windows were closed. Perhaps they had come down the chimney. Then he realized how unlikely that was. Someone had put them there.

Moving slowly, Hawthorne crossed the room and opened the French windows. The birds flew back and forth, frightened and unaware of the open door. The chickadee settled on a curtain rod. It was cold and the wind blew snow into the room. Hawthorne crossed to the door and tried to drive the birds toward the terrace. What was the point? What was he meant to think? Hawthorne felt only anger.

After a few minutes the chickadee found its way out into the snowy evening. The dove took longer and Hawthorne had to pursue it with a towel as the bird flew from one side of the room to the other and small gray feathers floated down to the rug. But at last it flew out through the French windows as well. Hawthorne closed them and put several sheets of newspaper over the snow that had blown onto the rug. He had just begun to clean up the bird droppings when Floyd Purvis had appeared, hammering on his door. He had found a boy drowned in the swimming pool and Hawthorne had to come right away.

Sunday morning, shortly after breakfast, Jessica walked over to the kitchen to talk to LeBrun. The day was sunny and the snow was beginning to melt, even though it was cold. As she walked along the path from her dormitory cottage to Emerson Hall, Jessica kept her eyes squinched against the glare. The mountains seemed to shine and the trees were all snow-covered, although now and then the pines on campus would shed their mantle of snow with a rush. The paths had been plowed and made curving black lines across the whiteness. Jessica wore a red down parka and her boots were bright purple.

She didn't want to see LeBrun, she was growing increasingly afraid of him, but that morning when she woke there had been a note under her door. She had thought they were about to go down to Exeter and rescue her brother. She had even begun to pack some of her clothes. But the note said it couldn't be Monday after all. It would have to be Friday. Jessica didn't like that and she wanted LeBrun to reconsider. If they changed the date, she'd have to call Jason. There wouldn't be time to write him. And if she called, there was the danger of reaching Tremblay or even her mother, though her mother wouldn't be so bad because she'd probably be drunk, and it was easy to put Dolly off if she was drunk.

But there was another matter bothering Jessica and that was her kitten, Lucky, which had recovered from its experience in the pool. What worried her was how Lucky had gotten into the water in the first place. She knew that LeBrun disliked cats and she knew he had a passkey, so he could easily have taken the kitten from her room. The implications of that were dreadful, however, because it suggested that LeBrun had thrown the kitten into the pool. And Scott had probably gone into the pool to rescue Lucky and had drowned. But how had Scott gotten into the pool unless LeBrun had let him in? Perhaps Scott had snuck in after him. But whatever the case, Scott's death and the kitten seemed inextricably entwined.

She felt awful about Scott—everybody did—and there was no way that she would get into that pool ever again. His death was still in the water. At dinner the night before, some kids had been crying and the rest had been somber. Although Jessica hadn't cried, she felt she should cry. Some kids had suggested that Scott had drowned himself on purpose, even that there was some connection between Scott and old Evings. And one girl, not a very bright one, had suggested that Bobby Newland had drowned Scott, getting even for Evings's death, and that Newland meant to kill them all one by one. That had been creepy even if it had been stupid. Jessica had liked Scott. He had been especially nice to her, even though he was younger, and he always offered her cigarettes when he had them. So she felt very much that she should cry and that perhaps there was something wrong with her— perhaps she really was a bad person after all—because she couldn't.

LeBrun was in the kitchen cutting up potatoes for lunch. He wore a white jacket, blue jeans, and a white cap. A student was helping him, a fat boy by the name of Phelps. One of the older women who worked in the kitchen was at the large metal sink, finishing up the pots from breakfast. The kitchen was bright with sunlight and the metal surfaces gleamed. There was the smell of garlic and tomato sauce. When the door swung shut behind Jessica, LeBrun stopped what he was doing and turned. He wrinkled his nose at her, then he came over, the knife still in his hand. Even his walk seemed crooked, as if he couldn't walk in a straight line. Jessica took off her cap, stuck it in the pocket of her parka, then shook out her hair.

"Hey, Misty, you want to help make lunch? We got a ton of work."

When LeBrun was about three feet away, Jessica said, "Did you throw Lucky in the pool?" She tried to keep her voice down, but the combination of anger and fear made it waver.

LeBrun raised his hands, as if in surrender, though he still held the knife. As he frowned, his dark eyebrows drew together. "You kidding? Why should I do a dumb thing like that?"

"Please, Frank, don't hurt my cat. I love it. I saved it and I want to take it away."

"You mean it's alive?" LeBrun shook his head in surprise.

"Dr. Hawthorne rescued it."

"For shit's sake, one life down, eight more to go."

"You *did* throw it in the water, didn't you?"

"What'd I just say?" LeBrun tapped the knife against his pant leg. They stood by two of the large refrigerators with stainless steel doors. Jessica's red jacket was reflected as a pink smudge on the bright metal.

"I want to take it with us when we get Jason."

LeBrun took a step closer, lowering his voice. "I sure as hell am not going to have a cat in the truck when we're driving down to Exeter, I can tell you that for damn straight."

"Please, Frank, I want to take Lucky."

"No way. The cat stays here. If you take the cat, I'll throw it out the window. I can't drive with a cat in the truck. Get serious."

Now Jessica felt like crying, even though she hadn't cried about Scott, but she wasn't going to cry and have LeBrun make fun of her. She swallowed and looked up at him crossly. "Why aren't we going tomorrow like we planned?"

"I got too much work. Larry took off, I don't know if you heard, and I'm in charge of the kitchen. If we go tomorrow, who'll make dinner? If we go later in the week, I'll get the chance to cook something ahead of time that can just be warmed up. I don't want to make trouble for Hawthorne. I'll be getting some more help in a day or so. And who knows, maybe Larry'll come back." LeBrun laughed abruptly, then stopped.

Jessica didn't like it but it made a kind of sense. The best plan would be for LeBrun to drive her to Exeter, help rescue Jason, then drive them to Boston, drop them off, and return to Bishop's Hill. That was a lot of driving, maybe seven hours all told. But LeBrun could come back in the night and nobody would know he'd been gone. But if he took off tomorrow and missed dinner, then everybody would know and they'd see she was gone as well. They probably wouldn't even get as far as Exeter before the police were called.

"Okay," said Jessica, "but don't do anything to Lucky. Promise me."

LeBrun reached out with the kitchen knife and slowly drew it a few inches down the red fabric of Jessica's parka. The fabric separated and white feathers pushed through the opening. "Don't tell me what to do. You hear what I'm saying? You don't want to make me upset."

Most of the students began coming back to Bishop's Hill from Thanksgiving break on Sunday afternoon, arriving by car with their parents or taking buses to Plymouth and getting picked up. A few flew into the small airport in Lebanon, then were driven to the school in a hired van. The snow made everyone late, though by evening most of the roads had been plowed. When the students arrived, they heard that Scott McKinnon had been found drowned in the pool on Saturday. A dozen or so had been friends with Scott, many liked him, all had known him. Coming so close after Evings's suicide, his death was especially upsetting and there was the question whether Scott hadn't committed suicide as well. Many theories went around and the students were agitated and disturbed. The homework that had been put off to the last minute didn't get done and students stayed up late talking. Those who had remained at school over the break couldn't remember exactly when they had seen Scott last, maybe Wednesday or maybe Thursday morning, but he had cut his math and English classes on Tuesday and he hadn't trailed anyone around trying to bum a cigarette.

At an assembly in the chapel during first period on Monday, Hawthorne talked about what had happened. He didn't talk about how Scott was found and he said nothing about the kitten. He spoke about grief and how it was a painful but necessary emotion. He said they all had every reason to be upset and the best thing they could do for Scott was to grieve for him, but they should also remember him and celebrate him and recall all that was good about him. The Reverend Bennett said several prayers. Many students wept and even several of the teachers wiped their eyes. Then Hawthorne canceled classes for the rest of the day and the students broke into groups to discuss their feelings. Many said how they were still upset about Mr. Evings, that he had been so unhappy that he had to kill himself, and they spoke about Bobby Newland's accusations and how distressing those had been.

Then the students began to realize that Mr. Newland wasn't at the school. He had been there for Thanksgiving dinner but had left either on Friday or on Saturday. According to the boys living in his dormitory cottage, the door to his small apartment was open and his clothes were gone.

As for Hawthorne, he was kept too busy to think about his conversation with Kevin Krueger. On Saturday he had begun trying to call Scott's parents, although he hadn't been able to reach the father in California until Sunday. And then he had to explain that he didn't know exactly what had happened or why Scott had been in the pool. He said the police were investigating. The father was angry and asked Hawthorne why they hadn't kept the damn place locked. And he said he meant to call his lawyer. The mother told Hawthorne that she would take care of the funeral arrangements. She wanted to get the body right away and she was upset when Hawthorne told her there had to be an autopsy. She said she didn't want her boy cut up, and Hawthorne could do nothing but give her Chief Moulton's phone number. And she, too, talked about lawyers and how she'd thought she could trust the school, when obviously it turned out that she couldn't. Hawthorne knew their anger masked their guilt—why, after all, had Scott had no place to go on Thanksgiving?—and he tried to be gentle with them and let them express their resentment and outrage.

Hawthorne's discovery that Bobby Newland had packed his clothes and disappeared was especially disappointing and made everyone's task more difficult, since Hawthorne needed him to talk to students. Bobby had the knack of making students feel at ease and express their emotions without constraint. He would have been useful that Monday when the students were saying how they felt about what had happened. All day Hawthorne went from one group to another, listening, for the most part, but also assuring them that their grief was necessary and natural. But it was more than grief. They all sensed that death was coming too close. First Evings, now Scott. Who would be next? A tenth-grade boy by the name of Skoyles asked if the locks shouldn't be changed and a twelfth grader, Sara Bryant, recalled that Gail Jensen had died at just this time three years earlier.

The notices that Hawthorne had written advertising for a new psychologist had begun to appear in the journals in November and already a few letters and résumés had arrived, despite the low salary.

Hawthorne recognized several names and one man had been a student of his in Boston. He realized that some applicants were responding to his own reputation, and he wasn't sure how he felt about that.

Fritz Skander also talked to students but he wasn't good at it and appeared stiff. The crying upset him and he told several students that they had to be brave, till Hawthorne explained to him that it was better to let them be emotional. It was Skander's idea that Scott had broken into the pool in order to swim and had accidentally drowned. His death was the grievous effect of a reckless cause. "It should remind us all," he told one group, "that we need to act like grown-ups." To another group he said, "A person who breaks into a cage of tigers must face the consequences."

A few faculty were helpful. Kate, of course, and Alice Beech. But also Betty Sherman, Gene Strauss, and Ted Wrigley. Bill Dolittle organized a reading of poems and other texts on grief and loss. The nurse went from dorm to dorm, just saying a few words; Kate came over to Jessica's dorm and talked to the girls in the living room, and she went to other cottages as well. But at least half the faculty stayed out of the way, though they, too, were shocked. Herb Frankfurter, for example, used the time to go hunting. Roger Bennett was also absent. Throughout Monday, Hawthorne hoped that Larry Gaudette would return and take some of the burden off his cousin, but there was no sign of him.

During the afternoon the Reverend Bennett told Hawthorne that Bill Dolittle was moving furniture into the empty apartment in Stark Hall. "And I hear him pacing above me," she said. "I didn't realize that you had given him permission to move in. I hate to think of the racket he's going to make."

Hawthorne went to look for Dolittle in the library and found him organizing the bookshelves. Dolittle's face lit up when he saw Hawthorne. "Have you heard something from the board?"

Hawthorne said that he hadn't. "I've heard you've been moving furniture into the apartment." They stood among the stacks. All the books looked dusty and old.

"That's not quite accurate. I only took a single chair, not even a comfortable chair."

"Why?"

"Well, you see, there's no furniture in the apartment and after I clean I like to sit a little and look out the window. There's a wonderful view, especially at sunset. Did you know there are three rooms as well as a kitchenette? I can walk from one side to another. It's not roomy, of course, but there's lots of space."

Hawthorne thought of Dolittle living in his small apartment in Latham for eight years. "Really, Bill, none of this is settled. We've no idea what the board will say. I'd appreciate it if you didn't move anything else up there."

Monday night Hawthorne telephoned Kate around eight-thirty, asking if he could come over. He had seen her during the day but they had exchanged only a few words. It had even occurred to Hawthorne that she was avoiding him.

He listened to her breathing. And he could hear a television somewhere in the background—a burst of artificial laughter.

"I think it's a bad idea," said Kate. "I'm still trying to think through some stuff."

"Is it what I told you when I was at your house?"

"I'm just not sure how much I want to complicate my life."

"I'd like to see you." Hawthorne meant to say that he needed to see her, but he couldn't let himself be that explicit. He stood in his living room and thought how empty it was. There were still small feathers on the chairs and rug.

"I'd rather you didn't. At least that's what I think right now. I don't know, it's all very confusing. Your life's full of ghosts."

After hanging up, Hawthorne put on his boots and heavy coat, grabbed a flashlight, and walked for several hours through the snow until he felt exhausted. He thought of the ghosts that populated his head. And wasn't one of them the person he used to be, the ambitious and self-confident clinical psychologist who believed he could do no wrong?

On Tuesday Hawthorne worked steadily in his office except for the hour he taught his history class in the afternoon. There were parents he had to write to and accounts he had to go over. In class, Scott's absence made everybody somber and little attention was paid to the Byzantine emperors. Hawthorne also had to telephone the trustees, and it seemed there might be a meeting. The school was supposed to close for Christmas vacation on Friday the eighteenth, and several trustees thought it might be wise to close earlier so that students could deal with their grief at home.

One of the trustees was a dean at Dartmouth, Carolyn Forster. Hawthorne had met her a few times at conferences when he had lived in Boston and it was Dr. Forster whom he had called from San Diego to say that he was interested in the position at Bishop's Hill. She was a humorless woman in her early sixties who had never married. Her father had graduated from Bishop's Hill in 1924 and she had worked hard to keep the school open.

After talking to her about Scott's death and the possibility of closing the school early, Hawthorne asked, "When the board decided to initiate a search for a new headmaster, I gather it wasn't a unanimous choice. What were the other alternatives?"

Dr. Forster was silent for a moment. "It wasn't certain that the problems at the school could be solved by a new headmaster, no matter how good, or by an increased financial commitment. Some of the board felt we were merely putting off the inevitable."

"And what did they suggest instead?"

"They believed we should look into the possibility of selling the school."

"Who thought this?"

"I expect many of us, though those members of the board who are alumni were the ones most solidly against it. And several others believed the school could still be saved."

"Do you remember who in particular wanted to sell the school?"

Dr. Forster cleared her throat. She had a deep voice for a woman and the practiced manner of someone with more than thirty years of experience in academic meetings. "You realize, of course, that once we decided to go ahead with the search and you were selected, then the board was entirely unanimous in your behalf."

"Yes, but earlier, who spoke in favor of selling?"

"There were three, maybe four. I don't know how strongly each one felt, but the most critical, I expect, was Hamilton Burke. He said that you don't treat a terminally ill patient with Band-Aids and Mercurochrome."

After his class on Tuesday Hawthorne spent several hours on the computer in his office going over school expenses and revenues. There seemed to have been payments for purchases that hadn't been received, or at least there was no sign of their having arrived—a commercial toaster for the kitchen, athletic equipment, office materials, even a trombone for the band. Hawthorne tried checking the paper files in the file cabinet but he still couldn't find an answer. Three times he called Skander to ask about certain discrepancies, but Skander was in conference or had gone home. When he finally called back, he said he would check his records and talk to the bookkeeper in the morning.

"I must say that I'm pleased that you're such a stickler for detail," said Skander, cheerfully. "It makes me far more optimistic that we'll all still be here in ten years' time."

"That's a five-hundred-dollar toaster. What do you think happened to it?"

"Oh, it will turn up," said Skander breezily. "Things always do."

Not for the first time Hawthorne regretted the absence of Mrs. Hayes, who had known so much about the workings of the school. Even though she hadn't handled school finances, very little had escaped her notice. Hilda Skander, while she knew about computers, didn't know much else, although she took calls, answered letters, and made sure that the office was stocked with Bishop's Hill stationery.

Shortly after five o'clock on Tuesday Hawthorne went looking for Roger Bennett, first going to his office, then checking the teachers' lounge, then the Dugout, and finally Stark Hall, where the Bennetts' apartment took up five rooms on the first floor. It was already dark and the sky was clear. The moon was cresting the mountains to the northwest.

Hawthorne waited in the small vestibule at the bottom of the stairs. After a minute or two, Roger opened the door. If he was surprised to see Hawthorne, he gave no sign of it. He put a finger to his lips. "My wife has her Bible study class."

"I need to talk to you," said Hawthorne. "We can go into the chapel." A door in the vestibule connected to a changing room off the choir.

"Can it wait? I hate to miss her classes. I find them so comforting." Bennett wore a gray sweater, khakis, and brown penny loafers. He leaned back against his door with his hands in his pockets. A lock of hair formed a blond fishhook across his forehead.

"Let's do it now," said Hawthorne as he opened the door to the changing room and continued on to the chapel. After a slight pause, Bennett followed him. Rosalind Langdon was practicing the organ. Hawthorne didn't think it was Bach. Perhaps Handel. It was muted and continuous like water flowing. Hawthorne saw a light in the organ loft. The rest of the chapel was lit by the golden chandeliers, which were turned down low, putting the far corners in shadow. Hawthorne sat down in a pew in the first row and waited for Bennett to join him. In the dim light the ceiling was nearly invisible.

Bennett sat down in the pew and rubbed his hands together as if they were cold. "So what's this about? More meetings?" His manner was hearty but cautious.

Leaning back, Hawthorne put his arms on the top of the pew. He tried to make himself appear relaxed, though he didn't feel relaxed. "Have you seen Chip?"

Bennett looked puzzled. "Campbell? I've run into him in Plymouth."

"Was that where you were yesterday?"

Bennett made an expression of mock sorrow. "I had a dentist appointment. Looks like I have to get a crown for one of my molars." He tapped his cheek to show Hawthorne the location.

"Isn't Chip a friend of yours?"

"We're friendly, that's all. I don't drink, which limits the number of possible meeting places. And he's unhappy with his friends at Bishop's Hill. He thinks we should have defended him more."

The notes of the organ reverberated through the chapel. The high notes made Hawthorne think of wind blowing down a chimney. "Why did you tell Mrs. Hayes that I meant to fire her?"

"I never did any such thing."

"That's not what she says."

Bennett stared at him with a fixed smile. "Then she's not telling the truth."

Hawthorne was surprised at the repugnance he felt for the other man. "Stop it. I know perfectly well that you told her several times, as did Chip Campbell."

"Is that why you asked about him? You think we're in cahoots?"

"And I know of other things you've done—spreading gossip and terrifying Clifford Evings. Don't you feel any responsibility for what happened?"

Bennett's smile seemed to tighten. "If you're going to abuse me, then we'll have to discuss these matters through my lawyer. You're still mad at me for knocking you down in basketball. I've told you over and over that it was an accident."

"Why is it so important to you to destroy the school?"

"You're mistaken. I love Bishop's Hill."

Hawthorne leaned forward and put one hand on Bennett's knee. "Roger, let me tell you something. I know exactly what you've been doing and I can prove it to the board of trustees. Your position at Bishop's Hill is no longer secure."

"You'd fire me?" Bennett opened his eyes wide, which made him look owl-like.

"Just like you say I fired the others."

10

Jessica didn't like the way LeBrun drove: too fast and jerky, turning the wheel abruptly and swerving, coming down hard on the brake. And in some places there was ice on the road. The car was a four-wheel-drive Chevy pickup and the front tires were out of line, or at least Jessica guessed that was what made it shimmy. The radio was busted and they mostly rode in silence. For a while LeBrun had been telling jokes but at last Jessica asked him to stop. Why do Canucks wear hats and why are Canuck women like hockey players? Then she had to beg. It was Friday evening, just after nine. For the past three days the police had been at the school driving everybody crazy. Dr. Hawthorne had announced that the school would be closing early for Christmas vacation, next Friday instead of the week after. Kids were calling their parents and trying to get their plane tickets changed. People couldn't stop talking about Scott's death. And when they weren't talking about it, you could tell they were thinking about it because their faces looked so serious. Somebody had murdered Scott and thrown his body into the pool. He hadn't been drowned after all. Had it been someone at Bishop's Hill or someone from outside? Several students said they had seen a suspicious man sneaking around the campus: tall and very thin and dressed in black. And then there was Larry Gaudette, who was still missing.

LeBrun had driven down to Concord on the interstate, then had cut across to Northwood on Route 4, heading toward Durham, then had turned south again. He seemed to know the roads and didn't need to look at a map. Jessica knew he was from Manchester but she didn't know much else. Questions irritated LeBrun. If he offered information, then she could ask a question—a "follow-up," she called it. Otherwise she let him alone. Twice she had begun to ask him about Lucky being thrown in the pool, then she had thought better of it. Even asking LeBrun to stop telling his jokes had been a mistake. But it was either ask him to stop or go crazy, Jessica had no doubt about that. One more joke and she would have jumped out of the truck. Jessica needed him; there was no one else to help her. But the sooner she was out of his company, the happier she'd be. She thought how in September she had seen LeBrun as easygoing and a little edgy—but not in a bad way. Then, scratching deeper, she had found someone who frightened her.

In the lights from the dashboard she watched his profile and at times she could see his lips moving and his cheeks going up and down as if he were arguing with himself. And his forehead would wrinkle. He drove with both hands at the top of the wheel and he tapped his fingers. He wore a dark hunting coat and a baseball cap. Now and then he glanced at Jessica but didn't say anything. Whether he was worried or angry, Jessica didn't know, though she could tell that something was bothering him and she thought it had to be the jokes, the fact that they had upset her.

"D'you think it's going to snow more?" asked Jessica at last, just to break the silence. Heaps of snow on either side of the road shone in their headlights.

"Snow? Sure, it's going to snow. It's not even winter yet. It'll snow for months. Everything'll get buried. A fuckin' graveyard of white stuff, that's New Hampshire in a nutshell." He spoke quickly, without looking at Jessica. She heard the irritation in his voice.

"Did those cops talk to you?"

" 'Course they talked to me, they talked to everybody. More'n once, too. They kept coming into the kitchen. I'm surprised they didn't poke their fuckin' heads in the oven. I would of given them a push and cooked them. Wouldn't that be a surprise. Baked cop."

The police had talked to everyone who had been at the school over Thanksgiving. It turned out that Scott had cut his classes on Tuesday and his roommate said that he had left their room only to go to the bathroom. And Scott had asked him to bring food from the dining hall. He said he was sick but he didn't want to go to the infirmary. Then his roommate had left on Wednesday, going down to Quincy to spend Thanksgiving with his family. Scott asked if he could come along but his roommate hadn't wanted to make his father angry. Now his roommate regretted it, of course. Jessica had heard that Scott had called Miss Sandler on Thanksgiving but she didn't know about what and she didn't know if Scott had been seen after that.

"Do you think the police have any ideas?" asked Jessica. She didn't want to keep asking questions but it was like a sore place and she couldn't stop fussing with it. She wanted to hear what LeBrun had to say. She wanted him to tell her something that would prove that he hadn't been involved, that he hadn't thrown Lucky into the pool.

"Sure they have ideas, they think Larry did it. That's why they're looking for him. Why would they be looking for him if they didn't think he did it?" Again LeBrun sounded exasperated, as if Jessica was just too stupid to understand.

Jessica watched LeBrun in the glow of the dash lights. It looked like he was angrily chewing something. "Do you think he did it?"

"He didn't tell me," LeBrun said, raising his voice. "Larry didn't tell me fuck. What d'you think, he's going to tap me on the shoulder and say he just killed the kid? You think he's going to wear a fucking sign? Or maybe it was that queer Newland. He's gone too, right? Or maybe it was that old bag who used to work in the office. Or maybe somebody snuck into the school, like a bandit. But I think it was Larry. It stands to reason, right? He must of killed the kid. I mean, he's disappeared."

"Why do you think he killed him?" Jessica kept watching LeBrun's jittery profile.

"Who the fuck knows? Maybe the kid kept trying to bum cigarettes from him like he did me. Maybe Larry just got fucking tired of giving him smokes. And he'd hang around, you know, always trying to get a cookie or something. Maybe Larry got sick of it."

"That doesn't sound like a good reason to kill a person." Jessica had mended the knife cut in her down jacket with a piece of silver duct tape and she kept picking at it.

"What d'you know about it? You an expert on killing people? Maybe Larry just got fed up. You hear what I'm saying? Maybe he was fed up right to here." LeBrun took his hand off the wheel and wiped a finger across the top of his forehead. "I seen it happen. You think someone doesn't have a reason to kill a person but there's always a reason. Like killing someone for the fun of it, even that's a reason, right? Maybe not a good reason but it's a reason. Maybe Larry killed him just for the fun of it. Like a sick joke."

"He didn't seem like that."

"Like what?"

"Like crazy, I guess."

LeBrun glanced at her angrily. "What do you know about crazy? You don't know shit. People aren't crazy, nobody's crazy. They're just not all the same, that's all. Fuckin' diversity, that's what they call it. Like tall guys and short guys."

"It seems pretty crazy to kill a person for no reason."

LeBrun hit the flat of his hand on the steering wheel. "The kid went and got himself killed. Maybe if he'd been minding his business, it wouldn't have happened."

Jessica kept silent for a moment, then she asked, "Do you think someone paid him to kill Scott?"

"Who the fuck would pay him?" LeBrun kept shifting in his seat, as if he were sitting on a broken spring.

"I don't know, maybe somebody who didn't like Scott. Maybe a relative."

"Shit, you're as bad as the fucking cops. I should make you sit in the back of the truck and freeze your ass off. That's what you'll get if you don't shut up."

Jessica kept silent. Her backpack with her clothes was by her feet and when she moved she could feel her money belt. She had given LeBrun a thousand dollars and had said she would give him another thousand when she got away with Jason. Actually, she had been surprised that he had trusted her. On the other hand, she wouldn't have the nerve to cheat him. She would hate to have him come looking for her.

"Maybe it was an inheritance," said Jessica after another minute, "maybe he was supposed to inherit some money and now it's going to somebody else. Maybe that somebody paid your cousin to kill him. You know, a contract killing."

"What did I say? You want to sit back there in the cold?"

"You think your cousin threw my kitten into the pool?"

LeBrun slammed on the brakes and Jessica was thrown forward again the dash. The tires squealed as the truck fishtailed. When the pickup came to a stop, LeBrun shouted, "I've had fuckin' enough! Get in the back!"

"No, Frank, please, I won't say anymore."

"Get in the back!"

Jessica opened the door. There were no lights on the road and it was cold. Once she had climbed into the bed of the pickup, LeBrun started up quickly so she slipped on the cold metal and banged against the tailgate.

Fortunately, she only had to ride in the back for about ten minutes. Still, it was freezing and she couldn't curl herself up tight enough to stay warm. The metal floor was like ice on her butt. The bumps were jarring and she had to hold on to the side, otherwise she would slide around.

At the edge of Exeter, LeBrun pulled into a supermarket parking lot and let her back in the cab. "Okay, show me where you live, but don't open your trap about anything else."

Jessica had sent Jason another letter, then talked to him twice on the phone. Jason had said that Tremblay would be out of town, that he was flying to Chicago. And by nine o'clock Dolly was usually so drunk that it was impossible to wake her. Jessica knew; she had tried. Jason had promised to leave the front door unlocked. They would get him and drive down to Boston to the bus station, where they would take the first bus going south. The next day, Saturday, they would be in Washington and she could call her uncle, at least to talk to him, if not to stay with him. And she would tell him about Tremblay, tell him about every awful thing that Tremblay had ever done.

The house on Maple Street was dark, but that didn't surprise

Jessica. It was past ten and Dolly was either in bed or asleep in front of the TV in the den. It was a tall late-eighteenth-century house, perfectly symmetrical, with no curving lines—a pretty, oversized shoe box was how she described it to herself. Jessica didn't think of the house as hers. It was Tremblay's house, even though her father had bought it after he and Dolly had gotten married. But Tremblay had put his stamp on it and it smelled of him. He had gotten rid of everything that had belonged to her father, except those things that Tremblay wanted for himself, like her father's leather chair and his shotguns and hunting rifles. Every time Jessica saw Tremblay in her father's chair, she felt angry. She had wanted to tell him that it was her chair now. Even the house was hers. One time she told him that when she got her money she would kick him out, but Tremblay had just laughed.

LeBrun parked in front, although Jessica would have preferred him to park down the street, but she was afraid to say anything and she was still cold from sitting in the back of the truck. When they got out, LeBrun shut his door too loudly. Jessica wondered what the neighbors would do if they saw them, whether they would call the police. The large Federalist houses had big yards and old trees. Maybe the neighbors wouldn't notice the pickup, maybe no dogs would start barking.

Jessica led the way up the walk to the front steps. The yard was covered with snow, though the walk had been shoveled. There was a snowman without a head that her brother must have built. Not too many years before, she had been building snowmen herself. Exeter didn't have as much snow as Bishop's Hill—only a few inches. Between the racing clouds, she could see a few stars. LeBrun walked noisily and again she wanted to tell him to be quiet. She had said she could get Jason by herself, that LeBrun should stay in the truck, but he insisted on coming. "I like seeing rich people's houses," he had said. "I want to see what I'm aiming for." As for Jason, she'd told him to pack a small bag and to take nothing that wasn't really necessary. Jason had said he had saved fifteen dollars and she had been touched by that. Jessica pressed down on the latch and the front door opened. Stepping inside, she smelled the stale odor of Tremblay's cigars and the cleaning detergent that the maid used. It made her recall other times, not nice times. LeBrun came in after her, scuffing his feet.

"Can't you be quiet?" she whispered angrily.

LeBrun snorted.

Jessica heard the grandfather clock ticking in the living room and the hum of the refrigerator. She had thought Jason would be down in the hall waiting for her. She couldn't believe he had fallen asleep, even though it was past his bedtime. She had told him to wait in the hall, but perhaps he was in the living room. She recalled several times when he had gone to sleep on the couch.

Jessica went to the entrance of the living room. "Jason," she whispered. She moved quietly to a floor lamp by her father's old leather chair and turned it on. The living room was empty. She turned the light off again. She felt angry and frightened. If it hadn't been for Jason, she would have gone down to Boston on her own.

"So now what're you going to do?" asked LeBrun when she had returned to the hall. "Looks like your little brother's let you down."

"Maybe he's in his room upstairs."

"I don't want to hang around here all night."

"It won't be all night. Wait here."

But LeBrun followed her as she climbed to the second floor. She wished she had brought a flashlight but she hadn't thought she'd need one. For that matter, she wished she had a gun. Several of the dancers at the club had guns. Gypsy had had a little chrome pistol that she kept in a tortoiseshell case in her purse. It looked like a makeup kit.

Upstairs it was dark, but the night light was on in the bathroom. LeBrun stayed behind her as she moved down the hall. He seemed to be mumbling to himself. The floor was carpeted and their feet made no noise. Her mother's bedroom was at the far end of the hall in the other direction. Jessica passed the closed door of her old bedroom and she shivered as she recalled the dreadful things that had happened there. Jason's room was just past the linen closet on the right. Jessica's legs felt funny—she hated being this far into the house, like sneaking into a bear's cave.

She paused before Jason's door.

"Is this it?" whispered LeBrun.

"Yes."

"Then what're you waiting for?"

Again she wanted to tell LeBrun to be quiet. Instead she slowly turned the knob and pushed open the door, which creaked slightly on its hinges. The room was dark.

"Jason?" she whispered.

There was no answer. She felt for the wall switch on her right. A sliver of light came from under the drawn shade but not enough to see if Jason was in his bed. When Jessica listened carefully, though, she thought she could hear him breathing.

"Jason?" she said again.

She turned on the light.

Tremblay was sitting on the bed smiling at her. There was no sign of Jason.

Her stepfather waved several sheets of paper. "Isn't it nice to have a little brother who saves your letters."

Jessica turned to run and bumped against LeBrun.

"He's got a gun," said LeBrun.

She looked over her shoulder at Tremblay, who held a small black automatic, not pointing it at her but holding it out so she could see it. "That's right, I have a gun. Haven't you read those stories where a husband or wife mistakenly shoots a loved one who came home without warning?" Tremblay smoothed his mustache with the back of his thumb.

"Where's Jason?"

"Elsewhere. I think we should have a little chat."

"We have nothing to talk about," said Jessica. Even though she wanted to appear defiant, she spoke in a whisper. She moved away from LeBrun, who shouldn't have stopped her from getting away.

Tremblay gave another smile. It was a meaningless expression, just something to occupy his face while he was being mean. "On the contrary, if you want to see Jason again, then we have to talk."

Jessica tried to look brave but didn't answer. Tremblay wore a dark sweater and dark pants. She realized he had dressed that way just so he could surprise her more easily. She almost expected him to have worn a hat as well, but Tremblay never wore hats. He was too vain about his thick silver hair.

"First of all," continued Tremblay, "I want to see this money belt that you've been bragging about to your brother."

Jessica didn't move.

Tremblay lazily gestured at LeBrun with his pistol. "Take it from her."

LeBrun reached under her down jacket and sweatshirt to grab the money belt. She could feel his cold fingers on her bare skin. Then he yanked the belt loose and she gasped.

"Throw it here," said Tremblay. LeBrun tossed it to him. Tremblay opened it, then shook it upside down so the money scattered onto the rug: three thousand dollars in fifty-dollar bills. "Not bad for showing your little tits."

"What are you going to do?" asked Jessica, staring down at her money.

"I'm afraid I'm tempted to shoot you both."

"I had no part in this," said LeBrun quickly. "She paid me to give her a ride. I had no idea she was going to kidnap anybody."

Tremblay's smile this time made his eyes crinkle with good humor. "I'm sure you didn't. You were just being nice." He nodded to Jessica. "Couldn't you find yourself a better-looking boyfriend?"

"That money's mine," said Jessica.

"What are you going to do?" asked Tremblay. "Call the police? I'll tell you what, I'll try to save it until your twenty-first birthday."

LeBrun began to chuckle, then stopped himself. He had been looking around the room, which had posters of Red Sox players and a Red Sox pennant.

"Where's Jason?" Jessica asked again.

"Why should I tell you?"

"Because I want to see him. He's my brother."

"We had a deal, right? Now the deal's off."

"No, Tremblay, please."

Tremblay's smile had great warmth. When Jessica had first met him six years earlier, she had been encouraged by it. Now it terrified her.

"Please don't touch Jason. I'll do anything."

Tremblay appeared to consider. He turned the small automatic over in his hand and seemed to study it. Jessica realized that it was one of her father's guns. Tremblay stretched his right foot forward and poked at the fifty-dollar bills on the rug. "I want your boyfriend to take you back to Bishop's Hill. I don't want any more foolishness. When you're here at Christmas, we can talk again. But don't count on seeing Jason. If you don't behave, I'll send him out to my brother's in Illinois."

Although Jessica was scared, she was surprised that Tremblay was letting her go so easily. But LeBrun was a witness, so perhaps he was acting semi-reasonable because of LeBrun. Or perhaps Jason had told other people that his sister was going to rescue him. But it was still a sham; everything that Tremblay said was a sham.

Tremblay lifted his chin. This time he wasn't smiling. "So it's a deal? You'll let this guy take you back?"

"You won't hurt Jason?"

Tremblay laid down more conditions—no phone calls, no letters. It was ten-thirty; they could be back at Bishop's Hill by one. Jessica felt exhausted. She didn't know if she wanted to cry or scream.

"Okay, it's a deal," said Jessica.

"Then get out of here."

"Can I have my money?"

"No chance. It's my money now."

Jessica's eyes began to water. She hated to have Tremblay see her tears. "Let me use the bathroom first."

"I can trust you?"

"I only want to pee."

She pushed past LeBrun without looking at him and made her way down the dark hall. She didn't really have to pee, but once she had locked the bathroom door behind her, she peed anyway. There was a phone in the bathroom and it occurred to her that she could call someone; she could ask for help. Then she realized she had no one to call. Maybe she could call Dr. Hawthorne but he was too far away and what exactly could he do? She washed her face in cold water. The sink, toilet, and tub were pink with gold-colored fixtures. There were framed pictures of toy poodles combing, primping, and putting on lipstick. She didn't flush the toilet. Let Tremblay do it. Jessica unlocked the door, turned out the light, and went back into the hall.

As Jessica approached Jason's room, she heard LeBrun and Tremblay talking. Then she heard Tremblay say, "What the hell did you bring her down here for? Are you nuts?"

Jessica couldn't hear LeBrun's answer.

"And when are you going to do it?" asked Tremblay angrily.

Jessica stood still and tried to make out what LeBrun said but his words were an indistinct mutter.

"Jesus, you're impossible," said Tremblay. "I don't know what the fuck you think you're doing. I should have shot you both after all."

She was surprised that anyone could talk to LeBrun so rudely and she waited for him to answer, but he said nothing and Tremblay didn't say anything else. Jessica waited a moment, then moved forward down the hall. When she reentered Jason's room, they were looking at her. Tremblay was standing by the bureau and LeBrun had moved to the window. LeBrun was shorter than her stepfather but wirier and dark-haired. His narrow face was hatchetlike.

"So you're ready?" asked Tremblay.

"I guess so." She looked at her money scattered across the bedroom rug. There didn't seem to be as much of it.

"Then you'd better get going."

Jessica and LeBrun left the house and walked back down the sidewalk to the pickup. It wasn't until they were driving out of Exeter that she spoke.

"Why didn't you do something?"

"I don't like guns. You didn't say there might be guns." LeBrun's voice was a low monotone.

"You still could have done something. You could have jumped him."

LeBrun laughed abruptly. "And get shot? You didn't pay me to get shot." The streetlights stopped at the edge of town and the interior of the truck suddenly grew darker.

"Are you going to give me back any of my money?"

"Hey, I just risked my life. That's worth a grand. Are you going to start in with the questions again?"

Jessica was quiet a moment, then asked, "What did Tremblay mean when he said, 'When are you going to do it?' What'd he mean by that?"

"He never said that."

"I heard him."

LeBrun continued to stare straight ahead. "What he said was, 'Why'd you do it?' Meaning why did I bring you all the way down here."

"That's not what he said." But Jessica wasn't one hundred percent certain and LeBrun must have heard the doubt in her voice. A few snowflakes drifted across the windshield. More were caught up in the headlights.

LeBrun put his foot on the brake and the pickup slowed. "You want to ride in the back? It's a long way. You could freeze to death."

Jessica slouched down in her seat and stuck her chin in the collar of her coat. She wondered whether she had misheard and what it meant if she hadn't. And she thought about what to do now. She couldn't even go back to stripping. Tremblay would do something horrible to Jason, she was sure of it. Her sense of defeat was like a stone on her heart. Everything felt pointless and wrong.

On Wednesday, December 2, the police had brought the results of the autopsy: Scott had been murdered. This fact gave new significance to Bobby Newland's disappearance. The autopsy had shown that Scott had been killed by a sharp object pushed up through the base of his skull. The state policeman in charge of the murder investigation was Harvey Sloan, a lieutenant in his midforties who wore dark suits and colorful ties. Over and over, Sloan heard how Bobby had accused the Bishop's Hill community of Evings's death. And again the possibility was raised of a link between Evings and Scott, though the police themselves said nothing. Bobby's description was sent all over the country. The fact that he was gay seemed to suggest that he might have had a special motive for murdering a young boy.

The commotion caused by Bobby's absence lasted till the next morning, when he was located on Martha's Vineyard, where he had lived before coming to Bishop's Hill. He had arrived on the Vineyard on Saturday, returned to the restaurant where he had worked, and asked for his old job back. Plenty of people had seen him and there was nothing to indicate that he was trying to hide. Even so, Lieutenant Sloan had him picked up, then he flew over to Martha's Vineyard with another policeman to question him. By late afternoon Bobby had been released, although he had been told to stay on the island.

Hawthorne called Bobby on Friday, after getting his phone number from Lieutenant Sloan. Bobby had been shocked by Scott's murder and angry that he had been a suspect. It also confirmed his belief that he had done the smart thing by leaving. He apologized to Hawthorne for his sudden disappearance, but he added, "What possible reason did I have to continue there?"

"I'm sorry you feel that way," Hawthorne said. He was sitting in his office and his desk was heaped with papers. "I thought you did a good job, and the kids liked you."

"I hated Bishop's Hill," said Bobby. "I was only there because of Clifford. It's an awful place and the people are awful as well."

Fritz Skander wanted to sue Bobby for breach of contract. "It will mean some additional money," he told Hawthorne. "Goodness knows, we need it."

"I have no intention of suing him," Hawthorne answered.

"Well, he certainly won't be receiving his November paycheck," said Skander, "and if he ever asks us for a recommendation, he'll find he's barking up the wrong tree."

The discovery that Scott had been murdered brought a number of police detectives to Bishop's Hill. Chief Moulton was often on campus as well, even though the state police investigation seemed to have passed him by. Lieutenant Sloan never consulted him and Moulton was allowed to poke around Bishop's Hill only as a courtesy. A state police lab crew spent much of Wednesday in Gaudette's apartment and sealed off Scott's dorm room. Bobby's small apartment was also taken over.

The psychological effect of the murder was disastrous. All pretense of teaching came to a stop. Larry Gaudette had been well-liked. It was shocking to think of him as a murder suspect. Bobby Newland's decision to quit heightened the sense of chaos. Four psychologists were brought over from Mary Hitchcock Hospital in Hanover, and counseling sessions were expanded. It had already been decided to close the school a week early for Christmas vacation, on the eleventh instead of the eighteenth. Hawthorne would have closed the school even sooner if it hadn't been for the various difficulties of changing plane tickets and travel plans and the disruption to parents' schedules. Quite a few kids would have had no place to go. Also, the police were reluctant to have the students who had been at the school over Thanksgiving suddenly taken out of reach.

Hawthorne was constantly on the phone to members of the board, trying to convince them that, despite the huge disruption, the school was continuing to operate. Gifts to the school had increased and the work on the roof of Emerson Hall would be completed by mid-January. Although applications were no higher than the previous year, at least they hadn't gone down.

Carolyn Forster, the trustee at Dartmouth, assured Hawthorne that he had the board's full confidence, and Hamilton Burke told him on Friday, "We have no intention of closing the school. We'll keep it going till the last dime is spent."

At the moment, it seemed to Hawthorne that he was operating on sheer will, with no thought beyond the Christmas vacation. The next semester remained vague; he needed to hire two new psychologists and he needed to have more of the faculty on his side. But at other times he was overwhelmed by pessimism and wondered why he was wasting his time. There was no guarantee that the school would make it, and really, how could they ever get over Scott's death?

The police interviewed everyone who had known Scott, which meant the entire school. Kate was questioned about Scott's call to her on Thanksgiving Day when he had been looking for Hawthorne. Had Scott seemed upset? Was he scared? A hundred times Kate blamed herself for not driving to the school right away and bringing Scott home with her. But how could she have known? Even Hawthorne regretted going down to Krueger's in Concord; if he had been at the school to receive Scott's call, then the boy might still be alive.

Hawthorne had coffee with Kate in the Dugout late Friday morning to assure her that she couldn't blame herself about Scott. Herb Frankfurter and Tom Hastings sat drinking coffee across the room. Hawthorne was aware of their quick looks and knowing expressions. Several students were playing video games and a dozen more were grouped around a few tables. Something by the Spice Girls was on the jukebox, although the volume had been turned down.

"It wasn't as if I'd been doing anything important," said Kate, explaining why she hadn't gone over to the school. "It was just laziness on my part."

"You didn't know anything was wrong."

"I could tell that something was bothering him."

Hawthorne, who had made many such explanations to himself, felt well acquainted with the if-only-I-had-done-such-and-such type of thinking. "I wonder if Scott called anyone else?"

Kate shook her head. "Do you really think Larry killed him?"

"I don't know. I can't believe it." They were silent a moment. Hawthorne sipped his coffee, which tasted burned.

"I'm sorry I said I didn't want to see you the other night," Kate said quickly. "I know you're going through a lot."

"I didn't blame you. After what I told you . . ."

Kate lowered her voice. "It wasn't that. The whole thing is just so complicated."

"My life *is* full of ghosts."

"I should never have said that."

"I'm afraid I still want to come over. I want it more every time I see you."

Kate reached out her hand and placed it on Hawthorne's. Looking at him, her eyes flickered across his face as if she were trying to memorize it.

Hawthorne put his other hand over hers. First he looked into Kate's face, then he glanced away. Across the room, he saw Frankfurter and Hastings watching them. They had faint smiles. Hawthorne began to remove his hand from Kate's, then he didn't.

Hawthorne planned to call a faculty meeting as soon as the students were gone, and he asked Hilda to put notices in the faculty mailboxes that a meeting would be held in Memorial Hall on the second floor of Emerson at 10 a.m. on Monday the fourteenth—just over a week away. "Say it's compulsory," he told her.

"I don't think that's wise," Hilda said.

But Hawthorne insisted. He would use the meeting to describe all that had happened: the appearances of Ambrose Stark, the phone calls, the bags of food. He would accuse Bennett, Chip Campbell, and others of lying to Mrs. Hayes and forcing her from the school, of telling Clifford Evings that he was about to be fired. Then there were the criminal offenses: wrecking Evings's office and supplying Jessica Weaver with tequila. He hoped he could make Bennett and Herb Frankfurter resign. He imagined wiping the slate clean.

Even though the presence of the police was a continual reminder of Scott's death, there was still the school's daily routine to take care of. Hawthorne suspended the twice-weekly meetings in which he and the faculty discussed the students. On the other hand, the expanded counseling sessions required careful orchestrating and the teachers needed some advice on how to organize their classes until the eleventh if little or no academic work was being done. In his history class the quizzes he had planned had to be postponed. Hawthorne had meant to talk about Justinian the Great, but if the students wished instead to talk about Scott McKinnon, Larry Gaudette, or the presence of the police, then that's what would be discussed.

In addition, supplies had to be ordered, bills had to be paid.

LeBrun needed help dealing with local food vendors and the book-keeping. And Hawthorne was still trying to trace certain items that had been ordered and paid for but apparently never delivered. After some searching, the commercial toaster was found in a stockroom off the kitchen. But why it had never been put into use Hawthorne didn't know.

As for the three-hundred-dollar trombone, there was no trace of it.

"We already have four trombones," Rosalind Langdon had told him. "Why would I order another? Only two are being played as it is."

And Skander said, "I always confuse the trombone with the French horn. Do you think the supplier could have made a similar mistake?"

On Wednesday and Thursday nights Hawthorne had searched the attics of Adams, Douglas, and Hamilton Halls. He told people he was looking for the portrait of Ambrose Stark that had been taken from Evings's office. He made sure his searches were noticed, then he waited for some response. By Friday a number of the faculty were talking about it—their eccentric headmaster prowling the attics with a flashlight. Because of the police investigation, Hawthorne's actions were thought to be connected to Scott's murder and Gaudette's disappearance. Indeed, on Friday morning Hawthorne had even told Hilda that he believed something significant might be hidden in one of the attics.

That afternoon, Skander dropped by the office looking for an explanation.

"What are you really doing up there?" Skander asked. He spoke lightly, as if Hawthorne were involved in some kind of practical joke. "Have you been reading *Sherlock Holmes*? I'm not sure that the role of detective suits you."

"I'd rather not say right now," Hawthorne told him. "Wait until the faculty meeting on the fourteenth and expect some surprises."

Skander looked doubtful. "It seems we've had enough surprises."

"I'd just like to do everything I can to help the police investigation."

"Ah, so you plan to be a detective after all," said Skander. He rubbed the top of his head and seemed about to say more, then he abruptly shifted to another subject. "Have you given Bill Dolittle permission to move into that empty apartment in Stark?"

"I told him there was no possibility of such a move until we find someone to take his place in Latham. I've been quite clear about that."

"Well, he's moving in furniture." Skander stood in front of Hawthorne's desk.

"Just a chair." Hawthorne paused. "And a book."

"I heard that he also moved in a lamp. I know that Bill's a great fan of yours but he hardly earns his keep. His two English classes are a disgrace. He does little more than read to his students for the entire period—Raymond Chandler, P. G. Wodehouse, Philip K. Dick. Those are his particular favorites. As for the library, it's in total disarray. If Bill's been stuck in Latham for eight years, it's only because he deserves no better. Old Pendergast absolutely despised him, and in my brief tenure as headmaster I came to share his feelings. I hate to criticize a colleague but I know he's pulling the wool over your eyes. Really, Jim, you're too softhearted. Now that Bill's got his foot in the door at Stark, he'll be impossible to dislodge."

Although Hawthorne was beginning to share Skander's feeling, he at first said nothing. Again, he wondered if he had been blinding himself to Dolittle's inadequacies out of gratitude for his support.

"I'll speak to him about it."

Saturday night Hawthorne went through the attic of Emerson Hall. It had been a long day, during which he had met with Lieutenant Sloan, several trustees, the psychologists from Mary Hitchcock, and Ruth Standish, who had been working with them. He had also spoken with Gene Strauss about the effect of Scott's murder on applications. Strauss apologized for bringing up his concern so soon after the death, but he dreaded the damage that it would inflict on enrollment. Already Strauss had heard from several parents that their children wouldn't be returning after Christmas vacation. In the evening, Hawthorne had finally been able to sit for an hour in his new chair, just thinking. He had meant to think about Scott and his possible connection to Gaudette. Instead he thought about Kate and how her hand had felt against his.

About 10 p.m. Hawthorne put on his overcoat, fetched his flashlight, and went out into the dark. As he walked over to Emerson, he ran into Floyd Purvis, who had become more active as a watchman since the police had been at the school.

"You want me to come along?" Purvis asked halfheartedly.

Hawthorne said he'd be fine by himself.

"Watch out for rats," Purvis warned.

Hawthorne climbed the front steps of Emerson and unlocked the door. There had been snow flurries all day and the night was cloudy. He wiped his feet on the mat and flashed his light around the rotunda. In the middle of the floor, the gold letters *B* and *H* of the school crest sparkled as he moved his light across them. Just beyond the rotunda the shadows skittered away, then re-formed themselves. There was no wind and the building was still. Hawthorne pointed his light upward. It was at least fifty feet to the ceiling beneath the bell tower and the light could barely distinguish it.

Hawthorne climbed to the third floor, then unlocked the door to the attic. The stairs were wide enough to accommodate the bookcases, mattresses, and general bric-a-brac stored under the roof. As he began his ascent, he thought he heard a rustling but he wasn't sure. Reaching the top, he flashed his light down the length of the attic, then located the light switch on the wall. There were three switches: one for the staircase leading to the bell tower, one for the east side of the attic, and one for the west. Hawthorne flicked the switch for the west side and a string of ceiling lights flickered on—dim bulbs that cast shadows into the corners and illuminated boxes of nails and buckets of tar left by the men working on the roof.

Hawthorne again heard a rustling. He expected there were red squirrels as well as rats. He had meant to order traps earlier in the fall but with one thing and another he had forgotten. It was cold and he kept his coat buttoned. The west side of the attic formed a long room cluttered with boxes, broken easels, and music stands, desks, chairs, bookcases, metal bed frames, mattresses, and rolls of paper. Hawthorne told himself that when he had a chance he would see about clearing out some of the clutter. He moved slowly along the passageway that ran down the center, looking behind boxes and heaps of debris. The floors creaked. Hawthorne realized he was breathing rapidly. He stopped and tried to catch his breath. He felt foolish and angry at himself for being frightened. He pushed an old desk away from the wall and looked behind a bookcase. There were papers on the floor—old brochures and school catalogs—and they crinkled as he stepped on them. A chair tipped over with a crash. Hawthorne kept thinking what a firetrap the place was and before he could stop himself he had begun to remember the fire at Wyndham School. Briefly, it absorbed all his attention.

It took Hawthorne twenty minutes to reach the end of the attic. His movements stirred up the dust and he sneezed. Despite the cold, he was sweating. He kept turning quickly, imagining he had seen something out of the corner of his eye—a shadow or a sudden darting.

Hawthorne had just bent down to look behind a dark oak cabinet with two cracked glass doors when the lights went out. It was like being struck blind. He stood up quickly and banged his head against a rafter. Even in the dark, he knew that his hands were shaking.

Hawthorne listened but could hear nothing. He flicked on his flashlight and shined it down the corridor. The space through which he had passed seemed unfamiliar; the boxes and piled chairs took on new shapes. Again he heard a rustling. He pointed his light in the direction of the noise. Then a door slammed, but seemingly far away. Hawthorne's heart was beating fast and he stood still, trying to calm himself. He wished he were braver, less of an academic. Dust motes floated in the beam of his light.

Slowly, Hawthorne began to make his way back toward the stairs, swinging his light from side to side. Several times he turned around to make sure there was nothing behind him. After he had gone twenty feet, the beam of his light picked up the shape of something ahead. Hawthorne paused. He wished he had a weapon. From a pile stacked against the sloping roof, he took a hockey stick, then he almost discarded it because it made him feel silly. But he held on to it. As he walked forward, the shape ahead of him took on substance and after he had gone another few yards he realized that somebody was standing in the passageway—a wavering shape in the uncertain beam of his light. Hawthorne was afraid that his legs might give way beneath him. He stood still, again trying to calm his breathing. Then he shifted the hockey stick to his right hand and continued forward. Getting closer, Hawthorne realized it was a man and in another moment he saw it was Ambrose Stark. The former headmaster was grinning at him with a bright red grin that disfigured the bottom half of his face. It was the same image Hawthorne had seen staring down at him from the window at Adams Hall.

Hawthorne forced himself to take another step forward, then another. The light jittered across the figure and Hawthorne saw that his hand was trembling. Then Ambrose Stark moved. Hawthorne crouched down, keeping his light focused on the dead headmaster, not daring to look away. He tried to force himself to relax. Stark was about twenty feet ahead of him. Hawthorne made himself stand up, breathe deeply, and then move forward. The next time Ambrose Stark moved, Hawthorne realized the image was swaying. Closer, he saw that it was a painting hanging from the rafters. He wanted to laugh at himself but the image was too awful. The gaping red grin was horrific: a red slash across the face. What frightened him now was the knowledge that the picture hadn't been there when he had made his way through the attic twenty minutes earlier. Someone had hung it up after he had passed.

As Hawthorne drew nearer, he could see that the portrait was attached to a cord stretched between the rafters. It was a full-length picture showing Stark standing by a desk with his right hand resting on a book. He wore a dark suit and behind him was dark red drapery. His face was so distorted by the red grin that even his eyes took on a demonic appearance. He looked as if he were about to burst into mad laughter. Hawthorne stopped about five feet away. Clearly, it was the same picture that had been in Evings's office. Moving forward, Hawthorne reached out and took hold of the edge of the canvas. Then he yanked it down so the portrait fell to the floor. He felt relieved, even moderately brave. He was certain that Ambrose Stark would frighten him no more.

Detective Leo Flynn was disgusted. It was a rainy Monday morning in Boston with wet snow forecast, and the skyline had disappeared into the murk. Sirens were blaring, cars were honking, and on the other side of the office one of his colleagues was calling a young black kid a "scumbag." Shouting it over and over: Scumbag, scumbag. It was Pearl Harbor Day and Leo Flynn remembered when there used to be parades. He liked parades. And he liked fireworks. He'd been known to travel a hundred miles for a good fireworks display, and on the Fourth of July he was always out in the harbor in his pal Loomis's boat, getting as close as they could so the rockets shot up right above them; sometimes the sticks would come whickering down onto the deck and once they'd had a flaming piece of paper. If Flynn had had more sense as a kid, he would have gone into fireworks design instead of being a cop. Explosions for the heck of it. You had to be an artist to be a first-rate fireworks designer; you had to have pizzazz.

Right now Flynn was in the doghouse. The homicide captain had chewed his ear off for wasting so much time in New Hampshire. Why'd he have to go himself? Coughlin wanted to know. Hadn't Flynn heard of the telephone? Or e-mail? Or departmental reciprocity? Boston was always doing favors for those podunk New Hampshire departments. It was time for them to give something back. Flynn was needed in Boston. He had other cases and court dates coming up. What the hell was he thinking of?

Leo Flynn had told Coughlin everything he could about Francis LaBrecque. He had even told him some of LaBrecque's jokes, knowing full well that Coughlin hated jokes unless he was the person telling them. And he told Coughlin he had been looking for LaBrecque's cousin, the cook, Larry Gaudette, but Coughlin had only said, "Can't you write it all down? You fuckin' lazy all of a sudden? Give it to me on paper." Coughlin was in his late forties, fifteen years younger than Flynn, and they weren't close. Coughlin didn't know squat about Pearl Harbor Day, for instance.

So Flynn had been writing it down and the information would be sent all over New England. Much had been sent already. The computers would get cracking and a lot of departments would communicate with one another electronically. For Flynn it was obvious that the time was coming when you'd never have to leave the office. Everything would be done electronically and when all the information was in place a couple of patrolmen would be sent out to nab the guy. And someday—Leo Flynn had no doubt about it—they'd be sending out robots. But by then he would be retired and living in Florida, or maybe pushing up daisies, worm food after a life of cheap cigars.

Of course, his wife was glad he was back. She'd suspected he had only been fooling around: smoking too much and talking to other old farts like himself. And the rest of his homicide team thought he'd been fooling around as well. In vain did Flynn try to convince them that LaBrecque was the man they were looking for and that they had to find him fast, because who knew how many people he'd killed. LaBrecque could have left corpses all over New England. But Coughlin still saw no reason for Flynn to drive up to New Hampshire. Once the information was sent out electronically, it would only be a matter of time before LaBrecque was picked up. Flynn didn't doubt that. He just wondered how many more people LaBrecque would stick in the neck before it happened.

And because Coughlin was unhappy with him, he had given Flynn a case concerning a Puerto Rican junkie who had been arrested after feeding slices of his aunt into the garbage disposal.

The junkie had been caught because he'd been using the garbage disposal for three hours straight between 2 a.m. and 5 a.m. and it had overheated and started smoking. A neighbor had called the Fire Department. And now Flynn could hardly talk to the junkie without the Department of Social Services, and the public defender's office, and soon probably even the Puerto Rican Defense League breathing down his neck. It seemed that because the junkie had an IQ of 75, he shouldn't have to go to prison. But that wasn't for Flynn to decide. He wasn't supposed to have opinions. He had his paperwork and court dates and miles of red tape and every bit of it was taking him farther away from New Hampshire, where Francis LaBrecque was probably icing some poor sucker at that very moment. At least that was how Leo Flynn saw it.

Shortly after breakfast on Monday, Fritz Skander showed up in Hawthorne's office saying he had to do something about Frank LeBrun, that the man was unstable and might easily poison the entire school. Hawthorne didn't usually attend breakfast and preferred to make coffee and eat something in his own quarters. That morning LeBrun had lost his temper and thrown four pots at the two students assigned to help him.

"You seem to be a special friend of his," said Skander with a worried smile. "You should march in there and set him straight." Skander stood in the doorway of Hawthorne's office, his rectangular shape making him seem doorlike as well.

Hawthorne couldn't imagine marching anywhere. "Was anyone hurt?"

"They were scared, frightened—isn't that enough? After all, they're just children."

As he made his way to the kitchen, Hawthorne assumed there was more to the altercation than what Skander had described, but it wouldn't do to have LeBrun throwing pots. He wondered why Skander hadn't spoken to LeBrun himself, and once again Hawthorne saw that he couldn't take anyone's actions at face value. There always appeared to be something lying underneath.

When Hawthorne got to the kitchen, LeBrun was alone. There were stacks of dirty dishes from breakfast and no sign of the women employed to wash them. The floor was strewn with pots and broken plates. LeBrun was sitting on a tall stool in the middle of the kitchen with his arms folded and his legs stuck out in front of him, smoking a cigarette, although smoking wasn't allowed in school buildings. It was a gray morning and the lights were on.

"Now I suppose you're going to yell at me, too," he said angrily.

"That wasn't my intention," said Hawthorne looking around and walking slowly across the kitchen. "You want a hand cleaning this up?" He stepped over a pile of scrambled eggs.

"I'm not fuckin' cleaning anything." LeBrun didn't look at Hawthorne but stared straight ahead at the wall where there were several refrigerators. His white coat was unbuttoned and underneath he wore a red shirt. His thick dark hair was uncombed and spiky. As he sat, he jiggled his knees so his black boots seemed to dance on the tiles.

"What's bothering you?"

"Those fuckin' kids won't do as I say. I told this kid to take the eggs off the stove and he wasn't paying attention so they burned. Then the other one burned the toast."

Hawthorne drew up another stool next to LeBrun and sat down. "They're kids."

"Hey, if I'd done that at their age I'd of had the shit kicked out of me."

"What happened to the dishwashers?"

"They were fucking staring at me and so I said, 'What the fuck are you staring at, you old bags?' You should of seen them scatter."

Hawthorne grinned suddenly. "I guess you made a clean sweep, didn't you?"

LeBrun grinned as well. "Damn straight."

"Skander's afraid that you'll poison the school."

LeBrun stood up and kicked a pot, which went skittering across the kitchen. "Fat chance. I'm not going to poison anybody unless I get paid for it." Then he grinned again.

Hawthorne climbed off the stool and picked up a couple of pots. "These hang from those hooks over there?"

"Yeah, those ones by the sink." LeBrun dropped his cigarette and ground it out with his heel.

Hawthorne hung the pots from the hooks, then went back and got several more. LeBrun watched him. When he had finished hanging up the pots, Hawthorne took a broom and began sweeping the broken dishes into a pile in the middle of the floor. They made a rattling noise as he pushed them ahead of the broom.

"Hey, you're not supposed to do that."

"Somebody's got to."

"But you're the boss."

Hawthorne kept sweeping. "So what?"

LeBrun got a broom as well. "You're just trying to make me feel bad."

Hawthorne walked over to LeBrun. "No, I'm not. We got about one hundred and twenty people who are going to want lunch in a couple of hours, so I'd better get started."

"You can't cook."

"I can make sandwiches."

"Not good sandwiches. Not with all the stuff on them like I do."

Hawthorne shrugged and leaned on his broom.

"Okay, okay," said LeBrun, "I'll make lunch."

"Tell me what you need and I'll get it for you."

LeBrun kicked at another pot, which landed against the stove with a bang. "I don't need your fuckin' help." He let the broom drop to the floor and lit another cigarette.

"Is something bothering you?"

"The cops have been in here half a dozen times. I just tell them to get the fuck out, that I'm busy. Nah, that's not right, I talked to them. I just don't like it, that's all. I don't like them nagging me about Larry and when did I see this person last and that person last."

"I'm sorry about that," said Hawthorne.

"It's not your fuckin' fault. Why does Skander think I'll poison the school?"

"I guess he's nervous."

LeBrun began sweeping the broken crockery. "What a jerk. He thinks he's got it all figured out. He doesn't know shit. Like, he's making a big mistake. Look, you go tell those old bags they can come back and wash the dishes anytime they want, and you can get those kids as well. I won't say a word to them. But don't expect me to apologize."

"That's okay," said Hawthorne, "I can apologize. You want me to hire some more people?"

"Nah, it's just till the end of the week. Saturday I'm outta here one way or the other."

Hawthorne found the two dishwashers in the small lounge used by the housekeepers. They were shapeless women in their sixties who wore light blue dresses and white aprons. They said they didn't want to work with LeBrun anymore. Hawthorne said that LeBrun had promised to behave and that, anyway, it would only be until the students left. He offered them each a bonus of two hundred dollars. Grudgingly, they returned to the kitchen.

As for the students who had been helping out, one of them absolutely refused to go back. The whole school was scaring him half to death. He was leaving for his parents' house in Framingham either Tuesday or the next day and he wasn't sure if he'd be coming back in January. He'd have to think about it. It depended on whether they found out who had killed Scott. The boy was a tenth grader named Harvey Bengston. He wore thick glasses that made his soft brown eyes seem huge.

The other boy, Eddy Powers, didn't mind going back to the kitchen as long as LeBrun behaved and Hawthorne got somebody to replace Bengston. Maybe two people. Powers was an eleventh grader, a tall, skinny basketball player with a stoop.

"LeBrun's okay as long as you don't talk to him and make sure you laugh at his jokes."

Hawthorne thanked Powers and started to walk away, then he thought of something. "I gather Scott McKinnon didn't come into the kitchen much."

"You kidding? He was in there all the time trying to bum cigarettes and stealing cookies. He and LeBrun would swap jokes and Scott's were always better. He had a great one about a dead old lady who's been reincarnated as a rabbit in Wisconsin."

After Hawthorne had found two more students to help LeBrun, he returned to the kitchen. The women were washing the breakfast dishes and the floor had been swept. LeBrun was kneading a mound of bread dough, hitting it with his fists. Hawthorne told him that the students would show up about eleven, then he said, "You told me you didn't know Scott. Now I hear he was in here often."

LeBrun stepped away from the bread dough and wiped his hands on his apron. He wrinkled his nose at Hawthorne. "I lied."

"How come?"

"Hey, if I said Scott was a friend of mine, the cops would be all over me. 'When was the last time you saw this? When was the last time you saw that?' I'd go fuckin' nuts. So he hung out in the kitchen and bummed cigarettes, does that mean I killed him? What reason would I have?" LeBrun began to reach for a cigarette, then stopped himself.

"So your cousin saw him, too."

"Sure. I mean, Larry couldn't stand him hanging around."

Tuesday evening Hawthorne worked in his office after dinner. The state police had visited the school during the day to search the buildings. Chief Moulton said they were also looking for Larry Gaudette's car, which struck Hawthorne as peculiar since he assumed that Gaudette had taken it with him. In any case, no car was found. Moulton said that none of Gaudette's family in Manchester had heard from him, nor had his friends. As a result, the police were revising their theories.

About eight-thirty, Hawthorne locked his office. Emerson appeared empty. Even though the hall lights were burning brightly, Hawthorne started at every sound as he walked toward the rotunda. His snow boots squeaked on the marble floor. Hawthorne kept telling himself that in another week everything would be all right. The students would be gone and he could concentrate on his problems with the faculty. And LeBrun, something would have to be done about LeBrun. Skander was right: there was no way he could remain in charge of the kitchen.

Hawthorne left through the front door of the building, and out on the driveway he could see stars. The light in the bell tower shone above the school like a beacon. It was cold and he turned up his collar. A dog was barking far away and Hawthorne heard music, the high squeal of guitars. He walked around the outside of Adams. Lights burned in the library in Hamilton Hall and he saw a girl in a green sweater standing at a card catalog. Lights were also on in the dormitory cottages, though many windows were dark. Farther on, Hawthorne could see that people appeared to be home in the faculty houses.

A man was standing on the patio by the French windows of Hawthorne's quarters, a dim figure illuminated by a light on the walkway. Hawthorne hesitated, then continued forward. When he got closer, the man called his name. It was Kevin Krueger.

"What are you doing skulking back here?" asked Hawthorne, hurrying toward him.

Krueger shook his hand. "I just arrived. I need to talk to you."

Hawthorne heard the seriousness in his voice. He unlocked the door and motioned Krueger inside. "Come in, come in, you must be freezing." Hawthorne began turning on lights. He was struck by how dreary his apartment seemed. Only his leather chair looked inviting, something he could take pleasure in. For the first time, Hawthorne wondered if Skander had left the apartment dreary on purpose. I have to stop this, Hawthorne told himself. I can't keep suspecting everyone.

"Would you like a beer? A cup of coffee?"

"Coffee's fine," said Krueger.

Hawthorne unbuttoned his overcoat as he continued to the kitchen. Krueger followed him. His cheeks were red with cold. "How long did it take you to get up here?" asked Hawthorne.

"Two hours." Krueger removed his coat and laid it across a chair.

"That's not bad. What's on your mind? I'm amazed that you drove all this way."

"I'll wait till I'm settled with my coffee first."

Hawthorne was struck by Krueger's tone. He looked at him from the stove. "I guess I'll have coffee as well," he said, turning on the faucet and filling the kettle.

Five minutes later they were seated in the living room. Hawthorne had insisted that Krueger sit in the new chair while he sat on the couch, which after several months of airing still smelled vaguely of cat urine. Hawthorne waited for Krueger to speak.

Krueger blew on his coffee, then set the mug on a small table to the right of his chair. "I heard today that Hamilton Burke has been in contact with the Galileo Corporation."

The Galileo Corporation was one of the for-profits Krueger had mentioned at Thanksgiving, a private company that ran about forty residential treatment programs for high-risk children and adolescents, as well as a number of homes for the retarded. The company's headquarters were in South Carolina.

Hawthorne held his mug with both hands, letting its warmth take the chill from his fingers. "Perhaps it's just a general inquiry. A contingency plan."

"Actually he's been in negotiation for several months, almost since the beginning of the semester. He's counting on Bishop's Hill not opening in the fall."

"He said the other day that he and the trustees don't intend to close the school."

Kruger pulled at his mustache with his thumb as he listened. "I don't know anything about that. Burke expects the deal to be settled within the next few months."

"Where'd you hear this?"

"You remember Ralph Spaight—he was in several of your classes at BU? He works for Galileo. I talked to him."

Hawthorne had a vague memory of a fast-talking graduate student with short black hair. "I never liked him."

"He's doing well," said Krueger.

"And he said Burke was negotiating to sell Bishop's Hill?"

"Spaight has spoken with him. He said Burke's flown down to Columbia twice."

"And this was a board decision?" Neither of them were drinking their coffee.

"No, that's the point. He's done it on his own. Most of the board wants to keep the school open. Of course, if you resign and the school falls apart, then there's no hope. Burke will talk about interested parties hoping to make a deal and the board will see him as a hero. I don't know the particulars, but it's clear that some people will stay on in managerial positions."

"Did Spaight say anything about Fritz Skander or Roger Bennett?"

"He didn't know any names other than Burke's."

Hawthorne considered what it meant to have Burke lying to him. "I wonder if he ever offered Clifford Evings that leave."

"I doubt you could prove anything."

"If he lied to him, then he as good as killed him. Why is he so keen on all this?"

Krueger didn't respond and Hawthorne realized that the answer was obvious. Galileo had presumably offered Burke a sizable amount of money to see the deal go through. Most likely he would also be retained as attorney. Hawthorne went on to tell Krueger about the faculty meeting he had planned for Monday. "I've invited Burke and the other trustees. The faculty is obliged to come. I'm thinking now that I'll also invite Chief Moulton."

"I'd like to be there, too," said Krueger. "And you should have a lawyer."

"Be my guest. I expect sparks will fly."

Krueger reached into his pocket and took out a folded piece of paper, which he held toward Hawthorne. "I've tracked down Lloyd Pendergast for you. He's working for the Chamber of Commerce in Woodstock, Vermont. You want to call him?"

Hawthorne took the paper and began to grin. "I'll do more than that. I'll drive over and see him. I expect there's quite a lot he can tell me."

"Do you mean gossip?"

"On the contrary, I'm hoping to find information that can be used in court."

Hawthorne drove over to Woodstock Thursday morning with Kate. He wanted her as a witness and he wanted her company. Her only condition was that she had to be back by three-thirty, when Todd got home from school. Ted Wrigley had taken Kate's classes, combining hers with his French classes, since half of their students had already left; he was showing *Breathless,* a kind of pre-Christmas tradition of his.

Hawthorne told Kate what he had learned from Krueger, then he described his years of friendship with Krueger in Boston. It was a sunny morning and the snow gleamed from the fields and between the trees, but it was supposed to cloud up that afternoon. The two-lane road from Hanover was slow because of a number of logging trucks. As he drove, Hawthorne felt constantly aware of Kate's presence beside him, as if she were a heat source. She wore dark glasses that he had never seen her wear before. From the corner of his eye, he noticed her hands resting in her lap and more than once he was almost overwhelmed with a desire to reach out and touch her.

"What would it mean to sell the school to the Galileo Corporation?" she asked.

"It would be the end of Bishop's Hill. Debts would be paid. The faculty would receive some sort of severance package. A few would find jobs with the new institution. You could probably get a job yourself. Kevin thinks that some people, like Roger Bennett and perhaps others, would qualify for managerial positions that paid quite well. Certainly much more than they earn now."

"No wonder they were sorry you took the job."

Hawthorne had nothing to say to that. He thought again how he had come to Bishop's Hill to hide. He had never imagined that he would have such a strong desire to see the school succeed, that he would come to care deeply about the students, that he would even fall in love.

It had taken an hour before Hawthorne could bring up the subject of Claire Sunderlin. "I have no excuse for what I did," he said, trying to choose his words precisely. "I loved my wife. I had no wish to jeopardize my family. I'd known Claire for about four years and was attracted to her. Then, when we began to touch each other, I thought, Why not? It seemed like something I could get away with, something without repercussions. I know that my actions with Claire didn't cause the fire, yet I feel guilty. They kept me from getting there earlier. It's something I can't forget. I think of it every day."

Kate stared straight ahead, listening to Hawthorne without looking at him. Her coat was unzipped and the seat belt cut across her chest. "Have you seen her since?"

"No. She called me after the fire. I was in the hospital. I didn't want to talk and she didn't call again." Hawthorne remembered the nurse telling him that he had a call from a woman. Thinking about it, he could almost feel the pain in his arm once again.

"And what do you want from me?" asked Kate.

Hawthorne was surprised by her frankness. "I'd like our friendship to continue. I hope we'll grow closer." Hawthorne hated how cut and dried it sounded. He wanted to say how much he liked her, that he couldn't stop thinking of her, even that he needed her, but he was afraid of frightening her away.

"You mean sex?"

He looked at her quickly. Kate was still staring straight ahead but she was smiling slightly. "Yes, if that's what happens."

"And you could touch me without thinking you were touching another woman, without thinking you were touching your wife?"

"Yes, I think I could do that."

"If you can't, then it won't work." She had turned and was staring at him. Her eyes were dark and unblinking. "Will you try?"

"With all my heart."

Hawthorne had called the previous day to see if Pendergast would be in his office but not to make an appointment. He had told the secretary that he was a businessman with a chain of cyber cafés and that he was visiting Woodstock with an eye to available real estate. Pendergast's secretary said that he would be in all morning except for a half-hour meeting at nine. She explained that, as development director for the Chamber of Commerce, Pendergast would be a mine of useful information. Woodstock was just the place for a cyber café. Before hanging up, she asked Hawthorne how to spell "cyber."

Woodstock was strung with Christmas lights and the shop windows were filled with decorations. Mounds of snow bordered the streets, nearly burying the parking meters. On the sidewalks men and women wore colorful ski jackets. Every doorway seemed to have a Christmas wreath and Christmas music played from speakers tucked among the greenery decorating the old-fashioned street lamps.

Pendergast's office was in the center of downtown, a two-story brick building near the city hall. In the same way that Woodstock seemed to be a quaint illustration from a greeting card, so did Lloyd Pendergast seem illustrative of bluff, hearty charm. He was a red-faced man of about sixty whose tweed jacket, tattersall shirt, and cavalry twill trousers appeared to have sprung from an Orvis catalog. His brown hair was gray at the temples. Pendergast strode heavily across the floor of his paneled office and took Hawthorne's hand in a fierce grip. On the walls were six prints of English setters among fallen leaves and corn stalks.

"Awfully glad to meet you, Mr . . ."

"Hawthorne," said Hawthorne, trying to give a hearty squeeze in return. "And this is Kate Sandler, a colleague. But I'm afraid that I've misrepresented myself."

Pendergast maintained his robust smile but a touch of suspicion appeared in his eyes. He released Hawthorne's hand. "Well, what's it all about?"

Hawthorne wondered if Pendergast recognized his name. "I'm the new headmaster at Bishop's Hill. I just started in September and I've had a bit of trouble with some of the faculty, ranging from general hostility to actual criminal behavior. I'd appreciate hearing what you have to say about them. And I was wondering about your own resignation, whether you felt it was forced upon you in any way."

Pendergast began to look alarmed, which wasn't the response that Hawthorne expected.

"Well, there was always a fair amount of grumbling and foot dragging. I'm sure some of them disliked me. One can't please everyone . . ." Pendergast glanced at his watch.

Hawthorne hoped for information about Bennett, Chip Campbell, Herb Frankfurter, and a few of the others in the years before he came to the school. And there were also certain aspects of Pendergast's departure from Bishop's Hill that Hawthorne was still hoping to understand.

"What was your relationship with them?"

"Cordial, businesslike—I felt as headmaster it wouldn't do to make close friends."

"You left rather abruptly."

"I'm not sure that it was all that abrupt."

"It was in the middle of the school year."

Pendergast's anxiety seemed to increase. He half turned toward his desk and seemed unwilling to speak. Then he shrugged. "Sometimes the thought suddenly strikes you that it's time for a change. I wasn't happy at Bishop's Hill after my wife died, all by myself in that apartment. It seemed right that I leave when I did."

"You gave them hardly a month's notice."

"I really don't have a lot of time this morning, Mr. Hawthorne— or is it Doctor?" The heartiness had gone out of Pendergast's smile. He looked suspiciously at Kate. "I simply believed I could do better elsewhere."

Stephen Dobyns

Hawthorne felt that Pendergast was lying. The realization led him to recall Mrs. Hayes's remark that the former headmaster wasn't a nice man, especially after his wife died. And she had spoken of his vanity, that he had tinted his hair and worried about his figure. Hawthorne glanced at Kate, who was unbuttoning her jacket. Her head was tilted and she seemed to be listening to Pendergast with all the care that she might listen to someone speaking in a language she barely understood.

"Did Fritz Skander put any pressure on you?" asked Hawthorne.

"Why on earth would he have done that? Has Fritz been saying anything about me?"

"You resigned in early December. I'm trying to understand why."

Pendergast's red face grew a little redder and he stuck out his lower lip. "I'm not quite sure where you are going with this, Mr. Hawthorne, nor do I welcome it."

On impulse, Hawthorne asked, "Can you tell me about Gail Jensen?"

"What was the name again?"

"Gail Jensen—she died two weeks before you resigned."

"Yes, yes, I do remember something," said Pendergast. "A student, isn't that correct? She died of a burst appendix . . ." He stood very still as his eyes moved back and forth between Hawthorne and Kate. The sound of Christmas music could faintly be heard through the window.

"She helped out in your office," said Hawthorne. "You must have seen her every day." He didn't understand why Pendergast wasn't telling the truth.

Pendergast spoke quickly. "Hardly that, and it doesn't mean I had anything to do with her. I don't care what Fritz told you."

There was a pause as they looked at each other.

"Why should Fritz have said anything about Gail Jensen?" asked Kate. Hawthorne noticed the chill in her voice.

"I don't mean just about her. Why should he talk about me at all? The girl was just someone who occasionally worked in the office. There were several students who did."

Hawthorne again thought about Mrs. Hayes's unwillingness to talk about the ex-headmaster. He decided to bluff a little. "That's not what Mrs. Hayes told me. Let me use your phone and I'll give her a call."

Pendergast stood as if rooted to the floor. Hawthorne watched different emotions pass across his face: anger, fear, despair.

"You're trying to trap me."

"I think you've trapped yourself," said Hawthorne. "You made her pregnant." Glancing at Kate, he knew that she had reached the same conclusion.

Pendergast made one last attempt at indignation. "You got the whole thing from Fritz, didn't you? You've been leading me on."

"She had an abortion and died. For Christ's sake, she was only fifteen!" Hawthorne paused. "Shortly after that, you resigned. I expect you were forced to resign."

Pendergast moved to his desk and stood with his back to Hawthorne and Kate. His gray tweed jacket had flecks of blue and purple. He put his hands on the edge of his desk and leaned forward as if resting. Then he turned back to Hawthorne. "What if I deny it?"

Kate spoke up first. "Then we'll go to the police."

Nodding, Pendergast raised a hand and rubbed his forehead. "Oddly enough, I've been expecting a visit like this ever since I left Bishop's Hill, but I thought it would be someone wanting money."

"I want to know what happened," said Hawthorne.

Now that what he had done was out in the open, Pendergast began to relax. He raised a shoulder, then let it drop. "One thing just led to another. She'd been doing work in the office. One night I got her to stay late. We'd been a little chummy all along. My wife had died, I don't know . . ." He seemed ready to excuse himself, then changed his mind. "I had sex with her once. She wasn't a virgin, I can tell you that much. Anyway, she got pregnant. She told me I was the father. Of course I had no idea if it was true or false, but I found her a doctor. She told him that the father was a boy her own age. She was frightened that her parents would find out. You have to believe me, I was devastated when she died. Fritz knew about it. He always knew about everything. And a few other people suspected. Fritz said that if I resigned, he'd keep quiet and make certain it went no farther."

"Aren't you trying to shift the blame?" said Kate, still with the anger in her voice.

"I've no excuse for what I did," Pendergast said wearily, "but Skander's no angel. He and Roger Bennett had plenty of little tricks."

"Like what?" asked Hawthorne.

"Fritz was bursar—I guess he's still bursar unless you've fired him. I was sure he'd been embezzling money. Not much. A few hundred here and there. Then in my last year he and Roger hit upon a particularly lucrative scheme. They pretended that we had one less student than we actually had, which meant the boy's tuition went into their pockets."

"How do you know this?" asked Kate.

"I was rather inattentive toward the end. It made them greedy. Actually, it was Mrs. Hayes who asked if there hadn't been a mistake in the figures. I confronted Fritz and he tried to blame Roger. Finally, they both admitted it." Pendergast held out his hands as if offering Hawthorne their very emptiness. "Sad to say, I had far more to lose. The Jensen girl had died and I was in no position to stand up to them. So we forgave each other, as it were. I took my retirement and departed."

"What was the student's name?" asked Hawthorne.

"Peter Roberts. He was a freshman. As far as I know, he's still there. And they might have had other hidden students, unless your presence scared them."

Hawthorne wondered whether Pendergast was just trying to get even for what he believed was Skander's betrayal. Then he thought of the trombone, a missing computer, a slide projector that had been ordered but had never arrived, the peculiar billing of his chair, the uncertainty about Chip Campbell's salary. And there was more—a variety of apparent oversights and clerical errors.

"And no one suspected?" asked Hawthorne.

"Fritz handled the books and he did it with a certain casualness, an affable sloppiness that was very cunning. He could conceal a lot. And the embezzlement, if it was discovered, he could blame on a sort of harmless negligence. But this business of hiding students could send him and Bennett straight to jail."

"What you did was even worse," said Kate, her voice rising. "It was statutory rape and the girl died."

"That's perfectly true, young lady. It was a criminal act, and I feel terrible about it. But imagine what would happen if it became public. Charges and countercharges. The Boston papers would have a field day. Everyone's reputation would be tarnished, even your own. Who knows who would wind up in court, or if the school could remain open." Although Pendergast remained watchful, he began to recover a bit of his former heartiness. He moved around his desk, opened a drawer, and took out a bottle of Martell cognac. He held it toward Hawthorne and Kate. The color was returning to his face. "I find these discussions utterly exhausting," he said. "Like a snoot?"

When Hawthorne and Kate got back to Bishop's Hill about two-thirty, Hawthorne wanted to see Skander right away. But Kate said he should wait. Hawthorne was angry and he needed time to calm himself. They had talked about Pendergast's accusations all the way back from Vermont: whether they were true, whether they were exaggerated, whether they were even worse than Pendergast had said. Hawthorne hadn't recognized the name Peter Roberts; Kate found it familiar. Not only did Hawthorne feel betrayed by Skander, he felt he had been made a fool of.

They were standing in the parking lot by Kate's small green Honda. The sky was overcast and it seemed to be already getting dark. "I'm as upset as you are," Kate said. "They should all be in jail. Not just Pendergast—Fritz and Roger, too, if he's telling the truth. But it makes more sense to wait till you have enough to take to the police. You don't know what Skander might do if you frighten him."

"I'd still like to hear his reaction to some of this. Anyway, I'm glad you came with me to Vermont."

She stared back at him without speaking. He thought how large her eyes looked. Without any plan, he reached out and pressed his hand to her cheek. It was Kate's own face he felt, not anyone else's. He was almost sure of it. She continued looking at him and he could see the question forming in her dark eyes.

Hawthorne returned to his office and spent an hour going over the student files. There was no trace of Peter Roberts, but then, why would there be if Pendergast was right? Hawthorne would have to ask the other teachers if they had heard of him. Then he studied the other names and tried to recall the names of students that he knew. Were there others who weren't listed? He couldn't tell. Then he went over the accounts, adding up items that had apparently been ordered but were nowhere to be found. Had Fritz really faked the order for a three-hundred-dollar trombone?

Students were leaving. Several parents wanted to talk to Hawthorne and he spoke to them in his office. Hilda showed them in with little trace of her former good humor. She glanced nervously at the stacks of papers on Hawthorne's desk and tried to see what was on the computer monitor before he shut it off.

Parents were concerned about the school and their children's safety. Hawthorne said he expected that the police would soon make an arrest. He talked about the two new psychologists who would be joining the staff in January. He felt as much a hypocrite as Lloyd Pendergast, trying to be hearty and full of optimism, but Bishop's Hill would have no chance of surviving if half the student body withdrew over Christmas vacation. That would be playing into Hamilton Burke's hands. And Hawthorne was sure an arrest would be made shortly, though he still found it hard to believe that Larry Gaudette was the killer. Beyond that, however, was the possibility of other scandals—Pendergast and Skander and Roger Bennett. Pendergast was right, the papers would have a field day.

Later in the afternoon Hawthorne taught his history class. Only four students showed up. They discussed fear and how fear could increase without there being any real cause. They talked about their feelings and their grief.

"All I know," said Tommy Peters, "is that I'll be awfully glad to get on that bus on Friday."

After class Hawthorne returned to his office. He tried to go over the accounts once again but he couldn't keep his mind on anything. Hilda had left early and there was only the faint smell of peppermint drops to indicate that she had been there at all. Before dinner he visited the dormitory cottages, chatting with the students and trying to keep their spirits up. Then he went to the library, which was empty except for Bill Dolittle.

"We might as well have sent them home days ago," said Dolittle.

Hawthorne still hadn't talked to him about moving more furniture into the empty apartment in Stark Hall. Even if Dolittle was ineffectual, he was at least friendly.

"It will be over soon," said Hawthorne.

"Storms must be weathered," said Dolittle. "At least that's what they say."

Fewer than sixty people were at dinner, half the usual number. Gene

Strauss and Alice Beech joined Hawthorne at the headmaster's table, along with two students. Usually during dinner there was talking and laughter, but tonight it was quiet. Hawthorne wished there were at least music and he imagined funereal organ music and almost smiled. Neither Skander nor Bennett came to dinner, although Bennett's wife, the chaplain, sat at the head of one of the student tables. From the kitchen came the sound of pots crashing and once a broken plate. The student waiters were jumpy and moved too quickly. Hawthorne restrained himself from going into the kitchen and speaking to LeBrun. About ten minutes after dinner had begun, Jessica Weaver came in and sat at a table with Tom Hastings and two girls. Students were expected to be on time for meals, but no one seemed even to notice Jessica's arrival. Hawthorne tried to make conversation with his colleagues and the students, but he kept thinking about Pendergast's accusations and what he would say to Fritz Skander. Toward the end of the meal a state trooper looked into the dining hall, then went out again.

After dinner Hawthorne decided to visit Skander. He still couldn't quite reconcile the Skander he thought he knew with the one in Pendergast's stories. Even if he didn't tell Fritz all that Pendergast had said, he might form some idea of the truth. After all, he was a clinical psychologist, a trained listener. Therefore, around seven, he walked over to Skander's house. The paths had been shoveled but there was still a foot of snow on the ground. It was cold and no stars could be seen. A small road curved past the dormitory cottages and faculty houses, with lights every ten yards. Skander's house was about a hundred yards past the farthest cottage, just fifty yards from the woods.

Hawthorne climbed the steps. The porch light was out and he felt around for the doorbell. The air had that damp feeling it gets before snow.

Hilda answered the door. She was hesitant about letting Hawthorne come in. "Fritz is working." She appeared to hope that Hawthorne would apologize and say that whatever he wanted could wait until morning. A dog was barking in a farther room.

"This won't take long." Hawthorne stamped his feet and removed his gloves.

When Hilda showed Hawthorne into the study, Skander hurriedly got up from his desk and came to shake Hawthorne's hand. "What a pleasant surprise." One whole wall was a bookcase. Several of the shelves displayed golf and bowling trophies.

Hawthorne was struck by how genuine his smile appeared. He began to think that Pendergast hadn't been entirely truthful. "I met Lloyd Pendergast today," said Hawthorne, after Hilda had left them alone.

Skander's smile widened. "Dear old Pendergast. You must tell me how he is."

"He told me you forced him to resign after Gail Jensen's death."

At first Skander made no response. Then he raised his eyebrows and leaned forward as if he weren't sure he had heard correctly. "And why would I have done that?"

"Because he believed you were embezzling money, pretending to order things for the school and keeping the money for yourself. Was that what happened to the trombone? Did you pocket the three hundred dollars?" Hawthorne had remained by the door. He kept his voice calm but his fists were clenched in the pockets of his overcoat.

Skander massaged his brow. For a moment he stared down at the rug, and when he at last looked up, he appeared concerned, though not for himself. "Jim, this is really embarrassing. You understand, of course, that I wouldn't be popular with Pendergast. He was terribly afraid of going to jail. I felt if I went to the authorities it would do great harm to the school. Even then we were barely keeping our heads above water. It seemed that if Pendergast resigned, if he simply went away, we would have a chance of hiring someone truly qualified. Someone like yourself. I promised him that I would keep quiet and I kept my word, even though it's hurt me to do so."

"You frightened Mrs. Hayes into quitting and you frightened Clifford Evings. Did you pay somebody to wreck his office or did you do it yourself? You or Roger got Jessica Weaver drunk and sent her over to my apartment so you could blackmail me in the same way you blackmailed Pendergast. And that business with the painting and the phone calls from my dead wife and all the gossip and slander . . ." Hawthorne stopped himself. Out of anger he was saying more than he had intended.

Skander continued to look stricken. He held out a hand toward Hawthorne as if imploring him to stop. "Jim, I don't know what to say. What painting are you talking about? Roger certainly hasn't confided in me about what he might or might not have done. And if you feel there's the slightest irregularity with the accounts, then I really demand that you have an audit immediately."

Although Hawthorne didn't trust Skander, he could see nothing in his face, his eyes, his gestures, even his words that convinced him the man was lying. Skander's earnestness, his apparent embarrassment, his concern for Hawthorne's well-being—instead of being angry at Skander, Hawthorne found himself growing angry with Pendergast. On the other hand, he couldn't rely on Skander's appearance. He needed facts.

"I'll see about an audit first thing tomorrow," Hawthorne said.

Skander took a handkerchief from his pocket and wiped his forehead. "Surely the wisest course. But, Jim, this is truly hurtful. I thought we were closer than this, that we trusted each other. I love Bishop's Hill. It's my entire life. Why would I do any of this?" There was no anger or fear in Skander's expression; rather, he regarded Hawthorne as one might look at a dear friend who has become ill.

Hawthorne pressed on. "Because if I quit and the school closes, then Burke can sell the facility to the Galileo Corporation. And you'll stay on, perhaps even as bursar or associate director. You'll make more money, won't have to teach, and won't even have to move from your house."

"Jim, Jim, forgive me for being blunt. You must not turn your back on your true friends. If we don't work together, then I don't see how the school can be saved. I'm completely bewildered by all this venom. Please, think hard before you do anything rash." He reached out to put a hand on Hawthorne's shoulder, but Hawthorne stepped back.

"One more thing," asked Hawthorne. "What can you tell me about a student by the name of Peter Roberts? He doesn't seem to be on the books."

Skander's face seemed to pause in its solicitude, then his expression of concern reasserted itself. "Peter Roberts? I don't believe I know the name. Is he new?"

11

Roger Bennett's palms were sweating and he kept rubbing them on his corduroy trousers. He leaned against the doorjamb, trying to appear relaxed, but in truth he was afraid. He felt a prickling on his skin, as if what he wanted to do most was to run: to rush down the stairs and into the falling snow. He had spent much of his adult life feeling confident of his superiority, telling students what to do and making them do it. He had no experience with being terrified of another human being. Fritz Skander, on the other hand—so Bennett thought—looked perfectly calm, but perhaps he too was frightened and had the sense not to show it. Bennett was unsure of this. He never knew what Fritz was feeling unless Fritz told him, and even then Bennett wasn't entirely convinced.

It had been Bennett's idea that they should keep their mouths shut or, if they had to speak, that they should deny everything. But Fritz said they no longer had a choice—Hawthorne's discovery of the Peter Roberts scheme and his insistence on an audit meant it was just a matter of time until Hawthorne uncovered the extent of their misconduct, including their arrangement with LeBrun. Luckily, Roberts had not returned to school that fall, but many teachers remembered him, and the family lived in Keene. It would take very little investigation to prove what had happened. The two of them would go to jail. And the unfolding of the evidence against them was a process that would begin with the audit on Wednesday. Far better, Fritz had insisted, to call on the services of Frank LeBrun again.

Frank LeBrun sat on his bed watching Fritz, his face expressionless, although now and then he glanced at Bennett and grinned. Each time, Bennett wanted to bolt. Bennett wondered if LeBrun had had sex with Jessica on that narrow bed or if they had done it on the couch. Most likely they had done it all over the room. The shades were drawn, although it was only shortly after breakfast on Saturday, and the ceiling light was on. The one picture on the wall was a calendar with a photograph of a covered bridge. Looking closer, Bennett thought he was wrong about the date, then he asked himself what sort of idiot would hang up a thirteen-year-old calendar.

Fritz was talking and his tone was gentle, as if he were addressing a child he loved. "It's truly incredible for me to realize what you have done. When I told you on Thanksgiving that the boy had come to me with those wild stories, I thought you'd simply be amused. At most, I thought you might speak to him. Ask him to cease and desist. After all, people gossip and the fact that Larry was nowhere to be found might make people imagine that he had indeed come to harm. So the boy's story, it had to be no more than an insensitive prank. Youthful monkeyshines. I would have told him myself to put a lid on it, but it was Thanksgiving and one thing led to another and we were having guests. A busy day for all of us, no doubt. Yet when the boy told me that he needed to find Dr. Hawthorne and that Jim might use this information against you, might in fact cause you an injury, I thought it my duty to tell you what the youngster had said. I thought you would just admonish him, scold him, urge him to keep quiet. Dear, dear, did you really have to murder him?"

LeBrun leaned forward with his elbows on his knees, looking up at Fritz with his head slightly tilted. He wore faded jeans and a white shirt with stains from the kitchen—oil and coffee, a bit of red jam. With his head tilted, LeBrun's thin face looked decidedly freakish to Bennett, like features stuck on the spine of a book. LeBrun didn't speak; he watched Fritz and gently rubbed one hand across the black hairs on the back of the other. Fritz leaned against the bureau with his hands in the pockets of his tweed slacks and occasionally jingled a few coins. He was smiling benignly, but with a trace of disappointment.

"Of course," said Fritz, "I wouldn't dream of saying anything to anyone, though I must say the police have been an utter nuisance. But you have us over a barrel, Frank, you really do. If I didn't like you and didn't feel you deserved far more than life, in its intrinsic unfairness, has given you, then I might be tempted to reveal what happened to that boy. And the cat, we mustn't forget the cat. But what would be the result? If the police arrested you, then *you* might be tempted to tell them about that unfortunate prank in Clifford's office. I remain astonished at my folly in encouraging you to do it, even giving you some small sum. I don't know what I was thinking. But here was this fellow being totally useless yet earning a good salary. That money could have gone to other places where it was desperately needed. Scholarships, for instance. I was frustrated, that's the most I can say in my defense, and of course I worried about what was best for the school. My hope was that he might go away, just as Mrs. Hayes had gone away. Surely, you were as horrified as I when Clifford chose to end his life—a spiteful act, in any case—though we can't say for certain that the damage to his office was the actual cause. And I wouldn't blame you for telling the police—after all, an exchange of information might make them more lenient. And the tequila and the girl, another piece of bad judgment— no, no, it's quite obvious that we overreached ourselves. The best plan is to keep quiet about you and poor Scott McKinnon. And Roger, too, is the soul of discretion. His lips are sealed. But, really, can we say the same of Dr. Hawthorne? If he is truly planning to dismiss you for what you said to those boorish students—and that is only what I've heard, he hasn't spoken to me about it directly—then what would he do if he knew that you had murdered Scott McKinnon? No, no, my friend, I'm afraid you can't count on him."

Still LeBrun didn't speak. He glanced over at Bennett and grinned. Bennett had to force himself not to jump, to keep his face still, and not to wipe his palms on his trousers. It was the uncertainty that disturbed him. He hadn't the least idea what was passing through LeBrun's head. In fact, he wasn't sure what Fritz intended, except that he hoped to plant the seeds of suspicion, even fear, so that LeBrun would do something about Hawthorne. Enlisting the cook had been Skander's idea from the beginning. Bennett had never felt quite right about him, but he hadn't been insistent enough. Now it was too late to turn back.

"You must realize, of course, that Dr. Hawthorne is a clinical psychologist," continued Skander, "practically a psychiatrist, though he can't hand out pills. Perhaps you've had contact with such people in your time—always asking how you feel and if you're happy. And psychologists often suffer from an inferiority complex about not having a medical degree. It makes them more devious. That's the thing about Hawthorne, isn't it? You never know if what he says is true. Perhaps he's saying it because he thinks that's what you should hear. For instance, if he tells you how good you look, who knows if that's what he feels? Rather, that's the strategy he's devised. In fact, he may have decided you could benefit from the deception. To me he's been quite open about you, and let me tell you that I've found it shocking. Just because you haven't had the educational advantages of the rest of us doesn't mean you aren't intelligent. I've been quite straightforward about that. Even blunt. Your French Canadian heritage, the way you speak, your lack of sophistication, even your jokes—no, no, I've told Dr. Hawthorne right to his face that he mustn't judge you. Indeed, I've told him that I didn't want to hear you verbally abused in my presence, that even if you weren't as fortunate as he, it didn't mean you could be turned into a figure of fun and ridiculed. He's not a trustworthy sort, if you see what I mean. And I think he rather liked young Scott."

LeBrun got to his feet and walked across his small apartment to the refrigerator. He opened the door and took out a bottle of Budweiser. "You want one?" he asked Skander.

"Much too early for me, I'm afraid."

LeBrun held up a bottle toward Bennett, who shook his head. "What's wrong, Bennett, you're not smiling. Aren't you the guy who's always smiling? You used to be a regular clown." Taking an opener from a drawer, LeBrun popped the top, put the bottle to his lips, and tilted back his head. Bennett watched him drink nearly the whole bottle without pausing. Then LeBrun lowered the bottle, wiped his mouth with the back of his hand, and belched. "So what you're telling me," said LeBrun, leaning against the refrigerator, "is that I have to kill Hawthorne. You're saying I got no choice."

The snow blew horizontally into the windshield and then clogged the wipers, forcing Hawthorne to roll down his window, reach around, and flick the wiper, knocking the snow off so he could see, at least for another five minutes, until he had to roll down the window and knock off the snow all over again. The usual thirty-five-minute drive from Bishop's Hill to Plymouth had taken over an hour and during that time the winter weather advisory had been upgraded to a storm warning. Hawthorne had brought four students to Plymouth so they could catch the bus to Logan Airport in Boston. Luckily, most of the other students had left the previous day. Concord Trailways had assured Hawthorne over the phone that the bus would be running, though it might be late. Hawthorne himself had been a little late, but he'd still been able to get the students to the bus station—a gas station and convenience store with a bench—by noon. That evening Hawthorne was supposed to visit Kate; her son was with his father. Hawthorne told himself that he would be there no matter what—snowstorms, hurricanes, tornadoes notwithstanding.

Jessica Weaver had come along. All week she had been skipping meals and looking depressed and anxious. Helen Selkirk had told Hawthorne, "Not even her kitten cheers her up." But Helen had taken the bus to Boston two days earlier, leaving Jessica alone in their dorm room. So Hawthorne had decided to bring her to Plymouth and buy her lunch after dropping off the other kids. Jessica's stepfather planned to pick her up at school either that day or the next, although Hawthorne thought that he might be delayed by the snow.

"He's got a Jeep Wrangler," Jessica told him, "it's one of his toys. He thinks he can go anywhere. He'll be there all right."

"You don't seem to be looking forward to it."

"I hate him," Jessica answered perfectly calmly. "I wish he was dead. But at least I might see my brother. If it weren't for Jason, I wouldn't be going home at all."

"Is that what's been bothering you?"

"Partly. Have you ever felt that you really deserved to be punished?"

"For what sort of thing?"

"I don't want to say, but it's about the worst thing in the world."

"Does it concern your stepfather?"

"Sure, but it concerns me a lot more."

Hawthorne had spoken with Jessica's stepfather over the phone, although he had never met him. Peter Tremblay had the genial and articulate manner of a professional speaker—a lawyer well-practiced in boardrooms and courtrooms. In this way, he reminded Hawthorne of Hamilton Burke. Hawthorne wondered how such people were when they became sad or wistful or sentimental, when they expressed anything other than authority and hearty assurance.

"What about your mother?" Hawthorne asked.

"Dolly's too scared of Tremblay to complain. But they're going to be flying to Las Vegas right after Christmas. Tremblay loves to gamble but he's not very good at it. And Dolly loves to drink. He's hired a baby-sitter from an agency to take care of me and Jason, which surprised me."

"Why should it surprise you?"

Jessica didn't answer right away. "Tremblay doesn't like to leave us together. He thinks we conspire against him."

"And do you?"

"Of course."

From the bus station, Hawthorne drove Jessica to a diner called Main Street Station, across from Plymouth State College. He parked and they waded through the snow to the diner, which had a bright yellow front, a green metal awning, and two green pillars. Inside were red booths trimmed with dark maple and thirteen red-topped stools along a marble counter. They took a booth by a window that looked out from about six feet above the sidewalk. Cars and pickups were crawling along with their lights on and there was the jingle of snow chains. Across the street and up the hill beyond the parking lot, the four-story Rounds Hall was barely visible, its clock tower a blur in the blowing snow. Four students passed on cross-country skis right down the middle of the street.

Jessica ordered a half-pound monster burger with guacamole, jalapeño peppers, and sautéed mushrooms, and a strawberry frappe. Hawthorne got the turkey club, French fries, and a cup of coffee. The young waitress smiled as if she thought Jessica was his daughter. At the counter, four men were drinking coffee, each with a puddle of melting snow beneath his stool.

"So," said Hawthorne, wanting to continue the conversation they had had in the car, "what's this thing that's the worst thing in the world?"

Jessica's hair hung in two braids. She had unzipped her down jacket and underneath she wore her blue University of New Hampshire sweatshirt. "I don't know, it's not that big a deal. I don't want to talk about it."

"Does it have to do with what happened before you came to Bishop's Hill?"

"Partly."

"And what else?"

"Just a lot of bullshit." Jessica seemed no longer interested in talking. She sipped her water, then set her glass back on the table. She stared out the window and didn't look at Hawthorne. Each window had a border of red stained glass running across the top. "I miss my brother," she said at last.

"You'll be seeing him tomorrow, won't you?"

"I guess so." Jessica tore open a packet of sugar, poured it into her hand, and licked it slowly. Her tongue was pointed and very pink.

"So it's more than that, isn't it?"

Jessica crumpled up the empty sugar packet. "You can probably figure it out." She again seemed to be deflecting his questions.

"What do you mean?"

"Your wife and kid were killed, right? Well, my father was killed."

Hawthorne remembered that Jessica's father had died in an accident in which he had been flying his own plane "You think about your dad a lot?"

"He was my best friend. He protected me."

"I'd like to be a friend as well," said Hawthorne. "I want you to believe that you can trust me."

Jessica's voice hardened. "You don't replace best friends as easily as that."

Hawthorne winced and Jessica resumed staring out the window. All at once he saw her sit up as if someone had jabbed her with a needle. Glancing out the window, he looked down on a familiar figure bundled up against the weather. He recognized the green hunting jacket before he recognized the man. It was LeBrun, with someone whom Hawthorne didn't think he knew, though from where he was, above them, he couldn't see their faces. They were talking. The other man wore a red ski cap and seemed older. Then they disappeared.

"Frank LeBrun," said Hawthorne. "Who was the other fellow?"

"I'm not sure," said Jessica.

Her tone seemed purposely vague. She began tearing open another packet of sugar. The father in Hawthorne wanted to tell her that it was bad for her teeth or would ruin her lunch or would give her pimples. He was impressed that LeBrun had driven into Plymouth in such weather. But LeBrun had been born and bred in New Hampshire. This was probably nothing to him.

"Frank's a friend of yours, isn't he?" said Hawthorne.

Jessica crumpled the empty packet and dropped it in the ashtray. "Not particularly." There was a tension in her face that hadn't been there before. She looked scared.

"I thought you liked visiting him in the kitchen."

"He frightens me."

"How?"

Jessica didn't say anything to that.

"It was LeBrun who gave you the tequila, wasn't it?" said Hawthorne, leaning forward. It wasn't really a question. "Who was the man with him?"

Jessica turned to him sharply. "Leave me alone, will you? What'd you do, bring me here to grill me? I can walk back to school, you know."

"It's twenty miles," said Hawthorne, trying not to smile.

"I don't give a fuck." She straightened her jacket as if she meant to zip it up, then she began to pick at the patch of duct tape on the front.

The waitress brought their lunches. "Isn't it a shame how it always snows on a Saturday instead of on a school day," she said, beaming at Jessica. Above the table was a hanging light with a red glass shade. It swayed slightly as she set down the plates. The French fries were awesome, she told them.

Jessica continued to look out the window as if the waitress weren't there. After the young woman left, Jessica began poking at the bun of her sandwich with her index finger, making deep indentations and causing the guacamole to ooze out at the sides.

Hawthorne started to say something, then took a bite of his own sandwich instead. He supposed it was impossible not to feel paternal with a fifteen-year-old. He thought of LeBrun. The cook had said he'd be leaving for Christmas and he wasn't sure if he'd be back. Although he liked his job, he had a lot that he needed to do. "I got business all over the place," LeBrun had said. Hawthorne hadn't asked what sort of business.

After Jessica had eaten half of her hamburger, Hawthorne said, "Frank told me he hardly knew who Scott was, then later he said that Scott was in the kitchen all the time. He said that he and Scott were always telling jokes to each other, that he hadn't wanted to tell me the truth earlier because he was afraid of the police." Hawthorne let the sentence hang and returned to his sandwich. It was cut into quarters and each quarter had been pierced with a toothpick ending in a red frazzle. There was also a pickle and a small cupful of cole slaw.

"You don't know LeBrun," said Jessica. "You don't know the stuff he can do."

"What sort of stuff?"

"Like you don't know he was the one who wrecked Evings's office. You don't know shit."

"Why did he wreck Mr. Evings's office?"

"Find out for yourself."

"How does that make you feel, not to tell me?"

Jessica pushed away her hamburger. "Don't give me that 'feel' shit. I've already been down that road. All I'm saying is that you got to watch out. I'm not saying more than that."

"It scared you seeing LeBrun with that man, didn't it?"

Jessica said nothing. She had turned away and had begun to free her hair from the two braids. Then she said, "Have you ever done something so bad that when something bad happens to you you think you must have deserved it?"

"Maybe." Hawthorne watched her carefully. It seemed obvious she was talking about herself and not him. "It digs at you, doesn't it?"

"It makes me think that I've got to put up with stuff."

"You don't have to put up with anything."

She ran her fingers through her hair, then shook her head so the hair swung free. It made her look older. "If you were bad enough, you do."

"Is this the thing that's the worst thing in the world?"

Jessica was looking at an old man at the counter who was putting on his overcoat. After another minute, Hawthorne said, "You need to trust me. You have to believe I'm on your side."

Jessica turned abruptly, knocking the glass with her strawberry frappe so that, if Hawthorne hadn't caught it, the sticky pink liquid would have spilled across the table.

"You're just like those men at the club," said Jessica in an angry whisper. " 'Trust me, believe me.' All you want to do is get in my pants."

"That's absurd," said Hawthorne.

"You're sorry you didn't fuck me when I was drunk. That's what everyone thought anyway, right? So now you're sorry you didn't do it when you could. Don't tell me you're on my side."

Hawthorne wasn't sure whether to laugh or be angry, but it also seemed that she wanted to distract him from talking about LeBrun.

"So who was the man with Frank?"

Abruptly, Jessica slid out of the booth and stood up. "All right, Dr. Smart Guy, you had your chance. I'm walking." She began to zip up her jacket.

Hawthorne thought how quickly she could lapse into what he imagined to be the tone, if not the language, of the strip clubs. "That's okay, I won't say any more. We'll have a hard enough time getting back to Bishop's Hill as it is."

"Well, better you than LeBrun," said Jessica.

Detective Leo Flynn hated driving in the snow. The back wheels of his Ford Escort slid a little to the left, then to the right, no matter what he did. He hadn't expected it to be this bad. In Boston it had been raining. Between Routes 128 and 495 there was sleet. Since crossing the New Hampshire border on 93, he had felt as if he were driving deep into the interior of a snowman. Cars slid off the highway into the median or into ditches. Flynn watched them do it, half dismayed, half in awe. They had a silent grace, like dancers in a ballet. A tractor-trailer had overturned near Salem.

Every time Flynn crept by a car stuck up to its fenders he crossed himself. What a foolish way to spend his day off, he thought. If he didn't go today, however, the whole business would have to be conducted over computers and the telephone. Nothing face-to-face, what

Leo Flynn thought of as police work handled the old-fashioned way. A boy had been found dead in a swimming pool near Brewster. An autopsy had shown that he had been murdered just like Sal Procopio, Buddy Roussel, Mike Ritchie, and probably some other guys. The man sought for questioning was Larry Gaudette. And Flynn knew that name. Gaudette was the cousin of Francis LaBrecque and it had occurred to Flynn that maybe ice pick murders were a family business or one of those inherited skills like playing the piano or juggling five apples at once. Anyway, Flynn was driving up to Brewster to surprise the local coppers with his information about the other killings. So what that he was ignoring protocol; Leo Flynn was an old-fashioned guy. But if Jack Coughlin, the homicide captain, had wanted to slow him up, he couldn't have done better than throwing this snowstorm in his face.

As for catching Gaudette, Flynn could help with that as well. He had talked to Gaudette's friends and family in Manchester; he had talked to a couple of the guys whom Gaudette had worked for. Everyone liked him, which didn't mean much—Flynn had met murderers who'd been the most popular guys on their blocks. And serial killers were often charmers—fellows who could talk their way into your living room. Still, Flynn hadn't figured Gaudette for a killer and he wondered if these yokels had heard of Francis LaBrecque, because that's what interested Flynn most: just where LaBrecque was hanging his hat and what sort of tricks he was up to.

Flynn had left home at eleven and it was now one-thirty and he'd only just passed Concord—normally a one-hour drive. Soon it would be getting dark, although all the cars had their headlights on already. The only pleasure was in watching the big sport utility vehicles whipping past him—the Explorers and Broncos and Wagoneers—then seeing them stuck in a ditch a few miles farther up the road with their owners staring at them stupidly, as if a portion of the true cross had turned out to be plastic. The salt trucks were out, of course, and the plows, but it was snowing so hard that the road got covered again in no time: two inches, four inches, six inches. And it occurred to Leo Flynn that the smart thing would be to pull off as soon as he could and buy some chains.

Three hours later, Flynn was still driving north. By now it was dark and the fat flakes seemed to fling the brilliance of his headlights back into his face. Through the snow-blanketed silence he could just hear the clink-clink of the chains he had bought south of Laconia. They had cost an arm and a leg, but they were cheaper than having his car towed out of a ditch or dealing with the ulcer that throbbed every time his car skidded, spun, slipped, or swerved. Now, though he was still creeping along, he was doing it in relative safety. Also, as far as he could figure from the radio, the snow would keep up all night and through Sunday, and at some point Flynn would have to drive home. "Major New England storm" was how the deejays described it with pride.

At the Brewster exit, Flynn slowed to a crawl and crept down the off-ramp. He hadn't phoned the police station, because he wanted his arrival to be a surprise, but now he was thinking that everything he had done that day had been stupid. He should have called. He should have stayed in Boston. He should have done what he could do on the computers, which meant telling one of the nerds what he needed, since the only thing Leo Flynn knew how to do on a computer was play solitaire. He passed a Sunoco station just off the exit—a yellow glow in the murk. The orange revolving light of a plow eased past and he could see the sparks from where its great blade scraped the pavement. Only a few other cars were on the road, a few Jeeps and four-by-fours. He could hear the other guys on his homicide team saying to him on Monday, "You nuts? You did what?" Well, if he learned nothing new, then he'd keep his mouth shut. No reason to let others know that he had been this foolish.

It was six o'clock by the time Flynn got to Brewster. He'd asked for directions to the police station, which turned out to be a two-room shack next to a diner. The police station was dark and a note was tacked to the door that said, "Back at six." On the same note was a message reading, "Please call me as soon as possible—Hawthorne." The diner was closed. Flynn sat in his car and kept the windshield wipers going so he could see. It occurred to him that he should have bought boots at the same time he'd bought the chains. He wore a pair of low black shoes with leather soles. As he waited, Flynn listened to the radio announcements of canceled bingo games, dances, basketball games, lectures at the college, and church meetings, until he came to think that the entire state was shutting down.

Chief Moulton turned up forty-five minutes later wearing a heavy blue parka and a matching cap. He was driving a black Blazer with oversized tires. Moulton didn't look like a cop, Flynn thought, more like a lumberjack. They shook hands outside the police station, then Moulton led the way in. Already snow got into Flynn's shoes and he tried to dig it out with a finger. He and Moulton were about the same age, which was in Moulton's favor because Flynn didn't trust anyone under fifty anymore. They didn't have the prerequisite historical knowledge.

"You drove all the way up from Boston today?" asked Moulton. His voice had a buttoned quality, as if he were trying to hide the humor in it.

Flynn tried to arrange his face into an expression that indicated he was perfectly happy about driving through a snowstorm. "It took a while. Anyway, it was my day off."

Before they were settled in Moulton's small office, the chief tried to call Hawthorne. He dialed the number, listened, then pushed the button down and dialed again. After a moment, he said, "Looks like the phones are out at Bishop's Hill. I tried him earlier and left a message."

Flynn knew nothing about Hawthorne or Bishop's Hill but he attempted to look philosophical. Then he told Moulton about the three other killings, trying not to surprise him too much. After all, small-town cops didn't have a lot of experience with murder.

"I'd already got reports on them from the state police," said Moulton. "Lieutenant Sloan was telling me about them this morning, but I'm glad to have the details."

"What about Francis LaBrecque?" asked Flynn. "Do you know anything about him? He's the cousin of this guy Gaudette that you're looking for."

"Not looking for him anymore. A trapper found him in the Baker River before the storm hit—all frozen in the ice except for the heel of his shoe. We had a devil of a time cutting him loose. Poor guy had been turned into a giant ice cube. Anyway, we sent him down to Plymouth. We thought he might be in the neighborhood because his car showed up yesterday. Somebody drove it way down a logging road and left it."

"What about LaBrecque?" asked Flynn, feeling some of his thunder had been diminished.

"I don't know anything about any LaBrecque," said Moulton. "But there's a Frank LeBrun working at Bishop's Hill. He's a cousin of Gaudette's as well. He bakes bread."

Kate began to worry when she couldn't get through to Bishop's Hill on the phone. Her own lights had been flickering since five o'clock and she wouldn't have been surprised if they'd gone out. All it took was for a branch to break a wire; in a storm like this, entire trees had been known to topple. And if the wires were broken in several places, they could take hours to fix.

Hawthorne had called from Plymouth early in the afternoon to see if she wanted anything from the supermarket. She might not be able to get to a store because of the weather. He had Jessica with him and they were about to drive back to Bishop's Hill. And he had mentioned seeing LeBrun in town.

"I'd like to stop and talk to Chief Moulton in Brewster. LeBrun wrecked Evings's office. Maybe I should talk to LeBrun as well."

"Jessica told you about that?"

"Yes, but she won't give me any details."

That was when Kate began to worry. She herself didn't like LeBrun, didn't like his jokes, didn't like how he looked at her, didn't like his friendship with Jessica. Now Hawthorne wanted to go back to the school to talk to him. Kate thought that Hawthorne believed too much in talk, just as he put too much trust in his four-wheel-drive Subaru, that it would take him anywhere no matter how deep the snow got. She recalled how ready LeBrun had been to beat up Chip in the parking lot. What was talk to LeBrun? Nothing but telling jokes and being evasive. For that matter, what was talk to Hamilton Burke and the others who wanted to wreck the school? Only a vehicle of deception, something to make their untruths palatable. And the gossip and slander—all of it had been talk. Hawthorne's innocence almost amused her. He came from a world where talk had value, where people told the truth as best they could. And although it exasperated Kate, it was also something she liked about him. Hawthorne believed that people were better for having the information, while the dishonest, mediocre, and fearful wanted concealment. Bishop's Hill was full of subjects that people preferred not to discuss—the school's decline, the pilfering, the bad teaching, the fact that the previous headmaster had gotten a fifteen-year-old girl pregnant. These were subjects best left in the dark.

Kate called the school and found that the phones weren't working. Her car was in the garage, and when she turned on the light in her driveway she saw that at least two feet of snow had fallen. Clearly Hawthorne wouldn't be able to come over that evening and the strength of Kate's disappointment surprised her. She wanted the two of them to be together without interruption. And if Hawthorne spent the night, that would be wonderful. It seemed only a possibility, but even so she had put her best white sheets on the bed.

It was impossible for her to drive anywhere in snow this deep. Even if she could shovel the car out, she wouldn't be able to get down the dirt roads and the plows wouldn't clear them until the snow stopped. Did she really believe Hawthorne was in trouble or was she exaggerating the danger? Was it just because she wanted to see him? She went to the phone again, only to find there wasn't even a dial tone. Then she began to collect candles and to see if her kerosene lamps were full. The wind was blowing and the temperature falling, although the snow showed no signs of letting up. She put the kerosene lamps on her kitchen table and went to find a flashlight. After ten minutes she had found two, and some batteries as well. The previous winter she had cross-country skied to Bishop's Hill a few times, but never when the snow was two feet deep. The boots were in her bedroom closet and her skis were in the garage. As she walked to her bedroom, she began to reason with herself. Bishop's Hill was three miles away and she would hardly be able to shuffle along. Did she really want to fight her way through a blizzard?

Hawthorne had gotten back to Bishop's Hill around four-thirty. A plow had been through, but not for some time, because nearly another foot of snow covered the road. For the last six miles from Brewster Village he had passed no other cars. Twice he had drawn to a halt so Jessica could clear his windshield. Hawthorne had stopped in Brewster, looking for Chief Moulton, but there had been a note on the door saying that he wouldn't be back till six. So Hawthorne had scribbled a message, then pushed ahead toward the school.

"What do you think happened to Scott?" Hawthorne asked as they drove along Antelope Road toward Bishop's Hill. "Do you think LeBrun had something to do with it?"

But Jessica had slid down in her seat and didn't appear to hear. Hawthorne considered the adolescent's ability to leap forward into adulthood when treated as a child and to leap back into childhood when treated as an adult.

"Do you think he threw your kitten into the pool?"

Again Jessica wouldn't answer. Hawthorne asked himself what he knew about LeBrun. The cook had been hired by Skander on Gaudette's recommendation before Hawthorne arrived at Bishop's Hill. After LeBrun had swung at Chip, Hawthorne had run a check on him but he had learned nothing. The man seemingly had no record. Still, Hawthorne was increasingly aware of a volatility that he found disturbing, as if LeBrun had no inhibitions, no moral or ethical controls. What was LeBrun's background? And he found himself remembering the tack that one of the students had found in his bread back at the beginning of the school year.

The students—there were still a few who needed Hawthorne's attention in addition to Jessica. A dozen or so remained at the school. Clearly, they needed to be fed and cared for. A number of the faculty had also left and so, ideally, the last students could be put together in one of the dormitory cottages. Ruth Standish and Alice Beech were still at the school, along with Bill Dolittle. Perhaps they could all camp out in Pierce, and soup and sandwiches could be brought from the kitchen. Hawthorne again wondered how many of those who had left would be coming back after Christmas.

"Do you think you'll be coming back in January?" he asked Jessica.

She wouldn't answer. She seemed hypnotized by the swirling mass of snowflakes.

"You have to trust me," said Hawthorne. "Really, I mean you no harm. If you're scared, then maybe I can help, but I can't do anything if you don't tell me what's wrong."

Jessica glanced at him. In the lights from the dashboard he saw tears on her cheeks. He wanted to reach out and touch her but he was afraid it would be misunderstood.

"There are things I've got to do," she said, "and you can't help me. I'm sorry, that's just the way it is."

Stephen Dobyns

Hawthorne took the turnoff to the school, crossing the bridge over the Baker River. A small truck or four-by-four had passed that way and Hawthorne tried to stay in its tracks down the middle of the road. Even so, the Subaru skidded. When he passed through the gates, he could see the yellow light from the bell tower on top of Emerson, but very faintly. Although a few other lights were on, the school appeared deserted. The truck seemed to have turned off toward the school garage. Hawthorne wondered who would have driven up to the school in this weather and if it could have been LeBrun. He plunged the Subaru into the white unbroken surface that he hoped was the driveway leading to Emerson, though it could easily have been the front lawn. Even as he accelerated, he knew the car wouldn't make it. For twenty yards it veered from side to side, then came to a stop. When he put his foot on the gas, the tires spun but didn't go forward. The car was about a hundred and fifty yards from the front steps.

"I'm afraid this is it," said Hawthorne. "We'll have to walk."

"I should have stayed in Plymouth," said Jessica.

"I'll go first and you step in my footprints. Then you can cut through Emerson and Douglas over to your cottage."

Even pushing open the car door was an effort. Snow blew into Hawthorne's face and he tucked his chin into his collar. He waited by the hood as Jessica climbed out and waded toward him. She appeared as a white shape rather than a person. He held out his hand to her but she refused to take it. "Just get moving," she said.

The snow reached above Hawthorne's knees. He half shuffled, then took big steps, lifting his knees high like a heron in a pond. He could hear Jessica grumbling behind him. Actually, he found the snow invigorating. Its drama outweighed the aggravation. Then he thought of Bennett and how he had to speak to him. Hawthorne was positive that Bennett was mixed up with the destruction of Evings's office, which meant that he was also mixed up with LeBrun. Perhaps it could wait till morning. But could LeBrun wait?

Hawthorne kept his hands buried in the pockets of his overcoat. Twice he lost his balance and almost fell. When he reached Emerson Hall, he was sweating, while his feet felt frozen. He climbed through the smooth surface of snow on the steps, hanging onto the railing. Again he nearly lost his balance. Jessica fell and he helped her up. She wore no gloves and her hands were like ice. The front door of

350

Emerson was unlocked. Once inside, Hawthorne stamped his feet; the sound echoed in the rotunda. Jessica stamped her feet behind him. Her cheeks were red and her hair was full of snow.

"I'm sorry I was rude to you," she said. "I'm just scared and, besides that, I'm not a very nice person. Thanks for lunch, at least." She stared down at her purple boots.

"It's not true you're not a nice person." Hawthorne wanted to say there was nothing to be afraid of but he wondered if that was true. Instead he told her to get over to Pierce. "I'll call and see what they want to do about dinner. I'd appreciate it if you'd stay with the others in the dorm."

"I've got to feed Lucky. I'll just stop by the kitchen for some milk."

"Do you want to tell me anything about LeBrun?"

"He scares me, he scares me a lot, and he should scare you too." The snow in her hair was melting and glistened in the light.

"Who was the man he was with in Plymouth?"

"I don't want to talk about that."

Jessica turned away and Hawthorne listened to her footsteps growing fainter. He had an impulse to call to her, to keep her by his side. Then he wondered, What do I know about what's rational and irrational in situations like this? All those years as an academic and working in treatment centers—they had been no preparation for what was happening at Bishop's Hill. Wouldn't Bennett be desperate? He had always thought of him as foolish and henpecked. But was he also sly and calculating? Surely if he had been embezzling money, then it was in his best interest to appear harmless.

The office door was open, although Hilda was nowhere in evidence. The red blinker was flashing on the answering machine. The first five messages concerned cancellations because of the weather—deliveries that couldn't be made, a meeting that wouldn't be held. The sixth was from Chief Moulton. "Call me as soon as you can, professor. I've got something to tell you."

By now it was nearly five o'clock. Standing at Hilda's desk, Hawthorne picked up the telephone. It was dead.

Hawthorne removed his coat, shook off the melted snow, and hung it over a chair. Stepping into his office, he smelled peppermint and almost expected to see Hilda appear out of a dark corner. Then his attention was taken by the computer on the table across from his desk.

The screen saver showed different paintings by Leonardo da Vinci. Hawthorne couldn't understand why the machine was on, since he had turned it off before leaving that morning. Then he noticed a scattered pile of diskettes. Nearing the table, Hawthorne saw the diskettes had been cut in half. Despite his shock, he was impressed by how neatly it had been done, as if someone had tidily destroyed them with garden shears. He took the mouse and clicked his way into the file manager program. Right away, he saw that all the Bishop's Hill files had been removed, not only the students' files but the payroll, expenses, budget, the financial records, everything he would need for the audit scheduled for Wednesday. Copies were in the bursar's office, as well as in accounting, though those too might have been destroyed. Additional copies, however, were in his quarters, where he had a laptop.

Quickly Hawthorne returned to the outer office to get his coat. He needed to make sure that his laptop was safe. It contained the evidence about the pilfering and fake orders. No, not pilfering, thought Hawthorne, theft. And without that information the audit would be useless. As for Peter Roberts, the invisible student, a number of teachers remembered him from previous years, but there was no record of his ever having been at Bishop's Hill.

Putting on his coat, Hawthorne hurried out the door of the office, only to bump into Fritz Skander, who was just entering. They both stepped back, startled.

"Thank God you're safe," said Skander. "I was terribly worried. How awful to be stuck out on Antelope Road and be forced to spend the night in your car. And with that girl as well. I should never have let you drive into Plymouth in the first place. Far too much confidence is placed in four-wheel-drive vehicles, if you ask my opinion. I was just coming to see if there was any sign of you."

It occurred to Hawthorne that Skander was making these rather pointless remarks in order to give himself time to think. "I made it most of the way back. My car's out near the end of the driveway."

"And you're not even wearing boots. Really, Jim, you're hardly equipped for our New Hampshire winters. As soon as the snow stops I'll have to take you into Plymouth and get you properly outfitted." Skander wore a dark brown parka and an Irish fisherman's hat. He began to unzip his coat. There were great lumps of snow on his boots.

His cheeks were flushed and his smile had a fixed quality that struck Hawthorne as unusual.

"I've boots in my apartment. You were looking for me?"

"I must confess I was worried. Just last winter a fellow from Rumney froze to death when his car got stuck in a drift and he ran out of gas. Hendricks or Hennessy—I can't recall the name. For a while I knew it as well as my own. But I was also hoping to catch dear Hilda. It seems that I missed her. I expect she marched off across the snow without even thinking of it. Native-born, of course—they never mind the snow."

"Where are the students?"

"The ones who're left have gathered over in Pierce with Alice. They're toasting marshmallows and having a grand time."

They were standing in the hallway. Skander removed his hat and shook off the snow. He continued to smile and his eyes seemed bright with pleasure.

"Have you been in my office?" asked Hawthorne.

"I just got here this minute."

"Somebody destroyed my computer files on the school."

Skander's smile faded. "Good grief, how awful. You didn't think I did it, did you?"

"I don't know who did it." Hawthorne recalled the smell of peppermint.

"Show me. What a dreadful thing to happen."

Skander followed Hawthorne into his office. The lights flickered, dimming, then brightening again. Hawthorne pointed to the destroyed disks. "And the files have been erased from the hard drive as well."

Skander seemed shocked. He picked up several of the floppies and turned them over. "This is a criminal act. It must have been the same person who wrecked Evings's office." He looked back at Hawthorne and his eyes were full of concern. "How dreadful for our friendship that we should come to distrust each other."

"Surely you have to see that you're a suspect." Hawthorne didn't take his eyes from Skander's face.

"I know this is hard for you," Skander said earnestly. "What with Clifford and Scott and those spiteful things old Pendergast told you. There's nothing worse than conflicting stories. But believe me, I'm counting the minutes till the auditor arrives. Don't worry, I won't hold a grudge. You're doing exactly what you should do. You need to get to the bottom of this. I've already explained that Pendergast had every reason to hate me. Who knows what other unsavory tricks he'd been playing."

"Pendergast raped that girl," said Hawthorne. "Even if she submitted willingly. And you became an accessory by not going to the police. It's quite likely there'll be charges against you."

Skander put his hat back on. It was crooked and gave him a clownish aspect even though he appeared to be in pain. "The awful thing was that she was already dead. I knew I was taking a risk, but if the police had been brought in, it would have damaged the school tremendously. Of course, I was frightened, but there was no way to bring Gail back. A wonderful girl, in her own way. And so Pendergast was persuaded that it would be in the best interest of all concerned . . ."

"Did you persuade him?"

"I spoke to him but the actual decision came from someone on the board."

"Hamilton Burke?"

"I'd rather not place the responsibility on his shoulders unless I absolutely must. You don't know how hard it was for us all. But Mr. Burke was the one who came to me and asked if I would consider being interim headmaster. I must say I was flattered. Naturally, I had spoken to Mr. Burke on several occasions but I'd no idea that he had taken any particular notice of my existence. It was quite a step up for Hilda and me, though of course temporary. I had thought that Roger would get the appointment—he had lobbied for it quite actively—and I believe he was a tad disappointed. But there was some question about his wife, that Roger's appointment, even if only for a short time, would give the school a greater church affiliation than a few board members thought prudent."

Hawthorne considered how Skander's explanations made everything even less intelligible. "Did you know that Burke was in negotiations with the Galileo Corporation to sell Bishop's Hill?"

Skander tilted his head, as if he found Hawthorne's question amusing. "You must see that the board has to engage in contingency planning. What if you're not able to put the school back on its feet? Every month the interest on the loans comes due. I wouldn't be surprised if Mr. Burke wasn't talking to half a dozen possible buyers. He hasn't confided in me. But there's always talk, of course, and believe me, the subject is upsetting to everyone. The closing of the school, the breakup of our little family. Is this what your meeting is to be about on Monday? No doubt it's an excellent idea to have these matters discussed. For my part, I intend to do everything I can to make certain that Bishop's Hill stays open."

"I'm not sure I believe you," said Hawthorne. There was nothing more to say for the moment. All he wanted was to go to his apartment and see if his laptop was safe.

Skander looked delighted. He reached out to take Hawthorne's hand but Hawthorne stepped back. "But you don't entirely *disbelieve* me, that's the main thing. When the audit is completed, you'll see how wrong you've been. Talk to Mr. Burke and the rest of the board. I don't want to speak too soon, but I really think—thanks to you, of course—that Bishop's Hill is almost out of danger and I plan to say as much at the meeting on Monday."

They were walking out of the office. Clearly, the audit would prove Skander's innocence or guilt—unless, that is, the records had been destroyed. As for Peter Roberts, Hawthorne would talk to a lawyer. Yet he dreaded it. Any investigation would necessarily lead to Pendergast and Gail Jensen, which would mean a storm of publicity and criminal charges. However, there was nothing else to be done.

"By the way," asked Hawthorne, "have you seen Frank?"

"I'm actually on my way over to the kitchen right now. I think he means to put together something for dinner. I must say I'm impressed by how helpful he's been."

Hawthorne decided to push Skander a little. "You know, he first told me that he hardly knew who Scott McKinnon was. Now several people have told me that he knew Scott quite well. I wonder if we can fully trust him."

Skander chuckled. "There you go again, playing detective. Really, you should leave these matters to the police. Frank is surely eccentric but he's one of the best people we have around here. Look at how he's working to make something special for us tonight. I'm sure he has a surprise planned."

———◆———

Five minutes later Hawthorne was hurrying down the hall toward his apartment. He began to go outside again, then decided to cut through Emerson to Adams Hall. Fifteen feet separated the doors between the two buildings but Hawthorne often avoided this path. He liked approaching his quarters from across the terrace, where the view of the mountains was especially splendid, and this route required what he saw as uselessly going up and down two flights of stairs. As he hurried down the hall, he again noticed the lights flicker.

The wind blew more strongly between the buildings. Hawthorne opened the door to Adams Hall and climbed the stairs. Normally Purvis locked the doors to Adams by five o'clock but today he must have been delayed by the weather. Entering his apartment, Hawthorne found himself trying to detect the smell of peppermint or evidence that someone had been in his rooms. Then he hurried to the bedroom. The laptop was in its usual place on the desk. Flicking it on, he determined that the files hadn't been tampered with. In the desk drawer were his backup files. He took the computer and put it in the bureau drawer under a stack of shirts. Then he hid the floppies under the mattress.

Hawthorne changed his clothes, putting on a dark purple ski jacket, dark ski cap, and high rubber boots. Before leaving, he checked the phone but it was still dead. He wondered if somebody had cut the wires, though it easily could have been the storm. He wanted to call Kate and apologize for breaking their date that evening and he wanted to call Chief Moulton. Didn't anyone at the school have a cell phone? Hawthorne tried to remember and made a mental note to get one for the office next week. He hurried toward the door, then paused and went back for the flashlight in the drawer of the telephone table.

Floyd Purvis had a small office in the school garage on the other side of Douglas Hall, and he also, Hawthorne recalled, had a cell phone. Hawthorne cut through Adams and out the door to the Common between Adams and Douglas. In his boots and ski jacket he felt himself ready for the deep snow but there was a minute when he was wading through the drifts between the two buildings when he could see neither. He couldn't even see the light on top of Emerson. Then Douglas Hall loomed out of the dark. No lights were on but Hawthorne cut through the building and exited on the other side. Once more he plunged through the drifts. He lowered his head to keep the snow out of his eyes and adjusted his scarf so it wouldn't get under his collar. After he had gone twenty or thirty feet, he saw the light over the school garage.

Purvis's office was locked but Hawthorne opened it with his pass-key. The night watchman was nowhere in evidence, nor did it seem that he had been in the office that day. The cigarette smoke smelled stale and the heater hadn't been turned on, although the room was warm enough that Hawthorne's glasses began to steam up. Wiping his glasses on his scarf, he searched the drawers of the desk for the cellular phone and found a full bottle of Jim Beam. He was tempted to empty it but he left it where it was. Purvis most likely had the cell phone with him and, seemingly, he wouldn't be coming to work this evening. His truck probably wouldn't make it down the unplowed roads. Hawthorne picked up the phone on the desk but there was no dial tone.

He decided to go over to Pierce and find Alice Beech. Perhaps the nurse had a cell phone or knew who had one. Hawthorne paused to tuck his pants into the tops of his boots and tighten the laces, then he shoved open the door. His footprints were already covered. He pushed his way forward, trying to lift his boots out of the snow. Ahead, toward the dormitory cottages, he saw the row of lights lining the walkway as glowing spheres—vague areas of light. He made his way toward them, lowering his head against the flakes that stung his face. Consequently, he didn't see the figure approaching him till the other man spoke.

"Fritz, is that you?"

Looking up, Hawthorne couldn't recognize the person, but the voice sounded like Bennett's. The moon behind the clouds gave the snow a haunting luminosity and at times revealed the outline of the trees when the wind changed and the snow swirled off in other directions. Hawthorne began to take his flashlight from his pocket, then left it where it was.

"It's me," said Hawthorne. As he got closer, he began to make out Bennett's features. Bennett wasn't wearing a hat and his long blond hair seemed to have turned white. "Do you have a cell phone at your house?" Both had to raise their voices over the wind.

Bennett was up to his knees in the snow. "Why do you want one? Have you seen Fritz? It's important that I find him."

"I just saw him in Emerson. He was on his way to the kitchen to see what LeBrun was doing about dinner. Anyway, the phones aren't working and I need to make a call." Then he made out the fear in the other man's voice. "Is something the matter?" He took another step toward Bennett, only to realize that Bennett was backing away.

"What's LeBrun doing?" Bennett's words seemed scattered by the wind.

"He has to take food over to the students in Pierce. Do you have a cell phone in your apartment?"

"I don't know. I think it's broken. Look, I shouldn't be telling you this, but you've got to get out of here. LeBrun's dangerous. He's gone right around the bend. You don't know what he'll do." Bennett spoke quickly, as if his fear were propelling the words from his mouth.

"I couldn't leave even if I wanted to," said Hawthorne. "The roads are blocked."

"You'd be safer going into the woods," said Bennett, his voice rising to a shout. "And me too. We've got to get out of here."

"Did you get Frank LeBrun to wreck Clifford's office? Did you pay him to do it?"

"You don't know. It's worse than that, worse than you can imagine. Listen to me, I'm doing you a favor. You'd be safer in the fucking forest!" Backing away, Bennett stumbled and fell. Then he got up and began running through the snow toward Douglas.

"Roger!" Hawthorne called. But Bennett kept trying to run. Hawthorne watched him fade into the swirling dark. He thought of how Jessica had gone to the kitchen looking for milk. He felt afraid, but whether it was for Jessica or himself he couldn't tell.

Hawthorne kept on toward Pierce, the third in the row of residence cottages. He hoped to find Jessica, to see if she was all right. The night, or what was fast becoming night, was without limit or order. Hawthorne knew the snow would eventually end, yet at that moment it seemed immense and endless. His anxiety increased. What was wrong with Bennett? Why was he looking for Skander and LeBrun? Or perhaps he wasn't looking for them, perhaps he only wanted to know where they were so he could stay out of their path. But why had he urged him to leave?

Alice Beech was the only adult in Pierce. Ruth Standish and Tom Hastings didn't appear to be at the school; at least there weren't lights on in the dormitory cottages where they lived. Alice had set aside her nurse's white uniform for faded jeans and a burgundy fleece sweatshirt. A dozen students were with her, including Tank Donoso, but Jessica wasn't among them. The students were camped out in the downstairs living room and had collected mattresses and blankets so they could remain together. There was a fire in the fireplace. The table was strewn with candles, kerosene lanterns, loaves of white bread, bags of cookies, packages of cheese and bologna, two gallons of milk, and two gallons of orange juice. The students were sitting on the mattresses with blankets over their shoulders. They seemed excited and cheerful. A radio was playing jazz from the Vermont NPR station.

"We raided the kitchen," said Alice rather proudly. "No telling how long we'll be stuck here. The lights will probably go out at any moment; that's what always happens."

"Has Jessica been here?" asked Hawthorne. His glasses had again steamed over and he held them in his hand. The room appeared vague and unfocused.

"I'm afraid not. Her kitten's here someplace. We gave it some milk."

"I've got it," said a girl in the corner, and she pulled back her blanket so Hawthorne could see the sleeping kitten.

"She was on her way over here," said Hawthorne. Could she have gotten lost in the storm? That seemed unlikely. The lights were visible from Emerson. "Do you have a cell phone?"

"I'm afraid not. I asked for one last spring but Fritz said it was an unnecessary expenditure." Alice was rosy-cheeked and looked immensely happy, as if a bit of chaos agreed with her.

"Have you seen anyone else? What about Bill Dolittle?"

"I haven't seen him. Fritz was here an hour ago but no one else," said Alice.

"He didn't even say yo," said Tank, who sat on a mattress with a dark blue blanket over his head and tucked around his chin, which made him look oddly nunnish.

Hawthorne accepted a mug of hot tea and a cookie from Alice, who had a thermos. They spoke of the storm and the difficulties it presented. Hawthorne brushed the snow from his jacket. A few drops fell on a table where two boys were playing chess. They looked at him severely.

"We've been telling stories, but no ghost stories," said Alice. "That's the rule. Nothing scary. You're welcome to stay if you like.

We've got lots of blankets from the other dorms in case the furnace stops."

But Hawthorne kept worrying about Jessica. After another minute, he moved toward the door and zipped up his jacket.

"I'll be back later," he said.

Tank got to his feet. "You want some company, bro?"

Glancing at him, Hawthorne was again impressed by his physical bulk. Then he said, "You stay here where it's warm."

"The radio says we'll get three feet," said Alice.

"Fucking A," said Tank. "We can chill here till Wednesday."

Hawthorne made his way back through the drifts. He wanted to see if the Reverend Bennett had a cell phone and he wanted to find Jessica. He couldn't guess what had happened to her. They had separated over an hour earlier. Hawthorne considered organizing a search but it would be nearly impossible in the snow.

It was past six o'clock, but it could have been much later or no time at all, a period outside of time—just wind and blustering snowflakes. Hawthorne's fingers were cold in his gloves and he tried to keep them in his pockets. Every minute or so he looked up to see if he was going in the right direction. He could feel the muscles ache on the insides of his thighs from constantly lifting his legs. Early in the fall he'd discovered a row of ancient-looking snowshoes on a back wall of the garage and he had laughed at the idea of ever needing them. Hawthorne had never used snowshoes; the closest he had come was cross-country skis, but even that had been on manicured trails.

He plunged across the lawn toward Stark Hall. The chapel was dark, but he could see a single light in the Bennetts' apartment. Off to the left, along what might have been the driveway, was a large snow-covered lump that Hawthorne guessed was his Subaru. As the temperature had dropped, the snow had gotten fluffier and easier to wade through. The light at the top of Emerson shone unsteadily.

Hawthorne climbed the steps at the rear of Stark. The door to the Bennetts' apartment was just inside the lobby. Hawthorne felt around for a light switch but couldn't find one. Turning on his flashlight, he saw the doorbell and pushed the button. From inside he heard a distant chiming. He removed his ski cap and slapped it against his leg. The radiator inside the lobby hissed gently. After a moment, he rang the doorbell again. Since he had seen a light, he assumed somebody was home. Hawthorne took off his gloves and set them on the radiator. Then he rang the doorbell a third time.

"Who is it?" came a voice. It was the chaplain's, but it sounded gruffer.

"Jim Hawthorne."

"What do you want?"

"Do you have a cell phone?" Hawthorne kept his flashlight pointed down at the floor, filling the lobby with a dull yellow glow.

There was the sound of the door being unlocked, then it opened about two inches. A chain kept it from opening any further. "What did you say?" One of the Reverend Bennett's eyes peered out at him.

"I asked if you had a cellular phone."

"Have you seen Roger?"

Hawthorne stepped back from the door. "I saw him outside half an hour ago. He was looking for Fritz. Do you have a cell phone?"

"I sent it back—too much static. What about LeBrun, have you seen him?"

"He should be over in the kitchen getting food for the remaining students." Hawthorne didn't want to tell her what her husband had said. "You haven't seen Jessica Weaver, have you?" He could see the shadow of the chaplain's body through the crack in the door. He wondered why she kept the door chained. She didn't answer his question about Jessica. Hawthorne could hear her breathing. "What's going on?" he asked after another moment. "What's Roger doing with Fritz and LeBrun?"

The Reverend Bennett continued to stare at him. Then she said, "You shouldn't have come here. You know that, don't you?"

"What are you talking about?" He lifted his light so he could see her more clearly.

Harriet Bennett began shouting at him. "Why are you plaguing me? Don't you see what you've ruined? Everything would have been fine if you hadn't come to Bishop's Hill." Her voice broke, then she slammed the door. Hawthorne heard the locks turning. He looked at the door as if expecting it to open again so he could ask for some explanation, but it remained shut. Hawthorne took his gloves from on top of the radiator and went back out into the cold.

He considered walking over to the faculty houses. Perhaps Skander had a cell phone, or Herb Frankfurter, or Ted Wrigley, even Betty Sherman. He was almost certain that Gene Strauss had a cell phone, but he was supposed to be away that weekend, although his wife might be home. But it would take fifteen minutes to get over there and Hawthorne wanted to look through Emerson once again. Perhaps Jessica was still in the kitchen.

He made his way along the driveway toward Emerson Hall. The spikes topping the metal fence outside of Emerson all had little caps of white. Hawthorne looked up toward the light in the bell tower, which shifted and grew dimmer, then brighter as the snow blew across it. He could just make out one of the gargoyles staring down at him and the scaffolding from the roof repairs. He continued to the front of the building and used the railing to help pull himself up.

The echoes inside the rotunda had a melancholy sound, more like the noise of a tomb than a school. Across the bright blue school crest were muddy footprints. Hawthorne turned toward his office. As he got nearer, he saw that the door was open. He even heard a voice, though it didn't sound right—there was a staticky quality. Then he heard what it was saying. "Call me as soon as you can, professor. I've got something to tell you." It was the answering machine with Moulton's message repeating over and over. "Call me as soon as you can, professor. I've got something to tell you."

Hawthorne hurried into the outer office. It was empty. The message kept repeating. He walked to the answering machine on Hilda's desk and shut it off, but the message didn't stop. "Call me as soon as you can, professor. . . ."

Hawthorne felt a chill, then he saw that the voice was coming from a voice recorder. He shut it off as well.

Then someone spoke to him from his own office, just beyond Hilda's: "As soon as you can, professor. Beep. As soon as you can, professor." Then there was a laugh. It was LeBrun.

With a mixture of relief and dismay, Hawthorne walked to the door. LeBrun sat in Hawthorne's chair with his boots up on the desk. He had a bottle of Budweiser in one hand and something small and shiny in the other. His dark hair was plastered down across his forehead. He wore his white cook's jacket unbuttoned over a white shirt.

"Making yourself at home?" Hawthorne tried to smile. Something had changed with LeBrun. It wasn't just his expression, it was his electricity. His face kept moving, he kept wrinkling his forehead and pursing his lips.

"You look like a fucking snowman. You got to watch out, professor, playing in the snow. You could catch pneumonia and die." LeBrun spoke quickly, clipping his words.

"I've been trying to see if anyone's got a cell phone. I have to call Kate." Hawthorne kept his voice relaxed. He didn't want to mention Chief Moulton, that he wanted to get the police over to Bishop's Hill as soon as possible.

LeBrun reached inside his green hunting jacket and drew out a cell phone. "Looky here, professor. My boss gave it to me as a present. Just so we could chat. Nice guy, right?"

Hawthorne took a step forward. "Can I use it?"

"Fat fuckin' chance. I'm expecting a call. My stockbroker's got a hot tip. He's got the Japanese on the line." LeBrun laughed and put the phone back into his coat. "Actually, your time's up, professor. The big finale. Guess it had to happen." LeBrun stretched both arms high into the air, holding the beer bottle up like a torch. He had put the shiny thing on the desk, where it glittered. "I don't want you here no more."

"What do you mean?"

"You got wax in your ears?" LeBrun took a drink, then clunked the bottle down on the desk. "I got work to do and I don't want you around. You'll distract me."

When LeBrun picked up the shiny object, Hawthorne saw that it was a small ice pick. LeBrun's movements were jerky and he kept recrossing his boots, as if someone had turned up his speed. And his voice was higher. It seemed clenched and barely under his control.

"I'm not following you," said Hawthorne. He wiped the snow from his coat and moved back to the door.

"It's a joke right? You're the professor and you don't know shit. I'm the idiot and I got all the answers. Beginning, middle, and end. Like all of a sudden I'm the fucking teacher. I'm the big chastiser. That's what they said in school when I was a kid, 'We're going to have to chastise you.'" LeBrun picked up a piece of paper and pretended to read. "Let me see, do I got your name here? This one, that one. Hey,

363

professor, you're not on the agenda. Let me tell you, that's good luck for you. You hear what elephants use for tampons?"

"Sheep. You already told me."

"That was the old elephants. The new elephants use Canucks." LeBrun leaned his head back and laughed. His teeth shone in the light.

Hawthorne waited for LeBrun to stop laughing. "What don't I know?"

"You don't know that Skander wants you out of here. Sewed up and put to sleep." The lights dimmed, then came back again.

"Fritz?"

LeBrun cackled, then scratched his head, mussing his hair. "What do you think, his fucking wife, the tub of lard? You're messing up Fritz's plans, you're keeping him from being boss of the bosses. He wants you dead. Him and that fag Bennett. Like you're a chalk mark on their blackboard and they want you erased. And guess who's the big eraser?"

"You wrecked Clifford's office."

"That's old news, that was last month. You don't know shit, do you? That's why I want you gone. Just go home and you'll be okay."

Hawthorne put his ski cap in his pocket. He needed to keep LeBrun talking. "I don't understand."

LeBrun starting shouting. "Because I don't want to kill you, you hear what I'm saying? I mean, I could do it. No fucking sweat. Like this!" LeBrun swung the ice pick down and hit the desk, then he withdrew his hand, letting the ice pick quiver in the wood. "But I don't like being told what to do. I don't like some scummy hunk of shit saying if I don't do something, I'll get arrested. I'll go to jail. I'll get buttfucked. I'll die. Fritz thinks he can scare me into doing his dirty work and he's too cheap to pay me! Two hundred fucking bucks for the office! I would of killed you for a grand—at least I think so. But maybe I wouldn't take the job. I mean, you haven't been in my face. But let me tell you, that's nothing in your favor. It doesn't pay to like people. A friend is just a guy who hasn't knifed you in the back yet. He's still working out the details." LeBrun laughed and looked angry at the same time. The words tumbled from his mouth. "Know what I got offered for the girl? Ten grand. Even if Fritz had come up with ten grand for sticking you, I might not of done it. And now the fucker's saying that, if I don't do it, I'll get fried. He said you were going to the cops. He said you'd bring in the fucking army!"

"You killed Scott."

"Doo, dah, doo, dah, professor."

"But why?"

"He'd seen something he shouldn't of, it was like an accident. But it was Fritz who told me the kid had seen it. The kid went to him when he couldn't find you. He told Fritz all about it. I mean, I knew somebody'd seen it. I seen him hiding in the bushes. But just a shape, you know what I mean? I didn't know who it was till Fritz told me. Then it was easy. I only had to be patient. You be patient and you wait for the other guy to be impatient. The kid's dorm room was on the first floor." LeBrun reached into his pocket, took out a key ring, and jingled it. "And I got keys, I got all the keys."

"He was just a kid." Hawthorne told himself that he had to make some sort of plan, but his mind felt frozen.

" 'Just a kid'—*exactly,* professor. Look at it this way: I saved him. A kid like that, a little dicking in his past, some old fart holding his mouth open with his thumbs and banging past his tonsils. I saved him from being sent away, from fucking up too bad, from going to jail, from a bunch of guys using his asshole like a revolving door, from being like me. I fucking liberated him, you hear what I'm saying? He'll never be like me. He's safe. Now he's one liberated little kid. Dead, though."

"Where's Jessica?"

"She don't like being called Jessica. Her name's Misty. She's fucking trouble. I thought it'd be a piece of cake." LeBrun pinched his lower lip, drew it forward, and let go. Then he took a drink from his bottle and belched. "You ever have a job you're supposed to do, that you're paid to do, but something's not right about it? You keep putting it off. You don't feel like it. I don't even like the little bitch and she's got that fucking cat. Well, maybe she's not so terrible. She just talks too much. But maybe it's because I never stuck a girl. Maybe I don't like the guy with the money. But it's business, right? No kill, no dough. And now she's figured it out. She saw us today. She knows what's coming. You got to do what you've been paid to do. That's ethics, right? The big fucking morality."

"Is that what you were talking about a few weeks ago? The thing you couldn't do?"

"Yeah, professor, I needed your advice. I wanted to make you an accessory before, during, and after the fact. A little boost. You were no help at all. Hot air, all you shrinks are like that."

"Where is she?"

"Forget the questions, professor. I can change my mind about you anytime—fucking dumb school in a fucking dumb place. Fucking snow. I got something I need to do and I'm not doing it. Sounds like a fuckin' hillbilly song. Even if she was my little sister, I'd make myself do it. You can't let stuff like that stand in your way. That's how they finally get you." LeBrun reached forward and flicked the ice pick stuck in the desk so it vibrated with a buzzing sound. "You should sympathize with my problem. Those shrinks when I was a kid were always talking about how I felt, what was going through my mind. I didn't feel shit. I never felt shit. Like ice, that's how I wanted to be. Ice feels nothing. It don't even feel angry."

"Where was this?" Again the lights dimmed. LeBrun didn't answer until they came up again. Now the lights kept flickering.

"In Derry. It's none of your fucking business where it was. Hey, Doc, give me a pill so I can stick the girl. Give me some medicine to commit devastation." LeBrun laughed and wiped his mouth with the back of his hand.

Hawthorne had no sense of what LeBrun would do next. He tried to quiet his fear so that he could think clearly. "Maybe you once knew somebody like Jessica."

LeBrun cackled and slapped the desk, knocking over the beer. The bottle rolled to the edge of the desk and fell to the floor, spilling on the carpet. LeBrun reached down to a bag at his feet, pulled up another bottle, and twisted off the cap, which he tossed at Hawthorne. "There you go again, getting all shrinky on me. Maybe in my tender years a girl like Misty was sweet to me. I can see it now, just like in the fuckin' movies—*Misty and Me,* staring Francis LaBrecque. Fuck you, asshole, I was never a nice guy. You know those vampire movies? I always wanted to be the bat. I wanted to fly down your chimney and stick my teeth in your throat. Suck you dry till there was nothing left. I like being the bad guy. You always know where you are and what you're supposed to do. Fucking Skander thought he'd scare me. What a jerk. You ever been dicked, professor? You ever have a bunch of kids hold you down on the floor? Or old drunken farts who're supposed to be taking care of you? Churchgoers, you hear what I'm saying? Either dick or get dicked is what it boils down to."

"Where's Fritz?"

"Fuck you, professor. I got one and a half problems. You're the half problem—just a fucking smidgen of a problem. Misty's the whole one."

"Where is Jessica? I want you to give her back to me."

LeBrun kicked his feet down to the floor. "Shut up, professor. Don't make me mad."

Hawthorne tried to keep himself still. He hated his fear—it brought back the bad times, the burning corridor, Meg's awful screaming. But he had to make LeBrun stop, to jolt him out of his sense of power and control.

"Did you hold those pictures up at the window?" asked Hawthorne after a moment.

"That wasn't me. You got to admit some of it was funny. The rotten food, I loved the rotten food. And the dead-wife stuff. Jesus, I laughed." Again LeBrun grinned. He put his feet back onto the desk, then he linked his hands behind his head. "That was Bennett; he got some woman to call. He used to laugh all the time, then he got scared. But Fritz thought he could drive you nuts, that you'd go running back to California. I knew it wouldn't work. So when you didn't go nuts, Fritz cranked up the heat. Fuckin' amateurs, they never know when to stop. Fritz figured he could make me jump."

Hawthorne's mouth felt like dry fabric. "Do you know when to stop, Frank? You look like an amateur to me. What have you done with Fritz?"

Immediately, LeBrun was on his feet, spilling the beer and knocking the phone from the desk. "I been nice to you, professor. I gave you the chance to go someplace safe and warm." LeBrun reached toward the ice pick, which was still stuck in the desk, but he was so jittery that at first he missed it. Then he got it and yanked it free.

At that moment the lights began to dim. Hawthorne and LeBrun looked at the ceiling, watching the globe light turn from white to dull orange. Then it went out. The lights in the outer office and hall went out as well. Standing in the dark, Hawthorne and LeBrun were silent, waiting for the lights to come back on. But they didn't.

"You there, professor?" asked LeBrun quietly.

Hawthorne began backing across the outer office. "I'm worried about you, Frank."

LeBrun shouted, "You think you can fuckin' play with me?"

By now Hawthorne was already out in the hall. "Hey Frank," he called. "I think you're cracking."

LeBrun began screaming, "You're a dead man! You're a dead man!" A chair was knocked over and something else slid across the floor and banged into the wall.

Hawthorne began to move off down the hall, trying to run silently in his boots. Now that he had challenged LeBrun's sense of his own power, Hawthorne had to escape from the consequences.

"I hear you, professor," shouted LeBrun, running after him. "You don't know how bad I can hurt you."

Now Hawthorne was running swiftly through the dark. Somewhere up ahead was the fire door leading to the stairs. Hawthorne could see nothing. He took the flashlight from his back pocket. He didn't dare turn it on but perhaps he could use it as a weapon. It seemed that LeBrun's heavy feet were only a few yards behind him.

Abruptly Hawthorne hit the door at the end of the hall. He fell back, holding his head. His glasses were knocked off. LeBrun crashed into him and they both tumbled against the fire door. Hawthorne freed the arm with the light. He grabbed the fabric of LeBrun's jacket and pushed him back. LeBrun was growling like a dog. Then he stopped and laughed. He broke Hawthorne's grip and they again fell against the door. Hawthorne swung the flashlight, clubbing LeBrun, once, twice. The flashlight slipped from his hand and clattered to the floor. He shoved LeBrun away, then opened the fire door and ran up the stairs.

"You're a dead man, professor!" shouted LeBrun up the stairwell.

Hawthorne paused at the second-floor landing. He heard LeBrun running up the stairs behind him. Opening the door to the second floor, Hawthorne hurried into the dark hall. Here the classroom doors were open and in each doorway the dark was a shade lighter. LeBrun slammed open the door behind him. Hawthorne ran into a classroom on his left, then began feeling along the wall to the back of the room. Many of the classrooms had closets in the rear and he hoped to hide there. Hawthorne found the closet door and gently pulled it open. He was terrified that LeBrun might hear him. Feeling around in the dark, Hawthorne discovered a mop and a pail, then a stack of books.

"Hey, professor, this is the part I like best," LeBrun said in a stage whisper from out in the hall. "This is when we begin to have fun. I got my bat wings, professor, I got my fangs. I'm going to stick them in your throat, professor." LeBrun paused to listen. Hawthorne could hear him breathing. "What about jokes, professor? I can make you laugh. We used to have some good laughs, didn't we? You remember the clown joke? This taste funny to you? You listening, professor? You gotta be listening. You hear about the Canuck who picked his nose apart to see what made it run?" LeBrun chuckled, a hoarse sound deep in his throat. "You're in one of these fuckin' rooms, aren't you? I can smell you. I can smell how scared you are. But I'm going to make you laugh, professor. I'm going to make you crack up. You know how you brainwash a Canuck? Come on, Doc, I'm waiting for the answer. You give him an enema. You fuckin' ram it right up his asshole!" LeBrun laughed. His boots scraped on the floor as he moved along the hall. "You're going to laugh too, professor, then I'm going to find you."

Hawthorne crouched down in the closet as LeBrun went up and down the hall whispering his jokes. "Hey, professor, what's the difference between a Canuck and a three-day-old turd?" Then LeBrun chuckled. His footsteps faded away, then returned. Why is a Canuck like a tampon? Had he heard of the Canuck who had to use three rubbers at once? LeBrun's laugh was a noise deep in his throat, half laugh, half growl. Several times he came into the room where Hawthorne was hiding, bumped into a desk, knocked over a chair, then went out again.

"Hey, professor, did you hear about the Canuck who shoved two aspirin up his dick so he wouldn't get the clap? How about the Canuck who went to Paris and jacked off the Eiffel Tower? Where are you, professor! Answer me! You lousy fuck, you're not making me feel good. I got work, professor. You're making me waste the whole fucking evening! I don't need to kill you easy, I can kill you so it hurts!"

LeBrun came into the classroom again, stumbled into another desk, and swore. He picked it up and threw it so it crashed against others. Something—a window—shattered. He went back into the hall. He had stopped telling jokes. Hawthorne could hear his boots tramping up and down the hall. He imagined him pausing at the doorways and listening. Ten minutes went by. At last Hawthorne heard LeBrun walk down the hall and open the fire door. Hawthorne still didn't move. He imagined LeBrun taking off his boots and sneaking back. Another ten minutes went by, then ten more. Hawthorne crawled out of the closet and moved quietly to the hall. He was afraid even to breathe. A cold wind blew through the broken window. Hawthorne listened at the doorway. Then he began to move down the hall in the opposite direction from where LeBrun had gone, making no noise. The darkness seemed full of shapes. At every doorway he expected LeBrun to leap out at him. He had no weapon, not even the flashlight. When he reached the fire door leading to the stairwell, he paused to listen again. There was nothing. Quietly he opened the door and hurried down the stairs, continuing past the first floor down to the exit. Hawthorne pushed open the door and the cold air was like ice against his sweat-drenched shirt. He ran out into the snow.

12

The left-hand side of the double doors of Stark Chapel stood open and indentations led down the steps through the snow. Hawthorne was sure the door had been closed when he had passed by sometime after six. It was now after eight and the snow was falling as hard as ever. The electricity still hadn't come on but there was a reddish glow from the chapel windows, a circle of radiance through the stained glass. Without his glasses, Hawthorne's sight was blurry. Objects had lost their precise edges and seemed to merge with one another. His spare pair was in his desk in Emerson but he lacked the courage to go back and get them.

He was breathing heavily. He had thought he would die up there on the second floor of Emerson Hall. LeBrun's raving, his intensity, his madness, had nearly paralyzed him. Hawthorne's body felt as if its very center had been ripped away. For nearly an hour after the terrifying encounter with LeBrun he had stayed in Adams Hall—not even in his apartment but in a dark classroom on the second floor—trying to recover. He thought of Bennett's remark that he would be safer running into the forest, into the deep snow, that they both would. But Hawthorne still believed that the more he could increase LeBrun's self-doubt and irrationality, the better the chance Hawthorne would have of stopping him. In addition, he was worried about Jessica—and even Skander. LeBrun must have them both, and an attempt had to be made to rescue them. As he thought this, however, Hawthorne's fear increased. Perhaps he could find somebody to go back into Emerson with him. Even Bennett might help now that he knew how brutal LeBrun could be.

Hawthorne worked his way up the chapel steps. Because of the light, he assumed somebody was inside. When he reached the top of the stairs, he looked back along the driveway at Emerson. Up in the attic he saw a dim glow that shifted from one window to another. LeBrun was prowling up there; most likely that was where he had Fritz and Jessica. Even the suggestion of LeBrun's presence in the attic of Emerson Hall made Hawthorne's heart beat faster.

Hawthorne entered the vestibule outside the chapel and kicked the snow from his boots. The noise was loud and he started. Cautiously he opened the door and stepped inside. The steeply banked rows of wooden pews descended toward the apse. At the foot of the center aisle, in front of the altar, a bright light pointed up at an angle toward a stained-glass window where a bearded disciple in a blue robe held a fishing net. Hawthorne's nearsightedness transformed the light to a blurred shimmering, and it wasn't for another moment that he saw a figure sitting in the front row facing the altar, slightly bent forward as if praying or meditating.

Briefly, Hawthorne was afraid that it might be LeBrun, but the coat was not LeBrun's and the person seemed smaller. Hawthorne made his way down the steps of the aisle, which were carpeted, so that his boots made no noise. When he had gone halfway, he saw that the light on the floor was a flashlight and that the figure in the front row was a man sitting completely still, as if his whole being were concentrated on the altar and the silver crucifix that stood upon it. The chapel was silent. Not even the wind made a noise and it seemed to Hawthorne that he could hear his own heartbeat. As he drew close to the man, he saw that the flashlight was his own, the one he had dropped when he had been struggling with LeBrun, and a second later he realized the figure was Roger Bennett. For a moment Hawthorne was full of hope.

"Roger," he called, "it's me, Hawthorne." He squinted, trying to make the figure and the light at his feet come into focus.

Bennett still didn't move. He wore a bright blue down jacket and sat with his hands in his lap. He seemed riveted so completely on the altar in front of him that he had no awareness of Hawthorne's approach. His hair in the glow of the flashlight appeared golden.

"Roger," said Hawthorne, and he reached out to put a hand on Bennett's shoulder.

At first Bennett appeared to be pulling away, but so hesitantly that Hawthorne was unsure. Bennett leaned forward with his head tilting and his whole body turning slowly, not looking at Hawthorne but continuing forward, until suddenly Hawthorne knew that Bennett was going to fall and he reached out to grab his arm and missed. Almost gracefully, Bennett rolled off the pew, turning and landing on his back with his arms flopping out at his sides, his head banging against the carpet and looking up at Hawthorne with a grin so horrible and demented that it was all Hawthorne could do not to scream. Bennett lay on the red runner, his eyes wide and unfocused. He was dead but his grin was huge, like the grin on the painting of Ambrose Stark, an open-mouthed leer, a homicidal clown grin, with his white teeth protruding over his lower lip as if he were about to guffaw or sing. Hawthorne snatched up the flashlight from the floor and pointed the beam at Bennett's face. At first he was unable to move, but then, bending over, he saw that Bennett's grin had been contrived by shoving toothpicks between his upper teeth at the corners of his mouth, which stretched his lips into this imitation of humor. And broken toothpicks had also been used to prop open Bennett's eyelids, making him appear wide-eyed and manic. A lock of blond hair lay diagonally across his forehead. There was no sign of violence, no blood, nothing to show how he had died. On Bennett's feet were great green rubber boots with their toes pointing toward the chapel ceiling. Hawthorne had no doubt as to who had killed him. He felt his horror increase.

There was a noise to Hawthorne's right, followed by a cry, a high wailing. Stumbling back, Hawthorne saw that the Reverend Bennett had come through a door at the rear of the chapel. She was staring at her husband with one hand over her mouth even as her cry continued to echo through the open space. Hawthorne stepped to one side but he felt that he was invisible to the woman. She hurried forward, clumsily because of her weight, then threw herself at her husband, dropping to her knees and grabbing Bennett's shoulders, trying to pull him up, even pull him to his feet. Bennett's head had fallen back and he seemed to be staring up at his wife. The toothpicks stuck from his teeth like tiny fangs. His eyes seemed full of cheer. Hawthorne wanted to remove the toothpicks but he couldn't make himself get any closer. In any case, the chaplain paid no attention to him. She released her husband so he tumbled backward, then she buried her face in his lap and sobbed with great gasps, which shook her body and shook Bennett's as well, as if he still had life in him after all.

Hawthorne set the flashlight on the first pew, then retreated up the aisle, trying not to stumble. He could do nothing here, give no comfort, make nothing better. He opened the door and stepped out of the chapel.

Again he plunged into the snow, making his way along Stark Hall, skirting Emerson, and going along beside Douglas toward the dormitory cottages and the faculty houses that lay beyond. Twice Hawthorne fell, then got up again, his jacket white with snow. He thought he might be on the road that ran in front of the cottages but he couldn't be sure. There was no sign of his tracks from earlier. He kept seeing LeBrun shoving toothpicks between Bennett's teeth and under his eyelids to fabricate a smile. The work appeared to be that of the devil himself. But Hawthorne didn't believe in the devil. It was sickness that Hawthorne had seen and he had to repeat this to himself.

Candles were burning in Pierce, where the nurse and the remaining students were weathering the storm. Hawthorne heard the sound of a guitar and voices singing. The high voices of the girls seemed to make shapes in the air. Hawthorne wanted to go into Pierce and stay until the storm was over and the police arrived. Then he thought of getting Tank Donoso to go with him. Hawthorne pressed forward through the snow. Cowardice, he thought again. He was full of cowardice.

Shepherd and Slocomb, the next two cottages, were dark, but in Latham there was a faint light visible in a second-story window where Bill Dolittle had his studio apartment. Hawthorne clambered through the drifts and made his way up the front steps. The door was unlocked. He entered the dark hallway and blundered across the living room to the stairs. Once on the second floor he wasn't sure which door belonged to Dolittle, but by crouching down he could see a glimmer of light through the crack beneath a door at the end of the hall. He knocked.

"Bill, it's me. Jim. I need your help."

Hawthorne waited.

"Bill, Roger Bennett's dead. I need you to help me."

There was no answer. Hawthorne knocked again and waited. After another moment, he ducked down. The gap under the door was dark.

"Damn it, Bill, answer me!"

There was still no response. Hawthorne turned the knob but the door was locked. He pushed against it, hitting it with his shoulder. The door stayed closed. He wondered if he had been mistaken, if his eyes without their glasses had been playing tricks. After another minute, Hawthorne hurried back down the stairs. Once outside, he paused by a small evergreen and looked back up at the window. He kept telling himself that he was in a hurry and had no time to waste. As he was about to leave and make his way toward the faculty houses, he saw a flare of a match reflected in the glass as whoever was inside again lit a candle. For a moment Hawthorne was overcome by anger. He wanted to go back upstairs and kick down the door. Dolittle's cowardice became his own, his own wish to go someplace safe and dark, to conceal himself as he had earlier concealed himself in Adams. He hated the temptation that Dolittle presented. As he stared up at the flickering light in Dolittle's window, Hawthorne urged himself to make the sensible choice, to retreat to some protected spot until the storm passed.

Instead, he turned toward the faculty houses. He couldn't afford his hesitation: He had to find Jessica. He had to search out someone who could help rescue her or he had to rescue her himself. Yet whenever he thought of returning to Emerson he felt weak with fear.

The first of the faculty houses lay about fifty yards beyond the last dormitory cottage and was occupied by Gene Strauss. It was a shadowy two-story shape in the falling snow, no more than the outline of a house. The house was dark and there was no sign of candlelight. At times when Strauss was away doing admissions work—meeting with school heads and talking to prospective students—his wife and daughter went with him. Even so, Hawthorne climbed the front porch and hammered on the door. He waited and hammered again. He tried the door but it was locked. Strauss had gone hunting in the fall and probably had a rifle. Hawthorne told himself that he should break into the house and look for it. But he couldn't bring himself to shatter the glass and force his way in.

Hawthorne made his way back down the steps and waded through the snow to the second house, where Ted Wrigley lived with his wife, Doris, and baby daughter. Wrigley had told Hawthorne that he would be away until Sunday night or Monday morning, although he promised to be at the faculty meeting. Hawthorne saw a light in the window. He climbed the front steps and knocked. It was possible that Wrigley had a cell phone, even a gun. Not for the first time, Hawthorne thought of the pistol that Krueger had urged on him.

The door opened a crack. Doris Wrigley stood in the hall holding a flashlight. "Is that you, Jim? You must be freezing. Come in here where it's warm. I've built a fire."

Hawthorne scraped the snow from his boots and entered the hallway. There was the smell of popcorn and wood smoke.

"Is the whole campus dark?" asked Doris.

"Everything."

"And of course the plows haven't been through. We'll be lucky to see them before Monday." She led the way into the living room. Doris Wrigley was bundled up in heavy sweaters and her baby, who was a little more than a year old, was sleeping on a blanket in front of the fire. A dozen candles were scattered around the room on tables and bookcases.

"So is this a social visit?" asked Doris. She and her husband had been moderately friendly and helpful to Hawthorne throughout the fall—straddling the fence until they could judge whether he would be successful.

"Do you have a cell phone, by any chance?" asked Hawthorne.

"Ted has one that he keeps in the car but he's got it with him. He's supposed to be back tomorrow, but what with the storm . . ."

"What about a gun, do you have a gun?"

Doris stared up at him and all at once she saw the fear that was in him and some of it reached into her. She took a step back. "No, we've nothing. What do you want it for?"

Hawthorne thought of the story he could tell her and how she would be terrified. Yet he could think of no lie that would be reassuring. "I'd just feel more comfortable . . ."

"What's wrong, what's going on?"

Hawthorne backed into the hall. He felt foolish and ineffectual.

Doris followed him. "Tell me what's the matter. Why do you want a gun?"

"I'm sorry I upset you. It's just our concern about Larry Gaudette. Stay in the house and you'll be all right." Hawthorne quickly opened the door. As he descended the steps he saw Doris's outline at the glass as she stared after him. He had done nothing but frighten her. He heard the clicking of locks. Then the shade was pulled.

Herb Frankfurter lived in the next house with his wife and two daughters. Hawthorne pushed his way to Frankfurter's door and knocked on the glass. He was the faculty member who seemed to - dislike Hawthorne the most, presumably because Hawthorne had interfered with what he saw as the prerogatives of his twenty-year employment at Bishop's Hill. He never talked to Hawthorne if he could help it and avoided his glance in the hall. He also had skipped several of the faculty meetings until Hawthorne told him that he had to attend. Yet Frankfurter also seemed indifferent to the rest of the faculty members and had no friends among them.

The door opened and Frankfurter stood back with a flashlight in one hand and his cane in the other. "What's on your mind?" he asked. He seemed to find nothing odd about Hawthorne's sudden appearance.

"Can I come in?" asked Hawthorne.

Frankfurter moved aside to permit Hawthorne to enter. He made a polite gesture toward the living room but the expression on his face was ironic.

"Do you have a cellular phone?" asked Hawthorne.

"It's broken, I'm afraid."

"Do you have a gun?"

"What's going on?"

"Frank LeBrun has killed Roger Bennett and I'm afraid he'll try to kill Fritz and Jessica Weaver."

Frankfurter's eyes widened slightly, but other than that he showed no surprise. "Where are they?"

"Over in Emerson. If you had a cellular phone, I'd call the police . . ."

"So you're thinking of tackling him yourself?" Frankfurter permitted himself a sardonic smile. "I'm afraid I don't have a gun. My brother down in Laconia borrowed my shotgun and several hunting rifles and he hasn't returned them."

Frankfurter spoke calmly, as if what was a crisis for Hawthorne wasn't a crisis for him.

"Will you come with me back to Emerson? Maybe we can do something."

Frankfurter lifted his cane, showing it to Hawthorne. "I'm afraid that's not part of my job description, Mr. Headmaster. Anyway, with this knee, I doubt that I could even make it through the snow."

"Fritz and Jessica are in danger."

"If this fellow's already killed Roger, then I'd prefer to stay out of it. I'm terribly sorry, but I can't do anything for you." Frankfurter's voice grew harder. "But go ahead, go after him yourself. I'd like to see what happens."

"Do you really hate me so much?" asked Hawthorne, more surprised than hurt.

Frankfurter had his flashlight pointed downward, where it made a bright puddle of light on the braided rug. "I don't hate you. You're a blip in my landscape. You simply don't exist for me."

"We work together. We both live here. Surely, you feel some obligation . . ."

"I feel no obligation to risk my life. As for our working together, that's no more than an accident of fate. I don't know why this fellow's gone on a rampage, but I'm sure none of it would have happened if you hadn't come to Bishop's Hill."

"I thought you were a friend of Fritz's."

"Friendship has its limits. Besides that, I find his ambitions boring. I'm sorry." Frankfurter looked uncertain for a moment. "Who am I to go after a killer, or who are you, for that matter? Stay out of it. Wait for the storm to finish and then call the police. Why get yourself killed?"

"And Fritz and the girl?"

"What about them? Look after your own skin." A trace of anger crept into Frankfurter's voice. "Skander hates you. He's been talking behind your back all fall. You were a fool to trust him."

"You might have told me about it."

"It was none of my business."

Hawthorne turned and left the house. He swore that if he and the school survived he would remove Frankfurter from Bishop's Hill the first chance he got. Then he began to calm down. Frankfurter was afraid and vengeful, but perhaps he wasn't wrong.

At Skander's house there were lights in the downstairs windows. Hawthorne briefly imagined that LeBrun might be having a joke, that he would find Skander seated before his fire. But even before he knocked on the door he knew that wasn't true. As he waited he began to think about returning to Emerson Hall. He told himself that LeBrun was sick, he wasn't evil. But the thought of going back seemed beyond bearing.

Hilda Skander opened the door. When she saw who it was she looked frightened but she didn't say anything. "May I come in?" asked Hawthorne.

"What do you want?"

"Fritz is in danger. Do you have a cellular phone?"

Hilda stood aside. "No, nothing like that." Her blue denim jumper and pink sweater made her look like a middle-aged eight-year-old.

Hawthorne entered and looked into the living room. Someone stood before the fireplace, where a small fire was burning. Squinting his eyes, Hawthorne saw that it was Chip Campbell. He held a whiskey glass and glanced at Hawthorne. The room was smoky and the candles flickered.

"I got here earlier and got stuck," said Chip, "looks like I'll be spending the night. You haven't seen Fritz by any chance, have you?"

Instead of answering, Hawthorne turned back to Hilda. "Do you have a gun?"

"No," said Hilda, her voice almost a whisper.

"What's wrong?" said Chip, not moving from the fireplace.

Hawthorne realized that they were both scared, that they had been scared when he entered. "Frank LeBrun has killed Roger Bennett and he's got Fritz and Jessica Weaver."

Hilda pressed her closed hands to her chest.

"That can't be true," said Campbell, but he didn't say it as if he believed it.

"LeBrun killed Scott McKinnon. I think he's in Emerson with Jessica and Fritz. Bennett's body is in the chapel." And as he said it, Hawthorne again saw Bennett's dead grin. "You have to help me. We can get Dolittle and maybe Tank Donoso. The four of us should be able to stop him." The candlelight, coupled with Hawthorne's weak eyes, created a sense of unreality. Hawthorne heard his own desperation and the absurdity of his plan.

Chip walked unsteadily to the couch and sat down. He wore jeans and a dark sweatshirt. He rattled the ice cubes in the glass and took a drink. "That's a pretty tall order."

Hilda took hold of Hawthorne's arm. "It's not true, is it?"

"I'm afraid it is." He turned to Chip. "You're mixed up in this. You've known what Fritz and Bennett have been doing."

Chip held up his hands in mock innocence. "You got me wrong. I've nothing to do with this place. You fired me, remember? Besides, I'll be moving out to Seattle in January."

"You put those clippings about San Diego in people's mailboxes."

"That was Bennett."

"But he told you. And I bet he and Skander told you about the painting and phone calls and bags of rotten food. And you probably wrote that letter to Kate's ex-husband."

Chip looked uncomfortable and shrugged. "I had no reason to be nice to you."

"And you probably knew about selling Bishop's Hill to the Galileo Corporation. Why didn't you come to me? You're no better than they are."

"You can't prove I knew anything. Some West Coast hotshot telling us what to do, planning to stick us in a book—how could you expect anybody to help you? You got dumped on us by the board. Nobody asked us if we wanted you or not."

"I need your help."

"I'm sorry, I'm not leaving this house. I've already tangled with LeBrun, and anyway," said Chip, lifting his glass, "I'm looped."

Hilda sat down. Her face was buried in her hands and she was weeping.

"You're a coward," said Hawthorne.

Chip took another drink and leaned back. "You're right, I am. There are times when cowardice makes sense."

"Are you going to let Fritz get killed?"

Chip looked embarrassed. "I'm not a cowboy. Before you fired me I was nothing but a bad history teacher. LeBrun has no rules. I'm frightened just talking about him. He's a monster."

The last of the faculty houses belonged to Betty Sherman, and her teenage son, who had been born with Down's syndrome. Betty's husband had been dead for some years. He had been much older than his wife and had taught history at the school. The boy was their only child. Hawthorne had seen him several times—a chubby boy both sweet and heartbreaking, who cheerfully introduced himself to everyone as Tommy.

Hawthorne climbed her snowy steps and rapped on the glass so it rattled. First Tommy came to the door, then his mother. "Jim, what's the matter? You look awful."

"Do you have a cellular phone?"

"No . . ." Betty wore a dark skirt and a dark long-sleeved blouse.

"What about a gun?"

"Of course not. What's wrong?"

"Frank LeBrun's killed Roger Bennett. He's also got Fritz and Jessica Weaver captive in Emerson Hall. I'm sorry to frighten you."

"Oh, no." Betty put one hand over her mouth. Her son looked at her quizzically, then his face took on a worried expression.

"I don't know what to do. You're the last person I can talk to." Hawthorne felt exhausted. "People are scared. Understandably. And there's no way to get out of here, because of the snow. I'm afraid of what's going to happen."

"But you can't let Jessica stay there. God knows what he's doing to her."

"He's trying to get up his nerve to kill her." It was warm in the hallway. The snow began to melt on Hawthorne's jacket. He took off his gloves and ski cap.

Betty's round face seemed to shrink with distress. "Is he the one who killed Scott?"

Hawthorne nodded.

"I can give you a knife. I have an old hunting knife of my husband's."

Hawthorne imagined trying to attack LeBrun with a hunting knife and almost smiled. "I wouldn't stand a chance fighting him. Maybe I can talk to him. I don't know. I don't even have a light."

"Wait a minute," said Betty. She hurried off. Tommy stayed in the hall grinning at Hawthorne. A kerosene lamp on the hall table was smoking. Hawthorne lowered the wick.

"No lights," said Tommy. "They went out."

"That's true enough," said Hawthorne.

"No lights," Tommy repeated and his grin widened.

Hawthorne tried to look affable, but he was tired and fear filled his heart. He had to talk to LeBrun, convince him to free Jessica and Skander. He had to take advantage of LeBrun's own instability. He had to try, even if he had no chance of success.

Betty Sherman hurried back into the hall. Going to the table, she put down a flashlight, a hunting knife, and a crowbar. "That's the best I can do. I'd go with you but I'd be more of a hindrance than a help. And I'm afraid of leaving Tommy . . ." Her sentence trailed off.

Hawthorne looked at the knife. "That's okay." He felt that if he touched the articles on the table, there would be no turning back. He remembered his wife calling his name from the burning hallway at Wyndham. Although faint, the sound filled his mind. Hawthorne picked up the crowbar and the flashlight. Then, after a moment, he took the hunting knife as well. "I guess I'll go back," he said. "If the telephone starts working again, make sure you call the police."

Jessica lay on her stomach in the attic of Emerson Hall, hog-tied with a torn-up sheet. It was dark except for a sputtering candle near the door to the bell tower, but Jessica didn't mind the dark. It meant that LeBrun was someplace else, someplace where he couldn't terrify her. Earlier that day when she had seen LeBrun and Tremblay together in Plymouth, she had understood something that she had suspected ever since she had heard them talking in Exeter. But that wasn't exactly true—she had known earlier without wanting to know. And yet he hadn't killed her, had he? In some strange way of his, he must have liked her. But LeBrun had her money and soon he'd have Tremblay's too. How could she have imagined that he liked her? He didn't like her, he hadn't even wanted to have sex with her. Now, though, he still didn't seem able to kill her. At least that's what he had been storming about.

But he had murdered other people—it was one of his favorite subjects. He had killed his cousin and Scott and at some point he would kill her as well. Jessica was certain about that. No wonder Tremblay had agreed to let her come home for Christmas. He had meant for her to be dead long before Christmas arrived. And Jessica thought what a piece of trash she must be if everyone wanted her dead. Not everyone. Her brother loved her. Lucky loved her. Even Dr. Hawthorne had been nice when he had every reason to hate her. And he didn't want to have sex with her either. In fact, nobody did and maybe that was because Tremblay had already used her so badly. That was another reason why Tremblay wanted her dead, to keep her mouth shut. Jessica thought about heaven and if it existed; surely that's where her father was and if she went there she would see him. But if there was a heaven, then there must also be a hell and when LeBrun killed her he'd probably be sending her there.

The building was quiet now except for the sound of the wind. Earlier there had been shouting, even screams, and the sound of running. Mr. Skander had been with LeBrun but Jessica didn't know why or what was going on, except that Mr. Skander had made LeBrun get her drunk. "He paid me for that," LeBrun had said. "I don't see why he couldn't have paid me for Hawthorne as well." Jessica didn't understand that, but there had been a whine in his voice, as if Mr. Skander had cheated him. It made her feel sorry for Mr. Skander, though she knew she had every reason to hate him, but she felt sorry for anyone whom LeBrun was angry at. And when there had been the shouting and running, she had heard Mr. Skander yelling for help and begging LeBrun to stop. And she had heard LeBrun telling his awful jokes. And she had heard him growling. It seemed like they had been running through the entire building, then it had gotten quiet.

Jessica was cold and the dust on the floor kept getting in her nose. It was almost funny that she might freeze to death before LeBrun had a chance to kill her. Then she thought of her kitten and how she wouldn't be there to take care of it, and she was afraid she would cry, and she hated crying.

The door to the attic banged open and there was the sound of feet on the stairs. Jessica's body clenched and a chill ran through her that had nothing to do with the weather. LeBrun was coming up again. She tried to move but her hands were tried behind her back and her left foot was tied to her hands. She could hardly even wriggle, and when she pulled, the torn sheet hurt her wrists.

"How's my little girl?" came LeBrun's voice from the dark. Then she saw the beam of his flashlight as he came up the stairs. "How's my snuff cake? Did I tell you what they call a Canuck girl with half a brain?" LeBrun chuckled. "Skander didn't like that one, he didn't even laugh." Then LeBrun shouted, suddenly furious, "What the fuck's the answer?"

"Gifted," said Jessica, but she didn't laugh either.

LeBrun cackled. "Don't you love it," he said, "don't you love it?"

The beam of the light focused on her face and she tried to turn away. LeBrun's footsteps got nearer. "How's my girl? Answer me!"

"I'm all right," said Jessica.

"That's better. I don't like people who're rude to me. I mean, it's one thing to die and it's another to die with a lot of pain." LeBrun sat cross-legged on the floor in front of her. He sniffed and wiped his nose on the sleeve of his jacket.

"Let me go," said Jessica.

"Fat chance. Hey, I need the money. I need some legs to get out of here. Don't take it personal. It's a job, that's all. Like the American way of life. I get paid for it and that makes it okay." LeBrun laughed again, an ironic bark.

"Then why haven't you killed me already?"

LeBrun was silent for a moment, then he raised his voice. "Because I'm preparing myself, that's all. And the money's not here. Don't worry, it's on its way. Your dad's having a little trouble with the snow, but he'll get here soon. I just talked to him."

"He's not my dad."

"Yeah, what a shame. Did I tell you why Canucks wear hats?"

Jessica didn't say anything. Whatever was going to happen, she wished it was over.

"Did I?" shouted LeBrun.

"So they'll know what end to wipe."

"Jesus, I could listen to those all night. Know which end to wipe, ain't it the fuckin' truth. All right, little Misty, your time's up." LeBrun reached over and cut the sheet securing her foot. "Let's get started. It's got to be done before he gets here. I'll be taking his Jeep. I've always liked Jeeps." He took Jessica's arm and dragged her to her feet.

"What're you going to do?" she asked, terrified again.

"We're going up to the top, up where the bell is." He pulled her over to the door leading to the tower. "Too bad you're not going to get a chance to admire the view. I hear it's fantastic."

Detective Leo Flynn and Chief Moulton were in Moulton's black Chevy Blazer making their way down Antelope Road, which still hadn't been plowed. They had spent an hour in Brewster Village waiting for a plow but it had never shown up so Moulton said he'd try to force his way through, even though the snow must be nearly three feet.

"I don't want to freeze to death out here," said Flynn, who had not meant to say anything, who had meant to seem confident.

"The heater works and I got a full tank of gas. We could be toasty all night."

"If this was Boston, I could get the entire Department of Public Works to clear the roads. I'd get them out here or I'd fucking have their jobs."

Moulton cleared his throat. "Too bad we're not in Boston."

Flynn thought he detected an element of sarcasm. He glanced at Moulton but the police chief's face in the dash light was expressionless. "Hey, this guy's a professional killer. You should of at least called out the National Guard."

"I called the troopers," said Moulton. "Everyone's tied up because of the snow, even the National Guard."

Again there was the whisper of sarcasm. "So how far do we have to go?"

"About seven miles."

"That should take us about an hour at this rate."

"Maybe you'd do better on foot," said Moulton. "I bet even your feet are better than ours. A Boston flatfoot, isn't that right? I bet you could walk on the snow just like you had snowshoes."

"Hey," said Flynn, "I don't need this. We got serious business to take care of."

After the autopsy had located a small puncture at the base of Larry Gaudette's skull, Moulton had meant to go out to the school and talk to LeBrun. But LeBrun had been only one possible suspect out of several. That is, till Flynn showed up.

"If you'd called this morning," said Moulton, "we wouldn't have to be fighting this storm."

"I wanted to be here. I been looking for this guy all fall. Anyway, I thought Gaudette was our man." That wasn't entirely true but Flynn didn't want to seem stupid.

The Blazer swerved, then straightened again. If its tires hadn't been more than twice the normal size they would have gotten stuck long ago. In its headlights there was nothing but white. The road was invisible. Only the trees on either side indicated where the road must be. The wheels skidded again and the car swerved to the right.

"Do you think this fellow has left dozens of corpses behind him?" asked Moulton. "He could have been murdering people for years."

"I doubt it," said Flynn, a little defensively. He wanted a cigarette and was annoyed that Moulton wouldn't let him smoke in the car. "Generally with someone like that it takes a while to get the nerve to do the first one, then it gets easier. At the end it's harder to stop killing than to kill. But he might of only started a year or so ago."

"A killer who makes bread," said Moulton. "Francis LaBrecque, a Canuck. I wonder who else he's killed by now. Why, he could wipe out everyone left at the school."

Even with cross-country skis, Kate could proceed only at a shuffle. If she had stayed at home, she could have been sitting in front of the fireplace with a warm glass of cider and a book. But her anxiety had made her realize that Hawthorne was dear to her and she wanted to be with him. She thought of him alone at the school with people who wished him harm, and after enough of such thoughts it seemed to make perfect sense to go there. She had dressed warmly and already she was sweating, although her feet were cold. The skis kept her from sinking all the way down in the snow, and slowly she was making progress.

She imagined arriving at the school and finding everything all right. Hawthorne would be reading before his own fireplace and he would laugh at her foolishness. But at least she would be with him. Deep within her, though, she knew that nothing was right, that he was in danger. The snow blew in her face and she had to keep her head down. Now and then she turned on her flashlight, trying to calculate where she was. But the snow had changed the landscape, erasing the usual markers, and the houses set back from the road were dark. Indeed, she was afraid she might miss the turn to Bishop's Hill and go on toward Brewster. The turnoff would be only a gap between the trees, a slightly different blanket of white. It might be easy to miss.

It was past eight o'clock. Kate didn't feel tired. Her anxiety was like an extra motor driving her forward. But she worried that she would be late, that something awful had already happened, that Hawthorne would accuse LeBrun and make him angry. She imagined LeBrun destroying him with as much concern as he might show a fly. The thought made her move faster, which only increased her sense of folly. She paused and scooped up a handful of snow with her glove and pressed it to her mouth. Then she turned on the light again. Up on the left was the turnoff. She was certain of it.

Hawthorne entered Emerson Hall by a side door. He was too frightened to go up the front steps. In an attic window he had again seen a glimmer of light that he knew was LeBrun. He still had no plan but he had to keep LeBrun from hurting Skander and Jessica. But wasn't that absurd? How in the world did he expect to stop LeBrun? He doubted he would be able to stab him with Betty Sherman's hunting knife, no matter what LeBrun had done; it was against everything that Hawthorne believed in. He had to be aggressive but he couldn't be threatening, and on another day the paradox might have amused him. But however clumsy he was, he had to make LeBrun think that he was acting in LeBrun's best interests. And it was true. If he could save LeBrun, then he *would* save him. He had to keep repeating to himself that LeBrun was sick and deserved help. Even the repeating of it helped allay Hawthorne's fear, if only a little.

He opened the first-floor fire door and stepped into the hall. Two hours earlier he had wrestled here with LeBrun. He had dropped his flashlight and lost his glasses. Now he could hear no sound. Blocking the beam with his hand, he turned on the light. He had almost expected to see LeBrun waiting in the shadows. But there was no one. And there on the floor by the wall were his glasses. He bent to pick them up. The pewter frames were twisted and the right lens was broken. Hawthorne poked out the glass with his finger, then straightened the frames. With his shirt tail he cleaned the left lens and put on the glasses. He still couldn't see well, but he could see better. Absurdly, it made him feel more confident, as if he had armed himself.

Turning off the flashlight, Hawthorne moved slowly along the hall. He didn't want LeBrun to be aware of his presence until he chose. The crowbar was stuck in his belt. It might come in handy; he might have to force open a door or a window. The hunting knife was tucked through his belt at the small of his back. Its blade was seven or eight inches long and the handle seemed to have been made from the horn of some animal—an elk or mountain goat. Hawthorne was aware of it at every moment; it filled him with repugnance, as if its very presence belied who he was and dirtied him.

After about five minutes, Hawthorne felt the walls fall away on either side and realized he had reached the rotunda, where the windows created a ghostly transparency. His eyes could distinguish the surrounding open space ascending three stories to the attic and the bell tower beyond. LeBrun was up there—Hawthorne could almost feel him—and why would he stay there if Jessica and Skander weren't alive? He thought of LeBrun's saying that he had been born evil, a claim that absolved him of responsibility. Yet his reluctance to kill Jessica meant that he wasn't just a killing machine. Jessica was different. She couldn't serve as his tormentor's stand-in, somebody to punish. She was a girl. She couldn't be other than victim. LeBrun seemed unable to justify killing her. And Hawthorne hoped this was something he could use.

Yet now that Hawthorne was here and looking up into the rotunda, he hesitated. He stood in the dark and cursed himself, and just when his memory began to summon up the awful hesitations of the past, he flicked on his flashlight and pointed it upward into the huge darkness.

"Frank," he shouted, "I've come back for you!" Then he paused as the echoes of his cry rushed through the building, and he felt horror at what he had done. Still, he shouted again, "Frank, answer me!" And he kept his light pointed upward.

Far above he heard the clattering of footsteps descending wooden stairs. Hawthorne knew that LeBrun was coming down from the attic and his body turned cold.

"Frank, what are you doing? Answer me."

The air around Hawthorne trembled with the reverberation of his voice. He tried to calm himself, exert some self-control. He needed to keep LeBrun off balance and use the man's self-doubt and instability, even his anger.

"Answer me, Frank! Why are you doing this?"

"Go away!" came a cry in response. "I'll hurt you, I swear I'll hurt you!"

Somehow, hearing LeBrun's voice, even in its awfulness, made LeBrun seem less awful. "Frank, you're not answering my question!"

"Go away, professor! I swear, I'll get even. I'll hurt you!"

There was a bumping noise and a grunt, as if LeBrun were lifting something heavy.

Hawthorne moved his flashlight around the top of the rotunda and it seemed he could just make out the whiteness of LeBrun's face looking over the low wall at the third floor. Then something came tumbling out of the darkness, tumbling into the beam of Hawthorne's light. For a second it was just a white shape, but as it spun and twisted through the air Hawthorne saw that it was a human body, shifting from indistinctness to clarity as he stared through his broken glasses. It fell with bare arms and legs outstretched, and its white feet seemed to shine. It tilted, falling headfirst, then turned again onto its back, falling horizontally. Was it LeBrun? No, it was gray-haired and nearly naked, and splotched with blood. It was thick and plump and its skin was pink—Skander. Hawthorne leapt out of the way and tripped, falling backward. Skander hit the marble floor on his back, hit the blue-and-gold school shield, and bounced slightly. The sound of the impact had a wetness to it, a damp heaviness, followed by a smaller thud as he bounced again. His head hit after him and he lay still.

Hawthorne stood up and pointed his light at Skander. He wore yellow boxer shorts and nothing else. There were half a dozen crescent-shaped teeth marks on his shoulders and arms. His body was crisscrossed with blood and his skull was broken, a red crack across his forehead that disappeared into his gray and bloody hair. He lay doll-like with his arms stretched out as if were attempting to fly. His legs were spread apart and bloody, and the bright yellow shorts made him look oddly childish. Skander's face was distorted and twin rivulets of dried blood extended from his nose down to his chin. He was slack-jawed and his eyes were glazed with dull surprise.

Hawthorne could hardly keep the light steady. His whole body was telling him to run. Gradually he took hold of himself and turned the light upward.

"Frank, how could you have done this?" He spoke loudly, making his voice stern.

"Go away, get out of here!"

"I'm coming up," called Hawthorne.

LeBrun's voice rose to a squeal. "I'm warning you, I'm warning you. Don't you know what I can do?"

Then he heard another voice. "Dr. Hawthorne!" It was Jessica.

"Let the girl go," called Hawthorne, both relieved and increasingly terrified.

There was the sound of feet high above him and the sound of something being dragged. "I want to help you, Frank," called Hawthorne. "Let Jessica go." Hawthorne began to ascend the stairs. He imagined how LeBrun must have pursued Skander through the building, laughing and biting his body. "I'm coming up, Frank."

A door slammed. LeBrun was going back into the attic, taking Jessica with him. Hawthorne reached the second floor. As he climbed, the hunting knife chafed and rubbed his back. He paused and took it out, feeling its weight as his light reflected off the blade. Then Hawthorne began to climb to the third floor. On one of the steps lay Skander's white shirt, spotted with blood. A little farther lay a boot, then another—rubber boots with high leather tops, the laces of which had been slashed down the center.

At the top of the steps Hawthorne listened, but he heard nothing except the wind. He looked over the wall. Shining his light downward, he saw Skander spread-eagled on the school shield in the very center of the rotunda. He moved to the door leading to the attic. It was locked. He began to break it open with his crowbar, inserting the blade in a space near the knob, but then he stopped and rummaged through his pockets for his keys. He unlocked the door and swung it open.

Hawthorne listened and heard nothing. "Frank, are you up there?"

He imagined LeBrun waiting for him in the darkness. "Frank, answer me!"

The wind seemed to rush down the attic stairs, picking up scraps of paper, flecks of dust and grit, blowing them against Hawthorne's face. He thought of the attic's clutter and all the places where LeBrun could lie in wait for him. But wouldn't Jessica call out to him again? And what if LeBrun had killed her? Then Hawthorne pushed those thoughts from his mind and began to climb the wooden stairs, still holding the knife and still offended by it.

When he reached the top he shone the light around the attic but he saw no one. With all the mattresses and bed frames and bookcases, LeBrun could easily be hiding no more than a few yards away, just waiting for Hawthorne to turn his back. Again Hawthorne stopped that train of thought. A candle sputtered on the floor and there were scraps of torn sheets.

"Where are you, Frank?" Hawthorne tried to keep his voice calm, almost conversational. "Are you up here?"

Hawthorne listened. He found himself hating the wind and the noise it made. He took a few steps into the attic and shone his light down the corridor.

"Answer me, Frank."

Then he pointed the light in the other direction. Nothing. The candle went out abruptly, and Hawthorne jumped, swinging his light back across where the candle had been. The wind must have blown it out; it had to be the wind. Again he tried to calm his breathing.

"I want you to come back with me, Frank. Let Jessica go."

Hawthorne felt sure that the attic was empty. It was only his fear that was haunting its shadowy space. Slowly, he approached the door to the spiral staircase rising through the bell tower. The door was locked and he didn't have the key. It was in his desk. He pushed the blade of the crowbar into the narrow gap by the lock and pried, then wedged the bar deeper and bent it back with more force. The door cracked and sprang open. The noise startled him and he held his breath.

Hawthorne listened and heard nothing. Then he began to climb the metal steps of the spiral staircase. Snow had blown through the louvers and the steps were slippery. Brushing against the bell rope, he pushed it aside. Because of his broken glasses, it seemed he saw everything twice: once with clarity and once as a blur. Slowly, Hawthorne went round and round, holding the hunting knife in one hand and the flashlight in the other, trying to keep his balance by pressing his shoulder against the inside column. He came to the trapdoor leading to the top. Again he listened and heard nothing. He tried to push the trapdoor open but it didn't move. Once more, Hawthorne inserted the crowbar into a gap and bent it back. One of the boards of the trapdoor broke. He pushed the bar into another gap and a second board broke. Hawthorne realized that if LeBrun was in the tower and wanted to kill him, he wouldn't have a chance, knife or no knife. LeBrun could stab him as Hawthorne tried to climb through the opening. He paused once more to gather his resolve, then he shoved upward. The trapdoor slammed back and a shower of snow fell onto his hair and face. Brushing the snow out of his eyes, Hawthorne noticed that he had lost his ski cap without even knowing it. The wind blew against him. Quickly, he climbed the next two steps, pushing his head above the floor of the tower. There were fresh footprints in the snow—the large prints of a man's boots, and Jessica's smaller footprints. They led to the wall, the very edge of the dark space. Hawthorne climbed another step and flashed his light around him. The tower was empty.

When Kate passed the mound of snow covering Hawthorne's Subaru, she could barely distinguish the outlines of the school buildings in front of her. Even though she had guessed they would be dark, their darkness surprised her, as if the school were dead. She shuffled forward on her skis toward Emerson Hall, planning to go around Emerson to Hawthorne's quarters in Adams. The snow was letting up, hardly more than flurries, and the sky seemed brighter. She could make out the line of trees at the end of the lawn.

Passing in front of Stark Hall, she saw that the chapel door was open and light was flickering through the stained-glass windows. She might have gone in, but when she turned her flashlight toward Emerson, she saw three figures standing on the steps. She continued toward them, holding both ski poles in one hand and her light in the other. The flashlight's beam reflected off the snow and shone on the iron fence posts. She turned her light toward the figures again. Almost with disappointment she saw that it was Betty Sherman and her son, Tommy. Standing behind them was Bill Dolittle.

"What are you doing out here?" Kate called. "What's going on?"

"Is that you, Kate?" said Betty, taking a step toward her. "Oh dear, you should have stayed home. Mr. Bennett's been killed. Frank LeBrun's in Emerson with Fritz and Jessica Weaver. Dr. Hawthorne thinks he means to kill them."

"Where is Jim?" asked Kate. Betty and her son stood on the steps above her. Tommy had stuck out his tongue and was trying to catch snowflakes on its tip.

"He's gone into Emerson to find LeBrun," said Dolittle.

"I lent him a hunting knife," said Betty. "We followed his tracks to the side entrance. I thought I could find someone who might help. Bill came with us. Nobody else would come."

"Jim's in there alone?" All the fears that Kate had imagined on her way to Bishop's Hill were dwarfed by the actuality.

"He went by himself," said Dolittle. He wore a dark overcoat and a sheepskin trooper's hat with the flaps down over his ears. His nose was bright red in the cold.

"Have you seen anyone else?" asked Kate, unfastening her skis.

"No, no one," said Betty.

"You should go home," said Kate. "You're in danger here."

"I want to stay," said Betty, "but I think Tommy and I will wait outside."

"Jim came looking for me," said Dolittle. "I just couldn't talk to him. I'm sorry." He turned up his collar and held it together with one hand.

Listening to Dolittle, Kate's own sense of purpose strengthened. She took off her skis and leaned them against one of the columns, then she continued up the steps through the snow, using a ski pole for support. The door was unlocked, but snow had blown up against it and she had to pull hard. She kept the ski pole with her as if she could use it as a weapon, yet knowing how ineffectual it would be. Once inside she shone her light around the rotunda. Fritz Skander lay sprawled on the blue-and-gold school shield.

Kate began to scream, then bit her lip. She slowly approached the body, holding her flashlight in front of her so that Skander's yellow shorts seemed luminescent. When she saw his torn flesh, she shut her eyes. For a moment she didn't move, not trusting her legs to carry her. Then, hesitantly, she advanced toward the stairs leading to the second floor.

Chief Moulton was able to drive a little faster. Another car had come onto the road from the cutoff across the Baker River to West Brewster and Route 25, a big SUV, by the look of the tracks, and it had made a path for them. Where the cutoff joined Antelope Road was an old cemetery now looking like a field with a few stones poking up through the snow.

"You telling me all this was once cornfields?" said Leo Flynn.

"Just on the south side of the road. There wasn't much farming on the mountain. Then farming got worse after the Civil War and folks started heading out west."

Flynn gestured toward the tracks ahead of them. "You think those belong to the state troopers?"

"Nope. Otherwise, I could of raised them on the radio. I don't know who they belong to. Whoever it is, they must have a powerful reason for being out on a night like this."

"What kind of shot are you?" asked Flynn.

Moulton sucked his teeth. Even staying in the SUV's tracks it was hard to keep the Blazer going straight. "I guess I can hit a barn door if I have to."

"That's probably better than I can do."

They rode in silence for a while. Flynn tried to remember the last time he had fired his revolver. He didn't even bother with target practice anymore. But at least it was clean, he knew that much. He'd oiled it just that morning.

"You get a lot of summer people?" asked Flynn, who had never liked silence.

"There's a lot up at Stinson Lake, a few miles north of Brewster Village. I get called up there about a dozen times during the summer. What they call domestic disturbances—"

"Those tracks are turning off to the right," interrupted Flynn.

Moulton slowed up to make the turn as well. "This's the turnoff to Bishop's Hill. Whoever's in that thing is going right where we're going."

Hawthorne leaned over the wall of the bell tower, looking down at the scaffolding more than twenty feet below. LeBrun was sitting cross-legged in the snow at the edge of the darkness and Jessica lay on her stomach facing him. LeBrun had one hand on the back of Jessica's neck as if pressing her against the wood. His flashlight was a little behind him, brightly illuminating his left side and Jessica's red down jacket. LeBrun was leaning forward and his head was bent. Neither was moving. Around them Hawthorne was aware of great dark space extending in all directions. The snow had decreased and there was a glow to the clouds from the hidden moon. Hawthorne thought how

Skander's conniving had come to this—Skander and Bennett dead, Jessica and LeBrun balanced motionless on the rim of a chasm.

Hawthorne began to call out, then stopped himself. The workmen doing the repairs on the roof had attached a ladder to the side of the tower, and the tip of it extended about a foot above the wall. Hawthorne still held the hunting knife and the flashlight, though the light was off. He set the light on the floor of the tower, then, after a moment of hesitation, he dropped the knife as well, feeling relieved even as his fear seemed to increase. He swung one leg over the wall, then grabbed the top of the ladder, which shifted slightly in his hand. He looked down at the driveway far below and felt his legs weaken. He looked away, toward the woods. Far in the distance, where the road should be, there was a faint glow; a car was coming. Hawthorne eased his right foot onto the ladder, gripped the top with both hands, and lowered his left foot down from the wall. Once he felt secure on the ladder, he took one step, then another. With each step it seemed that splinters of ice swirled through his belly. But as long as he didn't look down, he could keep moving. He had removed his gloves and his fingers felt numb against the cold metal.

After Hawthorne had descended about ten feet, LeBrun's light swept across him. "It won't do any good you coming down here." The anger seemed gone from LeBrun's voice.

Instead of answering, Hawthorne continued to climb steadily down the ladder. LeBrun's light moved away from him.

"You're a stubborn fuck."

Again there was no anger. Perhaps frustration and uncertainty, but also the kind of calm that at times results from bewilderment. Hawthorne took a quick look over his shoulder and saw that LeBrun was still sitting cross-legged, with one hand holding Jessica against the scaffolding. The flashlight was again in the snow, the snowflakes swirling through its bright beam. Hawthorne moved down to the next rung.

"I can go ahead and kill her, you know," said LeBrun. "One twitch of my hand and she's over the side." His voice was still quiet, as if filtered through his mystification.

Hawthorne reached the bottom and turned slowly on the planking, which was slippery and shook under his weight. LeBrun and Jessica were about ten feet away. The glow from the woods was brighter as the vehicle approached. Hawthorne paused to put his gloves back on, then he took several steps toward LeBrun. He could see the flicker of light through the windows of the chapel far below. Jessica's head was turned from him. She lay as if she were already dead.

"Don't get too close," said LeBrun, raising his voice.

Hawthorne stopped, then lowered himself so that he was sitting about five feet from Jessica. There was nearly a foot of snow on the scaffolding, more in some places where it had been sculpted by the wind. He sat cross-legged like LeBrun, with his hands in front of him so LeBrun could see that they were empty. He didn't speak. LeBrun's light seemed to be getting dimmer, yellowing at the edges of its circle. Jessica's jacket and jeans were turning white with the falling snow. They sat silently for several moments as LeBrun continued to stare down at the girl.

"Why can't I do it?" said LeBrun at last, turning toward Hawthorne. He removed his hand from Jessica's neck and wiped the snow from his face. He wore no gloves and his other hand was in his coat pocket.

Hawthorne didn't answer for a moment. He could see headlights slowly coming down the road out of the woods, approaching the gates of the school.

"Let's go downstairs, Frank. Let's just stop."

"Tell me. Why can't I do it?" Now Hawthorne heard the frustration more clearly.

"You already know the answer."

"Because she's a girl?"

"More than that."

"Give me a reason."

"You can't blame her for anything. She's a victim, just like you."

LeBrun's voice rose a little. "That's bullshit." LeBrun reached out and grabbed the back of Jessica's neck. Hawthorne heard her breathe sharply. He kept himself still.

"Look, I don't know what happened to you." Hawthorne paused, as if counting off the seconds. "Tell me about the school in Derry."

"I don't want to talk about it. All that's dead, it's over and done with. I hardly remember anymore."

"What happened before that?"

"It's a dead time, don't you hear what I'm saying? I fuckin' cut it out already."

The car was now at the far end of the driveway. It looked like a large Jeep. LeBrun glanced at it, then looked back at Hawthorne. He let go of Jessica and put his hand in his coat pocket.

Hawthorne leaned forward. "Let's go, Frank."

LeBrun reached out for his light and shone it in Hawthorne's face, then he lowered it. "I got no place to go. Anyway, it's too late for that shit."

"Perhaps I can help you."

LeBrun's voice hardened. "What the fuck are you offering me, prison?"

"There're other kinds of places. If you let Jessica go, it'll be better."

"A fucking loony bin."

"I'll try to help you."

"There's nothing you can do." There was no regret in LeBrun's voice, only resignation.

"Let Jessica go. Let her go home."

LeBrun made one of his croaking laughs. "She doesn't have any home." He pointed toward the car, which had stopped between Hawthorne's buried Subaru and the library. "See that Jeep? That's her stepfather. Fucking Tremblay. Five grand down and five on completion. He probably figures I've already done the job. I could go down there right now, get the money, and get out of here. Shit, I could even take his Jeep."

"He paid you to kill his daughter?" said Hawthorne, lowering his voice. He looked quickly at Jessica. Her very stillness made him realize that she already knew about Tremblay.

"Stepdaughter. He's just another of the world's assholes."

LeBrun's hands were back in his coat pockets and he was again leaning toward Jessica. "If she'd paid me to kill Tremblay," he said at last, "I probably could of done it, no problem. You hear what I'm saying?"

Now it seemed to Hawthorne that he saw the lights of another car. "Come on, Frank, let's go inside. I'll help you the best I can."

"What the hell would that be?"

"There'd be tests, doctors, you could talk about what happened to you."

"You don't get it. You don't know my world. You don't know what I've done."

"I can try."

"It wouldn't work. I've done too fucking much." The frustration came back into LeBrun's voice. "I don't like not doing what I been paid to do." He reached out again and grabbed Jessica's neck. Then he too saw the lights of the second car. "What the fuck?"

Driving in the tracks left by the Jeep, the second car was able to move faster.

"If that's the cops," said LeBrun, the anger growing in his voice, "this girl doesn't stand a chance." He twisted around onto his knees, then rose into a crouch.

"Come with me now," said Hawthorne, beginning to stand up as well. "Otherwise it will be too late."

"No, I can't."

"Come with me. Leave the girl. Let's stop this."

LeBrun looked at him, and it seemed to Hawthorne, just for a moment, that LeBrun was weighing the possibility. Then he looked back at the two cars. "Jesus, what's he doing?" The second car had passed the Jeep. At the same moment, Hawthorne and LeBrun became aware of the white lettering on the door and the light on top, even though it wasn't flashing. Hawthorne recognized Chief Moulton's Blazer. As for the Jeep, it was turning around and beginning to head back out the driveway. LeBrun was now standing on the scaffolding. "The fucker's leaving with my money." He looked back at Hawthorne. His eyebrows in the shadow looked ferocious and dark. "You tricked me! You planned this all along. God damn you!"

Then, suddenly, the bell above them began to ring—deep, resonant explosions, over and over. Startled, LeBrun looked up, and at the same time Jessica rolled away from him toward Hawthorne and staggered to her feet. Perhaps she bumped LeBrun or perhaps she only surprised him. Perhaps it was the ringing of the bell. Whatever the case, LeBrun took a step backward and there was nothing there, only dark space. He spun his arms, and the ice pick flew over his shoulder as he tried to regain his balance with just his right foot on the planking. Hawthorne tried to jump forward without slipping himself. The bell continued to ring. For an instant Hawthorne's and LeBrun's eyes locked and in LeBrun's there was astonishment changing to fear. Both men reached out, then Jessica screamed and LeBrun was gone.

Leaning forward, Hawthorne saw him fall. LeBrun made no sound, twisting with his arms out to the side. His snow-covered hunting jacket glistened in the lights of the approaching Chevy Blazer as he flipped through the air. It seemed to Hawthorne that as LeBrun fell, the spikes on top of the fence were reaching toward him. Some were gold-tipped, some wore caps of snow. LeBrun hit the fence with a sudden clang and was impaled through his back. He screamed, a short, choked-off roar as three of the spikes pushed through his belly. In the headlights, Hawthorne saw LeBrun thrash and arch on the golden metal, then he was still. A gush of blood reddened the snow beneath him. The bell had stopped ringing and the silence felt thick and palpable. The flashing blue light on top of Moulton's Blazer came on and swept across LeBrun's body. A small group of people was assembled by the steps of Emerson.

Jessica was standing back by the ladder, holding on to it. She had seen LeBrun fall but she hadn't seen him hit the fence. She pointed out across the snow-covered lawns where the Jeep's taillights were just passing through the gates of the school.

"Tremblay's getting away." Her voice was at the very edge of hysteria. "He'll kill my brother."

Hawthorne put his arm around her shoulder. "Moulton will radio the troopers. He's down below right now. They'll get your brother out of the house before Tremblay even reaches Plymouth. He'll be arrested."

The girl put her arms around Hawthorne and held him. He could feel her body shaking even through the thickness of her jacket.

"I thought he was going to kill me. I just knew it."

"It's over now. Do you think you can climb back up the ladder?"

"I'll try. I'm scared."

"I'll be right behind you." Hawthorne went over to get LeBrun's light. He couldn't imagine who had rung the bell. He pointed the light up the ladder so Jessica could see the rungs. She took hold and stepped onto the first rung.

"Don't let me fall," she said.

"I won't," said Hawthorne.

"You saved my life."

Hawthorne didn't say anything to that. He realized that he couldn't climb and hold the light at the same time. Then a light flicked on above them, not pointing down into their eyes but pointing to the side, letting them see the ladder and helping them climb. Hawthorne dropped LeBrun's flashlight back onto the scaffolding.

"Keep going," he said. "Whoever's up there will help you over the top."

It was Kate. He had to look a second time to make sure he wasn't mistaken. She reached down and grabbed Jessica's arm, steadying her. Then she helped Hawthorne. "You rang the bell," he said.

Kate touched his cheek. "I saw the knife and then looked over the side. When I saw LeBrun stand up I thought he was going to hurt you. And the police were coming . . ."

Hawthorne embraced her, then held her tighter. In his mind he kept seeing LeBrun falling and hitting the fence, then twisting on the spikes. He pulled away.

"I have to get downstairs," he said. "Help Jessica."

Hawthorne dropped through the trapdoor and hurried down the circular staircase. He could hear Jessica and Kate coming behind him. The light from Kate's flashlight bounced across the inner walls of the tower. Their boots rang on the metal steps.

At the bottom, Hawthorne felt his way uncertainly across the attic to the stairs, not waiting for Kate. Then he descended to the third floor. He could hear their footsteps falling farther behind. Now there were windows, and light coming through them. Hawthorne didn't pause. His mind was full of LeBrun and the inexorable progression of events.

On the first floor of the rotunda Hawthorne found Hilda Skander sitting by the body of her husband. She didn't look at Hawthorne, nor was she weeping. She had a handkerchief and was rubbing the bloody spots from Skander's corpse. She looked very serious and her brow was furrowed with concentration. She spat into the handkerchief and rubbed it against Skander's skin. Then she spat into the handkerchief again. Hawthorne hurried around her to the front door.

As he came out of Emerson, he saw Betty Sherman with her son and Bill Dolittle. A pair of cross-country skis was leaning against one of the columns. Betty came toward him.

"Where are Kate and Jessica?" she asked, frightened.

"They're coming."

"The police are here. LeBrun . . . ," said Betty, then she couldn't say any more.

Hawthorne looked over at the fence where LeBrun's body was arched across the spikes; his arms hung past his head toward the snow. The Blazer was just drawing even with him. Its blue light swirled across the body. Bill Dolittle stood in front of Betty's son so he wouldn't see. A light appeared above them, then Kate and Jessica emerged through the door of Emerson. Hawthorne began to run toward LeBrun, stumbling in the snow and getting up again. He heard Betty say something to Kate. Jessica was crying.

A spotlight on the side of the Blazer came on and turned slowly until it was pointed directly at LeBrun's body, casting the spider-shape of his shadow onto the wall of Emerson. LeBrun's back was broken, and the spikes pushed up through his stomach. Blood ran down the iron posts, steaming in the cold. LeBrun was alive, but just barely. His eyes were open and he watched Hawthorne approach through the drifts.

"Frank," said Hawthorne. He reached up to touch him, then stopped.

Very slowly LeBrun began to smile. He opened his mouth to speak. For a moment the smile hung on his lips, as delicate as smoke, then his face relaxed into meaninglessness.

Hawthorne felt that their conversation wasn't finished. There was more he wanted to tell him. "Frank," he said again. But LeBrun was dead; there were no words left. Hawthorne raised his arms, trying to push LeBrun up off the spikes, but he couldn't move him. Hawthorne's hands and coat were red with his blood.

"You're not going to be able to do that," said a voice behind him. "Too heavy."

Hawthorne turned. An older man in a dark overcoat was climbing out of the Blazer. Hawthorne didn't recognize him. Chief Moulton was getting out on the other side. Both men walked toward him. The man in the overcoat wasn't wearing boots, but he waded toward LeBrun's body without paying attention to the snow. He was heavyset, like a rolled-up mattress.

Looking back toward Kate, Hawthorne thought how dear to him

she was. The spotlight on the Blazer reflected off the snow caught in the brick and dead vines of ivy, so that the building shone. Its very brightness made Hawthorne hopeful that the school would have a future, that he could keep it going. He saw Kate fall in the deep snow, then get to her feet and keep moving toward him.

The man in the overcoat joined Hawthorne at the fence. He stared up at LeBrun with his hands on his hips. "This is the guy who made bread?"

Hawthorne nodded. "He made good bread."

When Kate reached him, Hawthorne took her hand, pulling her to him. Without gloves their hands were freezing, yet he could feel warmth in the closeness of their palms. He tried to concentrate on it.

The man looked at LeBrun for a moment, then he reached up and touched LeBrun's head, smoothing his brown hair and brushing it back over his forehead. His touch was almost affectionate.

"And he liked jokes, right?" asked Leo Flynn.

EPILOGUE

Leo Flynn sat in his kitchen with his feet in a dishpan of water hot enough that steam rose up around his bare knees. He had on an old plaid bathrobe, and a blue wool scarf was tied around his neck. His nose was several shades redder than the rest of his face—a strawberry in a field of pink. He took a Kleenex from the box on the Formica table and began to unfold it. Next to the box of Kleenex was a glass of orange juice and a bowl of chicken soup. Before Flynn had a chance to lift the tissue to his nose, he sneezed.

Junie stood in the doorway eyeing him critically. She wore a dark green dress and was just leaving for her women's club, which met on Monday nights. Her "hen club," Flynn called it, but only to himself. Although she was sixty, her dark red hair had only begun to turn gray in the past few years and she had kept her figure. Despite what he thought of as her carping, Flynn still loved her as strongly as when they had married over forty years earlier.

"And what about those snow chains?" Junie was saying. "They weren't cheap."

"I already told you I'll get reimbursed. Coughlin said he'd send off the paperwork." Reaching down, Flynn scratched the ears of his eighteen-year-old black cat. Rheumy-eyed and ragged-eared, the cat was named Curley after the former mayor.

"That's what you said when you bought that expensive flashlight, and you never got your money back."

"For crying out loud, I can only say what he promised. Without the chains I'd of been dead in a ditch. It snowed all the way back down this morning, leastways till Concord. The salt trucks had their hands full."

Junie crossed her arms and assumed a stubborn expression. "I don't see why you went there anyway. It was all over by the time you showed up."

"That was the weather, not me. I did the best I could." Flynn grabbed another Kleenex and blew his nose, making a sound like a motorboat. The walls of the kitchen were light yellow. On the wall above the table hung a photograph of Pope John Paul and another of President Kennedy. "Anyway," continued Flynn, "I'd been looking for this guy all fall. When I found him, he was dead. Sometimes it happens like that. Hey, it saved the state a chunk of change. Two states."

Flynn was just as glad to get away from the subject of snow chains.

He had arrived home with his cold around three. He'd called in sick, then gone to bed and slept for several hours. When he woke, Junie had made the chicken soup and began preparing the pan of hot water for his feet while he told her about his journey through the snowstorm and what he had found at Bishop's Hill.

"I never seen snow like that." Flynn shook his head vigorously to give a sense of the drama. Curley stared up at him with his head tilted, as if trying to construct a rudimentary thought but not quite managing. "It wasn't like snow down here. This was big-time weather. Snowplow didn't show up till midnight, with the troopers and ambulance right behind. I ended up sleeping in a dorm—some kid's room with rock and roll posters on the wall. Electricity never did come on."

"So why didn't you come home yesterday? Coughlin said you were supposed to work." Junie took her coat from the back of a chair. Her club met punctually at eight and it was now past seven-thirty.

"I wanted to talk to this guy Hawthorne. Dr. Hawthorne, they call him. He told me about LaBrecque or LeBrun—I can't keep the names straight. Like I had part of the story and I wanted the rest. I thought he'd be glad that LaBrecque was dead. But he was more upset about

LaBrecque than about those two teachers that got killed. Hawthorne couldn't stop talking about him. It made me suspicious, but this copper up there said Hawthorne was all right. A little eccentric, that's all. They call this copper a police chief but he's only got one guy under him. We had a couple of meals together. I like him. We might even go up there this summer. They got a lake."

Junie looked skeptical. "I like to take our vacations on the Cape." She began putting on her coat—dark brown with black buttons and a mink collar. "So everything's over and done with?"

"As far as Massachusetts is concerned, but New Hampshire's not off the hook. There'll be a grand jury investigation and they'll bring charges against three or four people—a couple of them lawyers. That'll drag on for a while. Statutory rape, sexual abuse—the whole business. But then a lot of white-collar crime. That Hawthorne's got his work cut out for him, I can tell you. Give me a good old working-class murder any day of the week. Nothing subtle or too complex. I mean, LaBrecque was a bad guy but he'd been a bad guy from the start. These teachers and lawyers, it's like they chose to be bad. Like they could pick one or the other and they decided they wanted to be crooks."

"They all sound the same to me." Junie tied her scarf around her neck. "I'll be back by eleven at the latest. Remember—no cigarettes, no beer, be in bed by nine, and keep the cat off the table." She crossed the kitchen to kiss his cheek. Flynn patted her behind.

"You look nice," he said.

Junie pursed her lips disapprovingly, then smiled. A moment later she was shutting the front door. Flynn waited about ten seconds, then removed his feet from the pan of water and padded over to the refrigerator, leaving wet footprints on the linoleum. Taking out a half gallon of milk and a bottle of Molson, he opened both, then got a saucer from the cupboard. He set it on the kitchen table and filled it with milk. "Like some milky?" he shouted. Curley had been deaf for years.

Flynn picked up the cat and set it in front of the milk. Then he returned to his chair and opened the window a few inches, letting in a gust of frigid air. Curley was staring at the milk as if he didn't know if it was meant to be drunk. Flynn scratched the cat under the chin. Black hairs floated down to the table. He would have to clean them up before Junie got home. Taking a pack of Marlboros from the pocket of his bathrobe, Flynn shook one out and lit it with a kitchen match. He inhaled deeply and bent over to blow a cloud of smoke through the partly opened window.

How strange, he thought, still brooding about Bishop's Hill. If going to prison or getting killed was how you ended up, why would a person choose to be bad?

He thought of LaBrecque's death again and how upset Hawthorne had been. Why hadn't he been relieved, getting rid of a guy like that? Hawthorne hadn't wanted to let LaBrecque stay on the fence till the ambulance came. They had to move the body—first Moulton and himself and Hawthorne, trying to push LaBrecque off the spikes where he was wedged tight, pushing until Flynn thought he was going to bust a gasket. Then they had gotten the other teacher that was hanging around, then this pretty woman, Hawthorne's girlfriend or something. The five of them pushing and shoving and grunting until LaBrecque had flopped over into the snow.

But there was Hawthorne, standing over the guy looking somber, practically in tears. He was mourning, for Pete's sake. Who the hell was this LaBrecque to make such a fuss over? Like he had told Junie, LaBrecque had been a bad guy from the start. It was as if LaBrecque had become the person in charge, as if the dead man lying there in the snow was making the rules. But Leo Flynn wasn't having any of that and so he had turned his back to the bunch of them and looked out at the night sky, where the snow was stopping and the moon was coming out.

RD12FF